Banebringer

Book One of The Heretic Gods

Carol A. Park

Shattered Soul Books

Pennsylvania

Shattered Soul Books
2600 Willow Street Pike North
PMB 259
Willow Street, PA 17584
www.carolapark.com

Publisher's Note: This is a work of fiction. Names, characters, places, and incidents are a product of the author's imagination. Locales and public names are sometimes used for atmospheric purposes. Any resemblance to actual people, living or dead, or to businesses, companies, events, institutions, or locales is completely coincidental.

Cover art/design © 2018 Brit K. Caley
Book Layout © 2017 BookDesignTemplates.com

Banebringer/ Carol A. Park. -- 1st ed.
ISBN 978-1-7321491-0-6 (paperback)
ISBN 978-1-7321491-1-3 (e-book)

FOR MOM

Who taught me to read

AND DAD

Who "doesn't like fantasy"

Contents

Acknowledgements

Writing is often thought of as a solitary endeavor, but as with most efforts in life, you don't get far without a team. The support each of these people has offered has been invaluable to me.

It is nerve-wracking to give your unfinished work to others to read, and many thanks must go to my faithful test readers, Wes Allen and Tam Case, for your valuable feedback. I promise this time there will be a sequel!

I am also grateful to Amy McNulty, my editor, fellow writer, and a long-lost friend, who I was delighted to reconnect with.

I must also thank another friend, Brit Caley, for enthusiastically embracing my request to create this book's awesome cover despite my having no idea what I was doing, and my brother-in-law, Andrew Park, for designing a super-cool logo for Shattered Soul Books and the interior chapter icons. I am lucky to have not had to look far to find such talented artists.

I cannot fail to mention those students who I will forever think of as my 8th grade Latin class, my original fan club, even though they had never read anything I had ever written. I guess it was just cool to have a teacher who was writing a book. This isn't that book—and none of you are in 8th grade anymore—but if this one ever lands in your hands, I hope you enjoy it more than Latin (difficult to imagine, I know).

Thanks also go to my mom and dad, for never saying I couldn't, and to my mother-in-law, who has been my constant cheerleader, along with other friends and family members too numerous to list.

And, finally, I must thank my husband, Calvin, whose only complaint about my writing endeavors is that I have trained him too well and forever ruined his ability to enjoy uncritically any book or movie that is anything less than above-average. He somehow manages to constantly encourage me while simultaneously critiquing my drafts until it hurts. This book wouldn't be what it is without your input, and I would never have come this far without your support. Thanks for keeping me from writing silly things like "a regular boat."

CHAPTER ONE

The Hunter

The tree limb Vaughn thought he had stepped onto dissolved into a puff of red mist. He lurched forward at the unexpected step, slipped on the damp undergrowth, and swore as the deadweight of the bloodhawk he was dragging behind him tugged out of his grasp.

The mist dissipated, though he knew the bothersome creatures the mist represented were still there. They flitted about in his peripheral vision, attaching to trees as random branches here or taking the shape of a butterfly there. He had counted at least a half-dozen following him—and making a general nuisance of themselves—since the bloodhawk had fallen from the sky with his arrow in its heart.

Since there was nothing else to glare at, he glared at the carcass of the bloodhawk, as though the misstep were its fault, and hefted it by its neck again.

He scanned the thinning forest ahead of him, his eyes involuntarily adjusting for the dying light. Smoke rose from the village chimneys above the trees. *Almost there.* And thank Rhianah for that. He had needed to range farther than before in hunting this one, and the bird—longer than he was tall—was getting heavy.

The things he did for a few coins, a real bed, and a good meal every once in a while—and if he had a woman to warm the bed for a night, all the better.

Or two nights. Two nights was all right, every once in a while, as long as he didn't make a habit of it. A well-deserved reward for the community service he provided freely, right?

He grinned, the memory of the soft skin of the farmer's daughter still fresh in his mind from the previous night.

He gave the bloodhawk an extra tug and continued on more carefully, determined not to let a bloodsprite trick him again.

The wind changed and the smoke he had seen tickled his nostrils instead.

He halted and squinted out of instinct rather than necessity. That wasn't chimney smoke.

He dropped the bird, dipped his hand into the pouch sewn into the inside of his vest, and used his index finger and thumb to crush one of the silvery droplets of hardened aether he kept there.

He crept forward, leaving the monster he had slain behind, wishing, when twigs kept popping under his feet, that he was as good at moving silently as he was at moving invisibly—with the aid of the aether, of course.

The forest petered out and he crested the rise that would allow him to look out over the quaint, sprawling village.

He sucked air through his teeth. *Burning skies.*

A blackened husk was all that remained. Charred timbers still smoldered, producing the smoke he had seen a few minutes ago, and on the far side of the village, flames were licking up the last of the village proper. Beyond, even the farms had been burned, including the crops in the fields and the barns that housed the cattle that the bloodhawks had been ravaging. Nothing moved save the scavenger birds that had descended, already hunting for flesh to pick at.

The fallen buildings made it easy for Vaughn to see directly into the village center, which the hard-working villagers had paved in stone over the years to create a more hospitable place for market day. A symbol encircled the well, proclaiming to anyone who would pass by that the town had been condemned by the Conclave for heresy. To his eyes, the symbol had an unmistakable luminescent sheen. Blood—and fresh, by the color.

Vaughn hardly dared to breathe. He wanted to close his eyes but was unable to tear them away from that sight.

There was no need to paint the symbol in blood. It wasn't standard practice. It was blood because someone knew a Banebringer—the only type of person who would be able to tell from this distance what it was—would see it. Blood always looked like this to Vaughn and those like him, even in daylight. And his extra-sensitive vision made it even more noticeable in lessened light. Someone also knew that.

He finally closed his eyes. *No. Rhianah, no.*

He ought to run—now. But he couldn't. He couldn't leave without seeing if there were any survivors. Perhaps the villagers had been allowed to flee. Perhaps their homes had been the only price they had paid.

He knew his hopes were in vain even as he approached and began walking through the ruins, as silently as he could. Too many birds had found purchase in too many spots around town.

He turned his eyes away from the birds, sickened, only to be looking in the right direction to see a figure step out from one of the more intact buildings. "So. I was right. You simply couldn't resist coming to see the damage you inflicted."

Vaughn froze. Had his invisibility failed? But the moon was nearly new, *and* it was daytime; it should be nigh on perfect right now.

"I know you're there. Your boots are already blackened with soot."

Vaughn glanced behind him. Footprints in the ashes led right to where he stood.

The ashes had adhered to his boots, damp from his trek through the woods. He was such an idiot. Why couldn't he have just run? He turned to look for a place to hide—for some way to flee without the footprints following him.

But it was as though a volcano had erupted. Had Gildas done this on purpose? Scattered the ashes so evenly, so that Vaughn could be tracked walking into the town?

He unhooked his bow from his back, reached into another pocket on his pouch, and started stringing it.

The figure walked closer. "Preparing your bow?" He spread

his arms out to the side, palms open. "Come. Why don't you show yourself? My hands are empty."

Right. Vaughn knew from experience how fast Gildas could produce his hand crossbow. And he didn't have to be accurate. If a bolt treated with the right substance grazed Vaughn's skin, he would be too delirious to even know he was about to be Sedated.

He eased back a few steps and then darted behind the nearest half-burned wall and crouched down.

Footsteps moved closer to his position, but Gildas was taking his time. Toying with him.

"If you're wondering why I did this, I thought perhaps a more powerful lesson was in order."

Monster. Vaughn half-stood to be able to sight Gildas with his arrow over the wall. He was looking in Vaughn's direction, but his eyes roved from side to side, no doubt searching for some sign of Vaughn's precise location.

Vaughn shifted, causing his bow to dip and scrape against the top of the wall. He jerked it back up, but a hand-sized chunk of wood crumbled into ash anyway. Vaughn ducked down in time to hear the thwack of a crossbow, and a moment later, the tip of a bolt had lodged itself in the disintegrating wood right in front of Vaughn's nose.

He shuffled backwards. As always, Gildas was playing a dangerous game. If he were unlucky, and one of those bolts killed Vaughn...

Then again, Vaughn had never been certain if Gildas cared.

The effects of the aether he had crushed earlier had almost worn off, and his supply was running low. Still, he was loathe to burn it from his own blood unless it became necessary...

He almost laughed. This wouldn't be a good example of necessary? He transferred his mental grasp from the aether he had crushed to the aether in his blood, and the crossbow thwacked again. The bolt flew over his head this time.

He must have flickered into visibility in the transfer. He ducked down farther and crept a few more paces down the wall, which was fast coming to an end.

This was bad. He could make a run for it, but his footprints would give him away. And the ground directly behind him rose steeply as it gave way to the woods. Knowing himself, he would slip as soon as he reached the wet grass and roll back down the hill and right to Gildas' feet.

He peeked around the edge of the wall and sighted Gildas once more. *Do it. Just do it, Vaughn.* He was standing right in the open, not even making an attempt to shield himself. Making a mockery of Vaughn's own cowardice.

"If there is blood on anyone's hands here, it's yours, Teyrnon. Treating with demons is a serious crime."

The use of his given name, that of the third son of the Ri of Ferehar, finally tore a snarl from his throat. He was no longer that man. "The only demon I'm treating with is you." He gestured with his bow, though no one could see it but him. "These people were innocent. They had no knowledge of what I am. I was hunting bloodhawks that had been harassing their livestock, and they showed me hospitality in return."

Gildas' smile grew grim. "I know what you were doing. It's what you always do. Flitting from town to town, seeking refuge in exchange for hunting bloodbane. You just can't resist trying to make atonement for your crimes."

Vaughn wanted to deny it, but the words stuck in his throat. Crimes? No. He didn't believe he or any other Banebringer had done anything warranting the notice of the heretic gods. They were capricious, if they existed at all. But atonement?

Yes. He wanted to believe he did what he did solely out of the goodness of his heart. He demanded no payment—only accepted what often poor villagers offered in return. Knowing he was helping to quell the plague upon the land that his existence— and that of other Banebringers—brought was reward enough. That, and a night or two of peace and safety, though it be a mere illusion of the normalcy he craved. But it also diminished, if temporarily, the ache caused by what had been lost on his account.

Gildas moved in his direction, still talking. "But there is no atonement. You're cursed. And those you associate with will pay the price for harboring a demonspawn."

Vaughn glanced behind himself again. Wet grass. Wet. Surely he could do something with that.

He chewed on his lower lip. He rarely used that part of his powers. He wasn't good at it, so it took more out of him. Could he handle staying invisible *and* harnessing the water from the grass at the same time? And what would he do with it once he had it?

Gildas had almost reached where he crouched. Much closer, and he wouldn't need the crossbow. He could reach out and stab him with the needle.

"You won't escape me this time, Teyrnon."

Just release the arrow.

His hand started to tremble. He tried to will it into submission—to will himself just to let go of the string...

But like every other time he had been handed this opportunity, he couldn't do it. He simply could not kill his own father.

He was wasting time on this. He knew he wouldn't do it. Frustrated, he secured the bow on his back and began to retreat. If he was going to attempt an escape, now was the time.

Gildas stopped moving and cocked his head to the side, listening to Vaughn's footsteps, which would soon become visible to him from over the remnant of the wall.

Vaughn concentrated on the droplets of water that sprinkled the grass and the dampness in the dirt. He gathered it together up on the rise and began pulling it closer, hoping Gildas wouldn't see the trickle as it came.

Gildas' eyes lit on a spot at Vaughn's feet, and he smiled.

Vaughn hurled the water at his crossbow and started running.

The thump on the ground and Gildas' curse came simultaneously.

Vaughn had been aiming merely to startle Gildas, thus gaining himself a few precious moments to scramble up the rise. If he had managed to knock the crossbow out of his hand, even better.

Unfortunately, his concentration on the water caused him to lose control of his invisibility, as he had feared. He slipped halfway up the rise and lost half the ground he had gained. It turned out to be in his favor, because a bolt hit the spot where he would have been standing had he kept moving in that direction.

He regained control of the aether to fade out of visibility again and weaved back and forth up the rise, hoping Gildas wouldn't be able to predict his next location. He only had to make the tree line.

Bolts flew far too close to him several times, but, finally, he reached the top and hurtled into the woods.

Gildas let loose a torrent of curses from behind him. "There will no longer be refuge for you, Teyrnon!"

In other words, the same fate would befall any town he tried to seek safety in from now on, if Gildas found out. Hundreds of innocents to prove a point. Gildas had been cruel in his hunt for Vaughn over the years, but this atrocity topped them all.

He stopped and leaned against a tree to catch his breath and closed his eyes, trying to block out the image of the burned town in his mind. *If there is blood on anyone's hands...*

He gritted his teeth and denied himself guilt. *He* wasn't the criminal here. And he would never know peace until his father—his own, personal Hunter—was dead. And if *he* couldn't—wouldn't—do it...

He clenched and unclenched his fist a few times. Perhaps it was time to spend that stolen fortune.

Ivana held herself still as the eyes of the eunuch in charge of Gan Pywell's personal stash of so-called companions slid over the lounging women. Almost all of the women—girls, really, most barely of age—followed his gaze: some anxious, some bored, some resigned, and a small few downright terrified.

The last were the girls Ivana had come in with. None of

them, including Ivana, had been broken in yet, though they had been there three weeks.

The girl closest to Ivana shrank back as the eunuch paced to where the three of them sat. Ivana lowered her eyes, as was proper, and waited.

She hoped he chose her this time. She was tiring of this place.

"You." The eunuch's voice was rich and commanding; he had obviously been castrated later in life.

She looked up to see which of the three of them he was speaking to, and found his eyes resting on her.

Excellent.

"The Gan is in the mood for something different," the eunuch said. There was neither pity nor enmity there. It was a statement of fact. He was a servant, as they all were. His eyes roved over her. "Fereharian?"

She nodded, though he hardly needed to ask. Her bronze skin was enough confirmation.

His skin, on the other hand, was the deep brown of southern Donia, yet had cool jewel undertones that pointed to Fuilyn heritage a few generations back. Ivana had puzzled over that as a way of entertaining herself upon arriving, since Donia and Fuilyn were on opposite ends of the Setanan Empire. It was an unusual mix.

"Good enough." He gestured to another of the eunuchs. "Prepare her."

While they saw to the cosmetic preferences of Gan Pywell, she considered the lot of the girls housed here. It was better than being in a whore-house in the city, she supposed. They were well-cared for, after all: kept in good health, fed choice food, and were expected to do nothing more than sit around and wait for Pywell's attention and convenience.

Then again, the same could have been said of the Pywell's pet dog. Perhaps Pywell should have turned to bestiality instead. It would certainly be less expensive to keep a collection of dogs than women.

She was forced to set aside such amusing speculations, however, as, perfumed and attired appropriately, she was ushered into Pywell's bedchamber via a side entrance.

She suppressed a grimace when she saw him. He sat at a small square table set up in front of an open window on one side of the room, finishing dinner. He wore a robe, but it was untied and he wore nothing underneath. She had only seen the Gan himself twice, once on an investigatory mission, and again when he had chosen the latest crop of companions. He was no better sight to behold unclothed than clothed, that was certain. His skin was saggy and spotted with age, but it wouldn't be the first time she had suffered a decaying old man.

No, it was the nearly-empty tumbler of amber liquid at his right hand and the dilated eyes as he turned to look at her that made her fight the shudder. It was a confirmation of the information she had, which was satisfying, but his breath surely stank of liquor.

Ugh. She hated that.

On second thought, maybe the dog had it better.

She lowered her eyes before he could catch her own for long, awaiting his command.

———

Ivana waited until Pywell's breathing became regular and steady before slipping out of his bed. She halted with one foot on the plush rug beneath, listening. Satisfied no one was coming, she stole across the room and bent down to wriggle two fingers between his writing desk and the wall. At first, she felt nothing, and she frowned. Aleena had never failed her before...

Ah. There we are. She pried a tiny packet of paper loose and then sat down at the table to unwrap it. She spared one moment to admire the clear, finger-nail sized disc that lay innocently on the paper. It was one of her more ingenious concoctions. Tasteless. Colorless. Odorless. And, most importantly, near instantaneous once ingested.

She set aside the disc, burned the slip of paper in the candle on the table, and swept the ashes onto the floor.

She then picked up the disc—*gently, gently*—she didn't want to compromise the gummy protective layer—and took it back over to the bed.

Pywell made it too easy. His mouth had lolled open to allow his half-grunts, half-snores out. She slid the disc under his tongue, waited a moment until she was sure it would have dissolved, and then pressed his jaw shut.

He snorted and shook his head, but she held his jaw firm and then massaged his throat firmly, forcing him to swallow a few times. His eyes flew open, and he stared at her in confusion and some indignation for all of ten seconds before his body went rigid, spasmed twice, and then lay still.

She could tell by the blankness in his eyes that he was dead, but she put two fingers to his throat anyway. In her profession, she had to be certain about the demise of a target.

The main door to the room opened, and a tiny *eep* and a soft *whump* issued from that direction.

Ivana jerked her hand away and whirled to face the door. A maid stood there, a pile of laundered linens lying at her feet. She stared at Ivana with wide eyes. "I thought—I didn't think he was here—"

Ivana's mind sifted through her options and went for the best possible scenario first: that she hadn't noticed anything out of the ordinary. "He just—he just fell limp," she said in response, feigning fear. "I was—I think he might be dead."

The maid was silent. She chewed her lip, and her eyes went back and forth between Pywell's corpse and Ivana several times.

She wasn't buying it. She was thinking too quickly. Whatever she had seen...

Had it been the expression on Ivana's face upon entering—too calm? Or had she hesitated too long before spinning the lie? Whatever it was, the maid's dark face had taken on a greyish pallor, too pale to be simply horror that she may have walked in on Pywell in the middle of his carnal pleasures, or horror that he was dead.

Frankly, from what she had heard, most of his servants would be relieved.

But that didn't mean they didn't have consciences.

"You—" the maid stammered. "Did you—who are you?"

Ivana surged up and shut the door. The maid backed away from her as she approached, which confirmed Ivana's guess that she had made the conclusion Ivana didn't want her to make. Ivana advanced on her, shoved one palm against her mouth before she could scream and the other against her throat, and pushed her back into the wall.

The maid thrashed against her, but Ivana held her firm, increasing the pressure against her throat.

The maid bit her hand.

Ivana cursed and instinctively pulled away, and as soon as she was free, the maid screamed.

Damn you, girl! Ivana shoved her across the room and then flung herself at her. Ivana wrestled the maid's flailing arms and legs until she had her in the right spot and then pushed her out the open window.

The maid screamed again as she fell to the ground below and then was silent. Ivana looked out. Her broken form left little doubt as to her state.

She gnashed her teeth in frustration. The maid's screams would bring guards sooner than she had anticipated, and she needed a revised plan, fast.

Ivana screamed herself and then hurried to the bed and pulled the corpse of Pywell out of his bed. He landed on the floor with a heavy thud, and Ivana lugged him as close to the window as she could before the sound of running and shouting floated down the hall.

She let go of Pywell, picked up the flimsy robe that had passed for a garment to cover her with, and held it to her chest just as the door was flung open and guards stormed in.

She cowered against the wall, feigning hysterics. "He killed her!" She gasped and shuddered and sank to her knees. "Threw her out the window, oh, Rhianah, help me..." She wished, not for the first time, that she could manage to whip up tears, but she had never been able to fake that particular reaction.

One of the guards went to her and took her robe from her hands. She shrank away, but he knelt and wrapped it around her shoulders, covering her up as well as such a garment could. "There now," he said. "Why don't you just tell us what happened?"

"He's dead," another guard said, bending over Pywell. "I don't see any injuries."

The guard's face went grim, and he raised an eyebrow at Ivana.

"She—she—the maid—she walked in—" Ivana squeezed her eyes shut. "The Gan became angry. He didn't even say a word. Just leapt out of the bed and shoved her. She went right out the window...oh blessed Rhianah, I don't know if he meant it to happen. He was drunk, oh gods, oh gods..." She wrapped her arms around her knees and buried her face there.

"All right, all right," the guard said. "But how did he die?"

Ivana shook her head and squeezed her arms around her knees tighter. "I can't. Oh gods..."

The guard stood. "Someone get the eunuch. He might be able to get her to talk."

There was movement in the room. Ivana remained trembling against the wall, calculating her options in response to the possibilities of what would happen next.

The guard hadn't even questioned her story about Gan Pywell throwing the maid out the window. Everyone knew his temper was vile, especially when drunk. As rumor had it, she wouldn't be the first servant to die in a fit of his rage. But he was nobility. He could get away with an awful lot before the law would be forced to deal with him.

"What happened, girl?"

The eunuch now stood above her. His voice was tight and face grim—almost too grim. Was he worried this would mean repercussions for him?

"I told them—" She choked out, and then shook her head.

"Girl, you need to tell me what happened," the eunuch said, his voice bordering on dangerous. *Interesting.*

"After he threw her out the window, I screamed..." she said. "And then he came for me, too." She swallowed hard. "I don't think he realized he would have witnesses. And then just as he got to me...he collapsed." She shook her head. "That's it. Just collapsed."

"Old bastard," one of the guards put in. "Heart probably gave out. Too much drink. Knew it would happen someday."

Another guard snorted. "Surprised it didn't happen while he was riding the whore. The gods only know how he had the energy left for that."

"Certainly had enough of them. Maybe now that he's gone we'll get the spoils..."

The guards laughed, and Ivana gritted her teeth against the hot flame that flared in her chest.

"Stuff it, boys." The firm voice of the chief of the guards entered the conversation. "Back to your posts, and keep your mouths shut about this until we have a chance to debrief."

The guards left, and the chief guard and the eunuch held a brief, hushed conversation, and then the eunuch excused himself. The chief guard turned to contemplate Ivana.

"Gave you a fright, eh?"

Ivana was now painfully aware that she was alone and unarmed with a large and heavily armed and armored man. She couldn't win an outright fight against this man, not with current resources.

But she nodded and eyed the guard warily. Was she to be a scapegoat? She might be able to run, if she could get past him—perhaps through the companion's door.

But he made no move to assault or apprehend her. He just stood at the door, regarding her with pity in his eyes. "All right," he said quietly. "Here's what's going to happen. Whatever happened in this room is going to stay in this room. Understand? The guards will be talked to as well. You—you're to be released, effective immediately. Mental instability from the shock, made you useless for further service, understand?"

She stared at him, feigning confusion, and shook her head.

"You've heard the rumors. She isn't the first girl to go out the window, figuratively speaking. But with his death—" He stopped and shook his head. "It'll be a blemish on the house, and that can't be tolerated. There'll be rumors, but that's where it'll stop. Understand?"

Finally, she nodded.

"Count yourself lucky. You could have been down there with the maid."

Scarcely a half hour later, Ivana had been deposited at the edge of the estate grounds, with nothing but a satchel holding enough food for one meal and the clothes on her back—which thankfully now consisted of more than that robe.

Gan Pywell's lands were at the edges of Setanan civilization, pressed up against the desert to the west and the Cadmyrian mountains to the north. He was a minor noble, but his holdings were of important strategic value in keeping watch over the western pass that led to the pagan nation of Xambria, and he carried out his duties well. It was why no one would be interested in prosecuting him for petty crimes such as the murder of servants.

It was also why, had she actually been a slave released in such a manner, chances were better than not that she would die or be gang-pressed into worse conditions before finding adequate food or shelter. She was sure that was their hope.

Fortunately, she was neither a helpless slave-whore set free in sparsely populated lands at night nor without resource. She only needed to make it to the nearest safe-house before a roaming bloodbane found her first. Frankly, she couldn't have asked for a better resolution.

She glanced back through the gates to the manor house. Torchlight illuminated one side, and while she couldn't see what was happening, she was certain they were removing the body of the hapless maid.

She slung the satchel over her shoulder and turned toward home.

Chapter Two

Blood Money

3 months later

Vaughn crouched in an alleyway between two abandoned warehouses. He was watching a derelict pier, trying to summon the courage to walk out onto it as instructed. His contact wouldn't show himself if he didn't go out there, but he hated this part of the exchange. Three times before, he had done something similar. They always wanted him to expose himself first, which he supposed was appropriate when dealing with people who spent their lives in shadows, but that didn't make it any less nerve-wracking.

He took a deep breath, stood, and walked out onto the pier, avoiding places where the boards had rotted away and hoping he didn't take a wrong step and fall through. He stood motionless for a moment when he reached the end and then removed a wrapped sweet from his pocket and set it down on the pier. He turned to look toward land, waiting for his contact to join him.

"Honeyed date?" a feminine voice said from behind him. From the *end* of the pier, toward the water. He whirled around. Sure enough, a figure stood there, all but eyes covered in a dark cloak, holding the sweet in a—her?—gloved hand.

How in the abyss had she appeared there without his knowing? Had she been treading in the water beneath him? But she wasn't wet.

As if his nerves weren't already wrung out enough.

"I prefer chocolate," the voice—yes, definitely a woman—continued. "But this will do."

He gaped at her. "Do you know how expensive chocolate is?" he spluttered, without thinking. It had to be imported from the pagans across the sea—already an expensive enough treat, even without the Conclave's current choke-hold on foreign trade.

She tilted her head, and her eyes glittered in the moonlight. "So are assassins," she said flatly, and then she turned away. When she turned back, the date was gone.

He swallowed, now thoroughly disconcerted. It wasn't unusual for him to have to produce some sort of symbol to show that he was the person the contact was supposed to meet. A particular flower pinned to his cloak. A certain feather in his hat.

This was the first time he had been asked to bring a sweet. He figured it was because the assassin he was attempting to hire was called Sweetblade.

"Was that—some sort of test?"

"No," she said. "I just like sweets." She brushed some of the honey crystals off her gloves. "Now. You've managed to buy your way into this meeting, so you can't be destitute. Who is the target?"

Please, please, please, don't be like everyone else. "A Hunter from Ferehar named—"

"A Hunter?"

Damn. "Yes."

"We don't deal with Conclave targets. Looks like you wasted your money." She turned to go.

"But—"

She didn't even turn around to consider him. She simply walked away. And his fourth meeting was over, just like that.

His shoulders slumped. He could no longer afford this. The bribes merely to get to this point, four times with four different assassins, had emptied his pockets faster than he had thought possible, and he had yet to actually hire an assassin. This had been his last chance. The entire venture had cost him a fortune. Literally.

The contact disappeared into the same alley he had hidden in earlier, and he gritted his teeth. *No.* There had to be a way to convince one of them.

He walked back down the street, ducked into the doorway of another abandoned warehouse, and crushed a flake of aether between his thumb and forefinger. He *would* have his meeting with an assassin, one way or another.

The dining room of Ivana's inn was long empty of customers when Aleena finally returned. Ivana looked up from the table she had been wiping down and caught the other woman's eyes.

Aleena flicked her eyes to Ohtli, who had the night shift and was folding table linens behind the bar, and headed down the hall without a word.

Ivana finished wiping off the tables before tossing her rag on the bar and nodding to Ohtli. "I'm turning in. The floors need mopped tonight, please."

"Yes, Da," Ohtli said.

Aleena was already waiting for Ivana in her study.

Waiting was too kind. It was more like *lounging*. She had her feet up on Ivana's desk and was leaning back on the rear legs of her chair with arms crossed behind her head. Ivana shoved her feet off the desk as she walked by. "Manners, Aleena."

Aleena just grinned at her as the chair came down on all four legs with a heavy thump.

Ivana settled into her chair, and Aleena tossed a leather purse onto the desk. It landed with a satisfying thud.

"No problems?"

Aleena shook her head. "That should be the balance."

That was a relief. Ivana had been concerned that the rumors surrounding the death of Gan Pywell might negatively impact her contract, since it was supposed to look natural, but so far, she had heard nothing about murder. At least, not murder of Pywell.

She poured the contents of the purse on her desk and started counting. "Good. What about the potential?"

"The target was a Hunter. I turned him down." Aleena's voice held a question, as if to confirm Ivana's standing orders on refusing targets associated with the Conclave.

Ivana didn't look up; she merely nodded. It was standard practice. No assassin wanted to chance bringing the wrath of the Conclave down on them, and Ivana had her own reasons for wanting to avoid their gaze.

She frowned at the coins and started counting again. There were too many; she must have miscounted.

"Is it short?" Aleena asked.

"No. It's over."

"Really? I thought he was jesting."

Ivana looked up at Aleena. "Jesting?"

"Said he included a bonus for the..." She looked at the ceiling and tapped her chin. "'Delightful scandal that accompanied the Gan's unfortunate demise.'" Aleena shrugged. "You know how Xambrians talk."

He could only have meant the rumors about the maid's death. Typical Xambrian. But the maid had simply been in the wrong place at the wrong time; Ivana hadn't planned it.

Aleena's eyes were on her, but she knew better than to ask about the details of a job.

Ivana pushed the extra coins toward Aleena. "Deposit it into the charity fund."

Aleena swept the offered coins into her palm without a word, and Ivana pushed the remaining coins back into the purse. "Anything else of note?"

"Ri Gildas of Ferehar issued a matching contract yesterday."

The last coin landed on the floor instead of the purse, and Ivana bent down to retrieve it, irritated at the involuntary betrayal of her hand, despite years of practiced self-control.

Ri Gildas. She hadn't heard that name in years. She would

have preferred never to hear it again.

She had left Ferehar twelve years ago and had never returned, not for any job. Had even turned down a few simply because she had no desire to see that place again.

Control. She shoved the unwanted memories away and focused instead on the unlikeliness of Aleena's words. "Really? Isn't he the Ri that became a Hunter a few years back?" she asked as she came back up and placed the last coin in the purse.

It had caused quite a scandal, as she recalled. Though there were always back room alliances, the Ri technically served the king, so it was a bold move for a Ri to openly wed himself to the Conclave.

Still, Ferehar's political favor had decreased over the years in direct proportion to the Conclave's increase in power. The natives of the region had been worshipping the heretic gods when Setana claimed the land for its own, and while most of those natives had been fully assimilated into Setanan culture, rumors—rumors she knew to be true, having grown up there—abounded that worship of the old gods continued in Ferehar, which cast constant suspicion on the region by the Conclave. Becoming a Hunter might actually have improved the Ri's political standing in this case.

Aleena had paused to consider. "I do believe you are correct," she said at last.

Interesting. Apparently Gildas thought there was an active threat to his well-being. It seemed unlikely, not because he was a Ri—there were certainly enough people who would like to see a Ri dead—but because he was a Hunter. And as she had just been reminded, there weren't many assassins who would risk such a target. Nonetheless, by issuing a matching contract, the Ri had essentially announced that he had a strong suspicion someone was after him.

She tilted her head to the side. "Aleena," she said. "Did the potential client from tonight tell you the name of the target?"

"We didn't get that far." Aleena went on before Ivana could speak. "But I just had the same thought."

"It seems too coincidental, doesn't it?"

Aleena nodded.

"What are the terms of the contract?"

"Quadruple on proof of death."

Ivana blinked. *Quadruple? Burning skies.*

Aleena studied her. "You want me to try to find him?" she asked softly.

Ivana hesitated. "Tell me your impressions of the potential client."

"Nervous, obviously not used to this sort of thing. If I didn't know the target was a Hunter—and potentially a Ri—I'd say he didn't have enough money anyway."

An expensive proposition, indeed. Hunter aside, to go after a Ri...

The regional lords of Setana were collectively second in power only to the king. One didn't hire an assassin to kill a Ri casually, not least because of the repercussions. Though collectively powerful, individually there was a great disparity between Ri. The jostling for position and influence with the king—and more recently, the Conclave—was a constant give and take that sometimes turned bloody.

In theory, Ri were elected by the literate population of the region. In practice, the title was often passed down from father to son, or sometimes to a brother or cousin. But if the political climate of a region was unstable—or if the subjects had a particular distaste for the family of their Ri—the untimely death of a Ri could mean a fast, bloody succession war at best, and all out civil war between nearby regions at worst.

Ri were aware of all of this. They didn't leave easily exploited gaps in their security, and they were high-risk targets.

The potential must have known that would be expensive.

Which meant that *quadruple* would be all the more lucrative for any assassin lucky enough to be approached by the client while the contract was in force. If it weren't the Ri of Ferehar, she would have discarded the contract as wishful thinking. However, while Ferehar itself was a backwater region on the other side of the desert, it produced a disproportionate amount of the wealth of Setana compared to the other six regions.

The reason the region had been claimed by Setana in the first place had everything to do with the valuable cualli deposits at the edges of the rocky wilderness that defined most of the region's borders to the south. What the Ri of Ferehar lacked in political power, he made up for in wealth.

Yes, if anyone could afford quadruple the cost of hiring an assassin to murder a Ri, it would be the Ri of Ferehar.

Ivana closed her eyes. No. No amount of money could tempt her to take blood money from that man.

"If you're going to attempt to turn in the contract, you'd better do it quickly," Aleena said, interrupting her thoughts. "It's already been several hours since I left him."

Ivana shook her head. "No. Not worth it. It's still dealing

with the Conclave, however you look at it."

Aleena shrugged, and then nodded.

"Anything else?"

Ivana had trouble concentrating as Aleena related the latest news from the king's court—political alliances and betrayals, and the like—most of which Ivana had little patience for. When Aleena finally left her, she remained at her desk, staring down at the purse of coins.

She almost called Aleena back to have her find the potential client—not so she could take Gildas' blood money, but to take the contract for his death. The prospect of being *paid* to murder him was tempting. But it wasn't worth the risk—either the risk of tangling with the Conclave, or the risk of opening herself up to everything she had put behind her. It was why she had never gone back to do it for herself, once she had the means to do so. She wanted to pretend he didn't exist. She didn't appreciate him intruding on her well-maintained fantasy by inserting himself, in whatever small way, into her world again.

Her musings were interrupted by the sound of a heavy thud outside her study. She lifted her head and focused on the gap between the door and its frame. Aleena had left it open a handspan, and Ivana hadn't closed it.

"Aleena?" she asked softly. When there was no response, she rose silently from her chair and padded to the door, one hand sliding a dagger out of its hiding spot under her desk as she passed by. She held it point down behind her back; there was no reason to startle someone who wouldn't expect her to have it.

The door opened farther of its own accord just as she reached it, and she stepped back, hand tightening on the dagger instinctively.

Beidah, her cat, slipped into her study. The cat paused to look up at her, as if questioning why she was standing motionless at the door.

Ivana leaned down to scratch the cat behind her ears. "Damn cat," she muttered, but Beidah merely bumped her head against Ivana's hand a few times, accepted the token of affection with an obligatory purr, and then stalked away, leapt up onto Ivana's desk, and settled herself down on top of the coin purse without a second glance at her mistress.

Still, Ivana would feel better if she knew what had made the sound.

Vaughn tried to peel himself off the wall, but he was shaking so hard that he only succeeded in jerking his head a little. He had plastered himself there after a flying orange fur ball with claws had landed without warning on his head, giving him such a scare that he had skittered backward into the coat rack and knocked it over, which had scared him even more.

As far as he knew, his invisibility worked against animals and people alike, and other than the fact that the vicious beast had landed on him, he had no reason to believe that this cat was an exception. Indeed, once he managed to fling the fiend off his face, it hadn't given him a second glance. It had merely sniffed, as though offended by its arrested flight, and sat to smooth its ruffled fur before slinking into another room.

He managed to calm his tremors enough to rub a hand lightly over the gouges the cat had left in his cheek. He had had to bite his tongue to keep from crying out earlier, and the wounds were bleeding; at least, they *had* been bleeding. When his hand came away, all that transferred to his fingers was a dusting of silver: the blood-turned-aether that was the telltale mark of a Banebringer.

He picked at the dried aether on his cheek absently and then pressed a crushed sliver of bindblood aether into the wounds to heal them faster.

This might have been taking things a bit too far. Following an assassin's henchman—or henchwoman in this case—was insane enough; following her into a room without any idea of who might be in it, if he would have any place to hide, and if there would be a way of easy escape?

Had he become so desperate?

Yes. Absolutely, yes.

The door to the room the cat had entered opened wider, and Vaughn froze again.

A woman stepped out, and Vaughn recognized her as the woman who had followed the assassin's contact a few minutes after the contact herself had passed through. The two had then cloistered themselves in the other room, door firmly shut, and so little sound came from within that the room had to have been soundproofed.

The wooden plaque hanging on the outer door had proclaimed these the private rooms of the innkeeper; if that were the case—and given the dagger the woman in front of him held in her hand—Vaughn suspected that the "innkeeper" was none other than Sweetblade herself.

And looking for him. He tried not to contemplate what she

might do if he were caught here.

So, unable to do anything more useful than pray to whatever god was listening, he watched as she spotted the coat rack lying on the floor and moved to set it aright. He hardly dared move, but he had to edge away from her, or she would come too close to him for comfort.

He took one careful step to the side, and his back brushed the wall with a barely audible rustle.

Audible enough, apparently. She turned to look in his direction.

Damn. He had never been good at sneaking.

He held his breath, hoping she couldn't hear his heart hammering in his chest as well.

She moved closer to his position and finally stopped right in front of him, so close he could see the intricate metalwork on a rose-shaped pendant she wore on a chain around her neck, just brushing the low neckline of her dress.

He had thought assassins were supposed to be small and wiry. She was on the shorter side, to be sure, but that generous bosom was anything but wiry.

Burning skies—not now, Vaughn. He could only hope his invisibility didn't choose that moment to ghost. With the moon being almost full, it could, at times, flicker, shimmer, or even show a brief outline. Usually that was while moving, however. As long as he stayed still...

Thankfully, she looked right through him and then around the room again, before shaking her head and re-entering the side room.

She left the door open a handswidth, and when he felt calm

enough to move, he tiptoed over to the door and peered through the gap.

She was running her hand along the back of the orange terror, murmuring to it. He could have sworn the phrase "damn cat" was included in her words.

Well, at least he wasn't alone in that assessment.

She nudged the cat to the side and picked up a coin purse that it had been sitting on. The cat furiously licked an imaginary spot on the fur Sweetblade had disturbed before settling back down again.

Sweetblade, on the other hand, pushed aside a painting that was hanging on the wall behind her desk, revealing a safe. She unlocked the safe with the pendant—some sort of key, apparently—and deposited the purse inside.

She set the painting back into place and then sat down in the chair, absently stroking the cat again while she stared off into the distance. It closed its eyes halfway and purred so loudly Vaughn could hear it from across the room.

If he had come here hoping to find information he could use to blackmail the assassin into helping him, he had succeeded, in the worst sort of way, since the information was useless to him. He could hardly confront her about her secret identity, as that would probably get him killed. And while the thought of trying to seduce an assassin so he could steal her key was a bit thrilling, he judged the odds of success to be slim.

And also likely to get him killed.

There had to be something else, something a little less dangerous for him, something he could use...

He shook his head. For now, he had tempted Temoth

enough. He carefully backed away from the door, pausing every few steps to be sure she hadn't heard a noise and decided to investigate again. He unbolted and opened the hall door with one long cringe, waiting for it to squeak or give some other telltale sign of its movement, and waiting then to be confronted with someone outside in the hall, wondering how a door was opening of its own accord.

He was lucky on both counts; the door moved silently, and the hall was empty. He closed the door as quietly as he could, but his luck ran out, as it still made a soft *snick* as it latched shut. He gave up on sneaking and fled down the hall, not waiting to see if she had heard.

Beidah lifted her head, ears erect, and looked toward Ivana's study door. Ivana followed her gaze. She hadn't heard anything, but Beidah had better hearing than she did. After a moment, Beidah apparently decided it was nothing and settled her head back down on her paws.

Ivana could take no such chances. She rose yet again to investigate; the earlier incident, while having a plausible explanation—Beidah like to haunt the ledge above the door, and she could have jumped down onto the coat rack and then knocked it over—still had Ivana on edge.

As before, she found nothing out in the main living area. A mouse skittering in the walls, perhaps? Ivana hoped not, or she might have to recruit some of Beidah's friends. She prided herself on the cleanliness of her inn. No bugs or vermin at The Red Rose.

She had just begun to turn to go back to her study, when she spied a peculiarity in the pattern of the rug. No, not in the pattern—it was a foreign object. She picked it up and laid it flat against her palm. A thin length of a silvery material shimmered in the lamplight. She frowned. She had nothing among her possessions this could have come from, so unless she or Aleena had tracked it in on their shoes...

She glanced at the door. The bolt was open, yet she was sure she had latched it earlier.

Someone *had* been here.

She crumbled the substance between her thumb and forefinger, watching as it turned to powder and drifted back to the rug.

There was something familiar about the substance, in as much as she *ought* to have known what it was. The answer niggled at the back of her mind, and long-forgotten tirades surfaced, diatribes from the mouths of the so-very pious priests of Yathyn, blasting Yathyn's worst enemies, the Banebringers, and their unnatural blood...

She spun on her heel and went back into her study. Much to the protest of the dozing cat, Ivana picked her up and forced the claws from the sheaths on one of her paws. She stared at the claws. They were streaked with the same silvery substance.

Beidah wriggled from Ivana's grasp, jumped down from the desk, and gave Ivana a perfectly understandable glare before stalking out of the room.

Flecks of the silvery substance still clung to Ivana's fingers, and she rubbed them together, entertaining one of the worst possibilities someone in her position could have.

Someone had most *certainly* been here, and that someone knew who she was.

Chapter Three

The Babe and the Blade

Vaughn had retreated to the inn's dining room while trying to decide on his next move. If he were smart, he would give up this whole venture.

And go where? Back to roaming the countryside? He couldn't take up his previous activities, not without endangering anyone who helped him. Gildas had made that clear.

Should he flee Setana altogether? He had heard that the pagan nations Setana hadn't managed to conquer yet were less hostile toward Banebringers, but less hostile didn't mean sympathetic. And he doubted borders were of any concern to his father, anyway.

Back to the manor? He wasn't ready to admit defeat yet.

No, there was only one solution to his personal predicament, if not to the general one all Banebringers faced: his father had to be stopped.

It was late; the dining room was empty but for the woman who was mopping floors, and silent but for the *splash-swish-swish* of her mop. She was a sweet thing, with large, round eyes framed in long eyelashes that gave her a certain look of innocence. Vaughn grinned. More likely, the better to seduce men with; fortunately for her, he was easily seduced.

Once again, he had to berate himself. This was one of those rare instances when it truly was not a good time. At least, not for acting. Imagining, on the other hand...

Footsteps coming down the hall broke the hypnotic effect of her mop strokes, and Vaughn stiffened.

But it wasn't Sweetblade; instead, it was yet another woman, who looked worried.

What is this?

The newcomer made her way directly to the mopping woman, and the two held a hushed conference that ended with the mop being set aside and the two women disappearing together back down the hall.

Vaughn stood. He had taken a room at an inn in the next block over; it couldn't hurt to see what was happening before returning for the night.

Ivana sat at her desk again, a pathetic pile of only three books stacked in front of her, and one open on her lap. It was everything she had in her personal library that might mention Banebringers. She knew very little about them other than what the priests of Yathyn spewed in their warnings against heresy and false gods.

Her lack of information wasn't a personal deficiency; there simply wasn't good, factual material out there, and if there ever had been, the Conclave had probably destroyed it.

Were there Banebringers who could move undetected? She didn't know. For that matter, she didn't know why their blood was silver, why they sought to unleash terrors on the land, why they worshipped false gods, and where, if their gods were false as the Conclave claimed, they gained their powers from. Powers she also knew next to nothing about, other than that they were named profane.

For all she knew, everything she knew about Banebringers was lies. She had moved for far too long on the underbelly of society to put much faith in pure motives for anyone, let alone priests.

And her sad collection of books wasn't adding anything to her lack of knowledge. It had never bothered her until now, when it was possible that a Banebringer was spying on her. Worse, a Banebringer who could spy on her without being seen.

She looked around her study for what must have been the tenth time in an hour. She didn't like not *knowing*. Not knowing enough about Banebringers. Not knowing whether what little she knew was true. Not knowing why a Banebringer was watching her, and who might have sent him or her. Not knowing whether the Banebringer could be in her study right now.

She slammed the book on her lap shut. No. She had bolted the door from the inside, and even if she were wrong, and the person hadn't left, she would solve nothing by staring at shadows. What she needed was a way to find and dispose of this interloper.

The problem was, for all they didn't know, the one fact everyone *did* know was that it was dangerous to kill a Banebringer, because when a Banebringer died, the death spawned a bloodbane—or monster, or demon, depending on who was describing the fiends. *She* knew this all too well from one near-disastrous personal experience. It was why Hunters Sedated them, instead of killing them. Sedation simultaneously rendered their powers inert and caused the Banebringer to enter an irreversible comatose state. The threat would be erased, without spawning even more bloodbane—as if the land needed more.

But that meant that should she catch this Banebringer, she would have to be creative in order to get rid of him. She couldn't chance a vicious monster appearing in the middle of her inn. And how would she catch him, when she couldn't see him?

Whatever his—or his master's—purpose was, it obviously wasn't to kill her, or she would already be dead. Even she couldn't stop an invisible knife. So she would simply count on the fact that he would continue following her, and when the right moment came...

She fingered the sheath of the dagger hidden under her desk.

She would be ready.

A knock sounded at her door, and she glanced at the clock. Who needed her at this time of night?

The hallways of the inn were silent but for the padding of the feet of the two women he was following. Despite the circumstances, he felt strangely calm. For some reason, ever since he had become a Banebringer, walking at night, especially when it was still and quiet, calmed him. He attributed it to whatever connection they assumed he had to the heretic moon goddess, but he didn't know if that was really the case.

They still understood so very little about Banebringers, partially because most people were too busy hating them and hunting them down to care, and partially because the Conclave had destroyed most of the historical records that might have helped them.

The women stopped at Sweetblade's door, and he drew back, crushing another sliver of aether just in case.

The second woman knocked.

Sweetblade answered a minute later, looking tired and irritated. "Zyanya? Ohtli?" She looked back and forth between the two women. "What is this about?"

The two glanced at each other, but the one who knocked spoke. "It's Caira, Da. She...she's having trouble."

Sweetblade raised her eyebrow. "Having trouble?"

The mopping woman spoke up. "The babe won't stop crying, and neither will she."

For a moment Vaughn thought Sweetblade would dismiss them, but instead she nodded curtly. "Give me a moment."

She disappeared back into her rooms, and then after a few minutes, stepped out into the hallway, closed and locked her door, and retreated down the hall with the other women.

Vaughn hesitated. Was whatever this was about worth the risk? His curiosity was piqued. Who were these women Sweetblade employed at her inn, anyway? With the addition of the newest woman they had just mentioned, that made five women so far—no, six, since he had seen a woman working in the stables. Was the inn run by a gaggle of sisters or cousins?

And what was this about a babe? Did Sweetblade have children? *That* would be useful information.

He decided to follow them.

The women retraced their steps down the hall toward the dining room, but turned off into another hall before they reached it. At the end of that hall was a door, which Sweetblade unlocked.

Vaughn caught the door just as it was about to shut and slipped through.

Sweetblade glanced back, no doubt catching the extra pause before the door latched shut, and Vaughn froze, but she didn't seem to pay it much mind and continued on with the group.

The door didn't lead to a room; instead the hallway continued as though no door had been there in the first place.

Vaughn glanced back, frowning. He had noticed that Sweetblade's inn seemed to stretch farther back than the space he had seen allowed, but he had assumed a large kitchen or perhaps meeting area. He hadn't considered that there might be another section of private rooms back here.

In his hesitation, he had to hurry to catch up as the group of women disappeared through another door, and once again he snuck through at the last moment.

The contrast between this room and the hallway was startling. Almost immediately, the cries of a child pierced the air; he couldn't believe he hadn't heard it out in the hall. Soundproofing again, apparently.

The room was spacious and had a few rocking chairs scattered around, as well as an entire wall devoted to—incredibly—children's playthings. A plush rug covered one half of the room and hardwood the other.

A woman sat on the floor in front of one of the rocking chairs, doubled over to her knees, arms wrapped above her head, sobbing, and next to her in a cradle lay a young baby, screaming. He supposed, by the description he had overheard, that this was Caira.

Vaughn crept around the perimeter of the room to get closer.

Sweetblade went to the woman immediately. She knelt in front of her and gestured sharply to the two wide-eyed women behind her. "Is one of you going to pick the babe up, or are you going to let it scream?"

The worried woman stepped forward to take the child. "We've already tried to calm him." She shifted the child to her shoulder in what looked like a natural manner. "He won't stop crying."

Sweetblade glanced at the woman holding the babe. "Take him to the other room," she said. "I'll attend in a moment."

The woman nodded and retreated, patting the babe on its back and muttering soothing words.

The cries lessened and then cut off as they disappeared into a door on the other side of the room, leaving only the sobs of the mother.

Sweetblade sat silently until the woman on the floor's sobbing subsided. "What's troubling you, girl?" she asked softly.

The woman, Caira, shook her head, and wrapped her arms tighter around herself.

The mopping woman spoke, then, so softly Vaughn found himself reflexively leaning closer to hear. "We've been worried that she's going to hurt herself, Da."

Sweetblade didn't react to that startling announcement. Instead, she gestured sharply to the mopping woman. "Leave us," she said. "Go help Zyanya with the babe."

She obeyed, leaving Sweetblade alone with Caira...and Vaughn.

He inched back a little bit, feeling out of place and uncomfortable. It was like stepping into an entirely different world—one he had never seen or known. All these women, crying children...

Perhaps it would be best for him to leave. Could he slip out of the door without one of the women noticing? Unlikely, at this point.

"Caira," Sweetblade said again.

There was a moment of silence, and then, "He wouldn't stop crying. He won't sleep, and he won't stop crying..." She trailed off. "I can't do it," she said, her voice hoarse. "I can't do this anymore."

"Hush," Sweetblade said, "of course you can. You're not alone. That's why you're here. You need to ask for help."

Vaughn blinked, confused. That's why the woman was at the inn? To get help with her child? That seemed...odd, even for someone who wasn't an assassin.

But Caira didn't seem to hear Sweetblade. Instead, she had started crying again, this time the silent, wracking sobs of a pain so deep the sound just wouldn't come out.

Vaughn understood that, at least.

Caira pulled herself into a ball and whispered something.

Sweetblade sat back on her heels and closed her eyes for a moment. She then pushed herself to her feet and entered the door where she had banished the other two women.

A moment later, all three had returned. "Take her back to your room," Sweetblade was saying. "See that she sleeps."

"What about the babe?"

They all stopped to look at the child. He had finally ceased crying and was looking up at Zyanya with wide eyes, squirming restlessly.

"Give him to me for now," Sweetblade said. "Take care of Caira. Tell the others to keep watch on her and help her if it looks like she needs it. Don't wait to be asked."

Zyanya nodded and handed the babe over to Sweetblade.

Vaughn watched with a mixture of horror and fascination as Sweetblade cradled the child in her arms. He wanted to call out—let the other women know they had just handed over a child to a killer. But he remained silent.

Zyanya urged Caira to get up, and she finally complied, and all the women except Sweetblade left out the back door.

The babe had started whimpering again, and Sweetblade sat down in the rocking chair with it and began singing a soft lull-aby.

Vaughn felt frozen to the floor. He couldn't take his eyes off

Sweetblade's face.

Not the sharp intelligence and wariness he had seen in her eyes when she had been investigating in her rooms. Not the irritability and shortness she had expressed toward the women, despite her outward demonstration of concern.

But tired. Worn.

Not expressions he would have expected on the face of an assassin.

Transfixed, he found himself moving closer to the rocking chair.

The babe's eyes had closed, and Sweetblade, still rocking, was staring out in the room, eyes distant.

And then Vaughn tripped over a heavy object on the floor. He caught himself with his hands—but not before letting out a soft "oof."

Sweetblade's face changed from soft to sharp in an instant, and she turned her head to stare directly at the spot where he was crouched.

Clumsy fool! he berated himself, heart pounding.

"Who's there?" Sweetblade asked, her voice soft, but on the edge of dangerous.

Sweetblade rose from her chair, and Vaughn scrambled to his feet and edged away.

Her eyes narrowed when she reached the same place, and she turned in a circle, eyes darting back and forth, and then looked down at the offending object—a boat, lying on its side.

A moment later, the perplexing woman was holding a sleeping babe in one arm and a dagger in the other.

Not good. Definitely not good.

What would the best course of action be? Hide and wait till she went away—and hope he had an opportunity to escape this area before other women entered? Flee and hope for the best?

Sweetblade stood silent and still for what seemed like an eternity. Her eyes passed where he stood twice, and both times he squeezed his eyes shut and held his breath.

Finally, she moved with an impossible silence to the cradle, laid the sleeping child down, and started circling the room, looking into every shadow and every corner, until she returned to where she had started.

Surely now she was convinced that no one was here.

Then she went to both of the doors in turn and locked them—with a key she had tucked in her pocket.

He swallowed. No getting out now without the key. He was running out of options. He briefly considered tackling her—she couldn't see him, after all—but that was dangerous with a dagger in her hand. He could probably overpower her with sheer mass, but he had to assume a respected assassin could hold her own in a scrap, and who knew what other tools she had available to her? What if he failed and took a mortal wound?

There was a reason Banebringers avoided melee fighting.

All right, then. He just had to wait her out. Even if she happened to move too close to him, he could slip farther away. As long as he stayed hidden, he could continue to evade her.

"I know you're here," she said softly, the sudden speech into the silence startling Vaughn. "You were in my rooms earlier, and I know you're here now."

How...?

"I'm guessing you can't stay invisible forever," she said. "I'm a patient woman. I can wait."

Vaughn gaped at her. How had she come to the conclusion that there was an invisible person in the room, rather than that the noise had simply been her imagination? That didn't seem to be a logical conclusion for a normal person.

And she was right. He could stay invisible for quite a while—hours, even—but eventually he would run out of his solid aether and then be forced to burn it from his own blood. That might gain him a few more hours before he risked burning too much and fainting from blood loss. And he could only stay invisible if he were conscious.

So he had perhaps five or six hours? How long until sunrise? Would the women come back and try to get into the room before then?

Surely. And then she would have to unlock it, and he could slip away.

"If you're thinking you're simply going to wait until someone else needs to get into the room, that won't work. My girls know that if the doors are locked, I'm not to be disturbed. It will be a while before they become concerned."

Her girls? "Perhaps sooner since you have one of their children in here with you," Vaughn blurted out.

And in the split second he had to contemplate, with horror, the stupidity of speaking at a time like this, she had lunged in his direction. He barely managed to stagger out of her way and to the other side of the room, but he was no longer moving even at his level of quiet, and she was on him again before he could think of a next move.

He dodged again and hit his thigh on the corner of one of

the low shelves that held toys. He grunted and stumbled to the side, and a moment later she swept by, catching his smarting leg and causing him to lose his balance.

He fell, and in his panic and desperation he lost control of the aether.

It was so astonishing to see a man simply *appear* out of nothing that Ivana almost lost the opportunity to strike while she had him on the ground, and while he was quite visible.

Almost.

Her blade found his throat and her knee his groin before she allowed herself time to think further on it.

"Wait!" the man cried out, struggling against her.

She looked down at him, and her deferred astonishment from the previous moment returned as shock.

She *knew* this man.

He returned her gaze, a bit of fear, but mostly frustration in his eyes.

No. No, it wasn't him. He simply had some similar features.

Blood started to seep out from around her blade; she was pressing too hard. She released the pressure on the dagger, but held it there, stopping short of doing real damage.

She shook herself, annoyed that she had allowed herself to become rattled. "Who are you? Who sent you?"

He tried to speak, but it came out as a whimper.

She lessened the pressure on his groin. "Answer me!"

"My name is Heilyn," he said. "No one sent me."

She leaned in close to his face. "People don't stalk assassins for their own entertainment," she said. "Tell me what I want to know, or I'll castrate you before I kill you. Slowly."

Incredibly, he tried to *smile*, though it came off as more of a grimace. "Your options are so generous," he said. "But you can't kill me, unless you want to spawn a bloodbane inside your inn."

He was wrong, of course. She could, and would, kill him. Banebringer or not, she could never let someone who knew her identity go free.

She simply couldn't do it inside her inn.

The blood trickling down his throat had started to change to the same silvery substance she had found on her rug and on Beidah. She fought down the side of her that wanted to be absolutely fascinated by this phenomenon. She could indulge her curiosity when he was dead. "You're a Banebringer," she stated.

He nodded, and then winced as the motion scraped the edge of her blade further against his throat. "I swear it—I'm here on my own. I—I needed your services..."

She stared at him. *My serv...* And the pieces fell together. Of course. Why else would someone be desperate to remove a Hunter?

"You're the one who wanted to hire me to kill a Hunter," she guessed.

He looked relieved, as if her recognition of him would mean she didn't have to kill him.

She relaxed. This was going to be easier than she had thought. This was no enemy or family of a hit who had discovered her identity. It was one naïve idiot. *Perfect.*

"Yes," he said. "Exactly. I—"

She allowed her relief to bleed into her voice. "My second

turned you down, so you thought you would track me down yourself to convince me?"

"Well—"

"You're an idiot." Or a good actor. She was wagering it was the first. She tended to recognize good actors, since she specialized in it herself.

"Yes," he said. "I'm also desperate."

"What's the name of the target?"

"It's Ri Gildas of Ferehar," he said.

So she and Aleena had guessed right. Did Gildas know a Banebringer was after him? If he did, by issuing a matching contract, he had ensured that whatever assassin decided to take him up on it would get an unpleasant surprise upon executing the terms. It seemed an unlikely action for a Hunter, whose job it was to find and Sedate Banebringers so they didn't *have* to be killed.

Perhaps now that she *had* to find a way to safely kill him, she should go ahead and turn in the contract. But blood-money from Gildas? It was almost more satisfying to think of how his quality of life must have degraded of late, and how she could prolong his anxiety by simply not turning in the contract.

"Hm. A worthy mark," she said.

Both of his eyebrows rose. "You know him?"

"Of him. Let's just say we've had some...unpleasant dealings in the past." That was putting it mildly. But all she wanted was to make this man feel more comfortable, not to share her life's story.

"Then will you at least hear me out?"

She paused before answering, as though considering. "Perhaps," she said. "But not here."

With almost perfect timing, Caira's babe whimpered. Men tended to be more trusting of women whom they viewed as taking on the role of a mother.

It was a calculated risk, but she couldn't kill him here, for multiple reasons, and she had to get him to her rooms before the sedative took hold. She dropped her hand and stood up.

The man sat up. "Can't say as I've ever wanted a woman to get *off* me so badly," he said.

Unamused, she turned her back on him, picked up the babe, and cradled him in her arms, murmuring to him until his cries subsided.

"I do not meet clients in my inn, for obvious reasons," she said quietly, without turning around. "Can you turn yourself invisible again?"

"Yes," he said.

"Good. Do so, and follow me back to my rooms."

Chapter Four

Demonspawn

Vaughn knew with absolute certainty that this was a bad idea. While Sweetblade's determination to kill him naturally had subsided upon learning he was a Banebringer, would she really consider his contract? What if this was a trap so she could turn him over to the Conclave?

He chewed on his lower lip, watching while she handed over the babe to one of the women before heading back to her rooms.

It was strange, but for a seasoned killer, she didn't seem so bad.

No, he decided. She was a criminal. She would want to avoid the law, not draw attention to herself by handing over another criminal, however large the reward.

And if he sensed something was about to go wrong, he could still disappear.

Whatever the case, he had no other options left to him. It was either this or limp back to the compound and admit defeat.

Once they were in her rooms again, she invited him into her study and gestured to a chair across from her desk. "Sit," she said, and he obeyed. She paused at a cabinet in the corner that held a respectable collection of liquor. "Can I offer you a drink?"

"Thank you, that would be..." He paused and met her eyes. They were unreadable. *Don't you think you've had enough stupid for one day?* "Ah, actually, I think I'll pass."

She inclined her head to one side and sat down without getting anything for herself. She tapped the point of her blade lightly against the desk and then set it down in front of her. "So, tell me, Heilyn. Why are you seeking to remove Ri Gildas?"

"I should think that would be obvious," he said, watching her now run one finger along the flat of the blade, as though caressing a lover.

"Indeed. But surely you've realized the futility of having anyone associated with the Conclave eliminated."

"As I said. I'm desperate."

"Mmmm," she said. She was still watching him with those unreadable, glimmering eyes.

He shifted nervously. "So what do you want to know?"

"Time, place, method?"

"I, ah..." He hadn't thought it through that much. Did it matter? He felt oddly confused by the question. "I don't know as..." He blinked a few times. Was the room getting hazy?

"Is something wrong?"

"I don't feel well," he said, more to himself than her.

"Indeed?"

Damn! He lurched from his chair and stumbled to the side. "You—you—"

She didn't move. Just watched him as he sank to the ground, knees suddenly unable to support his weight.

How had she done it? He hadn't...had he? His head was cloudy. He couldn't think. "You tricked me," he muttered. He was on all fours now, head hanging to the ground. *No. No, no, no.*

He sensed her getting up and moving closer, and then after he finally collapsed completely onto the ground, something hard pressed into his back. He couldn't even lift his head to look, couldn't move his arms as she tied his wrists, and then ankles, together behind his back. Could only lay there, helpless, feeling like his entire body had suddenly tripled in weight.

Her hazy outline knelt next to him, and her face came into focus for a moment. "Understand, Heilyn—if that is indeed your name—this is nothing personal."

"Promise me you'll kill me," he heard himself say, though his speech was slurred.

"Pardon?"

He couldn't see her expression. His eyes had closed. "Don't turn me over to the Conclave. I would rather die. Please."

There was a lengthy pause, and then, "I give you my word."

The last sound he heard before blackness was her wry addendum: "For what it's worth."

—————

A few minutes later, Ivana stared down at the unconscious form of Heilyn—the poor, stupid man—Aleena now at her side.

She had been relieved that the sedative she had applied to her blade before leaving her rooms had worked on him. She knew virtually nothing of the powers Banebringers had; for all she knew they couldn't be sedated in the more traditional sense.

In any case, it *had* worked, and she had him at her whims. Now she had to haul him out of the inn and preferably out of the city without being seen by anyone who cared.

"I'm reluctant to involve you in this," she said to Aleena, "but I'm afraid I can't get him out on my own."

"I am ever at your service, Da," Aleena said.

Ivana snorted. "Insubordination, now? I've clearly given you far too many liberties."

Aleena grinned and opened her mouth to, no doubt, give some rejoinder, but instead, she turned toward the study door. "What's that?"

Ivana heard it as well. It sounded like shouting coming from outside. She stepped out of the study, crossed the living area, and pulled back the curtain on the single window in her rooms to look outside.

An orange glow flickered off the buildings near the end of the street.

Fire?

But that guess was proven wrong a moment later when the head of a mob turned the corner and began marching down the street.

At first, she couldn't see well enough in the dark to make out what was happening, but by the time they had reached the square, enough people with torches had arrived, and combined with the moonlight, she could see two men in the front of the crowd dragging a young woman between them who had obviously been beaten.

This didn't bode well.

Aleena joined her at the window. "What is it?"

"I don't know," Ivana said, "but it doesn't look good." She glanced toward the study. Heilyn could wait long enough for her to see what was happening. He would be out for hours.

She hurried out of her rooms and to the door of the inn, Aleena on her heels.

Her inn was one of a number of businesses that formed a ring of buildings around a large, mostly empty square. The square was used for free-standing markets and events during festivals; the raised platform in the middle sometimes became a stage for plays or a dais for royal—or religious—proclamations.

The mob was already spilling into the square from the narrower street beyond, filling it quickly. A few of her neighbors stepped out of their doorways in the square, rubbing at tired eyes and staring in astonishment at the mob. One of them took off running in the opposite direction—either to get help or to get away.

The two who held the woman shoved her to the platform, and the mob circled it.

Now that she was outside, and the crowd was closer, she could understand the shouting.

"Demonspawn!" one woman cried, echoed by a dozen others.

A low chant was behind it all. "Sedate her! Sedate her!"

Ivana knew immediately what was happening; it was a flash Hunt.

They usually formed after the annual sky fire, when that year's Banebringers had just been created. Eager to take vengeance on the cause of the fresh slew of monsters roaming the land, crowds would flare into existence, rounding up anyone suspected of having become a Banebringer. It didn't usually end well, whether the person accused was a Banebringer or not. Every once in a while, it happened at other times of the year as well.

The two holding the woman on the platform were joined by another, an older woman, who was yelling at the crowd. "...performed her demon magic on my son!"

The accused woman looked both terrified and furious. "He was injured!" she shouted. "I was just trying to help! It's all I've ever tried to do!"

One of the men holding her backhanded her, and she reeled backwards, falling into the second man, who shoved her forward.

She stumbled and sank to her knees, shoulders shaking.

The mob surged forward, pressing closer to the platform, eager for blood.

Ivana clenched and relaxed her fists as she watched the unfolding scene. This was bad. This was very bad. If that woman died, who knew what kind of horror could be spawned? She and everyone in the vicinity were in danger, and not from the mob.

But she could do nothing but watch and hope the crowd had enough sense to control themselves.

Not likely.

Then, a new sort of shouting heralded the arrival of the Watch. At least a dozen of them fanned out through the crowd, trying to keep peace before the mob got out of control, but they were too late. The incensed crowd paid almost no attention to the soldiers, armed though they were, and the tops of their tusked helms swayed this way and that as they themselves were swallowed into the mob.

The crowd finally parted for a single man riding on a horse. He had the double stripe on his shoulder of an officer, and he spurred his mount through the crowd and dismounted at the platform. He stepped to the top and held a conversation Ivana couldn't hear with the men holding the woman.

The men with the woman held their hands up, and the crowd slowly quieted.

"The Watch will take over from here," the officer said. "She will be properly tested and Sedated if need be."

A murmur of dissent moved through the crowd.

Even so, the officer gestured sharply to two of his men, who then made their way to the platform and took hold of the woman's arms.

"No!" she cried, struggling. "Please!"

"Demonspawn!" a man in the crowd cried. "Don't let her speak!"

The accused woman's voice rose an octave. "Please! Have mercy!"

And then someone threw a rock.

The rock struck the woman squarely on the side of the temple, and the soldiers let go and backed away as another rock sailed their way.

She felt Aleena tense next to her. Ivana had rescued her from this exact situation—only not because Aleena was a Banebringer. This couldn't be easy for her to watch.

The woman panicked and tried to flee, only to be met by a wall of shouting people on every side.

She was a caged animal, darting this way and that, trying to avoid the increasing hail of rocks and other airborne objects.

Ivana cursed. *Idiots.* There were few scenarios in which this would end well.

"Aleena," Ivana said, having to raise her voice to be heard above the crowd. "Go back inside, gather the girls and the children, and take them out through the kitchen. Rouse any guests on the way and make them aware of the situation."

"What about the...problem...in your rooms?"

"It will keep. If there is still a reason to deal with it later, I will do so then."

"What are you going to do now, then?"

"Remain to see what happens."

"And what are you going to do against—"

"You have your orders. All of them." Including what to do should the worst happen to her. Aleena would understand.

Aleena put a hand on her arm, as if to pull her away. "Ivana—"

Ivana rounded on her and shook her hand off. "Don't," she said, "test my patience."

There was a long pause. "Yes, Da." Aleena slipped back inside.

And then, someone in the crowd near to the woman

screamed and pointed upward.

Ivana followed her hand. A murmur of confusion ran through those in the back of the crowd, and then more in the front shouted as well, pointing, until it spread backward like a wave. The surging mob panicked, every individual finding him or herself as trapped as the woman in the middle.

And then Ivana saw it too. Fiery black shapes diving through the air, into the crowd, and then back up again, white, jagged teeth glimmering in featureless faces.

Demons? They looked far too much like the mythical depictions in storybooks to be real. And as she questioned what he saw, the feeling that they were real faded. She could see the shapes diving, but whereas before she could have sworn they were knocking people down, now it was apparent that they were passing harmlessly through.

Not everyone was as quick to see through the illusion. One man took his rock and beat another man over the head with it. Ivana didn't know what the man saw, but he obviously didn't realize it was one of his fellow rioters.

Hallucinations.

She glanced back at the woman. Another manifestation of Banebringer powers?

It didn't take long for more people to realize the creatures weren't real. A few from the mob looked around, puzzled and dazed, and soon the realization spread.

An almost surreal lull in the chaos fell on the crowd as it collectively grasped what had happened.

Then the crowd roared and swallowed the woman.

Chapter Five

The Bloodbane

The mounted officer was frantic. "Stop!" he shouted. "Stop!"

At least someone had sense.

The center of the crowd, where the woman had disappeared, roiled with a blind rage, and Ivana turned around to look up at her inn. She didn't see anyone peering out of the windows; at least they all had sense, unlike her.

A moment later a woman shrieked from the middle of the crowd. "Demonspawn! She's a Banebringer!"

And now we find out how bad it will be.

A jagged line of light split the air and then began to separate, from top to bottom, like a seamstress ripping apart a seam. Ivana could still see in between the two halves of the ripped seam, but it was distorted, as though looking through a pair of spectacles she didn't need.

Everyone there froze, transfixed, unable to do anything but watch with morbid fascination to see what would happen next.

The blur darkened, and then two pupil-less white eyes appeared against it. They roved one way in the darkness, and then the next.

A woman screamed, and the mob broke apart. Panicked people attempted to flee in every direction, not caring who they pushed down or stepped on.

The monster pushed its way through the tear, piece by terrible piece. Its frame was indistinct at first, edges licking backward into the tear like blurry flames, but the more of it that came through, the more concrete the details became.

She shuddered as she gazed up at the emerging form. *Burning skies.* This was about as bad as it could get.

"Da Ivana!"

She turned. It was the baker's son from next door, a pleasant man whom Ivana suspected had taken a fancy to her.

He was gesturing wildly at her. "Get inside!" he shouted. "What are you doing?"

She gave him a grim smile but didn't move. He shook his head and fled into the illusion of safety that his store offered. In reality, there was no safe place against this monster.

It wasn't the first time she had seen a bloodbane that had been drawn to the tear in the veil between worlds that the death of a Banebringer caused, though this was by far the largest she had ever seen. She knew the strength of even the lesser ones and doubted the inn would offer much protection. In fact, being inside might be worse.

The two strings of light that still hung dangling in the air now met together at the bottom end and sewed the blur back where it belonged.

No such luck in the case of the monster. Fully through the tear, it unfurled itself to its full height—a bipedal as tall as the second story of her inn—and let out a deep roar that vibrated the cloth of her dress.

It swung its head back and forth, watching the fleeing crowd with those terrible eyes, as if considering what course of action might produce the most chaos.

Watchmen ran up to the monster and hacked at its legs with swords, which drew its attention away from the civilians.

That didn't last long. It shook his head, like a horse flicking at flies with its tail, and with one arc of its arm, swatted a group of the Watch, sending them flying through the air and into the wall of the tailor's shop on the other side of the square. Only one moved after they landed, but that one didn't get up.

It stepped on others, and the last two, the monster picked up in one hand, opened its mouth to reveal a neat row of knife-like teeth and...

Even Ivana had to look away. The sound of the screams cut off abruptly, but echoed in her ears long after they had stopped.

So much for the Watch.

She pressed herself back against the doorpost to her inn, hiding in the shadows.

Burning skies, Ivana thought. *Aleena was right. There's nothing I can do against this thing.*

A terrific crash filled the air, and then another reverberating roar. She dared to peer around the doorpost. The monster had turned its back to her and was snatching at the fleeing mob. Most escaped its lumbering grasp, and it wasn't happy about that.

It smashed its arm into the wall of the nearest building—the tailor's shop and home. The side of the shop caved in, glass windows shattering and timbers splitting like twigs.

Illusion of safety, indeed. She could only hope that someone brought down the monster before it smashed this entire quarter of the city into splinters.

The square was starting to clear. The monster was vicious and strong, but slow. It swung its head and body around like a galley trying to turn on a coin, seeking another target, and its eyes lit on a small crying figure.

Burning skies, it was a child. Why a youngster had been in the mob in the first place, Ivana didn't know—curse the parents who thought *that* was a good idea—but now she had been separated from whoever brought her and was one of the few left in the square.

Ivana was closer to the girl than the monster. She was sure she could get there before it could.

Ivana pressed her hand to the side of the doorpost, eyes focused on the child. The girl either didn't know enough to run or was too afraid to move.

The monster took one lumbering step toward the child, the neatly placed flagstones of the square cracking beneath its weight.

Ivana darted out into the square, waving her hands and yelling to draw the attention of the monster and hopefully the child.

She succeeded with both. The child blinked teary eyes, and as the monster took another step and reached for Ivana instead, Ivana threw herself into a side roll, coming so close to the claws on its hand she could feel the wind of their passing.

She rolled to a standing position at the side of the girl, hefted her onto her hip, and then ran the opposite direction.

The stones of the square vibrated under her feet as the monster turned to chase her, but she didn't look back. Instead, she ran as though the abyss itself were at her back—then again, perhaps it was—and when she reached the inn, nearly tossed the girl through the doorway. She pointed and shouted, "Run out the back! Do you understand? Run out the back!"

The girl froze, staring at her with wide eyes, and at first Ivana was afraid she *didn't* understand. But, finally, she turned and fled in the direction Ivana had been pointing.

Ivana glanced up at her inn once more and was dismayed to see a shadowy figure standing at one of the upper windows that looked suspiciously like one of her girls. She didn't have any female guests that night.

She gnashed her teeth. What were they still doing there?

Ivana turned around to find the blank white eyes pinned on her. The monster raised a clawed hand toward the side of her inn, angry at being foiled.

"Oh, no, you don't!" she screamed. She rolled again, into its reach, and hopped up onto one of its feet. She felt for the hidden slit in her skirt, slid her dagger out of the sheath on her thigh and through the slit with a practiced hand, and then jammed it as hard as she could into the monster's foot.

Silver-red blood seeped up from the wound, but she hadn't really hurt it. She did, however, accomplish her goal of distracting it from smashing her inn—and whoever was left inside.

Instead, it lifted its foot, trying to step on her. She flung herself forward and grasped at its ankle like the neck of a bucking horse, while it continued to flick its foot in an attempt to fling her off.

She had always imagined her end would come at the end of a noose or at the point of a soldier's sword, rather than squished like a bug. This was a disappointing way to go, after all she had been through. Her aching arms started to lose their tenuous hold, and she closed her eyes, waiting for the inevitable.

Vaughn woke to a pair of almond eyes set in a furry orange head staring down at him, and he was certain he had gone crazy.

He blinked and groaned, and the eyes disappeared. Had he finally managed to drink enough to become senseless—and give himself such a headache?

But when he tried to move and found himself hampered by bonds on his wrists and ankles, he remembered what had happened.

The assassin had deceived and manipulated him, and he had followed her straight into her trap.

But where was she?

He craned his neck as much as he could, but the study appeared to be empty, aside from the owner of the almond eyes. The cat now sat on top of Sweetblade's desk, staring down at him with flattened ears as though ready to pounce.

Great.

He heard the faint sound of shouting from outside, guessed that's why she wasn't there, and blessed whatever god had sent the distraction. He doubted Sweetblade realized that whatever she had used to knock him out wouldn't last as long on him as on a normal person.

Now, he couldn't waste his good luck. He blinked hard several times, trying to concentrate past the pounding in his skull.

What could he use to get out of this? Invisibility was useless to him until he was free of his bonds, so that left water.

Once again, he cursed himself for not practicing it more. He surveyed his surroundings again. *Water. Water.*

His eyes lit on the liquor cabinet. *Water...content?* And glass bottles which might break and provide sharp objects with which to cut his bonds.

He chewed on his lip, visually selected one of the smaller liquor bottles, burned the aether in his blood, and *pulled...*

It trembled.

He *pulled* again, and it toppled over onto its side without breaking.

Damn.

He took a few deep breaths, rolled to the side, and hefted himself to a sitting position. The room swam crazily, and he groaned again.

The cat hissed.

He glared at the beast. "Don't blame me," he told it. "You want me out of your space, help me find a way out of here."

The cat started washing its face, casting Vaughn dirty looks every time he moved.

"Great," he muttered. "Now I'm talking to a cat."

He inched his way over to the cabinet and then slammed his body into it.

A few more bottles tipped, but still none broke.

Frustrated, he spread out his concentration widely and pulled as hard as he could on all of the bottles...

That only accomplished knocking them all over and making his head swim all the more with the rapid expenditure of blood.

He slumped back, defeated.

Sweetblade's cat stood up, stretched, and sprang to the shelf that contained the bottles. It pawed at one, causing it to roll around a bit. It paused, as though considering, and then pushed it off the edge. It watched the bottle fall to the hard wood—not hard enough, apparently, since it still didn't break—and apparently pleased with its efforts, began systematically knocking the bottles off the shelves.

"Is this something you frequently do in your spare time?" Vaughn asked the cat. "I can't imagine your mistress would be too fond of that hobby."

The cat flattened its ears again and renewed its activities with even more vigor, occasionally looking over at Vaughn with a wild look in its eyes.

Then, it happened. One of the bottles hit the growing pile of glass just right, and it shattered. The cat jumped, hissed at Vaughn—as though it were his fault—and then stalked out of the study.

"Crazy beast," Vaughn muttered.

Still.

He edged over to the glass shards, turned his back to the mess, and used his bound hands to gingerly feel for the neck of the bottle, which had broken off whole from the top. He managed to find it without slicing open his fingers, and then held the unbroken part in one hand and started sawing at the rope with the sharp edges.

It wasn't as easy as he thought it would be. He couldn't see what he was doing; the bottle kept slipping, and he was certain he was going to end up slitting his own wrists instead.

Fortunately, while his attempt at cutting through the rope itself wasn't working as well as he had hoped, his efforts *were* loosening it. He could feel the rope start to slip and burn on his wrists as tiny threads stretched and snapped.

A few more seconds...

There.

He wriggled his wrists—and a little bit of skin—free.

Whatever was going on outside the inn was escalating. He could hear screaming as he worked the bonds off his ankles, stood, and stretched.

He had to get out of here before she came back. He had a feeling next time she wouldn't be so foolish as to leave him alone with her cat. But it *still* felt like his brain was trying to bounce around his skull.

Liquor was good for something, at least. He picked up one of the smallest bottles and read the date. He whistled. Expensive stuff. He grinned, popped the cork, and downed it. "Why thank you," he said, setting the empty bottle on her desk. "Don't mind if I do."

But Vaughn's momentary merriment disappeared once he

found a window. He looked outside in disbelief.

An enormous bloodbane was stepping through a rift in the courtyard right outside the inn. He had never seen one so large; if the theory about the size and ferocity of the monster being correlated to how much the dead Banebringer had used their powers was correct, this Banebringer must have been quite active.

And this bloodbane was not only big, but savage. It had hardly stepped through the rift before it started looking for prey. This one wouldn't flee, not like a bloodwolf—this one was out for carnage, and in the middle of a city...

Vaughn felt sick.

Assassin or no assassin, he had to act. The bloodbane would crush half the city before the Watch would be able to bring it down with their mundane weapons.

He opened the window, slipped out, and ran for the alley where he had hidden his bow.

The inevitable didn't come. Instead, the monster roared again. It stumbled backward, stones crunching and cracking under its feet, and Ivana was finally knocked loose from her precarious hold on its foot.

She rolled again to the side, expecting to be squashed at any moment, and when she wasn't, she whirled around to see what had distracted the monster this time.

She followed its gaze up until she spied a figure standing on top of her inn, backlit by the nearly full moon behind it, drawn bow against its arm.

The figure let loose an arrow, and it struck the monster in one of its eyes, evoking another deafening roar. It was then Ivana saw the feathered shaft of a second arrow sticking out of the monster's other eye. The distraction from moments ago.

Ivana forgotten as nothing but a nuisance, the monster stomped its feet, and threw one arm out wildly in the direction of the archer. Ivana guessed it had been blinded, and alarm pulsed through her as the arm narrowly missed shaving the top floor of her inn off.

She screamed, leapt onto the monster's foot, and jammed her dagger into it again, and again, until her already sore arms trembled from the effort.

The monster's hand had been on a direct trajectory toward the archer, but her move caused it to falter, and it began its slow dance again, furious that the mouse had come back to nip at its feet.

The archer let another arrow fly, and it struck the monster to the side of the knee cap. Incredibly, the arrow slid through the heavy hide at the knee, and the monster's leg buckled. It fell with a crash onto the good knee, and nearly on top of Ivana.

She flung herself out of the way, and the ground met her right shoulder and arm with an inelegant skid. She stumbled to her feet, ignoring the sudden fire that ignited down her arm. Another arrow was already flying toward the monster's other knee, and then it fell forward. The entire square shook as its full weight hit the ground, and more timbers fell out of the crushed side of the tailor's shop, along with the crenellations on top of the building next to it.

But the monster was far from defeated. It thrashed on the

ground, trying to get up, and only succeeded in kicking through the wall of another building.

When she looked next, the archer had disappeared.

Ivana didn't know if he had gone to find a better vantage point, or if he had decided that was all he could do, but she wasn't going to lose the opportunity while the monster was disabled. Summoning every ounce of strength left in her, she pulled herself up its heaving side, plunging her dagger in again and again for a sturdy handhold for one hand, and grasping at divots in its hide for the other, and scrambled onto its back.

She had no idea what to do next, but she figured going for the head was always a good idea. She scrambled along its hide, half-crawling, half slithering on her stomach to avoid being thrown off, until she reached the center of its shoulders. She pulled out her dagger again, and jammed it into the side of its neck, hoping she would hit a vital area.

It thrashed even harder as more blood welled up, but not enough to matter. Frustrated, she jammed it in again, at a different spot.

The monster's arm tried to reach backward to grab her, but it simply didn't bend that way. So instead, it rolled over.

She used the momentum of its roll to fling herself through the air to avoid being crushed underneath and landed in a much more graceful crouch next to it. Blinded as it was, its arm flailed wildly at her, and she darted this way and that, trying to anticipate where it would fall next.

And then, all of a sudden, the monster let out one ear-shattering roar—so loud that for a moment the sounds around her faded. It tried to roar again, but it came out as an eerie, rumbling gurgle. It thrashed, shuddered, twitched, and then fell still.

Gasping for air, trembling from the energy pulsing through her overwrought body, she stared up at the monster's stomach.

The mysterious archer stood on top of the monster, bow in his hand.

Ivana shook herself and scrambled up the side of the monster again.

The shafts of three arrows barely poked up out of the hide of the monster in the center of its throat.

She turned to the archer and immediately recognized him. "You!"

Heilyn bowed deeply, like some noble bowing to the king. "At your service, Da."

"How did you—you should be—" She caught herself before she said more. Irrational rage pulsed through her, that he had escaped, that he had caught her unaware, that he didn't even seem to care. She settled for an unfair accusation. "You almost got my inn smashed!"

"Your cat helped me," he responded in answer to her unfinished question, a charming, crooked smile on his face.

A charming, crooked smile she had long since stopped dreaming about, stopped caring about, stopped *thinking* about—yet it hit her like one of his arrows, bounced off her walls...and left a crack.

She sucked air in through her teeth, finally seeing it. He didn't merely have similar features. This was no coincidence. Ri Gildas and a man who looked like Airell, his oldest son, showing up in context to each other?

She would bet her entire safe this man was closely related to him. A cousin? A brother, even?

His eyes slid down the length of her body and lingered below her waist; the skirt of her dress had torn at some point in her frantic movements and was revealing a long stretch of thigh. She glared at him and pulled the pieces of her skirt together.

Yes, definitely related.

The look did nothing to soothe her anger. She paced closer to him, dagger clenched in one hand, still dripping with the monster's blood. To her intense satisfaction, he backed away from her, finally looking nervous like he ought. "Whoa," he said, holding his hands out to the side, revealing the raw skin around his wrists where the rope had been tied. "I saved your life."

"I don't keep tally of debts," she said through clenched teeth.

He glanced back at the inn. "Is this really where you want to do this?"

As if to emphasize his words, the sound of jingling armor floated down the street. More Watch come, too late, to help.

He cast her another one of those grins. "And sounds like we have company. I'm sure they'll be fascinated to find that a humble innkeeper helped to take down this behemoth."

His eyes flicked pointedly to her dagger.

She was trapped, and she hated him for it. She couldn't kill him here, and not only because it would spawn another bloodbane. The Watch would see her, and potentially anyone who was still left in the square, watching. She had already revealed far too much about her other set of skills as it was.

Yet she couldn't let him go. He knew who she was, about her inn, about her girls. There were people who would pay to know those things—and do something nefarious with the information.

But of the two choices, only one had immediate consequences.

"This changes nothing," she spat at him, sheathing her dagger. "Don't think I won't find you."

And yet, how would she ever find an invisible man? She slid down the monster's side, anger almost to the point of boiling over, marched into her inn, and slammed the door behind her.

She was greeted by Caira, who was standing near the door holding a lantern. Her eyes roved to Ivana's arm, and Ivana followed her gaze. Her blouse sleeve was in tatters, the shreds sticking to one long, oozing scrape down her arm, from shoulder to elbow.

"Are you well?" Caira asked.

"I'll live," Ivana snapped. "Why are you still here?"

"Where else would I go?"

She didn't want to deal with this right now. She was physically and mentally exhausted, and worse, she felt that *crack* like a splinter beneath her skin. She wanted to tend to her wound, get a bath and go to bed, so that she could rise fresh and begin preparations for how she was going to handle this complication that had arisen in her life.

She pushed aside her own desires for the time being.

"Where are the others?"

"Nearby."

Too nearby, no doubt. "Then, since you were so foolish as to stay here, you can have the task of retrieving them."

Caira nodded again, and turned to go. But she paused at the

threshold of the kitchen. "Da?"

"What is it?"

"How...how did you learn to fight like that?"

Ivana rubbed one hand over her face and then turned to face Caira. "A long-forgotten diversion from my youth," she said. "I suppose it came back to me in my time of need."

Caira studied her for a moment, and then nodded and left through the kitchen door.

Ivana put her back to the wall, closed her eyes, and slid down it until she reached the floor.

"Don't worry. I'll make sure the story sticks."

Oh for— "The gods smite me ten thousand times over, why in the abyss are you still here? Did I not give an order?"

Aleena moved closer. "I followed it."

"Caira was still here."

"She wouldn't leave. I think she was hoping a monster would crush the inn with her inside. We took her babe with us, though."

Ivana exhaled. "Why did you come back? You shouldn't have left the girls."

"You weren't explicit on that point. I wanted to make sure you were well."

Ivana struggled to her feet. Why in the abyss did everyone suddenly care about her wellbeing? "Your primary task is always—*always*—to make sure the women and children are safe."

"They care about you, you know. We all do."

Ivan stiffened. "They shouldn't." She looked out the window. Dal Heilyn was gone. She turned to leave.

"Ivana—"

She whirled around. "You will address me as Da. Now, go help Caira find the others, get some sleep, and attend me first thing in the morning. We have something we need to discuss."

Aleena lifted her chin and met Ivana's eyes. "Yes, Da," she said, but there was no submission in her voice. She turned and left.

Ivana exhaled again. She had spent years meticulously crafting her world, keeping every piece under control and in its proper place.

It was unraveling, and she didn't like it.

Of course, it was bound to happen eventually. The world she had made would become the world she deserved.

She roused herself and started back down the hall. But that didn't mean it had to be this day.

Vaughn stood on top of the monster, watching the retreat of the assassin until she disappeared back into the inn, unable to help but admire her—in more than one way. She had fire, that was for sure. Then again, he supposed such qualities were useful for an assassin.

He shook his head. But it was a cold fire. She had stalked straight past half a dozen bodies, some mangled beyond recognition, without even pausing to look.

He looked. He always forced himself to. From his vantage, he could see the entirety of the destruction that the beast had caused. It could have been much, much worse, but that didn't mean it wasn't bad.

In addition to the corpses Sweetblade had passed, another

dozen were scattered around the square in various states of wholeness. Eight of those were the unfortunate Watch; the rest were from the mob: men, women, though thankfully no children. The reinforcements had started to arrive, and some were now moving among the bodies, checking for signs of life. Others were picking their way into the damaged buildings.

For most of the dead, it was their own idiotic fault. He would never understand it. *Everyone* knew if a Banebringer were killed, the death would pull a monster from the abyss. Yet, if the circumstances were right, people would still allow themselves to become whipped into a mindless fury, heedless of the danger to themselves or anyone else, simply because Banebringers were *that* hated.

But the carnage wasn't limited to those who had come with the mob. He didn't know if anyone had been killed when the monster had crushed buildings around it. And the Watch weren't part of the mob. They were merely doing their duty.

It was a bitter reminder of what could happen simply because he and others like him existed. He never wanted to forget that. Never wanted to be tempted not to care, like some others, simply because they hated him.

Someone called to him from below, and he glanced down to see two Watchmen and a rotund, balding man at the side of the monster. One of the Watchmen was an officer. The bald man was twisting a hat in his hand, casting fearful glances at the monster.

"Pardon, Dal!" the officer shouted. "Could you come down?"

Vaughn gave a brief wave to indicate his acquiescence, but before clambering down off the beast he retrieved his arrows.

The only reason they had slid so easily through the monster's flesh was due to the beastblood aether infused into the heads. While the suspicious silvery substance would be sealed inside, he didn't need to take any chances. He had already drawn enough attention to himself.

When he reached the ground, the two soldiers bowed deeply. "Dal," the officer said, "this man says you were involved in slaying this beast."

"I've some skill with the bow," Vaughn said, lifting his bow for emphasis. "I did what I could."

"Some arrows," the officer said, eyeing Vaughn's quiver.

Vaughn shifted and shrugged the quiver farther back on his shoulders, glad he had retrieved the arrows. "My cousin is a master smith," he said. "Sometimes it seems he can work magic at his forge." He wanted to be away from their scrutiny—and away from the assassin who was now going to be pursing him.

As if having his own personal Hunter on his tail wasn't enough.

"If I could, Watchman...?" the bald man interjected.

The officer waved at him, and the man scurried away. Thankfully, the interruption seemed to distract the officer from the subject of Vaughn's arrows.

"I'm told you're not from around here."

Vaughn's mind worked. "Ah, no. I was a guest at the inn over there." He waved in the general direction of Sweetblade's inn.

"Well, regardless, the Ri will want to know your name so you can be properly rewarded."

Vaughn paused. *Of course.* The king encouraged the Ri and Gan to give generous rewards to subjects who slew bloodbane.

He said it encouraged "citizen responsibility" to chip away at their numbers. What it really did was encourage young, foolish men to commit suicide. Still, every bit helped—and as a bonus, the nobles who had the luck of rewarding such subjects were recognized at court, as if they themselves had done the slaying.

But what a way to start his next stint at laying low. This was why he hunted monsters out where there were no nobles to use him as a trophy; only poor, grateful villagers.

At least, why he used to hunt monsters in such places. He *had* to disappear, and fast.

"And the shoemaker says there was a woman with you as well," the officer said before he could reply, raising an eyebrow in question.

An idea came to him. Could Sweetblade be convinced he wasn't a threat? Perhaps, but only if he had time to do so.

"My name is Heilyn. And, yes," he said. "There was a woman. And if she hadn't helped me, I wouldn't be standing here."

"Truly? We assumed he didn't see right, with all the excitement..." The officer shrugged. "Who is she?"

He did not, in fact, know her real name. "The innkeeper where I was staying."

The officer's mouth dropped open. "An *innkeeper* helped you take down this monster?"

"So it would seem."

The officer nodded again. "Well, Dal Heilyn, if you'll stay put for a day or two, you'll likely receive a message from the Ri."

Vaughn bowed again, and the two Watchmen turned to leave. He had just made an incredible gamble in order to keep the assassin off his back for a little while longer. It likely wouldn't turn out well, but with both a Hunter and an assassin after him, he would never be able to leave the safety of the Ichtaca again.

He ambled toward the inn, keeping an eye on the Watchmen, and then stopped on the other side of the monster's body, where they wouldn't be able to see him.

A silvery sheen coated the ground around a woman's body where a normal person's pool of blood would be—solidified aether from the Banebringer.

Some of the aether had already been crushed beyond his ability to easily transport under the feet of the mob—and monster, no doubt—but a good portion was still relatively intact.

He didn't know what kind of Banebringer she had been, but he could make an educated guess. Bindbloods were some of the Banebringers who were caught most frequently, usually because they couldn't resist using their abilities to help people. And if there was any truth to the correlation between the frequency of aether use and the strength of the bloodbane summoned...

He couldn't just *leave* without taking some of the aether. He glanced around. The Watchmen were still out of sight; he could hear them talking from the other side of the monster. He glanced up at the windows before him. Was anyone still watching? If they had sense, they would have fled.

His eyes roved to each window, checking to be sure there were no curious faces pressed to panes of glass, and he saw no one.

Reasonably satisfied he was out of sight from inquisitive eyes, he pried up a hefty chunk of the aether and then pocketed it. The priests, when they finally arrived to clean up the profane substance before it could do something completely fictitious like, oh, contaminate the water supply, wouldn't notice one piece of the aether missing amidst all that had already been crushed.

And with a final glance around him and at the windows again, he left the square and entered a nearby alley.

To anyone who would be watching, it would appear that he never left it.

Chapter Six

Buying Time

I vana drew the cup of tea she had been nursing closer to herself. It had gone tepid, but she took a sip anyway, and then wrapped her fingers around the body of the cup. She glanced out the window, taking a mental break from pondering her plans on how to deal with Heilyn beyond tasking Aleena with discovering his whereabouts.

The sun was well on its way to its place of rest. A group of priests had already been by to gather up the aether left behind by the Banebringer woman, and a group of workmen had removed the human corpses—or what was left of them. Then, a different group of men had stood around and argued for an hour, presumably about the best way to remove the monster's body, which was far too large and heavy to drag through the streets.

Finally, they had brought in a cart and secured the services of a priest, who was now moving about the carcass, touching joints and muttering whatever arcane words made his magic work. Now and again, a small puff of smoke rose from his hands, and some of the men came with large saws to cut through the weakened joint and haul away a finger or a toe. Currently, they were working on dragging one of its forearms over to the cart.

A slow process that would likely continue all week.

She sighed. Her inn was quiet and empty. Anyone with half a brain had fled; she hadn't seen a single guest since she had forced herself out of bed this morning, and likely wouldn't until they managed to get rid of that monstrosity—especially if they left it long enough to start putrefying.

Enormous, rotting carcasses in the square weren't exactly good for business.

That was why she was surprised when a strange man walked through the door of her inn as the sun was setting.

He wore the livery of the Ri of Weylyn—currently a man named Talesin—but had the dark skin of a man from the southern region of Donia, darker even than the deep bronze of her home region of Ferehar.

He made straight for her and bowed low when he reached her. "Pardon me, but I'm looking for the proprietor of this inn, a Da Ivana."

She put on her most gracious smile, rose, and curtsied. "That would be me, Dal. How may I serve?"

His eyes swept over her critically. "I bear a message from Ri

Talesin for you and a Dal Heilyn, a guest here."

She took one long, slow breath in through her nose. *To the abyss with him.* What now?

"All of my guests have fled," she said, "and none have returned yet that I am aware of. However, I will hear your message and pass it along should the guest in question return."

"Very well. My master would like you and Dal Heilyn to accompany me back to his estate, so that he might personally extend his gratitude for your recent service to the region."

"My recent service, Dal?"

"It has been reported to Ri Talesin that you and Dal Heilyn were instrumental in slaying the bloodbane which appeared here last night."

Reported, indeed. By none other than Heilyn himself, she was sure.

"Oh!" she said, putting a hand to her chest, feigning surprise while her mind skimmed through all her options. "I didn't know anyone even noticed." Public recognition for skills she preferred to keep quiet was the last thing she wanted. But she couldn't deny the messenger's identification of her as taking part in the slaying. All it would take would be for Caira to walk in and confirm his words in an idle comment. Neither could she refuse to go with him, as that would be unthinkably rude for a common, humble innkeeper like herself—not to mention she would draw attention to herself for the insanity of refusing a reward.

She was going to kill Dal Heilyn. Literally. But that was nothing new. Could she do worse than kill him? "I would be honored. What time should I be present?"

"The Ri already had plans to leave this morning for his country estate," the messenger said. "Therefore you and Dal Heilyn are to join him there at a banquet where you will be honored. A second caravan is leaving for his estate tomorrow; I will return in the morning to collect you so that you may join it. Please make sure Dal Heilyn attends."

As the messenger was speaking, Heilyn waltzed in from the hallway to the rooms, carrying a satchel and his bow.

That invisibility trick was *really* starting to annoy her.

"I heard my name." He bowed to the messenger. "Dal Heilyn."

"Ah. So you are still here. I will leave the explanation to Da Ivana, as I have other matters to attend to. Good day."

Ivana resisted the urge to sneer at the messenger's back as he left. The Ri's country estate. A day's journey there and back, not to mention the two or three days at the estate himself. *How typical of a noble.* If he really cared about those he was rewarding, he would have put off his plans to leave the city for another day. It probably didn't even occur to him what a hardship it would be for most commoners to simply go off gallivanting through the countryside at a moment's notice, even for a substantial reward.

But she had more pressing aggravations, the most important of which was standing just out of arm's reach.

Vaughn gave her a broad smile when she turned to look at him. "Ivana, is it?"

She didn't return his smile. He had trapped her—again. She couldn't dispose of him now, not without drawing additional attention to herself and the entire affair. It would have to wait until after they collected the reward, and eyes were turned the other way. "I suppose you think you're clever," she said.

"Not at all," he said. "Merely resourceful."

"All this does is buy you time."

"I'm aware. But I've bought a lot of time in my life." He winked. "I'm becoming quite the haggler."

Insufferable—

A trill of laughter sounded from the hallway, and a moment later, Ohtli's little boy ran into the common, straight for the front door.

Ohtli chased after him, dismay on her face. "Oh, no, no! Please don't go out there..."

He giggled and hurtled onward, glee at escaping his mother giving him extra energy.

He ran right past Dal Heilyn, who reached down to scoop him up as he passed by. He flew him through the air, much to the boy's delight, and right back into Ohtli's arms. "Oh no, you don't," he said.

"Oh!" Ohtli exclaimed, looking up at Heilyn with wide eyes. "Thank you, Dal..."

He bowed, giving Ohtli a charming smile; no, not *a* charming smile, *that* charming smile. "Of course, Da. Not a pretty sight out there for anyone's eyes, let alone a little one."

Ohtli blushed, returned his smile, and curtsied.

Ivana's stomach soured at her distaste for this man. "Ohtli," Ivana said. "Could you please find Aleena? Tell her to meet me at room four."

Ohtli looked away from Heilyn and to the ground. "Of course, Da." She curtsied again, this time to Ivana, and hurried away, child now snugged to her hip, but not without another backward glance at Heilyn, who winked at her.

"You will follow me," Ivana said to Heilyn. She just had to make it through this. And then...

"Room four?" Vaughn asked Sweetblade as he followed her down the hall. Sweetblade didn't respond.

Vaughn hoped that wasn't code for "torture room," or some such. He was reasonably certain Sweetblade wouldn't dare to murder him now, not while Ri Talesin was expecting both of them. Still, there was a lot a person could do beside murder.

"If you think I'm following you into another—"

Sweetblade stopped, unlocked a door labeled with a large numeral "4," and pushed the door open. "You will stay here until we leave."

He peeked through the door. It was, in fact, a comfortably furnished guest room. "Ah."

She held out her hand toward the room. "Please."

He hesitated. "You know, I actually already rented a room at another nearby—"

"That isn't what you told Ri Talesin's messenger, was it? Best to keep your story consistent."

She had caught him at his own game. "Right." He slid past her and into the room.

To his relief, another woman appeared just then and met Sweetblade outside the door before they entered the room together.

Sweetblade shut the door and faced the other woman.

"Aleena. I do believe you've met Dal Heilyn before."

Aleena inclined her head. "Indeed, though he may not know me."

He did, of course, since he had followed her to the inn, but they didn't know that. Average height, average build—in fact, she was pretty much average all around. She wouldn't stand out in a crowd and had the guileless, open face of someone you immediately felt you could trust. Plain, but pretty in her way. She didn't seem the degenerate sort.

"Please ensure our guest is comfortable for this evening," Sweetblade said.

"Is that code for, 'rip his fingernails off while he's sleeping?'"

Sweetblade ignored him. "We have been invited to Ri Talesin's country estate to be honored for our heroism and courage in dispatching the bloodbane last night." There was a touch of dryness in her voice, especially on the word "heroism." "I will be gone for at least four days; please see to the inn in my absence."

"Of course, Da." Aleena then proceeded to relieve Vaughn of his bow and quiver.

"Please don't lose those," he said. "They're...special." Aleena raised an eyebrow, but didn't reply. He wondered how much this Aleena was involved in her mistress' affairs. Was she only a contact? Was she also an apprentice?

She tucked his bow under her arm and waited, though Vaughn wasn't sure for what.

Sweetblade turned to Vaughn and started systematically patting him down, presumably looking for other weapons. "As for you, I have no way of *discreetly* locking you in a guest room until tomorrow. You will not, however, leave the inn."

"I wouldn't dream of it," he said. "Is breakfast included?"

Sweetblade met his eyes, and her own were hard and not at all amused. "May I remind you of the precarious nature of your circumstances?" Finding nothing on him that resembled a weapon, she then riffled through his bag. She found the knife he used to make solid aether and gave that to Aleena. She paused at the leather case carrying the qixli, opened it, but then closed it again without comment.

"Precarious and I are close friends," Vaughn said. In truth, while he was used to being Hunted, being expected to sleep while an assassin who was out for his blood lurked about? This was a new level of precarious for him. It was almost thrilling.

"I cannot decide if you are stupid, rash, or arrogant."

"Likely a bit of each," he said. "For instance, would it be stupid, rash, or arrogant of me to note that you have skilled hands?"

She narrowed her eyes, but he went on anyway. "Are you sure you found all my weapons? I wouldn't mind if you checked again."

She gave him a scathing look, but to his surprise, ran her hands over him again.

That was too easy. What was the catch? "If you're not doing anything tonight, I happen to have come into possession of a private room with a comfortable bed…"

"How fascinating," she said, and then moved even closer to him, tilting her head up a hair, as though waiting for a kiss. "You should know something, Dal Heilyn."

"What is that?" He leaned in toward her, unable to resist her bait. There was something dangerously intoxicating about this woman.

"Men who find themselves in bed with me usually don't get out again."

"That's all right," he murmured. "I don't mind the floor."

A snort issued from behind him, and they both turned to see Aleena covering up a smile.

Sweetblade didn't look amused. Vaughn didn't have time to be amused, because a moment later, crushing pain nearly sent him to his knees. She had ahold of his balls and was squeezing...

"I pulled the balls right off a man once," she said. "You don't want the floor either."

"I don't...believe you!"

She twisted. "Shall we find out?"

"No," he gasped. "No, I don't think so."

She released him, and he stumbled to the bed, sat down, and put his hands on his knees, waiting for the pain to subside. *Damn woman.*

"Sweet dreams," she said, and then turned and left.

"It's code for, 'don't let him out of your sight,'" a voice said from near the door.

He looked up. Aleena was still there, now leaning casually against the wall, and still looking faintly amused.

What was this? Why was she talking to him? "I see," he said slowly. "But I have this handy trick to take care of that."

She smiled, and it actually seemed genuine. "The inn is a place of safety for you right now," she said. "As long as you're here, she most likely won't harm you. I wouldn't chance leaving if I were you. Even the upcoming banquet may not be enough to save you if you make her angry enough."

"Most likely? May not?" He didn't want to hear qualifications right now.

"A word of advice: if you want her to trust you enough to let you go free, trying to seduce her is not the way to do it."

Was this woman offering him *help*? He felt a tendril of hope. "That suggests there might be a way to convince her to trust me?"

"Unlikely. But if there were, that wouldn't be it."

"She trusts you," he pointed out.

Aleena paused. "Yes."

"Should she?" he ventured.

She chuckled. "I am an excellent judge of character, Dal Heilyn. I don't believe you are a threat. But in this case, my opinion won't matter."

"So she really will kill me once she has the chance?"

Unfortunately, there wasn't the slightest hint of hesitation before she answered. "Absolutely."

"Will she give up the chase if I get away?

"No."

Great. He had come into this hoping to get rid of one pursuer, and instead would come out with two. He *had* to find a way, before this was over, to convince Sweetblade he wasn't a threat to her. "I don't suppose you would talk to her?"

"Good night, Dal Heilyn." She moved toward the door.

"Wait—"

She turned and raised an eyebrow at him.

"Did she really tear off a man's balls?"

Aleena smiled. And left.

Vaughn shuddered and tried not to think about it.

He flicked his eyes up to the mantle over the fireplace. A full bottle of lupque rested there. Probably came with the nicer rooms, like this one. Either that or Sweetblade was trying to entice him into drugging himself.

If only. He walked over to the mantle, picked up the glass bottle, and after considering the milky white substance inside, unstopped it and downed the entire bottle in a half-dozen gulps. It was enough to knock a normal man out cold.

He tilted his head, the neck of the bottle still dangling from one hand, and waited, hoping that this time it would be different. But it wouldn't be. It never was.

And sure enough, aside from the pungent taste and the burning in his throat and stomach, he felt fine.

He refrained from hurling the bottle across the room, which was a vast improvement in his self-control compared to eight years ago. Instead, he set it back on the mantle and walked over to the window. He pulled back one curtain and looked up at the moon, hanging half-full in the evening sky.

"Is the lot you gave me not bad enough, without also giving me some way of escaping it?" he asked it, not for the first time. As usual, it lazed about silently, unconcerned with him and his problems.

He let the curtain fall back in place, the familiar feeling of despair rising within. Sweetblade was right. He had bought himself some time, and that was all. Would the three or four days he had with her be enough to convince her he wasn't a threat?

He smothered the darkness with a practiced hand. Well, if

he had less than a week to live, he might as well make the best of it.

"Da?"

Ivana didn't look up from her books. She had spent the past two hours furiously trying to glean anything there was to know, anything she might have missed, about Banebringers before taking this trip. Was there a way to thwart his invisibility, for instance?

Bah. She shoved the current book she was looking at away. Useless, all of them. She would be better off researching how to fight various bloodbane, should it come to it. At least material existed on that. "Why aren't you watching our guest?"

"I thought you might be interested in his activities since leaving him."

"Not at the expense of his slipping away," she said, rising in a physical effort to contain her frustration. Aleena knew better.

"He's not going anywhere for a few minutes."

"What is that supposed to mean?"

"He left his room shortly after we did. He then spent the next hour in the dining room socializing—"

"Socializing? With *whom*?"

"Who do you think?"

Ivana pressed her lips together. "Where is he now?"

"Back in his room. With Ohtli."

Ivana swept by Aleena, out of her rooms, and marched down the hallway toward room four, pulling out her master key ring as she walked.

Aleena kept pace just behind her. "Ivana," she said. "Don't do anything you'll—"

Ivana unlocked the door, flung it open, and stood at the doorway, surveying the scene inside.

Dal Heilyn was putting his comfortable bed to good use, as she had suspected.

Ohtli let out a muffled gasp at the sight of her mistress and scrambled to cover herself.

Ivana folded her arms across her chest and pierced Ohtli with what she hoped was a suitably withering gaze. "Out," she snapped, pointing to the hallway. "Now."

The girl didn't even bother to dress—she gathered up her clothes, threw on her robe and was already hurrying toward the door even as Ivana spoke.

She curtsied when she reached Ivana. "I'm so sorry, Da. I— I'm so sorry."

Ivana shook her head. She had known Ohtli would have trouble with the requirements for working here when Ivana took her in—but she had wanted to give the girl a chance. At least she seemed genuinely distressed. "Later," Ivana said.

Ohtli curtsied again and rushed out of the room.

Ivana turned her gaze to Heilyn. He had stood up to clothe himself without even a moment of hesitation or apparent embarrassment, far too skillfully donning decent attire in the short span of time Ivana's conversation with Ohtli had lasted. Obviously, a man used to being found in bed with women.

Once he finished, he had the gall to remark, "Is it normally your habit to burst into the rooms of your guests unannounced?"

She didn't give him the courtesy of a response. Instead, she glared at him and shut the door. "He doesn't leave the room," she said to Aleena.

"What are you going to do about Ohtli?" Aleena asked.

"I don't know yet. For now, I'm going to go to bed. I have a feeling the next few days will be long."

Chapter Seven

Expectations

Ivana waited while Ohtli pushed a biscuit around her plate, ostensibly soaking up the dregs of her gravy.

She had been waiting silently the entire time Ohtli ate her breakfast. She was patient.

"I'm sorry, Da," Ohtli said finally, mushing the last of her biscuit into a gummy mound without looking up. "I...I don't know what came over me."

"A charming smile and a talent for flattery, no doubt," Ivana said.

As she knew too well.

She folded her hands on the table in front of her, as if she could physically suppress that unwanted thought. "You agreed to the requirements I set for those in my employ, did you not?"

Ohtli bit her lip. "Yes, Da."

"When I took you and your son in, it was not an invitation to add to the population under my roof."

Ohtli's eyes flew to meet Ivana's. "Oh, no, Da. He took precautions..." She trailed off and bit her lip again, averting her eyes at Ivana's look.

Ohtli stared down at her empty plate, seeming very young.

Sometimes it was hard for Ivana to remember that the girls she employed were, on the whole, not much younger than herself. Not all were as naïve as Ohtli, but she still felt decades older than any one of them, save, perhaps, Aleena.

"He said I was beautiful," Ohtli said softly. "Even after..." She lifted one arm and trailed it along one shoulder, and then let it drop. "Said they looked like rivers of liquid pearl."

Ivana took her meaning well enough. She had seen the thin, white scars that crisscrossed the girl's back and shoulders—a gift from her last place of employment.

Ivana closed her eyes briefly and sighed. "Do you work today?"

Ohtli's throat worked. "Yes, Da," she said, voice tight with trepidation. "Morning shift, here in a few minutes—"

"Has Garin been to see the circus yet?"

Ohtli paused, brow furrowed, and then she shook her head.

Ivana slid a setan across the table. "It will only be in the city for another day. Take the day off and take him to see it. Every little boy needs to see the circus."

Ohtli stared at the setan, and then at Ivana, her eyes wide and liquid. "Yes, Da. I-I will. But—"

"In fact..." Ivana flicked her eyes over to the window directly across the room from her and added a couple more setans to the table. "Round up all the girls and their little ones and take any that desire it with you. I'd wager we're still not going to see much business today."

Ohtli tentatively stretched out her hand to take the setans, as if afraid they would bite her. "Yes, Da. Thank you," she said, tears filling her eyes.

Ivana flicked her wrist in dismissal of her gratitude. "You're beautiful, Ohtli. But not because any man tells you so. Take one look at your little boy and tell me he wouldn't still adore you if you had two heads, five hands, and a giant wart on both your noses."

Ohtli's stifled a giggle. "Yes, Da."

"Don't let it happen again."

Ohtli stood, curtsied, and scurried away.

Yes, it was better to have the girls and the children gone for a while. The carcass of the monster wasn't a sight they needed to obsess over.

Movement in the room caught her attention, and she turned to see Aleena headed her way. The woman slid into the chair that had recently been vacated by Ohtli, across the table from Ivana. "Your turn," she said.

Ivana glanced down the hall to the guest rooms. "Ri Talesin's man should be back to retrieve us soon, anyway," she said. "No movement?"

"No. Or sound." After she had been certain all the girls were asleep, Aleena had strung bells on a rope outside Heilyn's door and window; if he opened either, the bells would ring loudly, on the off chance she fell asleep while keeping watch.

"Good."

"That was sweet of you—what you did for Ohtli," Aleena said, settling back in her chair, a grin splitting her face.

Ivana frowned. "*Sweet* has nothing to do with it," she said. "I'm annoyed. I'm extra nice when I'm annoyed, lest I accidently take someone's head off."

Aleena snorted. "No, I don't think so. I've seen you take plenty of people's heads off when you're annoyed." She gave Ivana the slightest wink.

Ivana rolled her eyes.

"Let's face it," Aleena said. "You're an old softie at heart."

Aleena had a way of seeing through facades. It made her an excellent informant, but a downright irritating second. "Don't be ridiculous. I might as well be a cold-hearted killer, for all the softness I have in my heart."

Aleena wagged her finger in Ivana's face. "You don't fool me."

"Yes, well, whatever you may think, don't go spreading rumors. I have a reputation to maintain."

Aleena merely grinned again.

Ivana glanced around to make sure the room was still empty. "And while we're on that subject, when I'm trying to intimidate someone, *laughing* rather ruins the effect, don't you think?"

Aleena's grin turned sheepish. "Sorry. I find him amusing."

"And you wonder why I don't take you with me...places."

Aleena raised an eyebrow. "I thought that was because you don't want me involved in that way."

"It is. I was..." She trailed off and sighed. "Reverting to my previous point—"

"Was that a joke? Were you making a *joke*?"

"—don't grow too attached."

"Do you really think he's that bad?"

"I found him in bed with one of the girls."

"If that's the worst sin you can ascribe to him..."

This was a strange turn of conversation. Ivana looked at Aleena, hard. "If I didn't know any better, I would think *you* were sleeping with him as well. Why this sudden interest in our guest?"

She shrugged. "Honestly, I don't think he's a threat."

And that was why she was the assassin, and Aleena was her informant. "This isn't about who or what he is, other than, perhaps, foolish. This is about the fact that I cannot afford the luxury of trust. You know that."

Aleena looked out toward the hall, as if considering.

This was unusual, for Aleena. She had never questioned Ivana's judgment before and certainly had never tried to convince Ivana not to kill someone.

The situation obviously didn't sit well with Aleena, and *that* didn't sit well with Ivana.

"You trust me," Aleena said.

"I trusted you before there was more at stake than my own well-being," Ivana said. Aleena had been the first whom Ivana had taken under her care—and wasn't precisely under her care anymore.

"So you're saying that you trusted me because of the circumstances at the time, not because of who I am?"

Ivana rubbed a hand over her mouth. *No,* she wanted to say. She had trusted Aleena in a moment of weakness, because she had been the closest thing she had to a friend. Which was also a luxury she couldn't—shouldn't have. "Yes. That's exactly what I'm saying."

Aleena looked skeptical. "And what if I decided to leave your employ?"

"You are not a prisoner."

"Really? I could leave? Just like that?"

There was a tense silence while the two women locked eyes, until finally it was Ivana who had to look away. She rarely felt so anxious about anything. Not even Dal Heilyn.

Not that she hadn't considered the question before. What if Aleena betrayed her, whether for coin or conscience? She had never answered the question satisfactorily in her mind, and she didn't like it that Aleena was bringing it up. Why right now, of all times?

"Why would you ask me something like that?" she asked finally.

Oddly enough, Aleena looked triumphant at that response. She stood up, put her hands on the table, and leaned over it to speak softly to Ivana. "Because you and I both know that no one in your position should ever—*ever*—hesitate to answer that question."

She strolled away from the table and down the hall. "Still your turn," she called back before disappearing.

Ivana found her hands clenched so tight in her lap that her fingernails were digging into her palms. What was the point of that? To prove she could trust someone else? To prove that Aleena trusted *her*? To expose the one flaw in her carefully constructed world, her one weakness?

Bells rang down the hall and a moment later Dal Heilyn walked into the room, followed immediately by the bell of the door tinkling as the messenger also arrived.

She unclenched her hands. Even if it were true that she could trust someone else, she would never trust a man like him again.

Ever.

Vaughn might as well have not existed, for all the attention Sweetblade paid him on the first leg of their journey that morning. They had ridden in silence for the first half of the day, Sweetblade, by all appearances, sleeping—with her head resting back against the wall of the carriage behind her and eyes closed.

As mid-day approached, Vaughn dared to speak at last. "I hope I didn't embarrass you last night."

She snorted and responded without opening her eyes. "I can assure you that I am quite comfortable with the sight of the male body, Dal Heilyn, even one as unremarkable as yours."

Perhaps not the best opening. "I noticed that I haven't seen a single man in your employ yet."

There was a long moment of silence, long enough that he shifted uncomfortably, before she spoke.

"That's because there are none," she said.

Interesting. He waited for her to elaborate, but she didn't. "I also noticed a few of your women with children."

"All but one, in fact."

He blinked. "That's rather unusual."

She finally opened her eyes. "A woman with a child? Did your mother not explain to you the way these things work?"

"That's not what I meant," he said, and he was certain she knew it. "I meant so many of them...and unmarried, I presume."

She met his eyes, and her face was harder than before. "I imagine that as long as there are men more eager to spill their seed inside a woman than to accept the consequences, there will be no lack of unmarried women with children."

The comment was pointed, and he felt his defenses rise. She made it sound like every woman who spread her legs to a man was forced into it. So he snorted. "And do the foolish women who let them bear none of the responsibility?"

There was a long moment of silence while she stared at him. She excelled at those.

"Indeed they do," she said softly. "In most cases, I would say they end up bearing all of it."

He couldn't respond to that. He doubted protesting that he was always careful would matter. So, instead, he tried to redirect the conversation. "I find it ironic that *you* are lecturing *me* on morals."

She raised an eyebrow. "Lecturing? I was merely making an observation. I cannot help if your conscience is so guilty that you need to point out the obvious in order to assuage it."

"I don't need to—" he began, but broke off as she turned away to look out the window, one corner of her mouth turning up.

She was baiting him. And he had taken it.

Half of him was outraged. Half was embarrassed. The other

half admired her, which was a dangerous—and thrilling—feeling.

That was more than a whole, but right now he didn't care. He had her talking and wasn't about to lose the opportunity. He would never prove he wasn't a threat if he didn't talk to her. "I don't suppose you would be interested in elaborating on your choice of workers?"

She shrugged. "It's no secret. As you so astutely pointed out, they are young, unwed mothers. Such women often fall into unfortunate circumstances, and so I provide employment that is kind toward the difficulties of raising a child alone."

The contrast between her two jobs was so stark that he laughed before he could help himself. "*You* run a charity?"

She turned back to frown at him. "It's no charity. They receive room and board for themselves and their children, along with a small allowance. In return, they work hard at honest employment and abide by certain expectations."

He refrained from pointing out the further irony of her providing honest employment. Instead, he latched on to her final statement. "Expectations? Like chastity?"

"That would be one requirement, yes."

He couldn't help himself. He gave her his most charming smile. "And does their employer abide by the same standards?" *Idiot. Don't you remember what Aleena told you?*

Indeed, she gave him one long, unblinking stare—her face turned from cool to frigid—and then went back to staring out the window.

He heaved a heavy internal sigh. He wasn't giving up. He had dodged Gildas for far too long to, in the end, be killed by the same assassin he had tried to hire to kill him. What irony that would be; his father, if he heard of it, would be pleased.

That thought alone was enough to keep him holding on.

What if she could be persuaded with coin? They were both about to receive a substantial reward for slaying the bloodbane; what if he offered her his share to keep her away?

He rejected the idea almost as soon as he had it. If she were interested in his coin, she would have suggested it already. It was probably more advantageous to her to have the threat gone.

Maybe he could blackmail her. He knew her secret; he would keep quiet as long as she agreed to leave him alone.

Or...she could just kill him and not have to worry about it.

When he considered it from her perspective, her plan to murder him made a lot of sense.

Except, of course, that he knew he wasn't actually a threat to her.

The carriage slowed and then came to a halt, and the door opened a moment later. The head of one of the servants appeared in the doorway. "Dal, Da, we're stopping to rest the horses and eat. You are, of course, welcome to join us."

Sweetblade rose and gave him a gracious smile. "Of course."

The servant offered his hand to her, and she took it and descended without a word to Vaughn.

He ducked out of the carriage after her and surveyed their surroundings for threats instinctively. A well-traveled road, but they were in between villages. An olive tree orchard hugged one side of the road, and a dense patch of woods stretched out along the other.

Those with the caravan—a healthy contingent of guards and

the rest of Ri Talesin's servants that were accompanying him to his country estate—clustered together on a patch of ground in the orchard. They were kind enough to make room for him and Sweetblade.

Situations like this always made him uneasy. It was one thing to socialize; it was another for a group of people to include him in on their everyday activities, as they ate, joked, and generally acted like normal people.

Because what they never knew is that he wasn't normal. If any one of them knew what he was, at best, he would be rejected from their group immediately amidst looks of fear and hatred; at worst, he would find himself in the hands of the Conclave, after being beaten just enough not to kill him, as any demonspawn deserved.

Sweetblade, on the other hand, a person whom he had previously thought of as aloof and cold, made easy conversation with the guards and servants. When they expressed admiration for the rumors of their slaying a bloodbane, Sweetblade blushed and demurred, saying it was luck and a pinch of irrational outrage at the thought of her inn being smashed, and nothing more.

She carried herself with such a sweet persona that if he didn't know better, he would have believed without doubt she was an innocent but delightful and intelligent young woman, enjoying a rare excursion outside the safety of the city to a new place.

Relative safety, he revised. Nowhere was ever truly safe.

He, of course, knew it was a charade. But was she really the cold woman whom he had encountered thus far, or was that a persona as well? Perhaps the brooding, weary woman he had watched rocking the babe was closer to the truth.

He riffled through his bag while eating, making sure everything sensitive he had brought along was still safe inside after it had been stowed on top of the carriage. At least he had managed to retrieve his bow and arrows before they left, by asking in front of the Ri's messenger. Sweetblade hardly had a public reason to keep them from him, especially since he was now known as a bloodbane slayer.

Guards would take any help they could get, if it came to it.

Everything looked to be in order, until he flipped open the flap on the qixli's leather case. He frowned, pulling the device halfway out while still in the bag. The aether in the qixli was shimmering slightly.

He rolled his eyes to the sky. It was a sign that someone was trying to contact him. It wasn't the first time over the past few days, but he had ignored it thus far. Whoever it was—and he had his suspicions—was persistent.

He glanced at the guards. He couldn't take it out right now, but neither could he let it go. It was too large to fit in the hidden flap in his coin purse, where he had stashed his supply of aether. If they searched him upon arriving at the Ri's manor and found a glowing qixli...

It might raise some questions, to say the least.

He stood, bag, bow, and all, and started walking away from the group, toward the woods on the other side of the road.

"Dal?" one of the guards asked.

"Need to relieve myself," he said. He grimaced. "Might be a few minutes." He then waved his bow in the air. "I'll be fine."

The guard chuckled. "Have it your way." The guard turned back to the group, but Sweetblade watched his departure with narrowed eyes.

He walked a little ways into the woods, found a rotting tree stump, and sat down on it. He slid the qixli, a circular device about the size of his palm, out of its case. At first glance it appeared to be a small cosmetic mirror. A wooden frame surrounded a polished glass center, and when he looked into it, he could see his reflection.

But that was where the similarities stopped. Upon close inspection—and especially if the damn thing were glowing—one could see that there were, in fact, two panes of glass, held in place by the frame, and in between was a silvery substance that swirled slowly when the device was tilted—liquid aether.

He held each side of the device firmly between his hands and waited.

After a moment, the shimmering subsided, and then the indistinct shape of a face appeared in the aether, slightly raised, as though someone were pressing the face of a doll to the back of the substance.

The mouth of the face moved. "It's about damn time, Vaughn," a tinny voice said. "Where are you?"

It was who he had thought: Yaotel. Vaughn fought back a grimace, though neither he nor Yaotel had the sufficient profile to able to see each other's facial expressions clearly on the qixli.

"Do I have to report everywhere I go now?" Vaughn asked, only partially feigning annoyance.

The qixli made an odd metallic sound, like someone coughing into a sheet of aluminum. It didn't transfer sound perfectly—at least, not for him. But Vaughn had used these devices enough by now to know that it was the sound of Yaotel snorting. "Don't get smart with me, moonblood. You know why I'm contacting you. Where are you?"

Vaughn ground his teeth together. "On the road."

"Uh-huh. You got a woman with you?"

"Do I look stupid?"

"You really want to know?"

Vaughn grunted, but couldn't keep a smile from creeping onto his lips. Vaughn was the only one among the Ichtaca who was of noble blood, and Yaotel was the only one who didn't seem to care.

"You're going through with it, aren't you?"

"None of your business."

Now it sounded like the aluminum being waved gently in the air. A sigh. "Look, if it's not too late, I'm telling you: get out. This is a foolish scheme. It can't go well."

Yep. Definitely too late.

"However, I know you don't care about my opinion. So here's something you might listen to: he knows."

Vaughn's stomach dropped into his knees. "What? How?"

"You've got a lot of skills, Vaughn, but sneaking around isn't one of them." There was a pause, no doubt while Yaotel had the same thought Vaughn did. *Ironically.* "How many assassins did you try before you found one who'd take the job?"

Vaughn said nothing. Sweetblade was the fourth and had been his last hope.

"Right," Yaotel said, interpreting his silence. "Well, you're in over your head. Whatever you've said and to whom, he's heard about it. And he's not happy. If you know what's good for you, you'll get your ass back here where you're safe."

Safe. He was tired of being *safe*. He had just wanted to be *free*. What was so wrong with that?

Vaughn closed his eyes briefly, trying to figure out where he'd gone wrong. It had to be one of the women—either a plant, or someone eager for a few coins in exchange for useless information. But what had he said?

Who knew. *Damn*, it was always a woman.

"Vaughn?"

"Thanks for the information. I'll be extra careful going forward."

Yaotel heaved another metallic sigh. "I hate to do this to you, but no matter what happens, we can't be associated with it. And if it goes poorly..." Yaotel didn't speak the additional words Vaughn knew were implied. *You're on your own.*

"I know."

"I'm sorry."

"I understand."

"All right. Well. Here's hoping I see you again this side of the river."

The aether swirled, and the face sank back into it. The aether no longer shimmered.

Vaughn put the qixli back into his bag and stared at the ground, hands clenched into balls. This kept getting worse.

If his father knew he was looking to have him assassinated, that probably also meant that he had learned the name Vaughn had been using for himself the past few months. A name he had just given to the Ri of Weylyn. And if his father heard of his recent adventure, he would know exactly when and where to find him in the next couple days.

But surely he was being paranoid. It was impossible for his father to both hear about the slaying *and* travel to Ri Talesin's manor in time to catch Vaughn. It hadn't even been two full days since the bloodbane fell.

Unless his father was already in the city for some reason.

He should have pressed Yaotel more. How had Yaotel found out that his father knew, for instance?

"Who were you talking to?"

He jumped up and whirled around. Sweetblade stood directly behind him, a hand resting casually on her thigh.

He relaxed when he saw it was her, though that wasn't a logical reaction.

"Damn you, woman, don't you have *any* respect for a man's privacy?"

"Who," she asked, eyes glimmering dangerously, "were you talking to?"

His gut reaction was to deny that he had been speaking, but she obviously had overheard him, so that would clearly be a lie. "Myself," he said. "I find myself good company."

"No," she said flatly. "It sounded like one side of a conversation, and I heard another voice as well."

So she hadn't understood Yaotel's words. That didn't surprise him. The tinny voice that came through the qixli wasn't very loud and didn't carry well.

She was scanning the trees. "Also, you lied about needing to relieve yourself."

She had followed him immediately, then. Of course. She

wasn't going to let him out of her sight. What excuse had *she* given the guards?

"Is another of your kind here, invisible?"

He almost laughed, but it would have been bitter. His *kind*? It was an apt example of how deep prejudice against Banebringers ran, that even an assassin held some subconscious bias against them. "We can't all turn invisible, you know."

"In fact, I know very little about it," she said calmly. Still, her hand rested on that thigh, probably because she had a dagger hidden there, and she moved a little closer to him.

He swallowed nervously. She wouldn't kill him here, would she? Far too close to the guards, right? And so close to all those innocents?

"I could, you know," she said softly, as though reading his mind, still moving closer. He backed away and promptly bumped into the tree behind him. "Accidents happen. A bloodbane *could* strike at any time."

"Unlikely, this close to the main road out of the city," he said.

She stepped even closer, made a swift movement with her hand, and then the point of her dagger was digging into his ribs. "But not impossible, wouldn't you say?"

"But what were you doing here?" he countered. "And why weren't you hurt? An innkeeper doesn't get so lucky twice in a row."

"Tell me who you were talking to," she said again, pronouncing each word slowly and deliberately. "Or I start cutting into sensitive body parts." The dagger drifted lower.

Damn, the qixli wasn't worth that!

"All right—all right—I have a device that allows me to speak over a great distance. No one was here. I was using the device."

"A device that allows you to speak over long distances," she repeated, incredulity in her voice.

"Yes."

"Show me. Now."

Vaughn waved in the direction of Sweetblade's dagger. "Could you...?"

She took one step back. While keeping a wary eye on her, he shifted to pick up his bag, pulled out the qixli, and then offered it to her.

She didn't take it. "That's a mirror."

"Just look at it."

"Hold it up for me to see."

He did as she asked, and she examined it more closely.

"Very well. Then..." She flicked the hand not holding the dagger. "Speak to someone."

He hesitated. That was drawing awfully close to a line he wouldn't cross.

"*Now.*"

But not over it yet.

He held the device in his palms again, as he had before, and willed it to call out to Yaotel's qixli.

The silvery substance started to shimmer. He moved it around so that she couldn't see what he was looking at—and more importantly, so that Yaotel couldn't see her. She looked like she was about to protest, but stopped abruptly when a voice came out of it.

"Vaughn? What now?"

"I forgot to tell you," Vaughn said. "Make sure I'm not contacted again. I'm going somewhere where the qixli could fall into hands it shouldn't. I don't want it glowing and attracting attention."

"You already get yourself into trouble?"

"Just being extra cautious."

Yaotel snorted. "Right. Because that's normal for you."

Vaughn smiled, but his throat felt tight. "Give Danton a hard time for me."

"Do it yourself, when you get back." The image faded.

Ivana was staring at the qixli, and for a moment, Vaughn saw neither carefree young lady, cold assassin, nor world-weary woman. "Burning skies, you were telling the truth," she whispered.

He shoved the qixli back into the case and tossed it into his bag.

"How?" she demanded.

"Let's just call it Banebringer magic," he said.

The cold persona snapped back. "My original question remains. Who were you talking to?"

"A friend."

She pressed the dagger against his ribs again. "Not good enough."

He set his jaw. "I'm sorry. That's all I can tell you."

"I'm not above torture."

He closed his eyes just long enough to steel himself against the nausea that swept over him. "Go ahead. It wouldn't be the first time."

She didn't move the dagger, either to remove it or cut into him.

"Or kill me, if you must," he continued. He met her eyes. "There are some things worth dying for."

"And there are some things worth killing for," she responded.

He snorted. "Indeed, I imagine for you, it's shiny and has a nice weight in your hand."

Her eyes flashed, and in an instant, the hand not holding the dagger had seized his throat and jaw. The heel of her hand pressed painfully into his throat, and her fingernails dug into his jawline. "Don't pretend to understand me," she hissed. "Because you don't."

He swallowed, trying to dislodge her hand. This was clearly the wrong time for making wry observations. "Look—I'm not a threat to you. I don't know how to convince you of that."

"You can't."

A tendril of hope died. But he took a guess that he hoped was right. "But you're not going to kill me here, are you? Would you really take that chance?"

She pushed herself away from him by shoving his head back, and then put away her dagger. She seemed more annoyed than angry, now.

He breathed out and rubbed at his jawline. "I wasn't talking to anyone about you. My friend was contacting me to tell me that my—Ri Gildas knows that I've been shopping for assassins."

Sweetblade remained silent.

"But...you already knew that," he guessed.

She looked at him askance. "Ri Gildas issued a matching contract on you three weeks ago."

"A...what?"

"He has offered to quadruple any offer an assassin receives for a hit on him, if he or she refuses the contract and instead turns in your head."

Vaughn's throat went dry at the same time his hands started to dampen. It was a rational move on the part of his father, having discovered that Vaughn had gone on the offensive. It also meant that Sweetblade...

She was holding her dagger up, examining it as though looking for mold on a loaf of bread.

This was worse than he had thought.

"I see," he said. "That's...just great." He stood up. "Lucky you."

She shrugged and turned away from him. "Perhaps."

He furrowed his brow. *Huh?* Was she saying she wasn't planning on cashing in on that contract, even though she was planning to kill him? That made no sense.

Then again, nothing about this woman made sense. Why had suggesting that she killed for money—which she obviously did—anger her?

If he could figure out who she really was, he might have a chance at knowing how to convince her to leave him alone.

Whatever it was, he had a feeling her "girls" were the key to understanding her. He knew what she did, but didn't understand why an assassin would take on such a project. Was it all a cover for her true identity, since no one would suspect the charitable innkeeper was really a hired killer?

Or...

A curious thought hit him.

Perhaps the assassin was the cover for the innkeeper.

As the carriage started moving, Ivana closed her eyes again, blocking out the sight of Heilyn—or whatever his name was. She was irritated at herself that she had let him get under her skin. Irritated for momentarily losing control.

And irritated that he looked *so* much like Airell.

He had to be a brother; the resemblance was too close.

The relation was hardly his fault—and he obviously had no love for the father he was trying to have killed—but she couldn't help despising him for it all the same.

She wanted this entire affair to be over. The banquet, the reward, disposing of Heilyn...so she could repair the crack he had managed to put in her walls before it grew any larger.

Chapter Eight

The Steward and the Maid

The man who met them as they stepped out of the carriage late that afternoon was as charming as any snake before it showed its fangs. While his clothes were fashionable, he wore the colors of Ri Talesin, which meant he wasn't a noble himself, but he could have fit in among them easily.

"Da Ivana, I presume," he said, taking her hand and kissing the back of it. She offered him a sweet smile and low curtsy in response, despite the way that his eyes lingered on her bosom before turning to Heilyn.

"And Dal Heilyn. You are most welcome in my master's house. I am Dal Allyn, Ri Talesin's steward, and will assume charge of you while you are here."

Interesting that the Ri was putting them—as far as he knew, two insignificant commoners from the capital that happened to have the good fortune to slay a monster—in his steward's charge.

The steward made a motion to the carriage driver, who spurred the horses down the drive, and began walking back toward the enormous manor ahead of them—without looking back at them or asking them to follow, which, despite such personal care, put them in their proper place as guests, but not highly regarded ones.

He swept one hand in a wide arc around him. "The grounds and manor house have been in the Ri's family for four hundred years," he said. "They are vast, and I would ask that you stay close to the manor, should you decide to wander while you are here, and stay close to the rooms allotted to you inside, lest you become lost."

Ivana studied the back of the man as they walked. The request was offered graciously, but the dual meaning was clear: *Be impressed with my master's wealth. Be assured that you are nowhere near his level in society. Therefore stay where you are told.*

Honored guests, perhaps, but only within limits.

It didn't take too much effort for Ivana to keep up the façade of the enraptured commoner. A slight opening of the mouth, wide eyes, and she could let her mind wander while she gazed around.

The manor house was far too large for the seven people that the Ri of Weylyn's immediate family consisted of, and the Ri no doubt had far more servants than they required to live comfortably.

And the steward was sure to enumerate all of the estate's features as they mounted the stairs into the great hall. Stables. Gardens. Hunting grounds. A large lake for fishing. Thick walls to keep out roaming bloodbane—oh their safety was quite assured.

She was sure to ask many hesitant questions, becoming more bold as he answered them, gathering as much information as she could while keeping up her role. The steward seemed to appreciate her interest and flashed her a smile or two that left no doubt as to his.

That was one to keep away from.

Ivana followed the steward through the great hall and up a back stairway. Marble. Gold. Crystal. And were those diamonds set into that mirror? *Good gods.*

She spared a glance at Heilyn. What was his reaction to all of this?

He didn't appear overly affected, which didn't surprise her. A minor noble family might have a modest manor, but rarely had the means to be so extravagant with their wealth. Even the noble her father had worked for—well-off enough to hire a highly educated and respected personal tutor for his children—hadn't been so garish.

If Heilyn were Ri Gildas' son, his family had a much higher ranking than the noble her father had worked for, even if Gildas hadn't been a Ri whenever Heilyn had left home.

Still, he ought to act a little more awed. There was no reason for the Ri, his steward, or any of the many servants passing through the halls to think that they were anything but the lowest of low. It would start rumors.

And servants did like to gossip.

If anything, he looked tense. As though he expected an assassin to jump out of a darkened stairwell at any moment.

She held back a dark laugh. Or plunge a dagger into his back from right next to him.

When the steward stopped his long tour of the manor to speak with a maid, Ivana leaned over to Heilyn and whispered in his ear, "Look impressed."

He started. "What?"

She gave him a look she hoped he would understand as irritation with him and then gave her most charming smile to the steward as he finished his conversation with the maid and turned back to them.

He bowed and returned Ivana's smile. "Idel will show you to your suite, just down this corridor," he said. "The Ri has timed your arrival to coincide with a banquet he was already giving for a friend of the family. You will be honored there tomorrow night." The steward took Ivana's hand, kissed it again, and then disappeared back the way they had come.

The maid curtsied. "This way, please."

They followed her a short distance down the hall until she stopped at a door. She opened it and allowed them inside. "Dal, your room is on the left, and Da, your room is on the right. You will be informed when your presence is required tomorrow." She curtsied again and gestured to a long rope secured to the wall. "I am assigned to your needs. Please let me know if you require anything until then."

"Thank you," Ivana said to the maid warmly. Heilyn gave her

a curt nod, let his eyes sweep over her once in an appraising manner, but otherwise ignored her.

The maid gave Heilyn a wary look, Ivana a shy smile, and closed the door after them.

They stood in an elegant—if sparsely decorated—sitting room. True to the maid's word, there was a door on the left of the room and a door on the right. In the middle, two couches and an armchair were positioned near a fireplace against the wall, and a long, full bookshelf graced the other wall.

The meager belongings they had brought with them had already been transported to the room and set against one wall. Vaughn tucked his bow and quiver, which he had insisted the guards let him keep with him for the rest of the journey, in the gap between the bookshelf and the corner where it wouldn't be of much notice. He then turned to watch while Sweetblade paced the length, breadth, and then circumference of the room, peering into every nook and cranny, and then disappeared into each of their respective rooms for a time. Finally, she emerged, managing to look both satisfied and displeased at the same time.

She stopped in front of Vaughn. "You should try to act a little less like you own the place," she said to him.

"Your pardon?"

"I know having maids bow and scrape to you in the middle of this lavishness was probably normal for you, but here you're just like me: nothing, and no one. Act like it, or you'll draw attention to us."

He blinked and wetted his lips. How did she...?

But she was probably right. He needed to look like he was unused to this environment. "Ah," he said. "Not exactly *normal...*"

"Come now, Heilyn. You obviously are—or *were*—noble. Let's get that out of the way."

He gaped at her. Had he said something to give that away?

She rolled her eyes and started ticking off her fingers. "You are well-spoken. You are clearly of mixed Fereharian and Weylynian ancestry. You have exceptional skill with the bow. And..." She gave him an appraising look. "You had enough money to hire an assassin."

Well, there was that. "Oh."

"And for the love of Temoth, *please* keep your raging need to conquer any attractive female under control while we are here."

He frowned. He had barely *looked* at the maid. "I don't need to *conquer—*"

She turned away from him, cutting him off. "The Ri obviously doesn't trust us—probably because he expects us to rob him while here, but you never know what other reasons he might have."

"What makes you think he doesn't trust us?"

"Aside from the fact that most nobles expect all commoners to be criminals of some sort or the other?" She ignored the look and raised eyebrow he cast her. She had a knack for saying such ironic things.

"Because he put us in a shared suite. Easier to keep an eye on us."

True.

"But mostly because there are at least two servants tasked with following us around."

That, he *hadn't* noticed.

She went to the bell pull and gave it a firm tug. A chime sounded from the hall, and a few minutes later, the maid knocked on their door.

Sweetblade opened it. "I was wondering...would it be possible to have a bath?" she asked, by all appearances hesitant and unsure of herself. "I couldn't find a place to heat water."

"Of course, Da," the maid said. "There is a bathing chamber off your room. I will send servants to draw a bath immediately." She turned to Vaughn. "Dal?"

"Um," he said. "Sure. I mean, a bath would be nice. And food, if you have it." He hoped that was sufficiently uncouth for Sweetblade. He didn't know if he could feign the innocence she put on so well, but uncouth...that he could do.

The maid curtsied. "I will have dinner brought up after your baths."

Ivana waited until the last hints of daylight were gone from the twilight sky, and then a few hours after that, until she could be relatively sure there wasn't an excess of people moving about the Ri's manor. Then, she went into the bathing room, slipped out of the window there, dropped down onto a ledge below her, and crept along the wall until she found an unoccupied room to enter.

Having thus avoided anyone who had been assigned to watch their door, she proceeded to map the layout of the entire manor.

On the first floor were rooms for entertaining. The second, the family living areas. The third, their own floor, housed the guest chambers—though the wing their chambers were in was much less elegant than its opposite on the other side of the manor.

The manor had, of course, a basement as well, housing the cellar, safe-room, and servants quarters, and in one wing, even two prison cells, though those were currently empty and un-guarded.

The Ri had also built a passageway out of the safe-room. That wasn't uncommon for the wealthy who could afford the extra expense; a safe-room was nice, but a safe-room with a back door was even better, should a monster break through the heavy metal door into it—or, the gods forbid, spawn inside of the room itself from one of its occupants.

The back door of a safe-room was also useful for other nec-essary escapes. Ivana made a note to explore the passageway farther the following day to see where it would spit the escapee out.

Satisfied she had an adequate knowledge of the manor should she need to make a hasty exit, she began to make her way back to the unoccupied room on the third floor that she had re-entered the manor through.

To her chagrin, as she approached the door, the steward himself turned the corner of the hallway. She hadn't seen an-other soul for the two hours she had been exploring, and she had nowhere else to go, so she turned and faced him. "Oh, thank Temoth," she said, hurrying toward him. "I thought I would never find my way back to my room."

The steward stopped, obviously taken aback to find her out of her room. "Da Ivana," he said, bowing. "What brings you out at this time of night?"

She, in fact, wondered the same thing about him, but she chewed on her lower lip and averted her eyes. "I...I couldn't sleep. I thought a walk might help, and I'm afraid I've become turned around. I'm so sorry if I've been impertinent in doing so..."

The steward relaxed and chuckled. "No, no, quite all right, my dear." He gave her a sidelong look. "Perhaps I can show you back to your room."

"Of course, Dal," she said, curtseying. "That would be such a relief."

The steward put one hand on the small of her back, ostensibly steering her in the right direction, but he didn't remove it as they walked.

Ivana bit back a grimace. So. He was *that* kind of man. She had suspected but had planned to avoid making herself an easy target for him. Such as being alone at night in an empty hallway.

"A pleasant evening, wouldn't you say?" he remarked.

"I suppose, my lord."

"Well," he said, "not so pleasant if you are unable to sleep." He gave her a sympathetic look, and she gave him a grateful smile in return.

"Indeed, Dal." *Worm.*

"Please, my dear. Call me Allyn."

"You are too kind."

"Ah," he said after another moment. "Here we are."

The door they stopped in front of was *not* the door to their rooms. Ivana feigned confusion. "I...are you sure? This doesn't look right."

"The hallways can look so much the same," he said, but he made no move to leave her. Instead, he stepped closer. "A sweet thing like yourself should avoid wandering at night."

Ugh. What a nuisance.

Vaughn stared up at the ceiling of his room, wide awake, even though it was well past three in the morning. His mind refused to settle, replaying the events of the previous few days, torturing him with scenarios of what he could have done differently, wondering if the decisions he had made recently would see him dead—or Sedated.

He squeezed his eyes shut against the pervasive pale light in the room—light no normal person would notice, but that his eyes always perceived. He had grown used to it over the years, and it no longer bothered him most nights—except on nights like these.

He turned over, buried his face in the pillow, and muttered a curse at the heretic gods who just couldn't let go of their mortal playthings.

Sleep. Must sleep. He would need to be as alert as possible in the days to come, lest he miss whatever trap his father was going to lay for him.

He lay still and silent, willing himself to sink into unconsciousness, but it didn't work.

He sat up in frustration and punched his pillow a few times.

That didn't work either.

Finally, he sighed. He had found only one remedy. Time for a late-night walk.

Even a truly naïve girl would have caught on at this point. "Th-thank you, Dal. I...I'll just be..." She felt for the doorknob behind her, but he pressed himself against her, trapping her before she could reach it.

"Now, we can do this two ways, dear. Easy, or difficult. I would advise taking the easy way. No screaming, no struggling. Perhaps even pleasant. Yes?"

Ivana shoved down the bile that rose in her throat. *Right.* "Dal?"

"Remember, I am a steward of the Ri of Weylyn. You are nothing. Thus, your word means nothing."

She allowed understanding into her eyes, let him see it, and then lowered them. "Just so," she whispered.

"Ah, there we go, dear. Now, I happen to know that the room behind us is unoccupied and quite comfortable. Shall we?"

He pushed open the door and guided her into the room, hand still on the small of her back. He didn't even bother to close the door before pressing himself into her.

Ivana mentally prepared herself as he nuzzled her neck. This was *not* what she had been expecting this evening. To the abyss with men like Allyn, along with the nobles who employed them, probably knowing full well of his lecherous ways. She wondered how many of the maids he was used to victimizing. Theirs, certainly—she had been far too wary of Heilyn. She felt herself start to tremble with anger.

"There, now," he said, "no need to be afraid. The easy way isn't so bad, and I can be gentle."

Well enough, that he thought she was afraid. That would be natural.

If only he knew that he ought to be the one quaking with fear.

Her hand itched to reach for the dagger strapped to her thigh under her skirt. But she restrained herself, trying to think about other things while his hands moved to the buttons on the back of her dress.

"Hello?" a voice suddenly said, and the door creaked open farther.

Ivana blinked. *Heilyn?* What in the abyss was *he* doing up?

The steward pulled back, a sneer curling his lip, but he quickly regained control of himself. "Ah. Dal Heilyn. As you can see, we are quite busy..."

"Yes," Heilyn said, a frown touching the corners of his lips. "I can see that."

They exchanged a long stare, and then the steward gave up. No doubt, Ivana wasn't worth enough to him to risk getting into a scuffle with another man. He straightened his tunic, glared at Heilyn, and left the room.

Heilyn said nothing. He just stood there, staring at her, brow furrowed.

Anger spiked through her. She supposed he thought he was being magnanimous, *rescuing* her from a man only slightly worse than himself. She glared at him and pushed herself away from the wall.

Without a word, she marched down the hallway.

Vaughn followed close on Sweetblade's heels, at once aghast and perplexed at the scene he had encountered. There was no way in Temoth's realm that she had been a willing participant. Yet he doubted she was unarmed. Why hadn't she just...knifed him, or whatever it was she did?

As soon as the door closed behind them, she turned on him. "Don't you *ever* interfere with my business again!" she snapped.

He opened his mouth in surprise. "But he was going to—"

"Yes, thank you. I am aware of the nature of the situation. Do you really think I was incapable of handling it myself?"

"But you weren't!" he protested. That was the confusing part. *Why?*

She pressed her lips together and advanced on him with a cold fury that terrified him more than she ever had thus far. "And what do you think would happen, if I killed or maimed the Ri's steward?"

"I suppose that wouldn't be good. But if you had, ah, dealt with him, no one would have suspect—"

"Yes. Yes, they most certainly would have. New guests, having just killed a monster, a steward who is known for victimizing the maids, and suddenly he's dead? And I hardly had the means at that moment to make it look accidental."

"But...but you're saying you would have—"

She had backed him against the wall now, and he didn't miss the way her fingers twitched at her thigh.

How had he landed in so much trouble by trying to be chivalrous?

"Yes. That is precisely what I am saying. I will do whatever is necessary to protect my identity. Sometimes that means doing things that aren't so pleasant."

He flinched back, as though she had spit at him, but no moisture left her mouth. "I was only trying to help." Burning skies. Wasn't it better that he had interfered? It still saved her the—

"I don't need your help, I don't want your help. Especially *your* help."

"What is *that* supposed to mean?" Was this woman so damn prideful that she couldn't be grateful for the happenstance that prevented her from having to do something unpleasant, as she put it?

"I am sure the number of maids *you've* seduced rivals that of the steward."

"Now, that's just unfair," he said indignantly. "Seducing is very different from taking it by force."

She snorted and pressed one finger into his chest so hard it hurt. "You," she said, "are everything I hate about men."

And then she turned on her heel and re-entered her room, slamming the door behind her.

Vaughn stared open-mouthed at the door. What had *that* been about?

Ivana tried to steady herself as she entered her room.

The nerve, insinuating that he was better than that worm!

In truth, she was relieved Heilyn had stumbled upon them.

She may have been used to such situations, but that didn't mean she *liked* it. She was simply furious that it was *Heilyn* who had found them.

She slammed her fist into the wall, heedless of the way it smarted as a consequence. And *why* did he infuriate her so much? She usually had a much better reign on her emotions than this.

What was happening to her? Why had he unhinged her so?

She knew why, and it was unfair of her to blame him for it. It wasn't his fault that his smile and manner reminded her of *him*, and that even in her fury, every nerve had tingled at their proximity a moment ago. It wasn't his fault that his presence was a constant reminder of events and emotions she had—up until now—successfully buried.

It was as though he were a ghost from her past sent to haunt her, to punish her for daring to escape the pain she deserved.

She would never be happier than when this was over and she never had to deal with him again.

Chapter Nine

Cracks

"Slouch," Sweetblade said, shooting a look at Vaughn.

"Slouch?" Vaughn replied.

"Yes. Look a little less like you've been raised to sit and stand and walk perfectly at all times."

Vaughn tried to stoop over a bit. "How's this?"

Sweetblade stared at him and then rolled her eyes up. "Never mind. Just...stand however you want." She turned away, folded her arms across her chest, and began tapping her foot impatiently.

He straightened up to his normal posture. No matter what he did, he couldn't seem to please her. His hopes, already dim, of getting her to trust him were fizzling out.

The expected knock came, and Ivana immediately folded her hands delicately on top of one another at her middle.

Vaughn straightened his tunic, wondering again at her ability to change personalities so quickly, and opened the door.

It was their maid. "Your presence is requested in the dining hall," she said.

Sweetblade curtsied and Vaughn bowed, trying very hard not to look at the maid, lest Ivana accuse him of more indecency.

"Thank you," he was careful to say to the maid, while looking at a point behind her shoulder that most definitely did *not* include a view of her cleavage.

He didn't know if the small sigh that issued from Ivana was exasperation or relief at finally having this entire situation move forward.

If the latter, he understood. For his part, he was desperate to get this over before his father heard of it.

They followed the maid down the hall, and unlike the winding course the steward had taken them on when they had arrived, she led them directly to the dining hall.

He shook his head slightly. The steward. A vile man. Whatever Sweetblade might think of him, he had never forced or intimidated a woman who was unwilling, and he had a low opinion of men who did. And he still didn't understand why his saving her from the steward had earned him such ire.

The dining hall was as grand as the rest of the manor. The ceiling stretched the height of two full floors, and the table in the middle took up the entire length of the room. Vaughn did a quick count and guessed it could seat at least fifty people.

Impressive, but had heard his father's could seat seventy-five.

He pushed thoughts of Gildas out of his mind. That could wait.

The footman at the door bowed as they approached. "This way, Dal," he said.

They followed him to a spot about two-thirds of the way down the table, where he pulled out Sweetblade's chair. She thanked him prettily, and once she was settled, he led Vaughn to the opposite side of the table, where the footman indicated he should seat himself.

If their arrival had been noticed, no one spoke of it. Conversation continued in a low murmur, with the occasional spate of laughter from one end of the table or another. Ri Talesin was already there, at the head of the table with, presumably, his wife and daughter on the ladies side, and his four sons on the other.

His daughter was a sight to behold; she was the very definition of gaudy. Her dress sparkled with hundreds of golden sequins, her necklace was set with large stones, and her hair was pinned up in a towering style he had never seen before.

Was this the fashion for noble ladies now? It had been awhile since he had been in such company.

The men on either side of him didn't seem inclined toward conversation, so he glanced down the table at the other women there. Indeed, many had their hair pinned up so high it was a wonder the ensembles didn't come tumbling down with the slightest twitch of their heads.

Temoth. It must be new; usually what the nobles did, the commoners mimicked, to the degree they were able, and he hadn't seen it reach the streets yet.

Then again, the commoners might not be able to afford the hundreds of pins and vats of hair ointment that must be required to keep such a style in place.

Finally, his eyes drifted to Sweetblade. Her hair was pinned up, but not so ostentatiously. Combined with her simple but flattering dress, she was out of place among the row of peacocks she sat with.

He found he liked her appearance, in contrast. Especially the tiny curls left down that tickled her neck as she spoke with the woman to her left.

She glanced his way and frowned when she caught him looking at her.

He couldn't resist winking, and her frown deepened.

He averted his gaze to his own side of the table and noticed for the first time that a large section of seats had been left empty, close to the Ri.

Perhaps left for the guests the steward had mentioned? Fairly important ones, if they were seated so close.

The Ri's sons were stately, sitting with rod-straight backs as they conversed quietly amongst themselves.

Suddenly conscious of his own similar posture, he tried to hunch down a little.

"Are you quite all right?" the man to his right said to him.

"Ah, pardon? Yes, of course."

The man tilted his head. "I wasn't sure. You looked as though you might be doubled over in pain."

He groaned internally. "A spasm, nothing more. Occasionally my stomach gives me fits." Vaughn coughed a bit for good measure.

The man gave him a sympathetic look. "No doubt your food is not what it should be."

While Vaughn was puzzling out the meaning of that comment, the man continued on. "Heilyn, is it? I heard about your daring defeat of the bloodbane spawned in the capital."

"Luck, I'm afraid."

"Well, my friend, your luck may well bring you enough money to supplement your options and clear up that stomach problem."

Supplement his—oh. Right. He was a commoner, and therefore destitute. Even though that wasn't at all true of many commoners, at least here in Weylyn, it was the perception among many nobles. Vaughn blinked and gave what he hoped was a grateful smile. "That would be wonderful."

The man inclined his head. "The name is Dewain," he said. "I extend my gratitude to you and your friend." He nodded across the table. "My daughter was visiting in the capital last week. Who knows what could have happened if the monster had been allowed to rampage?"

Vaughn sincerely doubted his daughter was anywhere near the quarter of the city where the monster had appeared, but he smiled anyway. "As I said, luck." He glanced across the table to Sweetblade. "And, she's not my friend. Just the innkeeper where I was staying." It sounded dumb the moment the words left his lips, and the man gave him a quizzical look.

Thank Temoth Sweetblade hadn't heard that.

"Well then," the man said. He turned back to the more interesting person on his right.

Vaughn breathed out and found himself hunching down out of pity for himself. This was an awful experience. He had never sat at a table in a noble's hall and tried to pretend to be a commoner before.

The conversation at the table quieted at the sound of the Ri clinking his spoon against his glass, a broad smile on his face. "I have just been informed that our guests of honor have arrived."

Was he referring to them? But, no, the Ri was standing and looking toward the door.

The entire table turned toward the door to view the guests.

There in the door, surrounded by guards, stood two jewel-encrusted women, one younger, and one older.

And to the right and back of the older one stood none other than Gildas himself.

Damn.

A flood of long-buried emotions crashed into Ivana's wall, rending the crack with a violence that mirrored itself so painfully in reality that she had to choke back a gasp.

She struggled for control, grasped for it even as it swirled around in the whirlpool, taunting her, telling her the past decade had been a farce.

It had been 13 years since she had last seen Gildas, and though he had aged, he had the same self-important bearing and superior countenance. It was almost as if he were still standing above the bleeding body of her father, sword dangling from a careless hand, ready to move on to the next inconvenience he had to deal with that day.

Except this time, the flash of pain quickly morphed into rage. It took every ounce of self-control she had left not to leap across the table and stab him right then and there.

She gritted her teeth. She should have just taken Heilyn's job. Who in the abyss cared if Gildas was Conclave? He was a monster, and if anyone deserved a bloody end, it was him.

A muffled moan floated across the table to Ivana from Heilyn.

He was staring at Gildas, face as pale as death. He had never looked anywhere close to that afraid of her.

A sudden stab of pity pierced her rage and calmed her riot of emotions to a reasonable level, which was as much a relief as it was an outrage. Pity! For *him*? Where had that come from? *Open the flood gates, and the whole damn lot comes through.*

She took deep breaths until the flood subsided enough that she could think clearly again; it would take more than that to put it back where it belonged. However, she was finally satisfied that she had herself under temporary control, at least.

She knew Gildas wouldn't recognize her; she was no longer the wide-eyed, innocent 15-year-old his eldest son had seduced.

Heilyn sank down into his chair as the company passed by, headed for the empty seats.

Ivana tried to catch Heilyn's eye, but he wasn't paying attention. His eyes followed Gildas until the party sat, and then they darted around the room.

She knew that look. Panic. Desperation. She had seen it on the faces of targets that were coherent enough to realize they were about to die.

Ri Talesin waited until the party was settled and then began his introductions. "I am so pleased to introduce to all of you Da Aphria and her daughter Da Lavena, of Ferehar." He beamed at the son sitting closest to him, no doubt the eldest. "I am even more pleased to publically announce for the first time that Da Lavena and my eldest son have recently become engaged.

"I wish them happiness, and of course, look forward to the many years of friendship to come from this alliance between Weylyn and Ferehar."

And many years of even more wealth, no doubt—as if the nobles in Weylyn or Ferehar needed more of that.

But what was the connection to Gildas? He was surely there because he had heard of Heilyn's presence, but he wouldn't have attached himself to the party for no reason. Was he connected to the noble house these women came from? Where was Aleena when she needed her?

Thankfully, the Ri was happy to elaborate. He turned to Gildas. "I would be remiss if I neglected to mention another honored guest, my good friend Ri Gildas of Ferehar. Gildas had graciously agreed to perform the marriage ceremony in his Conclave role three months hence, and was eager to be present for our announcement." He nodded to Gildas.

Gildas nodded his head. "It is indeed *my* pleasure to be present on such a joyous occasion," he said, all manners and grace. His gaze drifted around the table, meeting the eyes of many of those there with a smile and a nod. And though Heilyn was still staring at him as though he had been spawned from the abyss, Gildas' eyes drifted over him without a flicker of recognition.

That was...interesting.

Why did Gildas not call him out?

Gildas continued his speech. "It always warms my heart to see children mature to this stage of life; it reminds me of how much I still mourn that I have two less weddings to preside over in my own family." He infused his voice with a hint of grief, and it had the desired effect on the company, who all murmured in sympathy.

Ivana frowned. Two less weddings? She searched her mind for the details that would make sense of that statement and then remembered that two of Gildas' four sons were dead.

"Please make our guests welcome," Talesin said, and then sat down and leaned over to whisper in his eldest's ear.

His eldest suffered a brief smile, glanced at Lavena, who was too occupied with comparing her sparkling teardrop earrings with those of Talesin's wife to notice her fiancé's glance, and then looked away.

A solely political marriage, then. There was no love between those two.

The first course was served, and Heilyn looked as though he were going to be sick as a plate was placed in front of him. He repeatedly glanced toward the door, and it was clear he wanted out of this room. But he could hardly make an inconspicuous exit at present.

There was nothing to do but eat, which she was happy to do. Nobles didn't skimp on their banquets, and the food was delicious.

On the other hand, Heilyn hardly touched his dinner. He picked at it and pushed it around his plate, until the man next to him leaned over and said something.

Vaughn gave him a tight smile and nodded.

When the final course had come and disappeared, Ri Talesin stood again. "It is also my honor to introduce two others to our company tonight. As you may know, we have with us two unlikely guests." He spoke quickly, as though eager to dispense with the duty of recognizing them—though he had brought it upon himself.

"Dal Heilyn and Da Ivana? Would you stand for a moment?" The Ri turned his gaze in their general direction. He had made no attempt to contact them prior to now, but their seating location as well as their more common dress no doubt gave them away.

Ivana stood, ducking her head to feign embarrassment. Heilyn stood, stiff and unblinking.

"As many of you have heard, these two recently dispatched a bloodbane summoned to the middle of our capital. They call it luck, but I call it courage. I am pleased to award such courageous subjects living within my realm, and thus each will return home with a purse of fifteen hundred setans."

A murmur went around the table, no doubt a mutual acknowledgement of the generosity of their host—a heavy purse for any commoner, indeed, but Ivana doubted it even put a dent in his own treasury.

The Ri motioned to his steward, standing nearby, and the man bowed and walked first to Ivana, handing her a heavy leather pouch without meeting her eyes, and then walking around the table to do the same for Heilyn.

There was a smattering of applause and then Gildas spoke up. "If I may, my friend?"

"Of course," Talesin said.

"I would also like to extend my gratitude. While our Watchmen work hard to keep the borders of our cities safe, it is the bravery of such as these that mean we may all rest peacefully in our homes at night. I applaud you, honored citizens."

It was a pretty speech for a monster as bad as any bloodbane, but Ivana curtsied and smiled all the same. Gildas didn't give her a second glance.

However...

Gildas met Heilyn's eyes and smiled, for all the world a grateful ruler. But Ivana didn't miss the hardness in his eyes and the slight smugness of his lips. Still, he said nothing.

Heilyn glanced away almost immediately—toward the door again.

Ivana and Heilyn sat back down, and the Ri spoke again. "Just so, Ri Gildas, but it is you and your order who truly keep us safe."

Gildas inclined his head once in acknowledgment, and muscles jumped in Heilyn's jaw at that proclamation.

He hates him, she realized. That seemed an obvious conclusion in retrospect, but up until now, Ivana hadn't put much thought into the relationship between the man she had to kill and the man she wished she could.

Well. It seemed she and Heilyn had something in common.

Conversation at the table resumed, and the formalities of the banquet thus discharged, Ri Talesin rose along with his wife and children, no doubt preparing to retire to their parlors to greet their guests, as proper hosts should. He was stopped, however, by Gildas, who also rose and then whispered in his ear.

Talesin frowned and cast his eyes around the room, and then nodded. He gestured to the chief of his guards, who stood nearby keeping watch, and in turn whispered in *his* ear. The guard bowed and left the room through a doorway in the back of the dining hall.

Was Gildas so polite that he wanted to catch his prey without disturbing Talesin's banquet? Ivana found that hard to believe.

"If I may suggest we retire?" Talesin said above the general hum of the room, and a moment later chairs scraped against the hardwood as the entire table stood up, the women heading toward their parlor, and the men toward theirs.

Gildas followed the chief of the guards out the far door, while a good number of guests filtered out of the main door, not intending on staying past dinner. When the room was satisfactorily disordered, Ivana sidled up to Heilyn, who was attempting to slip out of the room unnoticed.

She hooked her arm in his and maneuvered them to the middle of a throng waiting to exit the hall. "Going somewhere, Dal?" she said into his ear.

"Gildas is here," he said, eying the guards that had appeared at the far door and two parlor doors.

Curious. Why were there none at the main door?

"Indeed. Why would that be, I wonder?"

"I don't know how he got here so fast. He must have been in the city. It's the only explanation." It was clear Heilyn was talking to himself, not her.

"You *knew* it was possible he could be here?" she asked, incredulous.

He cast her a nervous look. "He must have known the name I gave Talesin. I need to get out of here," he said, craning his neck to look behind him. "Where did he go?"

This was more than unfortunate. Her plan had always been to collect the reward, and, upon returning home, drug Heilyn and finish what she started.

Now, she had a dilemma. He wanted to leave now, for obvious reasons. She had no way to keep him here, couldn't kill him here, and she could hardly go with him. If ever there was a way to draw suspicion upon herself, it would be to flee right along with the Banebringer.

She again had to choose the path with the least immediate consequence, and that meant she had to let him go and attempt to find him again later.

She gritted her teeth in frustration. She *knew* she should have killed him in the woods and blamed it on a bloodbane.

The crowd finally started to move, and as they were swept out the dining room door themselves she saw what had caused the delay leaving the dining hall. Guards blocked the front doors, keeping guests from departing. Those who hadn't gone to the parlors were milling about the great hall, some clearly annoyed, many too drunk to care. Gildas was standing near the entrance, dispatching guards to block the rest of the exits to the hall.

Gildas glanced their way, and his eyes immediately roved a different direction, as though it were happenstance that they landed on them in the first place.

It wasn't happenstance. He knew exactly where Heilyn was and wasn't about to lose track of him.

Heilyn saw it too. "Damn," he whispered.

This presented another problem. She could, under no circumstances, let Ri Gildas get his hands on Heilyn. Heilyn had mentioned torture; what if the Conclave tried to get information out of him, such as the assassins he had tried to hire? For that matter, what if Heilyn tried to use the information to his advantage, as a stalling or even bargaining tactic once caught?

If he couldn't die at her hands, then she needed to see him safely out of anyone else's until then.

"Talesin's safe room has a back door," she said. "That would be one option for escape, though I don't know where the passage will put you out. I didn't have time to explore that far."

He turned to her as if seeing her for the first time. "Why are you helping me?"

"Only long enough to get you free from here so that I can deal with you on my own terms, I assure you." She let go of his arm. "Go, before it's too late."

He didn't argue. She turned away from him and started walking toward a nearby powder room, as if aiming to refresh herself. The next time she glanced back, he was gone.

There was something off about this. Ri Gildas had had opportunity after opportunity to identify and arrest Heilyn, yet he had passed on them all.

Ivana touched the sleeve of a passing guard. "If I might ask, Dal," she said, widening her eyes and allowing the slightest tremor to enter her voice, "what is happening?"

The guard hesitated and then nodded toward Gildas. "Ri Gildas has reason to believe there might be an assassin about.

Kind of him to take Ri Talesin's safety to heart while here, given that it's not his duty."

Ivana blinked, taken aback. An assassin? Not a Banebringer? She glanced at Gildas, mind racing. What was his game?

Ivana started acting in earnest. "An assassin...!" She placed a hand on her chest. "Blessed Rhianah."

The guard kept talking. "We're keeping the guests from leaving, trying to account for everyone."

Ivana sank against the wall and fanned at her face. "I...this is terribly unsettling."

The guard gave her a sympathetic look. "Begging your pardon, Da. I didn't mean to worry you."

"No, no, not your fault..." She waved him away, and he bowed and left.

The feeling that this didn't sit right was growing, and it wasn't because she loathed Gildas. Why wouldn't he simply declare what he knew to be true? He was a Hunter; if he knew a Banebringer were there, he would be within his rights to do whatever necessary to catch him or her, even if it caused half the company to grumble. He didn't need this subterfuge to see his son Sedated—or dead.

And then it hit her. Dead. Of course.

Having been presented with a live son of Ri Gildas, she had, of course, never considered that *Heilyn* was one of the sons that was presumed dead, but rather had assumed that the two dead sons were two *other* sons.

Ri Gildas—Heilyn's father—must have declared Heilyn dead, probably to hide the fact that he was a Banebringer to preserve his own reputation. Which meant no one knew, which in turn meant he couldn't make a public display of it, lest, having nothing more to lose, Heilyn use it against him.

So instead, he needed a reason to keep guests contained so he could find Heilyn on his own terms.

Her first reaction was relief. So he didn't actually suspect an assassin was about.

And then she realized he had arranged everything here to allow himself the opportunity to confront Heilyn alone.

All the guards had been dispatched to guard either Ri Talesin, which was unnecessary, or exits from the great hall. Unfortunately, the exit to the basement was now conspicuously sparse on guards.

She turned back to the entrance. Gildas was gone.

Chapter Ten

The Second-Worst Disaster

Vaughn tried not to run. Though there was a good chance his father had been watching him when he disappeared, he knew the only advantage he had by way of stealth was invisibility; in every other way, he might as well have been a bloodgiant hurling boulders at unfortunate travelers, for all the stealth he held in his body.

Actually, bloodgiants might be more *stealthy.* At least travelers were usually unaware of their presence until rocks began raining down on their heads.

And it was night, and the moon was nearing full. That meant his invisibility, while still useful, was not always complete. A keen observer might notice a shimmer in the air, or even see a flash or blur.

And Hunters, of all people, were keen observers.

So his heart was pounding as he slid past servants and guards on his way to the nearest staircase down, hoping no one would hear his footsteps or notice the sigh of air caused by his passing.

If anyone did, no one turned to look.

It took him more time than he wanted to find the safe room—the footprint of Ri Talesin's basement was as large as the manor itself, and even with his especially perceptive night vision, Vaughn almost missed the metal door hidden behind rows of barrels and crates stacked in the cellar.

The door was, of course, heavy, and the hinges were rusty from disuse. About half of the way open, it started to shriek in protest. He immediately stopped, but the sound it had made resounded as loudly in his ears as the bloodgiant's boulders against the ground; he was certain the entire company upstairs heard it.

Vaughn started to breathe a bit easier when he heard no immediate pursuit.

He could make out the outline of another door in the back of the room; the back door Sweetblade had mentioned.

He was about to slip through the partially opened door and into the room, when he sensed a change in the amount of light available to him, and shadows began dancing on the wall behind him.

"Now, Teyrnon. How impolite of you to leave so suddenly. Not even a greeting for your dear old father?"

Damn.

He turned to face his father. He hadn't pulled out the syringe with the hideous concoction that would make him permanently comatose, nor his hand crossbow. He was, however, staring vaguely in Vaughn's direction—no doubt because he had seen the door open of its own accord.

A lot of good his invisibility did when Gildas was blocking the only other way out—the door he had come through. With the maze of crates and barrels in the cellar, it would be dangerous to get close enough to try and slip by him. But his other option was to back into the impenetrable metal box behind him and hope he could fling the back door—certainly as heavy as the other—open fast enough to flee.

He didn't like the choices available to him. He was a fool to have come here. He should have run in the woods and taken his chances with Sweetblade.

Of course, he had more than invisibility at his disposal; but he used his other power so rarely that he often forgot he even had it. And was there even any water in the cellar for him to use?

He inched backwards until he stepped fully into the darkness behind him.

Gildas moved closer. "You've been busy, I hear," he said. "I hope you've realized by now the futility of your attempts to circumvent justice."

Justice. Right. He fought the bitterness that rose in his throat, trying to concentrate on the situation at hand, rather than Gildas' words. He stepped backwards until he reached the other door, not daring to turn his back on Gildas, and felt for the handle.

If only he had his bow. It would be so easy...

Forget it. He knew he wouldn't do it. He had had the chance to kill Gildas a half dozen times over the past few years, and he had never been able to bring himself to do it. No matter how many monsters he had slain—when it came to his father, he was a coward.

Now Gildas was standing near the doorway of the saferoom, lifting his arm to let his lantern shed light on the dark room. "Why don't you show yourself? Are you such a coward that even in the face of the inevitable, still you hide?"

The verbalization of his own thoughts stung. He wanted to retort, if only to speak a denial, lest his silence make it true, but he bit it back. His father always managed to get him to speak. Not this time. He tugged as hard as he could on the back door to the safe room.

It didn't budge.

Panic shot through him. *What...?*

He turned around and pulled harder, but it was stuck fast. Behind him, the other door screeched again.

Vaughn swallowed and glanced desperately at the only other way out of the room, which Gildas now fully blocked with his large frame.

Gildas stepped into the room. "You're a damned nuisance, Teyrnon, just like you've always been. I'm tired of it. It's time to dig this splinter out of my finger."

The words jabbed at him in spite of himself. *Just let it go, Vaughn. Ignore him.*

Perhaps he could simply hurl himself at Gildas. He might get lucky and knock him over and escape. It was his only hope, if a slim one. His father was not someone you scrapped with and came out unharmed, and all it would take was for him to plunge a syringe into any part of Vaughn's body. Didn't matter if it were his thigh or big toe.

The worst part was knowing that death wasn't even what awaited him. It was spending the rest of his life trapped in his own lifeless body.

Gildas swept his eyes across the back of the room, no doubt watching for a chance shimmer in the air that would give away Vaughn's position, and then finally pulled the syringe out of his dinner jacket with his free hand. "No, 'splinter' is too kind. You're a rabid dog, every bit the son of that bitch as you ever were. I'll be glad to put you down."

Vaughn could feel the rage building in him. His father was baiting him, and he knew it. Turning from insulting him to insulting his mother.

"I never wanted other sons, you know," Gildas said. "I wanted a daughter or two to sell in alliance, and that was all I ever wanted. I had my son, already being groomed by the time you and your brothers were born."

Vaughn did know that. His father had made the inconsequential nature of his and his two other brothers' existence quite clear growing up. Gildas didn't want children. He wanted tools.

"But you—especially disappointing. Always clinging to your mother's skirts, whimpering when Airell gave you the beatings you deserved. And then when I threw Cheris at you, you went and turned into a simpering fool."

Hurt and anger warred in Vaughn's chest. He always knew his father had preferred his oldest brother, had never entertained hope that his father cared for him in the least. But that he had *despised* him so...

"I'll grant you one use," his father said. "You kept the fourth one out of my hair."

Vaughn couldn't take it anymore. He clenched his fists and stepped forward, dropping his invisibility. "Leave Teryn out of this," he said.

Gildas flashed his teeth at him. "Was that his name?"

The anger won. Vaughn hissed and nearly threw himself at his father.

Except at that moment, the room exploded into chaos.

Ivana crouched behind a crate near the door of the cellar. Of course, Ri Gildas didn't know she was there. No one ever knew she was there unless she wanted them to. She had caught up with him just as he had stepped into the saferoom, imploring someone—Heilyn, she was certain—to show themselves.

Why hadn't Heilyn fled through the back door already?

She didn't hear him reply, but that didn't mean he wasn't there.

Gildas was speaking again. "You're a damned nuisance, Teyrnon, just like you've always been. I'm tired of it. It's time to dig this splinter out of my finger."

Teyrnon? Yet another name, probably his name by birth, coming from Heilyn's father.

"No, 'splinter' is too kind. You're a rabid dog, every bit the son of that bitch as you ever were. I'll be glad to put you down."

Ivana bristled as though the insult had been directed at her. As if, instead of throwing slurs against his wife, he were repeating the careless words he had spoken over the body of her father to the watching crowd. *That's what comes of letting your daughter whore herself.*

"I never wanted other sons, you know," Gildas said. "I wanted a daughter or two to sell in alliance, and that was all I ever wanted. I had my son, already being groomed by the time you and your brothers were born."

Daughters to *sell?* Her vision blurred red. The hypocritical, arrogant bastard—

She found herself creeping closer, her hand drawing the dagger hidden under her skirts without conscious thought. He had already given everyone a good reason for death; an assassin lurking about. A well-placed dagger, and she could slip back upstairs without anyone the wiser.

"But you—especially disappointing. Always clinging to your mother's skirts, whimpering when Airell gave you the beatings you deserved. And then when I threw Cheris at you, you went and turned into a simpering fool."

The hatred she had tried to set aside so that she could deal with this situation rationally boiled up in Ivana again. She had always despised him, for obvious reasons. But she had never known how truly foul this man was, and she was viciously pleased to see the dagger already in her hand.

"I'll grant you one use," Gildas said. "You kept the fourth one out of my hair."

Vaughn suddenly spoke, the loathing boiling in Ivana's chest bleeding out in his voice. "Leave Teryn out of this," he hissed.

Ivana didn't know who Teryn was, other than by context, his fourth son, perhaps, but what he said next—or more likely, how he said it—snapped something in her.

"Was that his name?" Gildas sneered.

She hurled herself at his back.

Instead of leaping forward, Vaughn stumbled backward, out of the way of his father, who suddenly pitched forward, Sweetblade on his back.

The syringe flew out of his hand and spun through the air. It cracked against the stone and then landed on the ground, and aether began seeping out.

He did a double-take.

"Sweetblade?" he asked aloud. What in the abyss was she doing here?

But Gildas wasn't one to go down easily.

Even with her dagger buried in his back, he managed to throw her off him and rise to face her, the shock of the assault quickly turning to disbelief.

She yanked her dagger out of him as she rolled away, and then scrambled to her feet and fell into a crouch, hatred smoldering in her eyes—not at Vaughn, but at Gildas.

Gildas swayed and fell back down to his hands and knees. Blood soaked his back, and after a moment, he collapsed to the ground and didn't move again.

Vaughn stared in shock. It had happened so fast he still couldn't believe it. He didn't understand. He had offered to pay

Sweetblade to do this, and now she had done it of her own accord.

Sweetblade moved forward, knelt, and placed two fingers at Gildas' throat. She waited a moment, and then stood, seeming satisfied.

That was it, then. His father was dead. He swallowed, feeling dizzy with relief? Grief? Shock? He didn't even know.

But now would be a perfect time to flee, if he could get that back door open...

Sweetblade was still standing there, no longer looking at his father, but instead staring grimly at him.

That...wasn't good.

"Your turn," she said softly.

He blinked, and then stepped back. "Now, hold on. Let's not be hasty. You can't—"

"If ever there were a good place to spawn a demon, a safe room would be it," she said.

"Damn you, woman! I'm not going to betray your secret!"

"I'm still in shock," she said, moving closer to him, backing him into a corner. "A Banebringer, under the roof of my own inn? And most likely the assassin Gildas was seeking, no less. They struggled, and he must not have known..."

Could he win a fight against her? He didn't know. He was likely stronger, but she was, simply put, deadly. Not to mention, fist fighting wasn't exactly his strength, and she had a dagger.

Now would be an excellent time to turn invisible. He might get lucky if he just—

The back door to the safe room squealed and buckled, and then fell off its hinges with a terrific crash, half-blocking the passage out.

Vaughn jumped back, and for the second time, a woman barreled into the room and landed on his father's body.

Vaughn gaped. The woman's eyes were wild, and Vaughn had the impression she wasn't entirely sane.

She spoke, and her voice was raspy, as though from disuse. "No," she said. "Such a death is too good for you..."

She raised her hand, and a moment later there was a scratching sound, like someone dragging a stick haphazardly over the ground. It grew and magnified, until the floor was writhing. Bugs and worms of every shape and size streamed and slithered into the room from the safe room passage behind them, swarming over the crushed door...and over Gildas.

The insects quickly ran out of open space on Gildas' body and started to spread out, toward Sweetblade, toward himself...

Water, Vaughn, water! Danton was right, he should have spent more time practicing.

The barrels outside the saferoom...wine?

He didn't stop to contemplate further. He reached out and *pulled.*

He could feel the wine straining against its confines in the barrels, the pent-up energy burning away his blood as he continued to pull on it, so he knew he was right about the water. But it took longer than he would have liked for it to escape. Finally, the red liquid burst out of half a dozen barrels from the room beyond, seeking the person who called it, until he redirected it to slam into the carpet of bugs covering Gildas, and then beyond.

The scrabbling sound stopped, and Vaughn swore he could

hear a thousand tiny screams as the bugs struggled and drowned in the wash, which he manipulated until all of the bugs had been caught up in it. He pushed the flood of wine with its tiny victims back down the saferoom passage.

The room spun as he turned back, and he knew he was close to over-doing it. His un-practiced, desperate solution had burned a dangerous amount of aether from his blood. He needed a moment to rest, which didn't seem likely...because the bug-woman had shifted her gaze, now murderous, to him.

Ivana had never liked bugs. She was half horrified and half fascinated at the scene unfolding before her; she had never seen Banebringer powers in action so dramatically.

She shook her head. Enough with scientific curiosity.

The newcomer—the crazed woman—had shifted her gaze to Heilyn. She didn't seem pleased he had foiled her attempt at...

Well, Ivana wasn't sure what.

She looked back at Gildas' corpse.

Her eyes widened. He was pushing himself off the ground, coughing.

No. There had been no pulse. He was *dead!*

Unless...

She glanced at the woman. Some sort of Banebringer magic? It had to be.

The woman didn't seem to care about Gildas now; she was preoccupied with Heilyn. And, oddly enough, Gildas didn't seem to care about Heilyn. Instead, Gildas rose to his feet, swayed, blinked, shook his head, and then turned to face Ivana, a grim look on his face.

"Sweetblade, is it?" he said softly.

Ivana was an assassin. She did her killing from the shadows, or in secret, and with surprise on her side. She knew how to fight, but she avoided it when at all possible. Especially head on fights with men twice her own size. But this was one man she couldn't risk letting go.

She hurled herself into him, hoping to land her dagger in such a way that would cause him to reel back and give her an advantage, but with unbelievably fast reflexes, he caught her arm. After a moment of grappling, he twisted her wrist back in a crushing grip and forced her to drop the dagger. He held her there for a moment, while she thrashed against his superior strength, trying to get enough purchase to kick him in the groin. But he held her away from himself, his eyes cold. "You should know better than to cross the Conclave."

He backhanded her across the face and then shoved her so hard that her breath failed her when she hit the wall.

She collapsed to the ground and gasped for air, tasting blood in her mouth where her teeth had cut the inside of her cheek. The room spun around her, and all she could do was raise her head and watch helplessly while someone infinitely more dangerous to her than Heilyn had ever been simply walked away.

Had his father really just risen and walked away? He had been dead, hadn't he? Sweetblade wouldn't have left him lying there if she hadn't been certain, would she have? And after all of this, why was he just leaving Vaughn?

The woman's glare turned into a crazed grin, and she flexed her fist. "Fasss...cinating..." she rasped. Then she closed her eyes and breathed deeply through her nose, saying something else Vaughn couldn't make out.

Vaughn glanced desperately around himself, searching for another solution to this problem. But he was already faint, and even if he could come up with a workable idea, he might well kill himself in the attempt. He didn't even know if he could turn invisible right now without risking himself.

He didn't know why the woman didn't just attack him. Was it because he was a Banebringer as well? Was she sane enough to care? But, now, the woman had ceased paying attention to him at all. Instead, she became interested in a commotion beginning outside the door. Shouts rang out, and before he could wonder what this new development portended, half a dozen guards in the livery of Talesin burst into the room.

The guards turned on the woman and Vaughn, drawing swords. They ignored Sweetblade, who was still slumped against the metal door where she had fallen.

Vaughn's throat went dry, but the woman grinned, snarled and stepped closer to the guards, causing the three in the back to deliberately block the doorway. The space in the safe room was too cramped to be able to effectively slip away, if he even dared; a few wild slashes of their swords in the right direction would easily land a blow on him.

So he backed farther into the safe room, as far as he could, until he bumped against the crumpled metal door. Perhaps he could use some of his pre-made aether, turn invisible, and worm his way through the opening while they were distracted.

The woman grabbed the sword of the nearest guard, and heedless of the gash it sliced in her hand, pulled him toward her and placed her bleeding hand on his chest.

The guard gasped, started coughing, and before Vaughn's eyes, his face *shriveled*. The woman dropped the guard, clearly dead, on the ground, and let out a shriek of hysterical laughter that set Vaughn to shivering even more than he already had been.

It took a moment for the other five guards to regain their composure at what the woman had done, but the first one who did lunged at her and bowled into her.

She stumbled back, but then lashed out and tossed him across the room like a doll. The third swung his sword and slammed the flat into her back with a blow that should have broken her spine, or at least exploded some sensitive organ, but she merely swatted him away.

Burning skies. He didn't know who this woman was, why she was here, nor how she had such extraordinary powers for a Banebringer, but since her focus wasn't on him at present, he did know that now would be an excellent time to flee.

Sweetblade had gained her feet and apparently had the same thought. She had already squirmed her way through the half-blocked passage out of the safe room and was disappearing into the darkness.

He followed suit.

Chapter Eleven

Reluctant Companions

Ivana ran from the second-worst disaster in her life as fast and far as she could, staying off the road and in the woods, until she had to stop from exhaustion.

She found a tree with branches sweeping down to the ground and crawled underneath the boughs where she would be hidden from view. She laid her head back against the trunk to take stock. She had nothing with her except the increasingly tattered formal dress she wore—a horrid dress to run in as it was—the dagger strapped to her thigh, and a purse of fifteen hundred setans.

The irony of that situation was such that she almost laughed aloud. A lot of good fifteen hundred setans did her right now.

But she stopped short of laughing. Now that she had a moment to rest, and the thrill of her flight had worn off, the injuries she had sustained in her brief struggle with Ri Gildas had started to manifest themselves. Her cheek was tender and swollen from where he had struck her; she moved her hand to touch it experimentally, and pain shot from her wrist up her arm. She sucked in a quick breath through her teeth and closed her eyes, holding the injured wrist close to her chest. She moved it, just a bit, with the same result.

Fantastic. And she wouldn't be able to find star-leaf at night. She would have to wait until morning.

She was in no condition to do anything but find a place to hole up and lick her wounds.

And yet, she was headed back to the one place that was the worst possible place to go.

She had to. She had to check on her girls. What would happen to them? Despair squeezed her throat in a way that hadn't happened for years. This was her fault. She had let anger cloud her judgment, and it might well mean harm would come to the only people she cared for.

She should have never gone to the estate, never followed Heilyn, never tried to kill Gildas.

She hoped that, whatever happened, they would leave her girls alone. It wasn't their fault that their mistress was an assassin. None of them knew about it, except Aleena, and she could feign innocence as well as Ivana. Hopefully Aleena could take over. Hopefully they wouldn't reap the consequences of her failure.

But the Conclave was known for its swift brutality when it came to people who crossed them, and she had to make sure.

She couldn't run without knowing what she had done this time.

She felt herself starting to drift off, and she hoped fervently as her mind clouded over that the branches would hide her from the view of any pursuers...or bloodbane.

A stick cracked, and Ivana jerked out of her half-slumber.

She pulled her legs up to her chest so she was a smaller visual target and leaned over to peer through the branches. Probably an animal, but you never knew once you were outside inhabited areas.

She frowned, seeing nothing. Yet she continued to hear the rustle of leaves and the snap of twigs.

She inspected the ground near the tree. These woods weren't tightly packed, and the almost-full moon shone through the leaves with enough light to see tolerably well. And so she could see the press of undergrowth, moving seemingly on its own. And as she peered closer, a faint shimmer in the air.

Heilyn? Temoth, how had he managed to come across the same path as her? She had hoped to lose him, once and for all, since his knowledge of her identity no longer mattered.

Then again, it wouldn't do to assume, and the branches wouldn't hide her forever from someone determined to find her. Surprise would be her only chance, especially while injured.

She slid her dagger out of its sheath as the leaves compressed right near where she was sitting and held it in what she considered her off-hand—though in reality she was nearly as good with her left hand as right.

The footsteps stopped. The leaves moved as though the person were turning...

She took her chance.

Heilyn appeared a moment after she crashed into him. She kneed his groin and shoved him backward onto the ground as he crumpled.

Unfortunately, before she could get her dagger all the way to his throat, he had grabbed her injured wrist to try and wrest it away from him.

She cried out, and darkness passed in front of her eyes.

The next she knew, *she* was glaring up at *him*.

She had dropped her dagger, and he kicked it out of the way. He had pinned her to the ground, one hand on each forearm, and a knee in her stomach.

He didn't look angry or grim; simply satisfied. "Looks like I'm the one on top of you this time," he said.

Fury boiled up again. "Get—off—me!" she snarled, trying to knee his groin again, but he had been prepared for that and shifted his weight from his knee on her stomach to both knees on her thighs.

She glared at him. "You let me up," she said, "and I'm going to kill you."

"Best not let you up then."

She gave another perfunctory struggle, but he was stronger and heavier than her, and she was both wounded and exhausted.

She gave up, chest heaving. She was emotionally wrung out; she couldn't deal with this right now. "Fine. Let me up, and I *won't* kill you."

He raised an eyebrow at her. "Really?"

"Really."

"And how do I know you're not lying?"

She gritted her teeth and closed her eyes, to hide his face, the face that reminded her so much of Airell. She wanted him *off* her! "You can take my dagger," she said.

"As if that's the only way you have to kill me."

She couldn't take it anymore. She screamed through clenched teeth. "Get off! Get off now!"

The pressure on her thighs released, and a moment later his irritating face was gone from above her. "You have anger issues, you know that?" He bent down and picked up her dagger.

She sat up, seething. She didn't. She didn't have anger issues. She wasn't supposed to have emotional issues of any kind. And yet here she was, raw and laid bare, in a way she had never wanted to be again.

She pushed herself to her feet with her good hand. "Get away from me. I never want to see you again."

"Wait, so you're really not going to kill me?"

"Ri Gildas, who is infinitely more dangerous to me, already knows who I am. Killing you would now be a waste of my energy."

"Well," he said, relief in his voice. "I wouldn't want to waste your energy."

"If you'll excuse me," she snapped, "I have more pressing matters that require my attention."

He failed to take the hint. Instead, he kept pace with her. "Where are you going?"

"I don't believe that is any of your concern."

"Wait—" He took hold of her arm, and she jerked it out of his grasp.

That had been a poor decision, as her wrist protested so loudly that she almost cried out. Instead, she clenched her teeth together. "What," she said, finally stopping to face him, "do you want?"

His eyes flicked over her face and then down to her arm, which she was holding close to her body out of reflex. "You're hurt."

"Thank you for that perceptive assessment."

"I have something that could help."

"I believe I said this before: I neither need nor want your help. Now go away."

"You may not want it," he said. "But you need it."

She snorted and started to turn away.

"You're no fool," he continued. "You don't stand a chance out here by yourself for long, especially injured. You know that." He held up her dagger. "And, you're unarmed."

Burning skies, he was irritating, and even more so because he was right. She would have to be out here overnight, and since she couldn't travel near the road, it would take her longer to get back to the city than it had to get to Ri Talesin's estate, which probably meant a second night.

Every night in uninhabited lands increased the odds a roving bloodbane might find her, and she knew her limits.

She had little to do with bringing down the behemoth in the city; if it hadn't been for Heilyn, they would all be dead by now.

She glanced at him and realized for the first time that he had his bow and quiver again. When had he retrieved those?

He offered a placating smile when he saw her glance.

She gritted her teeth. She hated the idea of accepting his aid. But she hated the thought of dying more.

That was something, at least.

"I can find things to help with the pain," she said.

"What I have will do more than help with the pain. It will help it heal faster."

"Banebringer magic?"

"Something like that. But ideally I'll need water and a fire." He pointed. "There's a creek that runs about a quarter mile that way. I know a good spot to take shelter for the night."

She ran her tongue over her teeth. *Ugh.* She was tired, she was injured, and the defenses she had spent a decade building around herself were in ruins. She needed to regroup, rest, re-bury and re-build. She could do it, she knew, but she needed the time and space to do so—time and space away from *him* and everything he represented. And a few good assassinations wouldn't hurt.

But she nodded curtly. "Fine."

She let him take the lead, and, thankfully, he didn't insist on further conversation on the way.

They reached the creek a few minutes later, and then walked along it for a good twenty more before he finally stopped. Heilyn immediately knelt and started rooting around in the dirt.

Ivana surveyed the area. A tumble of boulders lay along the creek here; the boulders would shelter them on two sides while the creek was on a third. It wouldn't stop a determined bloodbane—or anyone who might have followed them, which she was just as concerned about—but it was better than sitting out in the open.

"There we go," Heilyn muttered to himself. He pulled a tangle of sod, weeds, and branches out of the way, and then did the same at another spot nearby, revealing two holes in the ground.

He reached down into the holes and pulled out handfuls of debris. When he seemed satisfied, he set to filling the larger hole with firewood and kindling.

She found herself drifting closer, curious in spite of herself.

That was all right. Intellectual curiosity offered a cool detachment that she welcomed right now.

She eyed the holes critically, considering the sunken fire pit and what must be a ventilation shaft connected to it underground. *Huh.*

"You're building a fire that can't be seen," she said at last. She was...well, she hated to admit it, impressed.

"Thank you for that perceptive assessment," he said, a smile tugging at the corner of his mouth.

She frowned. "A bit less obvious of a conclusion than my bruises."

He brushed off his hands and pulled something out of a coin purse at his waist. "Not to me," he stated matter-of-factly.

Hmm. No, she supposed someone used to running would have acquired a handy set of survival skills.

He rubbed his fingers together, and a fine powder floated down into the hole. A moment later, flames licked at the sides, and a small but functional fire crackled in the pit. More Banebringer magic?

He got up and started looking around the immediate area. He came back with two flat stones about the size of her palm and a few long, smooth sticks. He dropped one stone into the fire pit, but the other he set to the side. He drew another *something* out of the pouch and crushed it between his fingers over the second stone. Again, shimmery powder trickled down, this time making a pile on the stone.

He lifted the hem of his shirt and used her dagger to rip a hole large enough for him to get his fingers into, and then tore a large piece of cloth off his shirt. He went to the creek and soaked the cloth, and then came back and dripped some water onto the stone. With his finger, he stirred up the mixture until it formed a silvery paste. Then, he folded the cloth a few times and wiped the stone clean of the paste with one side.

He held up the cloth and touched it to her injured cheek.

She flinched back and held up a hand to fend him off. "I can do it myself."

"You can't," he said. "Not yet. It won't work."

She frowned. "Why not?"

"It has to be activated, and you can't do that. It will know you're not a Banebringer."

She raised an eyebrow. "The...salve...is sentient?"

"No," he said. "Not precisely. We're still trying to understand it, but as far as we know, non-Banebringers are unable to burn—activate—aether."

He wasn't making much sense to her, but she forced herself to hold still and let him administer the makeshift compress. True to his word, a few seconds after he had pressed it gently against her cheek, he gestured for her to take it.

She did, and gingerly held it there.

"That should help with the bruising and swelling," he said, sitting back on his heels. "If it's going to work, it should start to feel a little better within a few minutes."

If *it's going to work*? "I was actually more concerned about my wrist," she said.

"That's more complicated," he said. "But I'm working on it next."

He pulled more of the same substance out of the pouch and held it in his hand. He cringed, and then he plunged his hand into the fire.

What—!

But when he brought his hand back up, it was undamaged. He was holding the stone he had thrown in earlier, and he dropped it to the ground, seeming relieved.

Even *more* Banebringer magic? She had never seen it, not like this. People knew Banebringers had 'heretical' magic, but rare was the person who had seen the magic at work.

Once again, he reached into his pouch—obviously *not* a coin purse—and this time, she saw what it was, because he set it on the hot stone.

He had produced a few fingers worth of tiny chunks of some silvery substance, which, once on the stone, melted rapidly into a viscous, silvery liquid.

She stared at it. It resembled the blood Heilyn had bled when she had first cut him with her dagger.

Heilyn was ripping off another piece of his shirt, this time more precisely attempting to tear off a long strip around the hem.

She removed the cloth he had given her and eyed the silvery paste again. "Are you having me put your blood on my face?" she asked.

"Perceptive. You should keep that on for a little longer."

"I'm rather adept at noticing details," she said, putting the compress back on her cheek.

A wry smile touched his lips, but he refrained from commenting. Instead, he held up the cloth and eyed the length of it, and then started ripping off another.

Did it not bother him at all that he was setting up camp—such as it was—with an assassin? Then again, he had never seemed particularly terrified of her, even knowing she had been looking for an opportunity to dispose of him.

In fact, sometimes he seemed downright determined to act rash and irritating enough to provoke her to kill him.

Still, he appeared to think that their common trials warranted a level of familiarity that she neither wanted nor was comfortable with.

"Not my blood," he said, tying the two lengths of cloth together. "A bindblood's. And it's not exactly blood anymore. We call it aether."

There was that name again. At least she knew what it was called now, but that wasn't a helpful answer. "I don't know what any of that means."

"It's difficult to explain."

"Try me."

"Why?"

"Because you're asking me to put it on my skin. I want to know what it is." She told herself that was true, and it was, in part. But a tiny part of her was also fascinated. Knowledge of something new, something other people knew virtually nothing about? How often did she have that opportunity? Her father would have already been eagerly interrogating him on the subject.

She shoved that thought away.

He shrugged. "A bindblood is one class of Banebringer," he said. "Their particular abilities lie in the areas of healing and hallucinations." He held out his hand, palm up. "Give me your hurt hand."

She hesitated.

He held up the double length of cloth. "I'm going to make a splint."

Once again, she gritted her teeth, but accepted his aid. She gingerly placed the hurt hand in his palm, trying not to wince at the movement, but failed.

He was exceedingly gentle as he laid the sticks along her wrist and lower forearm, and then started wrapping his makeshift bandage around them. It was unnerving. "Do you typically bandage your wounds all by yourself?" he asked as he worked. "Because you'd think you'd never let anyone help you before."

"Doctors tend to ask prying questions, such as, 'How did this happen?'"

He chuckled. "Fair. What about...Aleena, was it?"

"She's not usually around when I'm hurt."

He opened his mouth to reply, but then he stopped and stared at her forearm.

She knew immediately what he was looking at, and she forced herself to remain still.

"Where did you get those scars?"

Despair. Guilt. Blood. "I went hands first through a glass window," she lied. How had he even seen them, especially in the dark? They were so faded by now, a casual observer wouldn't notice.

He studied her arm for another moment and then flicked his eyes up to hers. He was looking at her as though he thought that if he just peered hard enough, he would be able to penetrate her protective layers and find something different than what she was underneath.

It was unnerving and refreshing all at once. To her horror, it stirred up something inside her, something that shouldn't *be* there at all. Yet it was there, and it reached out, straining to touch something genuine, to be *known*...

She shifted to distract herself. She was *far* too vulnerable right now. She wanted this to be over. "I don't see how this is going to help it heal more quickly. Only keep me from injuring it further."

"Patience." He picked up the stone with the liquid...aether...and then slowly poured it on the outside of the bandage, while gently rotating her whole arm and using his fingers to smear it evenly in a thin layer around her wrist. "Don't move," he said when he finished.

She obeyed. A minute later, he tapped the bandage where the aether was, and it clicked against his fingernail.

"You think *this* is going to suffice as a cast?" That would break with an accidental flick of her arm.

"It's not supposed to be a cast. It's a focus."

Ivana hated feeling ignorant. "I think this is where you

should go back to telling me what exactly this stuff is. You said it was blood—aether—from someone called a bindblood."

He settled back onto the ground, knees up and arms draped across them, and nodded. "It's what we call our blood outside our bodies—after it turns to this silvery stuff."

"We?" That wasn't the first time he had used the first person plural. Other Banebringers? Did he frequently speak with them?

He just looked at her.

She dropped it. She had no reason to waste energy trying to get him to divulge his secrets. She tapped the "cast." "So, what did you do with it? How is this supposed to help me heal?"

"Like bindbloods themselves, aether *from* a bindblood has the ability to heal, even apart from the person it comes from." He stood up, paced over to the stream, and looked up at the moon. "Of course, there's no telling exactly what it will do, but with the bandages as a focus—"

She got stuck on the first part of his sentence. "What do you mean, there's no telling what it will do?"

"Don't worry. Bindblood aether is about the safest there is." He looked back at her and shrugged. "Trust me. It will be fine. Probably."

Laughter bubbled up from those too-recently-ripped open scars. "*Trust* you? And why should I do that? I don't even *know* you—Dal Heilyn"

"Here's a start. It's Vaughn," he said. "At least, that's what *I* call myself now."

She spat the words out like bitter herbs. "I don't care."

They didn't seem to affect him. "So, where are you headed?"

"I believe I said that was none of your concern."

"I can help you get where you're going. I'm no healer, but if it works the way I hope, I'd say it's going to be a couple days before that mends completely." He nodded toward his bow, which he had set against one of the boulders. "You might be thankful for my help in the end."

She just didn't understand this man. Why was he here? Why did he even care? "Why would you want to help me? A few hours ago, I intended to kill you. Do you not believe that?"

"I believe it."

"Then—"

"Because for whatever reason—and I'm sure it had nothing to do with me—you came back to kill my—Ri Gildas, and saved me in the process."

"You're right, it had nothing to do with you. You owe me nothing."

"But mostly because I can't help but feel somewhat responsible for the fact that you're running."

"Don't. Ri Gildas knows who I am because I chose to attack him. My choices are my own."

"You would never have been at the estate if I hadn't shown up."

"Correct. I would be dead." She stood up, moved over to a spot next to one of the boulders, and brushed away a number of rocks and pebbles until the area was relatively smooth.

A grin split his face. "Wait, was that an admission that you needed my help back in the city?"

She lay down the ground. "I'm going to get some rest. If you need me to watch at some point, wake me."

"If that happens, you might want this." He tossed her dagger in front of her. She took the dagger, but raised an eyebrow at him.

He shrugged and smiled. "I trust you."

Vaughn's words seemed to irritate Sweetblade. She glared at him and turned her back on him this time when she lay back down. She fidgeted and shifted around, no doubt trying to get comfortable on the hard stone.

There was definitely more to this woman than she let on. An assassin who had a cover as an innkeeper? Sure. But an assassin who used that cover to employ and house single women and their children? He had never seen her act in a manner that might be called affectionate toward any of her women during his stay at her inn, but there had to be some measure of compassion beneath that cold exterior for her to even entertain such an idea.

And was it his imagination, or had her interest in what he was doing with the aether extended beyond the practical concern of knowing what she was putting on herself? Curiosity, perhaps, from the hardened assassin?

And why had she gone after his father after all, even when there was nothing in it for her? And with such sudden rage? There must be a history there he knew nothing of.

And those scars...

He glanced back at Sweetblade; it looked like she had finally fallen asleep. He rolled up one of his sleeves to look at the faded scars on his own arm. He knew how *he* had obtained them;

there was only one way to obtain aether from a Banebringer, and that was to let their blood. He could, of course, burn the aether in his own blood without having to spill it, but there was a theory that the more a Banebringer did that, the stronger the pull on the other side of the veil, and thus the greater the quantity—and ferocity—of the monsters that would come through at the sky-fire in the fall.

Since there was no way to link a monster to a particular Banebringer at the sky-fire, the theory was supported only by the apparent reality that when a Banebringer died, the same was true—and the monster his or her death spawned *could* be concretely linked to that Banebringer.

The woman in the city was a good example. She had been caught using her abilities to heal people—his guess was that she had been secretly doing that for a long time. And what had been spawned in exchange?

One of the worst kind of bloodbane in existence.

It was still anecdote, of course, but he didn't like to take chances. He didn't like to think that his use of his own powers might bring even worse monsters into the world.

The bloodbane spawned when he had been "gifted" had caused enough death.

His father's mocking words came back to him. *Was that his name?*

His stomach tightened in anger and a pang of grief.

He took a deep breath, willing the grief back into the persistent but almost ignorable ache of long felt sorrow, and looked at his scars again.

So he let his own blood, so he didn't have to burn his aether directly except when necessary.

Why did Sweetblade have those scars?

She would have told him if she were a Banebringer as well, wouldn't she? He had never met a Banebringer not glad to meet one of their own.

One of their own. As if they were not human.

And that was another thing about Sweetblade. The word *demonspawn* had never left her lips. She had never judged him, never asked what he had done to deserve this curse, never assumed he was in league with demons.

She treated him like any other person. Well, any other person whom she hated, but at least her dislike of him didn't revolve around his state as a Banebringer, which colored every other relationship in his life. Even among the Ichtaca it was always there, lurking. How could it not be? Yet she didn't seem to care.

He supposed that was the real reason he was still hanging around her. It was pitiful that his desperation for company had brought him to following around an assassin who, until recently, had been determined to kill him.

But he knew what it was to be alone.

He turned away from Sweetblade to watch the woods, as he should have been doing.

There was no perfectly safe place to spend the night outdoors, but Vaughn had been running from one place or another for years; he knew enough tricks that he had almost become comfortable with it.

It also helped that bloodbane were a bit of a specialty of his; he knew their weaknesses, strengths, and the relative danger they posed given the location, time of day, and circumstances.

Right now, the likelihood of an unprovoked attack by a bloodbane was low. He was more concerned about the people who might be following them. Would his father send men after him? Gildas had seemed remarkably unconcerned about Vaughn after that strange Banebringer woman had covered Gildas in bugs and healed him of whatever dire injuries he had suffered.

And it *had* to be only injuries. No Banebringer magic could bring the dead back to life.

He felt just a bit responsible for whatever might happen to Sweetblade's inn and employees. His father had burned down a village because one family had harbored him unaware. What would he do to punish her?

The least he could do was help her reach her destination safely.

The worst that could happen would be that it would delay his return to the Ichtaca—which he had been avoiding anyway.

He sighed. At least Sweetblade didn't want to kill him anymore.

A small comfort.

Chapter Twelve

The Color of Blood

The night passed without incident. Vaughn woke Sweet-blade after a few hours and took his turn to gain what little sleep he could. In the greyish light of pre-dawn, he rose and left her for about two hours to see what he could find out about any pursuers.

He ranged out from their position as far as he dared and was surprised to find that the search was half-hearted. He ran across only two units, one searching the road and its immediate surroundings—as if they would be stupid enough to follow it—and the other spread out across the span of a half-mile due north, directly toward the city—as if they would be stupid enough to go there.

He almost took the risk of closing enough on a group to

overhear their conversations, but invisible though he may have been, he was far from stealthy, and worry about drawing attention forced him to abandon that plan.

He saw no other sign of a search, and he wasn't sure if that encouraged him or discomfited him. As he had proven many times before, and, indeed, had just proven again, his father was crafty. It made Vaughn wonder if some sort of trap were being laid.

But he could do nothing about it at present, aside from continue on.

Sweetblade seemed to grudgingly accept the fact that he planned on tagging along with her, making no comment when he immediately joined her as they left their camp that morning, or even when he insisted on walking close behind her. Vaughn could extend his invisibility to people he touched—and in turn people *they* touched, within limits—at the cost of burning additional aether. He wanted to be sure he could reach her quickly should the need arise.

Despite their proximity, she said virtually nothing the entire day. Attempts to engage her in conversation were met with silence, scathing looks, or at best one- or two-word answers.

She still hadn't offered up where she was headed.

It started raining early afternoon—a steady drizzle that would likely last the rest of the afternoon and evening. The woods had thinned into patchy copses, so what little protection the leaves had offered had all but disappeared.

After about an hour of slogging through mud, Vaughn was getting tired of constantly wiping water out of his eyes. "Well," he said, drawing to a stop.

Sweetblade stopped as well and turned to face him. "What?" she asked, sounding annoyed—but then again, perhaps that was how she perpetually sounded.

"We could try to keep going. Or, we could look for shelter." He wiped at his face again, flicking water away with his hand—for what it was worth. "I vote for shelter."

Her hands clenched and unclenched repeatedly before she answered. "Fine," she said. "What would you suggest?"

He glanced around, trying to remember the lay of the land. They had traveled as far off the road as they had dared, and so he wasn't sure of their precise location. He would guess the capital lay about 25 miles or so to the northwest, and if that guess was right, there was a village about a mile due west. They might be able to beg shelter there.

Or, better, borrow it, when no one was looking.

Despite the price that had been exacted from him, being able to travel invisible had advantages.

He opened his mouth to suggest it, when a shadow overhead darkened the greyish pall that passed for light.

Sweetblade yanked him down as a gust of wind accompanied by a chilling screech passed right over their heads.

Vaughn knew that screech. He burned aether reflexively, hiding both of them from the sight of the bloodhawk—but it already knew where they were and flew right at the spot where they had disappeared.

Vaughn had enough time to see the claws at the ends of its wings before it slammed into him, tearing him away from Sweetblade. He lost his concentration—and with it his invisibility—and crashed into the ground beneath the bird. It scrabbled at his face. One claw dragged across his temple, but he managed to grab the edge of each wing in his hands, barely keeping it from ripping his face off.

A moment later, a dark blur went hurtling across him, and the bird was caught in the momentum and pulled off Vaughn.

As soon as the weight was off his chest, he scrambled to his feet, reaching for his bow. It had fallen into the wet grass and slipped from his hands twice before he managed a grip strong enough to pull—

He paused as he sighted it on the bird.

Sweetblade was *wrestling* the creature.

She was sitting on top of it and had shredded one of its wings with her dagger. She was trying to find purchase with her blade on its neck, but its hide was too thick.

He moved his bow, trying to keep the bird in his sights, but it kept flapping wildly with its good wing, flinging her back and forth in an ever changing position, and he was afraid he would hit her instead.

The bird finally managed to dislodge her, and she rolled to the side, but not quickly enough—and it was furious. It flapped its good wing once and landed on top of her.

Damn! If he could just separate them long enough...

Stupid. Water. He always forgot.

He let go of the bow with one hand and stretched his palm out toward the sky.

The bird—if it could be called that—didn't like Ivana's dagger. The pain in its wing was probably a constant reminder of what it could do. So she kept stabbing toward it, even though she knew the blows wouldn't land. The bird jerked back, trying to avoid the blade with a chilling intelligence, but unwilling to let her go.

Then the rain started to do something odd—it was swirling *up* instead of down.

The bird, as startled as she was, hopped back, screeching in confusion. The tornado of water solidified into a wall that then slammed back into the bird, hurling it several feet away from Ivana.

The bird tried to take off, but it could no longer fly. A second later, an arrow pierced its skull all the way through.

It flopped to the ground, twitched twice, and then lay still.

Ivana blinked once, twice, and then slid down to the ground, the events of the past few minutes a blur.

Vaughn's feet appeared in her view, and he grasped her upper arm and hefted her to her feet.

"What was *that?*" she asked, brushing him off as soon as she had her balance.

He glanced at the corpse of the bird. "A bloodhawk. I've dealt with them before. Vicious creatures, though..." His brow furrowed. "They usually don't prey on humans, unless provoked." He shook his head. "Odd."

He picked his way over to the corpse of the bird, and Ivana followed, and they both stared down at it.

Its head and beak reminded her more of a vulture than a hawk, but it was easily four times the size of that mundane bird, and that was where the resemblance stopped. It had no feathers—more like a bat than a bird—and at the tip of each wing were needle-sharp claws.

"Bloodhawk? Looks more like a vulture-bat to me." She glanced over at Vaughn. Blood was trickling down his temple, over top of a growing patch of silver, but it was hard to tell with the rain and his hair how deep the cut was.

He grinned. "But bloodvulture-bat doesn't sound good, does it?"

She almost smiled.

Almost. "However," she said. "I was referring to the rain."

"Oh." He shrugged. "I don't know. It's one of the things I can do."

"Control rain?"

"Water. And things that contain water."

"Like wine?" she asked, remembering the exploding barrels in the Ri's manor.

"I guess," he said. "I haven't experimented with it much."

Her mouth dropped open. "You can throw around water and you haven't *experimented* with it?"

He turned away from her, and he didn't seem entirely stable on his feet, just like back at the manor after he had tossed the wine around. "It burns more blood than invisibility. Especially when I'm improvising like that."

Burns more blood? She thought they had to use aether to work their magic. "I don't understand."

"Okay, more precisely, the aether in my blood. But that destroys the blood it resides in, so might as well be the blood."

Ah. So he could use the aether in his own blood, internally. Why didn't people know these things about the abilities of Banebringers? Again, her thoughts drifted to her father. He would have been fascinated. "You seem ill."

He closed his eyes briefly. "I'll be all right in a minute. I also regenerate blood more quickly."

She moved to face him again. His hair was matted to his temple with water, blood, and...aether. She couldn't help but stare. The flow of blood had slowed, and most of what remained on his face had hardened into a silvery substance. The wound was red with irritation and raw inside, like one would expect, but there was no crusted blood.

She knew Banebringers bled aether. Everyone knew that. And she had seen him bleed once before. But it was still fascinating.

Vaughn now wore a sardonic smile on his face. "Ready to call me demonspawn yet?"

Demonspawn. It was what they called Banebringers because their blood was silver—or turned silver, as she had just observed herself—similar to bloodbane.

It was a particularly offensive insult when used of someone who wasn't a Banebringer. Like calling someone not human. She didn't particularly like Vaughn, but Aleena was right: he wasn't *that* bad. "There *are* people in this world who deserve such a moniker," she said softly, "but in my experience it has little to do with the color of their blood."

He didn't say anything. Just looked at her.

It made her uncomfortable.

She nodded toward the gash on his forehead. "Some of that aether might help." She touched her wrist for emphasis. When she had woken up this morning, the pain had already faded to a dull ache. She had used her off-hand to be on the safe side, but she was, once again, grudgingly impressed with his work, magic or not. "Do you have an actual idea about where to find shelter, or was that just wishful thinking?"

"If I'm not mistaken, there's a village about a mile due west of here, but..." He glanced at the corpse of the bird. "Perhaps it would be better to find something a little closer."

Vaughn led them to a cave to spend another night in.

Well, *cave* was generous. It was more like a large indent in the rock behind a waterfall of the same creek they had been following; it went about ten feet back, and the first two feet were flooded with puddles from the waterfall, but it was relatively dry, and better, hidden. She only hoped they would make better time the following day. The rain and their zigzag course had severely limited how far they had traveled that day; every day lost was another day Gildas could get to her girls.

Vaughn's eyes flicked down over her as they settled in, and he made no attempt to hide it.

"If you know what's good for you, you'll keep your eyes—and hands, in case you're stupid enough to need the warning—to yourself."

He grinned. "You should wear more modest clothing."

She glanced down at herself, observing the way her tattered wet dress clung to every curve and showed a generous amount of skin.

She glared at him. "I'm not responsible for your second—or perhaps I should say primary—brain, thanks."

His grin broadened. "Touché." There was a pause. "By the

way. Thank you."

"For what?"

"For getting that bird off me. If you hadn't, I'd be dead at worst, or faceless at best."

She shrugged. She hated to admit it, but if he hadn't been there, she would be dead too. "I need you—or at least your skills—for the time being."

A half-smile flickered across his lips before he turned to search in his pouch.

She frowned at his profile. What was that?

He retrieved a piece of aether from his pouch, crushed it between his thumb and forefinger, and mixed in some water from one of the puddles with his other hand, forming the pasty substance again. He then proceeded to smear it in the gouge on his forehead. "So...where are we going again?"

She rolled her eyes. He had been trying to get that out of her all day. Very well. Perhaps he wouldn't be so keen to follow her anymore. "Weylyn City."

He had just rinsed his hands and was lifting a cupped hand to drink, and she took some satisfaction in seeing him spray water everywhere. "Pardon me?"

"You heard me."

He stared at her, hand held limp and dripping in mid-air. "Why in the abyss would you want to go *back*? I thought you were running?"

"I am. After I check on my inn."

"By inn, you mean your girls."

She knelt to the water herself. It annoyed her that he was perceptive enough to understand her real reasons. "There's a reason assassins don't tangle with the Conclave," she said. Her girls were under her protection. It was her fault that they were now potentially exposed. She needed to see to it that they remained protected before she moved on—if it wasn't already too late for that.

She felt his eyes on her. She sensed he was about to speak, but then stopped. And then started again. "About that. Why did you try to kill Ri Gildas?"

She turned away from him. For a little while, she had managed to forget the real reason she was in this mess. But it was still too close to the surface. "My reasons are my own."

"But I offered to *pay* you..."

What would he say if she told him? *Because your father killed mine for attempting to defend my honor after your brother seduced and impregnated me.* "My question is how he survived. Is there some Banebringer magic that brings the dead back to life?"

"No. He must have only been injured. That...crazy woman must have healed him somehow."

"He was dead."

"He can't have been."

"I am quite adept at telling when someone is dead, I'll thank you."

He shook his head. "It's simply not possible. Not even the most gifted healer could do that."

"Then perhaps you don't know everything about your own magic."

He hesitated. "All right. I'll grant that, but—"

She scooted as close as she could get to one side of the cave and lay down with her back to him. Even though it was only mid-afternoon, she was exhausted from having so little sleep the night before. Besides. She wasn't going to suffer through hours of him trying to make more conversation with her. "I'm going to attempt to sleep. You can take first watch again."

Once again, Vaughn found himself watching the restless form of Sweetblade as she attempted to fall asleep. The more he learned about this woman, the more perplexed—and intrigued—he became.

Everything he had learned of her up until now told him that she was exceedingly practical, and yet, against every wise course of action, she was returning home to be sure her employees had been seen to.

And then, of course, still niggling at him was the question of why she had taken matters into her own hands as it concerned his father.

She had demurred on the question, but the look on her face when she had attacked Gildas had been unmistakable. She utterly despised him, and hatred that deep could only be borne out of some history. She wouldn't have risked herself otherwise.

It wouldn't surprise him if, at some point in the past, his father had indeed done something to earn that hatred.

And his latest 'example' of this was merely the most poignant—not only because of the innocents he had slaughtered to prove a point, but because he had robbed Vaughn of the only activity that had made him feel normal again. Useful. Whole.

If his father had wanted to torment him for daring to exist, and for taking away not one, but two of his sons, then he had chosen the best possible manner of doing so: by punishing everyone who had helped Vaughn, whether knowingly or not.

Vaughn had since realized that he would be able to turn to no one but himself for help—a lonely, haunted place already, even among his Ichtacan "friends."

A varied group of people, some of whom were nice enough, and some of whom...well, frankly, weren't. They agreed on one premise: Banebringers shouldn't be persecuted, but their abilities studied, for the good of society. Aside from that, anything went. Yaotel was a powerful force of personality keeping the group from fracturing into warring sub-factions, and keeping them to an agreed upon code of conduct. But Vaughn shuddered to think what might happen if Yaotel died.

Aside from the monster it would summon, of course.

He sighed. There was something refreshing about being around Sweetblade. Sometimes he felt like he would never be known for anything more than his status as a target of the heretic gods' warped sense of humor. Among non-Banebringers, if they knew what he was, he would never be accepted. Among Banebringers, he was accepted *because* of what he was.

Ivana, on the other hand, knew he was a Banebringer and frankly didn't seem to care, except in as much as his abilities appeared to intrigue and aid her.

Ivana. That was her name, wasn't it? She was more than the assassin, more than the innkeeper. Perhaps if he stopped thinking of her as Sweetblade, she would start acting less like her guises and more like whoever she really was.

He watched as Ivana's breathing became more regular. It was crazy to go back to the city, but if his aid would put even a crease in his father's forehead, it was worth it.

Chapter Thirteen

Bait

It took Ivana almost an hour to fall into a restless sleep on the hard rock she had as a bed, and, once again, she woke after too little time.

She sat up, feeling disoriented, but after a moment, realized it hadn't been Vaughn who had woken her. She didn't even see him—though, with him, that didn't mean he wasn't there.

Then she heard it. A howl.

A wolf? This close to civilization?

The howl came again, closer, and there was something *wrong* about it.

"That's not a wolf," Ivana whispered, more to herself than to a hypothetical Vaughn who might be around.

Vaughn appeared next to her, eyes focused on some distant

point outside. "Damn," he said.

"What?"

"You're right." He picked up his bow.

Great. Just great. Three monsters in less than a week?

"We can't stay in here," Vaughn said. "We'll be cornered." He set an arrow to the string of his bow and walked to the mouth of the cave, peering out beyond the trickle of water that passed for a waterfall. He turned his head slowly, eyes watching every corner of the forest, as if he could actually see.

She slid her dagger out of its sheath and joined him, hoping that whatever it was, it was small and easily dispatched. Not all bloodbane were angry behemoths, or crazed, clawed birds.

"There," he whispered.

She turned and looked in the same direction he was facing, but saw nothing.

"Move out into the open," he said, "and then don't stop running." And then he slipped out of the cave and disappeared—literally—into the trees.

"Vaughn?" she hissed. "What—?"

And then two white lidless eyes appeared, staring out of the trees on the other side of the creek, far too high off the ground to be small and easily dispatched.

And Vaughn had *abandoned* her? The coward!

The eyes came closer, and then the creature itself appeared. It vaguely resembled a wolf, but only because it walked on four legs, had two pointed ears, and a snout. Like the bloodhawk, that was where the similarities stopped. It was two times the size of an average wolf, for one, and fangs sprouted down from the top of its jaw. Instead of fur, its skin was covered in the same thick hide as the monster they had killed in the city and the bloodhawk. Large, vicious looking claws gripped the dirt under its feet.

And its eyes turned in her direction.

A chill ran through her. *Don't stop running.* For once, Ivana agreed with him. This was not a beast she could fight with a dagger, even if she weren't trapped in a cave. She just hoped Vaughn had a plan beyond using her as bait.

Ivana darted through the waterfall and into the trees.

The beast crashed into the woods behind her, giving chase, and a jolt of fear gave her extra speed. Twigs slashed at her face, and then she remembered the second part of Vaughn's instructions: *stay in the open.*

That seemed counter-intuitive to her, but she did it anyway. She darted for the creek bed, the only truly open spot in the woods, and splashed into the thigh-deep water, hoping it didn't like water. The wolf-monster splashed in behind her, undeterred. Cursing, she waded toward the opposite shore, but apparently the beast was also a good swimmer.

It lunged at her before she could reach dry land, and a moment later, she felt its fangs dig deep into her thigh.

She screamed and tried to wrest herself free from the creature's hold. She managed to avoid letting its claws take off her head, but the beast snapped its head back and forth, and then let go, flinging her onto the other side of the bank like a doll.

So this is how it ends, she thought in a pain-hazed blur, watching in slow motion as the creature lunged for her throat.

There was a heavy thud, and it howled and stumbled sideways in the water. And then again. And again. Just like the monster in the square.

Until finally, it lay in the water, thrashing, quivering, and then still.

Ivana sank back, gasping in relief and pain. But her blood darkened the wet dirt around her and trickled into the water in swirling lines as the current carried it away, and she tried to rise, only to be forced back down by the pain.

"Ivana!" she heard distantly. "Ivana!"

She roused herself to look. Vaughn splashed through the water, and a moment later, she felt herself being picked up.

She struggled in his grasp. He would *not*—

"Relax," he said. "You're not going to be able to walk on that."

She gritted her teeth, the pain of needing him to *carry* her almost as bad as the agony in her leg.

But exhaustion won out. She relaxed, and in the moment before she fell unconscious, she had the odd sensation that she were five again, being held against her father's chest.

Ridiculous.

Chapter Fourteen

Revelations

Hush, hush, sweet girl. Go to sleep.

    But, Papa...I want to stay up and study with you a little longer.

Hush, it's late. There's always tomorrow. Go to sleep.

Ivana woke, cringing against the light. She opened her eyes cautiously, shaking off the dream, and tried to move.

Pain lanced through her thigh and her head swam. She froze, taking a few deep breaths to steady herself.

She stopped trying to move and looked around. She was back in the alcove behind the waterfall, and Vaughn was nowhere to be seen.

She pulled aside the remains of her skirt so she could examine her leg, bracing herself for whatever wound she would find there. But she found that it was wrapped tightly, from just above her knee to the top of her thigh, with what looked like strips from her dress.

She squinted toward the daylight. She pulled herself toward the water and drank deeply. Mist tickled her face and clung to her hair in beaded drops when she had finished.

What time was it? She had no idea what direction she was facing, and so no clue as to what the sun shimmering behind the water meant—other than that it was low enough in the sky to not be the middle of the day.

She heard splashing, and a moment later, Vaughn sidled through the small gap between the waterfall and the edge of the rock. He was damp after his trip through, but grinning. "You're awake," he said. "That's good." He held several small bundles in his hands and offered one to her. "Hungry?"

Why did he have to be so chipper? It reminded her of Aleena in the mornings. "Where have you been?" she asked, feeling cross.

He jingled the second pouch that hung at his waist. "Spending some of my hard earned setans." He settled down next to her.

She gave him a critical look. "You walked into a village looking like that?"

He shrugged. "I told them I'd had a run in with a pack of bloodsprites."

"Does this happen often to you?"

"They like me." He eyed her. "Most people do."

She rolled her eyes. "Bloodsprites aren't people."

He unwrapped one of the bundles, revealing a few pears. He

took a bite of one and then tossed her another. She caught it, and though she wanted to fling it back in his smiling face, her growling stomach forced her to take a bite instead.

They munched in silence for a while, both eating second pears, until her burning need to have questions answered overruled her complete lack of desire to talk to him. She didn't like not knowing what was going on. "You abandoned me to be eaten by a monster," she accused him by way of start.

"The worst ones tend to avoid daylight," he said.

"I meant last night."

"Ah. Yet if you'll remember, I advised you to start running, did I not?"

She grunted.

"Everything was completely under control."

"Nearly having my leg torn off by a gods-cursed wolf does *not* constitute having things under control in my book," she said. She moved her leg and winced. It didn't hurt so bad if she didn't move it, which was surprising. She should have been in abject agony right now.

"Still hurting?" He didn't wait for a response. He rose and knelt by her side, and then started unwrapping it. "As I said, aether can be unpredictable. Let me take a look."

She grimaced as the makeshift bandage pulled at the wound. "Is that really necessary?"

He finished, set the dirty cloths aside, and then opened another package. He held it up to show her the contents: a spool of thick thread, a needle, and a bolt of new cotton cloth. "It is if you want me to stitch this shut, which I would advise."

She dared to look at her leg and wished she hadn't. It looked as though...well, she supposed it looked as though it had been gnawed on by a large, monstrous wolf.

Appropriate.

The white of bone showed through in some places. "Ugh." She looked away. She couldn't believe she was even conscious. That bindblood aether was impressive.

He raised an eyebrow. "Surely the sight of a little mangled flesh doesn't upset *your* stomach."

She frowned at him. "I'm not fond of the mangled flesh being on my own body."

Amusement flickered across his face. "Well, you don't have to look."

She settled for watching him as he worked. He dunked a clean cloth in water from the falls and began rinsing out the wounds.

She clenched her teeth and put her head back against the wall. "Why," she said, trying to ignore the pain, "must you be so rough?" Though in truth, his aether had to be helping. Otherwise, she would never be awake for this.

"Are you always this grumpy, or is that just the façade you show the world?"

"I have no idea what you're talking about."

"Mmmm."

She flinched as he touched a particularly sore spot. "Sorry," he said, and his touch was gentler from then on.

She opened her eyes again and found them drawn toward the gruesome sight of her leg and his ministrations.

"You're lucky the fangs of that particular beast weren't poisoned." He produced a jar and a bottle of amber liquid—liquor, no doubt—from one of the other packages. "I'm not sure that these would be enough, otherwise."

"Are you going to pour that on my leg?" she asked, pointing to the bottle.

"I need to clean it somehow."

She usually avoided alcohol—even nominally clouded judgment could be deadly in her line of work—but aether or no aether, that was going to hurt like bloodfire. She'd make an exception this time.

She stretched out her hand and motioned to the bottle, and he handed it to her. She uncorked it with her teeth and took a few long swigs, and then gave it back. "I don't know if a little bit of liquor and salve will be enough either," she said, taking a guess at what was in the jar. "No offense."

"Really? That's a change." He pulled out a few more slivers of the aether and crushed them. He mixed some of the powder into the salve and then dumped the rest into the liquor. "With this, it should be enough. The aether will better know what to do with the foci."

"The aether will know what to do," she restated in disbelief.

"Yes. If you give it something to focus its abilities on, it performs better, or at least performs more in line with what you want it to do." He pointed to her wrist—though the splint had been ripped off in her struggle with the bloodbane last night, she found her wrist didn't hurt anymore. "Like your 'cast.'"

"I thought you said it wasn't sentient."

He chuckled. "It's not, precisely. Yet..." He shook his head. "Well. I don't think we know enough yet to come to any conclusive theories."

"We?" she pressed.

He held up the bottle of liquor. "Ready?"

She was intrigued in spite of herself. Probably partially the liquor. But, in this case, talking helped keep her mind off the pain, so she didn't mind.

"Who are you?" she asked. And then she stuffed a piece of cloth between her teeth.

Vaughn dribbled the liquor over Ivana's thigh, trying to get it into every crevice of the wound.

Her entire body tensed. She squeezed her eyes shut, clamping down hard on the cloth with her teeth. Though he could tell she was trying not to cry out, a muffled groan made its way through the cloth anyway.

Vaughn shook the last drops out and sat back on his heels, considering her question. He supposed it didn't matter now. "My birth-name was Teyrnon, third-son of Ri Gildas of Ferehar—though he wasn't Ri when I was born, of course. Now I'm Vaughn, demonspawn fugitive son of Ri Gildas of Ferehar."

He said it calmly enough, but a hint of bitterness tinged his voice. And he was certain she heard it.

But she didn't comment on it. She spat the cloth out, eyes still closed. "Finally going to admit it?" she asked through gritted teeth.

"Admit what?"

"That Ri Gildas is your father."

"You knew?"

"I guessed." She didn't elaborate. "But he declared you dead."

"Yes. I've always assumed it was because he didn't want his growing prestige tainted by a demonspawn son."

"Is your other brother actually dead?"

"I have three other brothers. Teryn, the youngest of the four of us, is dead, yes." He tried not to falter in his work as he spoke. The image of Teryn's mangled body—looking much like Ivana's leg—had been seared into his mind in that moment of horror when he had realized what had happened—why a bloodbane had been pulled through a tear while they hid, ironically, in their own saferoom during the sky-fire. "I don't know about my other two brothers. I assume they're still alive."

She didn't say anything.

He hesitated. "You...don't seem to care much that I'm a Banebringer." He opened the jar of salve and started rubbing it into the wounds.

She glanced at what he was doing and then away again. "It would be the height of irony for me to condemn you for having an illegal existence."

That was surprisingly fair of her. "What, you don't theorize that I must have done something horrible to deserve it? Or that my family line is tainted?"

She almost smiled, but there was too much mockery in it to be a real smile. "Oh no," she said. "I'm sure you've done something horrible. Perhaps just not to deserve being cursed."

"Cursed," he repeated. "Did you know they used to call us Gifted?" That was a long time ago, before the Conclave had even existed. Back when the heretic gods were still worshipped.

"Doesn't seem like much of a gift to me," she responded. He could feel her eyes on him again. "Though invisibility...now that's something that could come in handy in my line of work. I'd give a lot to have that."

"I'd give a lot to not have it," he said, his voice rougher than he intended. What were a few magical abilities compared to family, acceptance, and love?

His throat tightened at the memories, especially of the last. They had haunted his dreams since the night he fled his own home. Since the night he subsequently fled the home of his ex-fiancée, who had no longer wanted anything to do with him the moment he had changed.

She was silent at his confession. Instead, she changed the subject. "You know an awful lot about these monsters."

"I've been fighting them for years."

Her eyes flicked to his bow, resting against the wall of the alcove. "If you can take down a twenty-foot monster with a few arrows, why don't you just stick one in your own father's back at an opportune moment? Doesn't seem you needed to waste money on hired help."

He put down the jar he had been using and wiped his fingers on a piece of cloth. "For one, I've never killed anything other than monsters and animals, and I don't know if I want to start now." He didn't look up to see her reaction, but he had a feeling it would be impassive, as usual. "For two, I'm really terrible at this sneaking around stuff. Ironically."

She snorted. "I hadn't noticed."

He allowed a small smile, but went on. "For three...I don't know if I could do it." That was a half-truth. He *knew* he couldn't do it. "He is my father, after all."

"A father who is determined to hunt you down and turn you

into a comatose husk?"

Vaughn didn't know how to respond to that. He didn't know how to explain. Yet he felt compelled to try. "He wasn't that bad when I was a child," he said. "At least, I don't remember him that way. Perhaps a little obsessed with making his sons into perfect specimens of nobility, but...he wasn't cruel." He paused, a few memories rising to the surface that contradicted that statement. "Usually," he revised. "But I wouldn't have thought he would have turned on his own family. But I guess...I guess some things are too much to handle."

"Sounds like you're making excuses for him."

"No," he said. "I'm..." Was he? In the end, his father proved that he cared more about his own power than his children.

He fell silent, once again, not sure how to respond. "How does it feel?"

"It doesn't, right now."

He raised an eyebrow. "At all?" That wasn't good; the salve should have only decreased the pain, not numbed her entire leg. Had there been nerve damage? He ran his fingers over the upper part of her thigh, where the skin was unbroken. "Can you feel this?"

He didn't even need to look at her to know the answer. He heard the sharp intake of air, felt her tense under his hand.

He looked up and met her eyes. It only took a few heartbeats of silence for him to realize she hadn't been tensing in pain, and for his own body to respond to the realization. And then—

"I misspoke," she said, shoving his hand off her thigh and seeming disconcerted for the first time since he had met her. "I meant it doesn't hurt."

"Ah." The salve was acting properly as a focus for the aether, then. "Good."

He wiped his hands again and then looked for the needle and thread, ready to stitch her up as best as he could; he wasn't a surgeon, and it wouldn't be pretty, but he had stitched together a few of his own wounds in eight years' time. Hopefully, in combination with the aether, the healed result wouldn't be that bad.

Ivana let out a slow, silent breath as Vaughn turned away to root around in the bundle of items he had bought.

Curse her body for its sudden betrayal.

Vaughn turned back, holding the spool of thread, but frowning. "Where did I put the needle..." he muttered to himself. He picked up his discarded dinner jacket, emptied the inner pockets, and then set it back down again.

"It's stuck in the spool," she said, and only barely kept herself from smiling. *Bloodfire. One too many draughts on that bottle, apparently.*

He looked at the spool in his hand, in which the needle had sunk almost to the end in the mass of thread. "Oh." He shook his head, pulled it out, and started threading it.

She glanced at the items he had discarded from his dinner jacket. "You had a *sheath* in your dinner jacket pocket? Who in the abyss were you planning on bedding that you needed it with you at *dinner*?"

He gave her that crooked, charming grin she hated so much.

She frowned at him. "Don't even think about it."

His grin broadened. "Sorry. Far too late for that."

"Tell me, Dal Vaughn, what would you do if you got a woman with child on one of your many conquests?"

"That won't happen."

"You know those things aren't perfectly effective, right?"

"The odds are better when I'm only using one—" he tilted his head as if considering, and then shrugged, "—*maybe* two per woman. And there's always tanthalia."

Great. The herb that could destroy a woman's womb if over-used—as she knew first hand. Then again, she supposed he would say he only needed one or two doses per woman. Burning skies, this man was unbelievable. Perhaps he *did* deserve the title 'demonspawn.' "You still haven't answered my question."

He started in on the worst of her wounds. "If you're asking if I would marry her, I can assure you that no woman, once they found out what I was, would *want* to marry me, even for the sake of a child."

"And what if you weren't a Banebringer?"

"Then...I'd already be married," he said. "I had a fiancée before I was changed."

She didn't miss the implication that his fiancée had broken it off with him *because* of his change. Interesting—but beside the point. "I'm speaking theoretically here."

He cast her a furtive glance, and then looked back down at his sewing. "I'm afraid if I answered honestly you'd decide you wanted to kill me again."

She gave him a suitably withering look.

He sighed. "Look—no, I probably wouldn't." He hurried on before she could reply. "But she wouldn't end up on the streets, to be plucked up by an eccentric assassin who runs a charity—if that's what you're getting at. I would give what monetary support I could."

"Bastards can get awfully expensive," Ivana said, trying to decide if she resented being called eccentric or not.

He jerked his head toward his jacket. "Hence, precautions." He tied off the thread for one wound and re-threaded the needle to begin on another. "Enough about me. What about you?"

"Pardon?"

"Who are you, Ivana?"

Ivana flinched, as if he had struck her. If she were able, she would have risen and walked away. As it was, she was stuck there.

"You know who I am," she said.

"I know *what* you are."

"There is no difference." She tried to communicate with her tone that if he pressed it, he might not want to go to sleep tonight.

"Come on. Play fair. What about siblings?"

"You're asking *me* to play fair?"

"You have to tell me something."

"I do not. But so you'll stop bothering me, yes, I had one sibling. A sister."

"Had?"

"I don't know where she is," she said. "Dead, probably." If she were lucky. Otherwise, she was likely still a slave, a fate Ivana herself had narrowly avoided.

Her throat contracted. By running. By leaving her sister behind.

Guilt? *Burning skies.* How long would it be before she could lose this man and everything he represented? Trying to regain her long-cultivated detachment with him around was like pouring water into a sieve.

"I'm sorry," Vaughn said.

She didn't like this subject. "I'm surprised you didn't save some for yourself," she said, nodding toward the empty liquor bottle.

"You're awfully talkative tonight," Vaughn observed.

It was the liquor, in part. It had been pretty strong stuff, and she had downed enough to relax a full grown man. She felt it around the edges.

She shrugged. "I'm trying to keep my mind off the fact that you've been digging your hands *into my leg.*"

"Actually, now I'm sewing up your leg."

"Ugh," she said. "Whatever."

He chuckled. "I don't really drink," he said.

She raised an eyebrow. "I find that hard to believe."

He shrugged. "What's the point in drinking when I can't get drunk?"

"You can't get drunk?"

"Alcohol doesn't affect Banebringers."

That was a revelation. And...it put him in a whole new perspective. "That's rough," she said.

He worked for a few more minutes in silence, their conversation having apparently run its course. Finally, he declared, "I'm done."

She examined her leg. It was a pretty ugly job—and she was sure she would have some pleasant scars on her leg after it healed, but it was better than nothing. "Thank you."

He seemed a little surprised at her expressed gratitude. She was a little surprised herself.

He looked at her for a moment, and then nodded. He went to his bundles and unwrapped another one, and while he did so, Ivana glanced toward the waterfall. The sun was setting.

Apparently it had been later in the day rather than earlier in the morning.

Vaughn returned with a long length of clean white cloth. "All right," he said. "Let's wrap it up again."

Ivana adjusted her position, lifting one knee so he could reach around her leg with the cloth. As she did so, her torn skirt fell to the side, revealing the entire length of her leg, from ankle, to thigh, to the scrap of cloth that still held the skirt of her dress at her waist.

He paused momentarily, eyes resting on the unbroken flesh there. She wore an undergarment, but it was a delicate slip of cloth, as though she were preparing for a tryst, not going to be running around in the woods fighting monsters. Though to be fair, she hadn't known she would be doing that when she had dressed for the banquet.

He glanced her way. Her eyes were him, and one eyebrow was raised.

He coughed, embarrassed to be caught staring at her like an unexperienced schoolboy, and started wrapping the leg.

"My," she said, humor in her voice. "You would think you've never seen a woman's leg before."

"I was observing that your choice of underclothes isn't very practical," he said, keeping his voice neutral.

"A woman wants to feel feminine now and again," she said. "Even if that woman is a hardened killer." She paused, a slight warning in her voice. "Perhaps especially if that woman is a hardened killer."

He finished the wrap, tying a knot and then tucking the loose end in at the top of her thigh. He wondered if her being slightly tipsy would make it more or less likely for her to follow through on her threats.

Warning or not, he found his hand lingering there again, tracing the skin at the top of the wrap. "Well, rest assured, hardened killer or not, you're quite feminine underneath."

He was in dangerous territory. He knew that. But her skin was so smooth. After he had touched her earlier, he couldn't get out of his mind the thought of what it must be like to run his hands over the rest of her...

She shifted, and he flinched, half expecting a dagger at his throat, but she said and did nothing.

He looked up to meet her eyes. He was surprised to find them half-closed.

She ought to tell him to stop. She opened her mouth to do so, but nothing came out. Instead, her lips remained parted as his finger traveled upwards, tracing a line up her thigh, onto her hip.

Her body was rebelling against her again. Sending all sorts of mind-numbing messages to her brain.

And he was moving from touch to caress. With eyes flicking repeatedly from hers to her leg, one finger turned to two, and then three...

Against her will, she felt herself relaxing into his touch. It had been so long since someone had touched her like this, in such a way that she could enjoy it. Not to get information. Not because she was about to assassinate them. Just because.

No! Stop! Her mind screamed. But her body simply refused to cooperate.

She found herself shifting again, trying to expose even more flesh, and he willingly accepted her silent invitation, following an invisible line from her hip to her upper abdomen, even pushing back her dress slightly to reach the skin there...

His hand paused, ran across her stomach again, and then stopped. "You have stretch marks," he said, surprise in his voice.

Vaughn cursed himself the moment the words left his mouth. It was as though he had doused her with water.

She sat up, shoved his hand away, and flicked what remained of her skirt back over her leg, glaring at him.

Still, he was so shocked, he couldn't help but press her. "You have a child?"

She struggled to rise to her feet, though he didn't know why. "No."

"But—"

"It's none of your business. Along with the contours of my leg." She limped across the alcove, about as far away as she could get from him, and slid back down the wall, resting her head back against it with a grimace.

He decided it would be wise to drop the subject.

"I bought a bundle of blankets," he offered.

She didn't reply.

And so he sat in the increasing darkness—not that it mattered to him, since his eyes adjusted to let in more light the darker it became—until he was certain she was asleep.

When that happened, he padded over to where she sat, gently lowered her to the ground, tucked one blanket beneath her head and draped another over her.

He couldn't say why he did it. Only that it felt right.

Chapter Fifteen

Star-Leaf

Ivana was sure every muscle in her body had been trampled when she woke up. Her back hurt from sleeping on stone, and her leg was aching again. And then there were the dreams. It had been years since she had dreamed of *him*, yet it was the same sequence of passion, heartbreak, and betrayal, crushed together in one distorted summary.

Except this time his face had been replaced with Vaughn's. It irritated her, even though he could hardly be responsible for her dreams.

She grimaced as she pushed herself to her feet and tested her leg. Thankfully, she was able to stand and walk.

Vaughn was missing again—not that she cared. She would just as soon that he disappear forever, and she sincerely hoped he didn't bring up the stretch marks again.

Temoth. What had come over her last night? She couldn't blame it all on the liquor.

She went over to the bundles he had bought the previous day, hoping to find another clean cloth, and she did, so she started the process of changing her bandage.

She examined the wounds once she had removed the soiled cloth. The angry red of the surrounding irritated skin had faded some, which was a good sign. She rewrapped her leg and went looking for the needle and thread. When she had found it, she proceeded to stitch as much of her skirt back together as possible. She didn't bother below the knee—no reason to be impractical—but she would be damned if she gave him an excuse to see her leg again.

It wasn't pretty, but it was functional.

She had just risen to put away the needle and thread when Vaughn returned.

Too bad.

He glanced at her. "You shouldn't be up on that leg," he said.

"You would prefer I sit around here and wait until the guards catch up with me?"

He shook his head. "They don't know where we are yet."

She raised an eyebrow, and he jerked his head toward the waterfall. "I did some scouting. I'm pretty sure they're pulling back to Talesin's estate."

After only a day of searching? Great. That probably meant they were concentrating on the city, hoping she would return, even though that would be incredibly foolish.

Apparently she was foolish.

"Good. Perhaps it will be easy to slip through then," she said, stepping toward the entrance.

"You're serious about going back to the city?"

"I never asked you to come. In fact, feel free to leave any time you want."

"I'm still coming, I just—" He shook his head. "We should at least wait until—"

She whirled to face him. "I don't have time to waste lying around convalescing. You want to stay here, be my guest."

"At least let me look at your leg again—"

He stopped talking when she glared at him. Instead, he held up his hands in surrender and turned to the bundles. He tied them up into a roughshod bag that looked like it used to be his formal tunic and slung the whole device over his shoulder, along with his bow and quiver. "All right. No reason to wait around longer then."

Three hours later, whatever Vaughn's aether-infused salve had done to help with the pain was wearing off: Ivana's leg was killing her. She could feel the stitches pulling with every step, and her entire thigh both ached and burned, but she wasn't about to admit that to Vaughn. Since it was becoming difficult to walk, she started watching the foliage more closely as they picked their way through the woods and, finally, found what she was looking for.

She stopped and plucked all of the leaves off a star-shaped plant growing at the base of a tree and popped one of them in her mouth.

Ugh. It was disgusting, but it worked wonders as a painkiller. It was a shame her father had never been able to publish his findings before he died.

She tucked the rest of the leaves into her bosom, drawing Vaughn's gaze.

"Star-leaf?" he asked.

"Painkiller," she said. She started walking again, fighting the limp.

"I've never heard of that," he said.

"You wouldn't have," she said.

He glanced at her as they walked. She could almost feel the curiosity beating from him, but she refused to indulge him.

"Is your leg hurting that badly again?"

"When mixed with the root of a dennil, it also makes a fantastic poison," she said. Conveniently, they were passing a patch of the aforementioned flower. She leaned down, collected a sample, and tucked it also into the bosom of her dress.

He didn't ask again.

Vaughn and Ivana crouched in the negligible shade of three trees, the last bit of cover before they would approach Weylyn City. The orange glow of the sun sinking below the horizon almost made the derelict tangle of buildings spilling beyond the outer walls look livable.

They had reached the city after they had already closed the gates for the night. Ivana had been unconcerned, assuring him there was a way in other than the gates; but entering through the outer city made him nervous. It wasn't exactly a place he relished wandering around at night, even invisible and with an assassin at his side.

They still hadn't seen any sign of patrols on their approach, and it was making Vaughn uneasy. He found it hard to believe that his father had given up, knowing he was in the area. Then again, his father also probably didn't think him stupid enough to return to the city.

But what of Ivana? Would they guess she would return to her inn? He half expected a trap, but when he had suggested the idea to her, she had merely rolled her eyes.

Of course it's a trap, she had said. *But a trap only works if you get caught in it.*

That was one of the longest speeches she had given to him today, choosing mostly to favor him with silence, speaking only when he spoke to her first. He continued to curse himself for losing control last night. It might have been his imagination, but she had started to seem like a normal person for a little while. So much for that.

He glanced at her as she pulled another star-leaf out of her bosom, ripped half off with her teeth, chewed, grimaced, and swallowed. It was the only indication he had that her leg was giving her pain again. He didn't know whether to admire her fortitude or the plant she was using as a drug. In an ideal situation, even with aether, she would be off that leg completely for at least a few days. As it was, she had withstood miles more of hiking today with no complaint and hadn't slowed them down much either.

If anything, he was the one who was slowing them down. He had used his extra supply of his own aether and had been forced to rely on burning the blood in his own body to turn them invisible—which occurred with increasing frequency once the cover of woods had petered out and they had approached more populated lands. He was tired, mentally and physically, and he didn't know how much longer he would be able to keep it up—especially with the added drain of extending his invisibility to encompass Ivana.

"Are you ready?" Ivana asked.

He gave the outer city a dubious look. "You sure about this?"

She didn't favor him with a response. Instead, she stood up, and he was forced to move to keep her invisible as well.

She skirted most of the outer city itself, until the buildings dwindled almost to an end against the city wall. There, a ramshackle old house—if it could be called that—sat pressed up against the wall. In fact, like many of the buildings here, it was most likely using the wall itself as its own backside.

It looked even less lived in than the surrounding buildings. The front door had a splintered cavity in the middle, as though someone had tried to kick it down. Lopsided shutters hung at the single window in the front, and the chimney was half-fallen in.

With a single glance around them, Ivana forced the front door open—without kicking it in.

Vaughn finally moved away from her once they were inside, which was as rundown as the outside. A three-legged table sat in the middle of what used to be the kitchen, and a rusted woodstove no longer had its vent pipe attached to the ceiling.

Most pleasantly, a foul stench emanated from a pile of rags in one corner, which hosted the remains of a feral dog's latest meal—though the dogs themselves were nowhere in sight.

"Nice place you have here," he said. "Summer home?"

She gave him a look and moved away from him to kick aside a rumpled, faded rug, revealing a trap door underneath.

She heaved it opened and jerked her head toward it. "You first."

He hesitated, a sudden thought striking him. What if the reason there had been no patrols was because she was working *with* his father to dupe him into being captured?

Perhaps that was why he hadn't died; maybe she hadn't actually killed him. Maybe it was all an act.

She raised an eyebrow at him and then shrugged. "Have it your way." She swung herself down through the trap door, not bothering with a ladder. She grunted as she hit the floor, probably because of her leg.

He took a deep breath. He had come this far.

He lowered himself down onto the ladder and shut the trap door above his head. It was pitch black for a split second before his eyes adjusted to whatever minimal light was filtering in.

They were in the cellar; broken shelves hung on the wall, and a few smashed barrels and boxes littered the floor. Ivana felt for a lantern; she obviously knew where it was, but he moved over to help her find and light it.

She grunted by way of thanks, and they moved on—to the back of the cellar. She shoved aside a stone—in the wall?—and ducked through the opening.

Again, he followed.

They stood in a small cavern. Mushrooms and moss dotted the damp, overgrown ground and walls. He stepped a little farther in while he waited for her to put the stone back, and then whirled around, sure he felt someone tickling his neck. It turned out to be a length of lichen hanging from the ceiling.

Ivana picked her way along the ground, and he followed. As they walked, he saw signs that they weren't the first to travel this way. A discarded tin can here, a chicken bone there, the remains of a fire tucked against a wall.

"Where are we?" he whispered to Ivana. He didn't know why he had whispered—only that it seemed appropriate given the circumstances. The cavern was so quiet, aside from a distant sound of rushing water.

She didn't whisper back, but her voice was low. "Under the walls," she said.

"I didn't know this was down here."

"You're not supposed to."

Not long after, she stopped in front of a mat of hanging lichen. She pushed aside the lichen, revealing a small grate. She pulled at it, and it came off easily in her hands. She jerked her head at him again, looked behind them as he ducked through first, and then replaced the grate.

They stepped out into a man-made passage. The sound of the water was nearby, now, though he couldn't see it, and the pervasive scent of rotting garbage made him wrinkle his nose. This time, he took a guess. "Sewers?"

"Upper level," she said. "We don't have to go far."

Indeed, they only walked for a minute before they came across an iron ladder attached to the wall.

He held the lantern while she ascended, and then he followed. They exited through a maintenance access point—which was conveniently unlocked—into a dark alley Vaughn would have been nervous about traversing alone and visible.

However, the city wall stretched above them, and they were now on the side of it they wanted to be. Ivana doused the lantern and left it on the inside of the grate leading to the sewers. They slipped down the alley, invisible once more, Ivana leading the way.

She wound through so many alleys and side streets that Vaughn would never have been able to retrace their steps, until finally, he recognized the quarter of the city in which her inn was located.

Before long, they emerged onto the other side of the same square.

She arrived first and halted so abruptly that he ran into her. "What...?" he asked, and then looked for himself.

All that remained of her inn was a skeleton of charred timbers.

Chapter Sixteen

Message in Blood

Ivana stared at the place where her inn had been, unwilling to believe her eyes. "No," she whispered. It was gone. Burned to ash so thoroughly, it couldn't have been an accident. Not here in Weylyn City, which was praised for its highly effective fire brigade.

Despair, anxiety, the pain of loss—they washed over her, and then at last...blessed numbness.

"Burning skies," Vaughn muttered.

She knew a catastrophe like this was a possibility, depending on how angry she had made the Conclave. But she had hoped merely to find guards swarming the inn, questioning or perhaps detaining her girls. Had hoped to be able to communicate with Aleena, get her feeling on the situation, let her know that the inn was hers, now, as they had planned, now that her identity had been compromised.

Instead, the square was dark—every street light, every window—and empty, which she found odd. Where were the curious onlookers, gaping at the terrible sight? Clucking their tongues, shaking their heads, whispering that they had known something was off about the innkeeper—even though they had thought nothing of the sort before today.

She felt Vaughn's eyes on her, and she pressed her lips together, refusing to look at him, lest he strip her protections again.

She stared at the inn until Vaughn looked away. "Ivana—"

"You've done what you said. You helped me get here undetected, and I'm not ungrateful. I think it's time you went your own way."

"But—"

"There is absolutely no reason for you to remain here further," she said. Perhaps she could *finally* be rid of him.

"I'm trying to tell you something."

She reluctantly turned her head to look at him.

"This wasn't only directed at you. It was directed at me."

She paused, parsing that assumption. "I don't follow your logic. It's my inn. How could that hurt you?"

He looked back at the remains of the inn, silent for a moment, and then spoke softly. "He once burned down an entire village because one family took me in." He paused, and his voice lowered another level. "They didn't even know I was a Banebringer."

"I don't think—"

"He likes to send me messages. If it weren't for me, your inn would still be there. He might have made an example out of one or two of your women, certainly would have ruined you and made sure you could never go back, but this is extreme even for the Conclave, if not for him."

Ivana shook her head. "I think, in this case, you may be seeing things that aren't there."

"No," he said.

"What makes you so sure?"

"Because I'm seeing something that *is* there." He pointed. "The wall of the building next to yours, to be precise."

She squinted in the darkness, and all she saw was the looming shape of the wall of the bakery, in contrast to the yawning spot where her inn once was. "I don't see anything."

"Of course," he muttered. "I forget." He glanced around. "Let's move closer."

She hesitated. This had to be a trap. But as long as they stayed invisible...

So she moved with him to skirt the square, his hand lightly on the small of her back, until they came to the aforementioned wall.

He pointed with his free hand, and she stared—there, painted on the wall in dark paint, was the symbol of the Conclave.

"All right," she whispered. "So the Conclave wants to make sure I know this is punishment for tangling in their business. I still don't see—"

"Look closer."

She shook her head, but obligingly reached out and touched the paint. Actually, on closer inspection, it didn't look like paint.

She scratched a bit off, touched it to her tongue, and then froze.

It was blood.

Her head started spinning. No. *No.* Surely, this wasn't some message that they had not only burned her inn down, but had hurt or killed her girls.

"It might be a message to you," Vaughn said, "but it's also for me. This is what my father does, for my benefit."

The numbness was starting to give way, and now anger filled the space. The bastard. As if he hadn't already done enough to ruin her life. She wouldn't let him ruin the lives of those girls too, not this time. This time, she wasn't running.

The sound of footsteps running in their direction snapped their attention elsewhere, and they pressed back against the wall.

A moment later a man came into view. He skidded into the ash, mouth hanging open. He spun around. "No," he whispered. "No, not now. I was so close. Where are you? Kayden, you've been such a fool..."

Ivana frowned. Kayden? She had heard that name before, from Caira's lips, and it couldn't be coincidence.

"Acquaintance?" Vaughn whispered in her ear.

She shook her head. But if he was looking for Caira...

"If you want to be useful one last time," she said to Vaughn, "cause a distraction at the right moment."

She stalked toward the man, who was now facing away from her, leaving Vaughn's invisibility behind.

"Ivana!" Vaughn breathed urgently after her.

She knew what he was thinking. It was crazy to reveal herself, when people could still be watching the deceptively empty square. In fact, she was quite sure they were. But she wouldn't be the marionette in Gildas' plan.

So without a noise, she slid her dagger out of its sheath, slipped up directly behind the man, and put the blade to his throat.

He gasped and started to fight back. In response, she pressed the dagger closer.

"I'm not going to hurt you," she whispered in his ear. "Not if you stop moving. I just want to talk. There are likely people watching, and this is just for show. I know you have no reason to trust me, so trust that I could slit your throat with one flick of my hand."

He went limp, but she could still feel him trembling.

"Are you looking for Caira?" she asked.

The man started to nod, but no doubt feeling the cool metal against his skin, stopped, and answered instead. "Yes. Do you know where she is? What happened here?"

"I know Caira," she said, without answering his second question, "but I don't know where she is now."

Even in his fear, his shoulders slumped.

"What business do you have with her?"

"We were...friends." The word sounded hollow in his mouth, and Ivana doubted that was the extent of the relationship. "I...did something foolish to hurt her. She left home, and I lost track of her. I've been trying to find her ever since. To tell her I'm sorry. To make it up to her."

Ivana was satisfied. He was either an excellent actor, or he was telling the truth.

"I know of a way you might obtain information," she said,

"but it may be dangerous."

"Anything. I'll do anything," he said hoarsely.

"You help me, I'll help you. There is a woman I know. She might know where Caira is, but I don't dare find her myself." If Aleena was alive and waiting, she couldn't risk putting her in danger again by being seen with her. She didn't know how extensive the Conclave spies and traps might be.

The man opened his mouth, but she shook her head. "It would be best if I didn't explain." She released the clasp of the chain she wore around her neck with one hand. At the end dangled a pendant—one Aleena would know well. "If the woman is alive and free, she'll be waiting at The Quay inn near the docks tomorrow night near midnight. Don't talk to anyone, just go to the back table. Her name is Aleena, but she won't respond to that unless you first ask for Tara." She pressed the necklace into one of his hands. "Give her this. She'll know what it means. Tell her you're looking for Caira. If she can help you, she will, but might require your help in return."

She felt the man swallow hard against her blade, as if debating who this strange woman was and why she was instructing him to go to clandestine meetings with another woman he didn't know. But he nodded slightly.

"Now," Ivana said. "I need you to follow some very precise instructions. In a moment, I believe there will be some unhappy guards who start this way. Use the opportunity while they are otherwise engaged to slip away. Circle this quarter, head to the next quarter over, and stop at The Bay Stallion Inn. Rent a room for the night under the name Edwyn Bitters. The innkeeper will ensure you can leave undetected. Only then, go to the docks. Do you understand?"

He hesitated, and then nodded again.

"Repeat what I said back to me."

He did, and she was satisfied.

Footsteps. The rasp of swords being drawn.

"If there becomes a point when the guards seem distracted," she said, hoping, for once, Vaughn actually *had* stuck around, "try to get away."

She turned him around to face the square. A moment later a dozen guards appeared.

They halted when they saw her holding the man.

The guards spread out around the area, encircling her, and then one stepped forward. "Let him go," he said. "And perhaps we'll be kind."

"Let me go," she said, "and perhaps I won't kill him."

One of the guards gave a grunt, and then rubbed his head. "Someone threw a rock at me!"

Half the guards spun to look in the direction that the rock had to have come from.

The man stomped on her foot, hard, and Ivana didn't have to feign pain. He wrested himself free from her loose grasp and fled into the darkness. One of the guards called after him, but he didn't stop, and they let him go, more concerned with her.

As she had hoped.

She held up her hands, dagger in the air. "You have what you wanted," she said. "Now what?"

"Put the weapon down," the lead guard said.

She raised an eyebrow, shrugged, and put it on the ground in front of her, continuing to hold her hands out.

The captain jerked his head toward two others, and they approached her cautiously, swords out.

She waited until they were within striking distance.

And then, in one fluid motion, she dropped to the ground, under their swords, picked back up her dagger, and swept it at their knees.

They stumbled back in surprise, and she rolled to the side and fled through the hole they had left in their circle, barely escaping the lunges of the nearest guards.

Shouts rang from behind her, but she ran. Her thigh screamed at her every time that foot beat into the ground, the star leaf simply unable to keep up with this kind of punishment. She kept running anyway, taking advantage of the surge of energy while she had it. She ran until she was certain no one was close enough to see her, and then she started to climb a building.

She was halfway up when she felt her stitches start to tear. She stopped, clinging to the side of the building as the agony of her wound ripping open caused darkness to obscure her vision momentarily. She waited until the wave of dizziness had passed and finished climbing. She reached the top of the building, ran along the flat roof, jumped over a narrow alleyway to the next one, and then climbed down the other side into a dark alley.

She stumbled as she landed, her leg giving way beneath her.

She leaned heavily against the building, and with a trembling hand, shoved another star-leaf into her mouth. It was dangerous, taking so much of it at once, but she couldn't afford to be stopped by pain right now. Her bandage was warming with fresh blood, but she could do nothing about it until she was relatively safe.

She waited long enough for the star-leaf to lessen the pain to a manageable level—it didn't take long, as much as she had recently taken—and then kept running.

A few minutes later, the thrill of the chase wore off so drastically she almost collapsed onto the ground.

She knelt there for a moment, gaining her bearings, listening for footsteps. She no longer heard the shouts of following guards, or anything at all, except a tomcat howling nearby and the sound of mice skittering away at her presence.

She turned her head toward the direction the mice were fleeing. There was an entrance to the sewers here. They were a death trap for someone who didn't know their way around them, but fortunately, she did, and she knew enough of where she was to know where this access tunnel would likely lead.

She limped over to the barred archway—large enough for her to crawl through—and examined the grate. Usually, they weren't permanently attached, since they were designed as access tunnels for the men who maintained them as well. And, sure enough, she found hinges and a keyhole without any trouble.

Unfortunately, she didn't have anything on her she could force the lock with. They weren't all open as the one they had entered the city through; only those frequented by people who needed to move surreptitiously. She searched the alley for a tool that would suffice, but it was dark, and here in the alley the buildings obscured most of the light the moon gave.

A hand on her shoulder nearly made her jump out of her skin.

She whirled around, blade out, and the person jumped back. She relaxed. It was Vaughn.

"You about got yourself gutted," she snapped. "What are you still doing here?"

"I need to escape as much as you do," he said. "I figured I'd follow you to see how you get out, since I haven't the foggiest idea how we came in."

It annoyed her that he was *able* to follow her, but she supposed being invisible helped.

Speaking of invisible... "Can't you just...walk out?"

He shook his head. "I'm starting to fatigue," he said. "If I try to keep burning aether so constantly for much longer, I'll risk making myself sick."

"I thought you said you regenerated blood faster?"

"It regenerates proportionately at about the same rate I use it—like trying to pour sand back through the same hole you poured it from in the first place."

She shook her head. There wasn't time to ponder this right now. She gestured to the locked grate. "You don't happen to have lockpicks on you, do you?"

He shrugged and shook his head, but then looked around the alley. He held up a finger, tiptoed to one end, and then picked something up off the ground. He came back and showed it to her. "Will this work?"

How in the abyss does he do that? He had the best night vision of anyone she had ever met, and she was beginning to suspect it wasn't entirely natural.

She examined the bit of metal, bent it in half, and then tried it in the lock. It took a moment, but soon the lock released with a satisfying snick.

Excellent. She glanced at Vaughn, who was waiting nearby. His frequent anxious glances at the ends of the alley were not comforting.

"Are they nearby?" she asked.

He nodded. "They don't know where exactly you went, but they were able to follow you to the general area."

In a timely response, she heard the rattle of armor in the street nearby, and then conversation.

She opened the grate. It creaked noisily, and she winced.

"I heard something over there!" a voice said, too near for her liking.

She crawled into the tunnel, and Vaughn followed behind. Any light they had was soon gone, but she crept forward, feeling her way through the darkness. She knew these access tunnels, and eventually it would end at a ladder which led down into the sewers, like the one they had entered through. The sewers themselves had sporadic light sources, enough to get her to one of the beggars' tunnels.

Sure enough, at one shuffle forward, the ground dropped out from beneath her hand.

She halted, turned herself so that she could swing her legs over the edge, found purchase on the ladder rungs she knew would be there, and started climbing down.

It was pitch black, so she didn't even bother looking up to see if Vaughn had managed to follow. A moment later, his boots scraped against the metal rungs of the ladder behind her, so her question was answered.

When she felt water soak into her boots, she stopped and

carefully lowered herself down. The water shouldn't be up over the maintenance walks at the sides of the sewers, but they had just had a heavy rain. It would be easy to be swept away if the sewers were flooded.

Fortunately, it only came up to her ankles. She felt for one of the metal handles built into the wall and pulled herself along it until she felt relatively secure on the walk.

She heard a splash as Vaughn reached the bottom.

She closed her eyes and listened. There was no sound of pursuit through the tunnel, thankfully.

"Did you close the grate after you?" she asked Vaughn.

He didn't reply.

"Vaughn?"

"Oh, sorry. Yes. I nodded."

She snorted. "In case you haven't noticed, we can't *see* anything, so you'll have to use more than body language."

She felt him shift, heard cloth moving, and then a moment later, torchlight flared.

She reeled back against the sudden light, eyes watering, and when she could finally see again, she stared open-mouthed at Vaughn. "How did you—where—"

He was looking at the torch warily, as if expecting it to explode. "I still had the torch I bought in my bag."

"But how did you *light* it? And in the dark?"

He finally looked away from the flame, seemingly satisfied that whatever he was worried would happen wouldn't. "First," he said, "I can see in the dark, as long as there is *some* light coming from somewhere."

That confirmed *that* guess.

"Second..." He held up his pouch, which she recognized as the one he kept his aether in. "I have aether from a fireblood."

"Let me guess," she said, "they can manipulate fire?" Like back at their first camp, with the fire pit.

"Something like that," he said. "But it's the most dangerous kind for someone who *isn't* a fireblood to use. It's volatile, and while foci"—he waved the torch a little for emphasis—"do help, if it goes wrong...well, the result can be rather dramatic."

So apparently he *had* been expecting it to explode.

She shook her head. At this point, she didn't even want to know. "All right," she said. "We have a ways to go now before we get back to where we came in."

He didn't question her; he let her lead them deeper into the tunnels.

Chapter Seventeen

Beggars' Refuge

Vaughn trailed right behind Ivana. He had heard of the dangers of becoming lost in sewers—especially a system as vast and labyrinthine as this one. He wouldn't have attempted it alone, but he trusted her expertise in this area. After all, she had just been prepared to traverse the tunnels without any light at all; he supposed with light, it would prove as easy for her as turning invisible was for him.

It wasn't long before they started to pass other tunnels. The only sounds they heard were their own footsteps as they sloshed through the murky water and the rush of water echoing around them.

The water was foul. It smelled foul, it looked foul, and in places, it rose dangerously in depth, no doubt due to the recent rain. At one point, they had to wade through it, gripping the handholds on the wall to avoid slipping off the walkways.

Ivana led them on, stopping at each tunnel to examine metal plates set into the wall—presumably markers of location. Finally, she turned down one, traveled a ways, and then turned down another. It was at this point that he saw, to his surprise, another light source ahead. The tunnel widened, the walkway began to rise in elevation, and her footsteps quickened. A moment later, they emerged into a large, cavern-like room. The water ran through a wide trough cut in the middle, but on either side was dry stone.

And then, to his even greater astonishment, he saw evidence of habitation. Dirty scraps of blankets tucked against the walls, recent cook-fires...but no people.

Ivana stopped. "It's all right," she said. "He's a friend."

It took a moment, but one by one, people started to re-enter the room from all of the various side tunnels leading out. They emerged slowly at first, but when neither he nor Ivana made any moves, they appeared content to ignore them and went back to whatever business they had—which didn't appear to be much.

Vaughn looked at Ivana, eyebrow raised.

"Several regions, including Weylyn, have outlawed beggars in the cities," Ivana said. "They have to go somewhere, don't they?"

She headed to the farthest corner of the room, where a ragged man sat muttering over an odd assortment of items spread out on a ratty blanket.

He knew Weylyn's rules about beggars, of course, though he

didn't spend a lot of time in the cities. He took a few extra steps to catch up with her. "I thought in conjunction with that law, the government set up workhouses."

She snorted. "Little better than slave labor."

"Don't they get an allowance?"

"I rescued one of my girls from a so-called workhouse. Do you want to know what condition she was in when I found her?"

"Surely better than if she had been living on the streets." He glanced around. "Or down here."

"Appearances can be deceiving," Ivana said, and, having reached the other side of the room, knelt in front of the man.

Vaughn remained standing and shifted nervously. The beggars in the room looked as though they were paying him no mind, but sharp eyes glanced his way every so often. Ivana, they ignored.

The man smiled. By the looks of it, he had only half his teeth. "Sweetblade," he said. "I don't like it when you bring friends." The man spoke with the refined accent of Venetia, but his skin was the lighter tan of one of the central regions.

"He's harmless, Tenoch," Ivana said. "I give you my word." She shot Vaughn a look, as if to warn him against making her into a liar.

The man grunted. "What do you have for me today?"

Ivana snapped her fingers and held out her hand to Vaughn. He frowned, but handed her their dwindling bag of supplies.

She opened a flap and pulled out the handful of dennil root she had picked earlier that day. She put it down on the blanket. "Dennil root," she said. "You remember how to make the tincture I showed you last time?"

The beggar flashed his toothless grin again. "Do you hear a cough?"

"Good," Ivana said. "This should be enough to last you and yours another month. After that, I'm afraid you may be on your own."

The beggar rocked back and forth. "Yes. I heard."

"I was hoping."

The beggar craned his neck to look at the bag. "Have any star-leaf?"

Ivana smiled, and oddly enough, it looked genuine. "Nice try."

"Ah," he said, closing his eyes, a half-smile on his lips. Then it faded. "Heard you've angered the Conclave," he said. "Tried to take out a Hunter. So I heard."

Ivana said nothing, so he continued. "They're saying you enlisted the services of a Banebringer to do it."

Vaughn started, and the man shifted his eyes to look at him. He swallowed and tried to smile.

"They say *she*," he emphasized the word and then looked away from Vaughn, "can suck the life out of you through her hands."

Vaughn raised an eyebrow. They thought that crazy Banebringer was *with* Ivana? Or at least, that's what 'they' were saying...

"That's preposterous."

The man shrugged. "It's what they say."

"Well, you can't trust everything you hear. What of my girls?"

He started rocking again. "Think one or two got away. They

say they took the rest to the workhouses."

"What do you say?"

"I say they've disappeared, to wherever the Conclave disappears worthless people."

"No bodies?"

The man shook his head.

Ivana frowned, and Vaughn was amazed at how remarkably calm she was, given that her entire life had been upended. Given that just a few hours ago she had risked being captured to send a stranger on what was likely a fool's errand.

"Anything else?"

The man tilted his head to the side. "They know you're down here."

How could he possibly know *that*?

Ivana grimaced. "Thanks." She stood up and started to turn away, when Vaughn spotted a coiled string on his blanket.

He picked it up. "This is bow-string."

"So it is."

He examined it more closely. It was odd looking. Sort of shimmery. And then he blinked. "Is this made with aether?"

"Well, now," the man said. "That would be illegal, wouldn't it?"

Considering it would have taken a Banebringer to do it and it was prohibited to keep aether—highly illegal.

They didn't have a weaveblood among the Ichtaca, but he knew a few who had managed to obtain such strings for their bows. They were nigh on indestructible. "How much?" he asked, reaching for the pouch inside the bag.

Ivana's hand shot out and gripped his wrist so hard he was

sure it would be bruised. She gave him a hard look, and the man's eyes grew even sharper.

And the beggars around them were no longer feigning disinterest.

Ivana pulled a few star-leaves out of her bosom and tossed them on the blanket. "A fair trade," she said. "Use it wisely." She tugged Vaughn away.

Vaughn could feel the eyes of everyone in the room on them as they left through one of the side tunnels that didn't have water running through it. "Did I do something wrong?" he asked once they were out of hearing range.

She turned the corner and flattened herself against the wall, shoving him next to her, and then peered around the corner. Out of caution, he handed her his torch and took the opportunity to string his bow.

"You don't let people like that know you have coin on you," she said quietly.

"Well, I thought..."

"You thought I trusted them?"

Yes, actually. She had seemed comfortable enough.

She snorted. "Not a chance, not even Tenoch, though he's helped me get out of a few pinches." She pulled back and laid her head against the wall, and then turned to look at him. "For someone who's been on the run for so long, you don't have much street-sense."

He shrugged. "I don't seek the company of beggars and thieves," he said.

"Oh? Then who *do* you seek the company of?"

"I don't have the luxury of company."

"What? Not even the occasional woman?" she asked, casting him a wry look.

"Well. There is that. But can you blame me?"

"Most certainly."

He tugged at the string a few times, making sure it was secure, and took the torch back. "You can't tell me you've never sought solace in the arms of a man."

"You assume I need—or even want—solace."

It was an act, an act so good he was sure she believed it herself. He knew it as surely as he knew the isolation that ate at his own soul. He didn't know how he knew, only that he knew. "I'm sure even people like you get lonely."

She met his eyes. "There is no solace for people like me." She broke the gaze to peer around the corner again.

He wanted to argue with her, but he sensed that would get nowhere. So instead, he asked, "Why are we standing here?"

"I'm making sure none of the beggars are following us."

"Ah," he said. "They seemed jittery."

"Wouldn't you be, when strangers are known to show up at random and haul you away to a workhouse?"

He blinked. "The authorities know they're down here?"

She let out an exasperated breath. "Of course they do. Sewers, workhouses—as long as no one can see them, do they care? But every once in a while, they think it a good show—or perhaps sport—to raid the sewers and drag a couple beggars back up where they belong."

She bit the final words off like they were her last, and again, he couldn't help but wonder at her. Why was she an assassin? She ought to have been a leader of some people's advocacy group, or the like, with her sensibilities running so sympathetic to the blighted of society.

Footsteps down the tunnel made him tense, and Ivana's dagger was in her hand in an instant, but she stepped out from the wall into the open. "Tenoch," she said. "Did you remember something else?"

"They're coming."

Ivana cursed. Why were they being so relentless? She had been hoping they would give her up for lost in the sewers.

"Let's go," she said to Vaughn. He followed her without question, which was a nice habit he had, at least.

She picked up the pace, casting looks over her shoulder every so often. She had to eat another star-leaf with the increase in movement, to ward off the corresponding increase in pain in her leg. She was going to regret the amount she had taken in a few hours, but hopefully, by then, they would be somewhere safe.

She heard activity farther down the tunnel and halted, holding up her hand to Vaughn to indicate he should be silent.

He drew up behind her, and they listened.

Yes, definitely ahead. It could sometimes be difficult to tell the direction of sound down here. And yet Tenoch had said they were coming, which meant they also had to be behind.

"Can you turn us invisible yet?" she asked Vaughn.

He scratched at his chin. "Well...I can, but I wouldn't trust moving with it right now. Not sure I can hold it perfectly."

"Good enough." She gestured to the ground. "Kneel."

He raised an eyebrow, and after securing the torch he was still carrying in a nearby wall bracket, did as she asked. When he was on the ground, she clambered onto his back.

"Well," he said, sounding amused. "This is exciting."

"Turn us invisible and shut up."

He did both, and they waited.

A moment later their pursuers came into view, two from behind, and two from ahead. They halted when they saw each other, brows furrowed.

Good, Ivana thought grimly. *Now come together, have a nice conversation about it...*

They did exactly as she hoped, meeting in the middle of the tunnel.

"You see them?" one guard asked.

Another shook his head, and then glanced at the out-of-place torch. "No, but I could have sworn..." He turned his back toward Ivana, and she leapt.

Vaughn grunted as she used him for leverage, but held steady, and she landed on the guard's back.

"What the—" he shouted as he stumbled backward, trying in vain to reach his sword, while his comrades gathered their wits, and then Ivana caught his throat in the crook of her arm.

As he lumbered around with her weight on his back, clawing at her arm and gasping for breath, an arrow flew through the air and lodged itself in the thigh of another guard.

The guard yelped and fell to one knee. Two more arrows followed soon after that one, disabling the same number of guards, until finally an arrow found the leg of her own.

He stumbled, and she lost her grip on his back, but still she clung to him with her arm, using her own dead weight to prevent him from drawing air until he fell to his hands and knees. He tried to buck her off, weakly, and even managed to get his fingernails into her arm and draw blood, but finally he collapsed onto the ground, unconscious.

She drew her dagger, slit his throat, and then stood and surveyed the situation.

Two of the guards had decided it wasn't worth fighting an invisible enemy and were limping back down the tunnel.

The last guard, on the other hand...

He had, apparently, at some point during her scrap with the first guard, hurled himself in the direction he had seen the arrows come from and was now wrestling with a visible Vaughn, bow knocked to the ground beside him.

She had just taken a step in their direction, when she heard the other two guards coming back.

She glanced that way, and her stomach dropped.

Not the guards. The Conclave.

Chapter Eighteen

Layers

Two priests stood in the tunnel, grim expressions on their faces, a cloud of incense already rising around them. One of the pair started intoning a rapid, snapping chant, and then raised his hand toward the torch. The flames at the head of the torch licked outward, as though seeking other fuel to devour, and then the priest jerked his hand toward Ivana.

She flung herself to the side just as a spout of fire streamed out from the torch and arced in her direction.

It fizzled against the sewer wall behind her, just as another spout headed her way, courtesy of the second priest.

She was forced to move again, and again, as they alternated chanting and throwing fire so that they could keep up an almost continuous offense.

To the abyss with the Conclave!

She used the moment of delay their magic required while finishing a chant to roll in close to them.

She came up right in the face of one. His look of surprise was still plastered on his face as he fell at her feet, blood spurting from his neck.

The second priest had time to begin a low, sinuous, drone before her arm flicked out toward him.

At least, she thought her arm had flicked out toward him. Instead, it cut through air.

She blinked and turned, finding the priest a foot away from where she thought he had been.

The drone rose in fervor, and when she tried again, she was hurled backward by what felt like an incredible gust of wind.

The priest's invocation changed again while she caught her breath, and he held one hand directly toward her.

She didn't have time to consider what that might portend, because a moment later, an arrow struck him in the chest.

His arm fell, and the incantation died on his lips. A split-second later, he fell to the ground himself.

She pushed herself to her feet and found herself trembling. She didn't know if it was the excess surge of energy caused by the frantic fight, the overuse of the star-leaf finally taking hold of her body, or if it was merely the shock of fighting such a foe.

Or perhaps all three.

She turned, expecting to see Vaughn standing with bow in hand, pleased at having saved her life—again.

Instead, she found him on the ground, blood running from

his nose and a purplish bruise growing at one eye. He had curled in on himself, except for one arm laying out limp to the side, silvery dust on his fingers. The last guard was standing over his quarry, satisfied that he had cowed the criminal.

He clearly had no idea that Ivana was still alive and that his two Conclave associates were dead, because he didn't even turn to look at her before she stabbed him from behind.

She knelt at Vaughn's side. "Vaughn," she said. "Vaughn!"

He opened one eye and tried to smile. "You look almost concerned," he croaked out.

She frowned at him. "Can you move?"

He grimaced and tried to sit up. "Temoth," he said, huffing a bit, and then managed to prop himself back against the wall. He pressed at a spot on his side and then breathed out. "Thought I might have had a broken rib or two, but I think it's only some nasty bruises," he said. "He was trying hard not to kill me." He let out a short-breathed chuckle. "That's something, huh?"

She didn't reply. It would be so easy to leave him here. He would just slow her down. It was clearly the most practical course of action.

His smile faded, as if he could read her thoughts.

She hesitated. But she might need his aether, yet. The warmth of the blood still oozing from her aching leg attested to that.

So, instead, she handed him a piece of star-leaf. "We need to get out of here before the other guards realize their comrades aren't coming back."

Relief spread across his face. He ate the leaf, made a face, and then struggled to stand. She helped him as much as she could, letting him lean on her.

Vaughn glanced at the ground, as if seeing the bodies for the first time. His eyes dragged over the two dead guards and then moved on to the priests. "They sent battle-priests," he said, disbelief coloring his voice.

"So it would seem." She had never fought priests before. She wasn't supposed to have ever drawn the ire of the Conclave.

His eyes lingered on the priest with the arrow through his heart, and then he looked away, eyes closed, lips pressed together.

"Get it out now," she said. "We were out of time fifteen minutes ago." And she was fading. She could feel the effects of the star-leaf starting to pull at her limbs, begging her to sit down for a little while, to rest.

He turned away from her, one hand bracing himself against the wall, and emptied the contents of his stomach.

She handed him another piece of star-leaf. "First person you've ever killed?" The aether on his fingers suggested he had used magic to do so. Impressive that he could be so clearheaded while being beat up.

He nodded, avoiding her eyes, and ate the leaf she offered.

"It's not supposed to be easy," she said. "If it were, you'd be like me. Can you walk on your own?"

He tossed his head, as if to fling off whatever was ailing him, in the process spraying a few drops of fresh blood from his nose onto her arm that mingled with her own blood.

He stretched a little, winced, and then stretched again. "I think I can make it for a little ways."

"Good," she said, letting go of him and turning away.

"You know, I can't seem to get ahead. Every time I save your life, you save mine," he said from behind her.

"Duly noted," she said. "Next time, I'll be sure to let you die." She plucked the torch out of the bracket and strode off down the tunnel, trying to ignore the pain increasing in her leg again. She couldn't take any more star-leaf, or she'd risk more serious complications.

"All right, all right!" he called, and his footsteps shuffled behind her. "Let's not be hasty…"

Vaughn was worried, at first, that he wouldn't be able to keep up with Ivana. He felt like…

Well, like someone beat me up. He grinned, though it wasn't at all funny.

It had been a long week.

But the initial pace she set tapered off rapidly, and she started limping. He couldn't see the bandage beneath her skirt, even as tattered as it was, but with all of the action she had seen since he had last wrapped it, he couldn't imagine those stitches had held. If they had a moment to rest safely, he'd try to get her to let him look at it again. At the least, it would need a new bandage and another dose of aether.

They wound through the sewers for a little while longer—long enough that he was thoroughly lost. However, before long, they were clambering through the same hole in the stone they had come in through, traversing the cavern tunnel, and entering the broken cellar.

Ivana smothered the torch on the cellar floor and climbed up the ladder to the main floor. At the top, she pushed aside the trap door. As she started to lift herself up, he put his foot on the bottom rung—and one of her feet slipped.

She swore and caught herself before he could reach up to do the same. But instead of climbing back up, she dangled there, putting her head against the top rung of the ladder.

"Ivana?" he asked, concerned.

She roused herself, muttered a string of curse words under her breath, and continued on.

When they had both reached the top, she went to the window and cautiously looked out through the crack left by the broken shutters. She then leaned against the wall. "We'll be safe here for a little while. The city guard doesn't bother with this area of the outer city."

An intact bucket lay on the floor, and he wandered over to look down at it. "Is there somewhere to get water?"

She closed her eyes. "Move that barrel," she said. "There's a well."

"That's handy," he said, doing as she said. There was a hole in the floor underneath, and a thick rope dangled down the edge. He pulled it up, but the end was frayed.

"Don't lose the bucket down the well," she said. "Or you'll have every thief and smuggler in the city infuriated at you."

Great. He tied the rope tightly around the handle of the bucket and then knotted it again. He lowered it down, and sure enough, heard the distant splash of water a moment later. He heaved the bucket back up and set it on the table.

He leaned down to inspect it. "Fresh?"

She nodded. "It's drinkable."

The taste was heavy with minerals, but it quenched his thirst enough. Then, he found a rag in the bag and went to a cracked mirror on the wall. He winced at his reflection. One eye was starting to turn black, and the other cheek had split and was surrounded by a nasty bruise. He peeled away the remains of the aether that hadn't flaked off his face from his nose, which wasn't broken, thankfully.

He turned back around in time to see Ivana sliding down the wall. She grimaced as she hit the ground, and then put her face in her hands.

"Ivana?" he asked again. She just shook her head slightly.

He brought the bucket over to her and set it down, and then settled down next to her. "Have some water."

She picked her head up and stared at the bucket. Then she leaned forward and cupped her hands to drink, but spilled half of it down herself as they shook.

"Here—" He helped her hold the water by cupping her hands in his own.

She drank, and then drank again, and then sat back, eyes closed.

"What's wrong?" he asked.

"Too much star-leaf," she said. "It's finally caught up with me." She opened her eyes and stared at the ceiling.

"Is that dangerous?"

"Can be. But I didn't have much of a choice. It was also dangerous to let myself be stopped by pain."

He didn't know what to say to that; only found that his sense of concern increased. "Is there anything I can do?"

She shook her head. "I don't think I took enough to cause any permanent damage," she said. "A few hours of rest and I'll be good as new." She moved her leg and grimaced. "Well. At least as far as the star-leaf is concerned."

He frowned. "Let me look at your leg again," he said. "At the least, I can apply some more salve and fresh bandages, if not try to fix the stitches."

She exhaled and jerked her head.

He took that as acquiescence and got up to retrieve the bag of supplies.

But when he returned, he found her head nodding to the side. "Ivana?" he asked, placing one hand on her shoulder. "Ivana." He shook her, but she didn't respond.

She was already sound asleep. He gently lowered her to the floor and stripped off the blood-soaked rags holding her leg together.

What he found was not encouraging. The salve had helped to bind the deepest wounds faster than they normally would have healed, but the entire area was an angry red and was starting to swell. The stitches had indeed pulled out in a number of places, tearing the skin further. He did his best to clean the wound off with water from the well, and then applied a generous helping of the salve, with an equally generous serving of bindblood aether mixed in. But despite his ministrations, he was no doctor, and by the looks of it, that was what she needed.

He dug out the last of the clean bandages and wrapped her leg back up again. At the least, it would help to numb the pain for a little while.

He then set to the task of examining his own wounds. He

dipped his rag in the water, crushed bindblood aether into it, and then pressed it against his face with a sigh. It could have been much, much worse, but he had taken one look at that guard and known there was no way he would win a fight with him. Knowing the guard hadn't intended to kill him—a distinct advantage of being a Banebringer—he hadn't given him a reason to apply more force than necessary to subdue him.

It was humiliating—his instinct was still to fight back, despite the circumstances—but he had learned to do what he needed to survive, and sometimes that meant fighting, most of the time it meant running, and occasionally it meant simply giving up.

At least Ivana hadn't left him behind. For a moment, he was certain she had been about to.

He turned his eyes back to her. Ivana.

Sweetblade had been about to leave him behind. Had Ivana intervened? She was a mystery to him. Sweetblade was a hard, cold woman. Her other identity wasn't particularly warm, but she didn't seem purposefully cruel, like some sadistic maniac who enjoyed hurting people for the sake of it.

Even so, she held herself aloof. There was someone else buried beneath those two layers, someone he hadn't been able to figure out yet. He didn't know if she knew who it was anymore, and he couldn't help but wonder about how she had come to the place she had in life. Could he pry it out of her? Could he get her to show a little bit more of herself—her true self?

Burning skies, why did he *care*?

He sighed. He was starved for company—real company—that was all. It had been half a year since he had been back with the Ichtaca, and even there, he had been lonely. His status as the son of one of the wealthiest noblemen in Setana had put a barrier between himself and most of the other Banebringers, even though it hardly mattered anymore—would never matter again. Yaotel was free with him, but Yaotel was their leader, and he also wouldn't hesitate to have Vaughn imprisoned if he felt Vaughn was going to threaten their cause.

He wanted the company of someone who didn't care if he were a Banebringer, or the son of a nobleman, or anything else.

He blew out the flame in the lantern, deciding to get some sleep himself.

When Ivana woke, natural light was seeping into the room through the window. Vaughn was sleeping a few feet away from her, and her leg felt strangely...well. She pulled aside her skirt to look at it and found fresh bandages. Vaughn had apparently tended to her wound again while she slept.

She sighed. Better that she had been asleep, than reminded of the last time he had bandaged the wound for her.

She tried to stand. She was a little wobbly, but she could walk, and without much pain. It was needed relief after the hours of agony she had just endured. Even better, the side-effects of too much star-leaf had mostly worn off. She still felt a little dizzy, but that could be as much from exhaustion as anything else.

She found the bucket and dipped fresh water from the well, and then went about splashing her face with the water. It felt good; she sorely needed a long soak in a hot bath, but just washing her face and rinsing out her mouth refreshed her a bit.

"You're awake," she heard from behind her. "And moving around. I assume that means your leg is feeling a little better?"

She didn't turn around. "Yes."

Vaughn moved over to the table and leaned against it to face her, arms folded across his chest. "I looked at that leg," he said. "There's only so much I can do, and it's not healing like I had hoped. You need to see a doctor."

"As much as I would love to secure professional treatment," she said, "that's out of the question until I'm well away from here." Ironic that she had a full purse, enough to pay the best doctor, and couldn't even spend it.

He bit his lip, but said nothing more. He had to know she was right. Still, he watched her, eyebrows furrowed slightly.

His gaze made her uncomfortable. "Stop looking at me like that," she said.

"Like what?"

"Like you're...concerned about me."

He raised an eyebrow. "I *am* concerned about you."

"Don't be. I'm not someone you should spare your concern on."

"No? Are you not a person?"

No, she thought. *I'm a wraith.* She turned away from him, so she couldn't see his face.

As she did so, she saw a shimmering raised patch on her arm. Perplexed, she craned her neck to examine it further. *Ah.* Vaughn's blood from earlier.

She picked at the patch and then peeled it off. She made to flick it away, but he stopped her, sounding horrified. "What are you doing? You can't just toss that! I can use it. It's valuable." He held out his hand.

Just to annoy him, she tucked the bit of aether snugly between her breasts. "Good. Perhaps I can sell it to Tenoch the next time I'm in Weylyn City."

He raised an eyebrow, a slow smile spreading across his face. "Do you really think that would stop me from retrieving it, if I wanted to?"

She drew her dagger and pointed it at him. "I wouldn't try it."

"You won't hurt me," he said.

"Why would you make such a dangerous assumption?"

"You could have left me behind in the sewers, and you didn't."

She snorted. "That's because you're still some use to me," she said, gesturing toward her leg with her dagger.

"Perhaps," he said. "But I think it's more than that. I think that blade is a part of your disguise." He held up one finger when she opened her mouth to protest. "An effective disguise, I'll give you that. But I don't believe for an instant that it's who you really are."

She rolled her eyes. What did that even mean? She was a professional killer. It was what she was, and who she was. She had left behind any other persona long ago.

"Fine," he said. "Let's pretend your motives were entirely selfish in not leaving me behind. What of your inn? Do you really need to hire the women that you do?"

"Who would suspect the altruistic innkeeper of something more nefarious?"

"No," he said flatly. "I don't believe it." He pointed at her midsection. "I think it goes deeper than that."

Her girls were her one weakness, and she didn't like it that he had not only discovered it but was trying to *understand* it. Hunger gnawed at the inside of her—hunger to believe his insinuation—that something of her old self remained—and it infuriated her.

She shoved him backwards, into the wall, pressing the tip of her dagger into his throat. "I don't know what you *think* you know about me, Dal Vaughn," she hissed, "but let me make myself perfectly clear: we are not friends. If I'm feeling generous, there are exactly six people left in this world that I would not betray, hurt, or kill if it became necessary for me to do so. You are *not* one of those people.

"I have one goal right now, and that is to find those people and see them to safety. I am tolerating your presence because for now, you are aiding me, rather than hindering me. Should that change..." She pressed the dagger in just enough to draw a bead of blood.

He met her scowl evenly. There was uncertainty in his eyes, but it didn't stop him from speaking. "Is that Sweetblade talking, or Ivana?"

Her rage lashed out, and she struck him on his injured cheek, and then again, and again, to punctuate each of her words. "There. Is. No. Difference!"

He gasped and reeled back from her, eyes watering, one hand to his cheek.

She re-sheathed her dagger and glared at him. "And the only reason you're not dead for your audacity is because I don't have the energy to deal with a bloodbane right now."

The events of the past week had thoroughly shaken her. She wanted him out her life, now. If she could disappear like he could, and slip away, she would do so, heedless of her leg injury.

Vaughn turned away from Ivana, went to the window, and peeked out, if for no other reason than to try and hide from her that she *had* finally rattled him.

Maybe he was wrong about her. Maybe. But he couldn't shake the feeling that the reason she had lashed out at him was because he had touched a nerve.

It wasn't that he didn't believe her. He did. He had no doubt that if he got in her way, she wouldn't hesitate to follow through on her threat, if only because he might push her far enough that she would snap.

Was the reason he had been so insistent on staying with her because deep inside he hoped she would?

He shoved away the ache in his chest and focused on the immediate future.

The sun had started on its downward slide to the horizon. He supposed it would be wise to wait until dark to begin his trek back to the Ichtaca. He had nowhere else to go, and though he hated the idea of slinking back with his tail between his legs, he desperately needed a chance to rest and think about his next course of action.

That gave him a few hours to work on building up another reserve of his own aether, should he run into trouble again.

He turned around, intending to ask Ivana when and where

she was planning on going, but she was nowhere to be found.

He spun around in a circle, scanning the room, but there wasn't anywhere for her to hide. Had she decided to leave without even saying anything? But he hadn't heard the trapdoor open, and he had been standing right next to the door...

Suddenly, her disembodied voice floated from a spot next to the table, right where she had been standing before. "Why do you look so bewildered?"

He blinked and stared at the spot. From the floor beneath, perhaps? But then how would she know he looked bewildered? "Where are you?"

"Right here?"

As she spoke, a ghost of her outline flickered in and out. It was what could happen, any time, not only when the moon was full, when a Banebringer that didn't have his profile used moonblood aether to turn invisible. It didn't work perfectly, especially when moving.

Impossible. That was...impossible! Unless...

He moved toward the spot and reached for her. Sure enough, his hand met solid flesh. He felt her try to jerk away, and the air shimmered again. "What—?"

But he tightened his grip, fear beginning to creep into him at this development. Why hadn't she told him? Had this all been some sort of elaborate ruse on the part of his father after all? He had feared it, but had brushed it off, finding it hard to believe his father would work with a Banebringer. But he hated Vaughn enough that he might, in order to achieve his goal...

"Let go of it," he said, and his voice came out hard as iron. "Tell me what you know. Are you working with my father?"

She broke away from him. The ghost moved to the other side of the room, and the shimmer of her dagger flashed before she disappeared entirely again. "I have no idea what you're talking about," she said. "And you had better—"

"You're invisible."

"What? That's ridiculous."

"Look in the damn mirror!"

There was a pause and then a gasp, and her dagger fell through the air and hit the floor with a clatter. Almost simultaneously, she reappeared.

He lunged for the dagger and reached it a second before she did.

She snarled and tried to kick him in the groin, but he had been ready for retaliation. He jumped back, grabbed one of her arms, and forced it behind her back. She flailed like a cat caught by its tail and almost got loose after she elbowed him hard in his bruised ribs with her free arm, but with the help of a well-placed jab to the wound on her leg, he managed to grab that arm as well, shove her against the wall, face-first, and press her there with his body.

"Let go of me!" she shouted, outraged, still struggling.

"Not so fierce without your teeth, are you?" he hissed into her ear, though truthfully, he was having a hard time keeping ahold of her. "Now tell me who you're working with."

"For the last time, I have no idea what you're talking about!"

"You're a Banebringer," he accused. "And you didn't tell me."

"I am not!"

Before he could think about it, he took her dagger and sliced it shallowly across her upper arm, and then jumped back to stand on the trap door, holding the dagger at ready. She whirled around, fury on her face as she touched her arm and looked at the blood on her fingers.

"You idiot!" she growled at him. "You've seen me bleed. Has any of it ever turned to aether before now?"

The logic she offered slapped him in the face, and he blinked, the anger draining out of him.

She was right. She couldn't be a Banebringer. And she had seemed shocked. He had chalked it up to her excellence at deception.

"Then how did you turn invisible?" he asked, throat dry.

"I. Don't. Know."

They stared at each other across the room, he brandishing her dagger, and she standing in a half-crouch, chest heaving, though with exertion or anger, he didn't know.

He flicked his eyes to the cut on her arm, unable to believe that in a moment it wouldn't turn to aether. But it didn't. Red blood continued to trickle out of the slice.

He dropped his hand, and then the dagger, too stunned for more words.

She had retrieved the dagger in an instant, and he flinched back, expecting to feel it dragging across his throat, monster or no monster. But instead, she sheathed it with a snap and backed away from him, eyes wary.

"Do it again," he said.

"I can't," she said. "I don't know what I did in the first place."

He rubbed one hand over his face. She had to have used the aether she had inadvertently taken from him. It was impossible, yet he had just seen it happen.

"Where is the aether you hid?"

She searched for it, but came up empty-handed. "It's not there," she said finally.

"You used the aether," he said, his guess confirmed.

"I thought you said that was impossible," she said.

"It is. It was supposed to be." He glanced toward his bag, where his knife was, and hesitated. He wasn't particularly keen on turning his back on her right now. "Can I have your dagger again?"

"You must be out of your mind."

"Fine," he said. "Understandable." He bared his forearm. "Prick me. Enough to draw blood."

She hesitated, and then moved over to him and made a nick in his arm. A drop of blood welled up, and he waited a few moments, until it started to shimmer, and then turned to aether. He picked off the resulting flake and handed it to her.

She took it between her thumb and forefinger.

"Now try it," he said.

She looked at him and then the aether. "I honestly don't know what to do."

"What did you do before you turned invisible before? What did you think?"

She looked at him out of the corner of her eye. "I wished I could turn invisible," she muttered.

He wanted to comment on that, but he forced his mind back to the matter at hand. "Okay. Wish it again."

She stared at the aether, brow furrowed. It was almost cute. Not a term he would normally apply to her. "Am I invisible?" she asked.

He shook his head.

"Then it's not working."

"Yet I know what I saw," he said. "You didn't see yourself in the mirror, did you? Am I crazy?"

She shook her head. "No." She was still staring at the aether, and her frown deepened. "If it's true that I used that aether..." She hesitated. "Have you ever tried mixing the blood of a Banebringer with a non- Banebringer?"

He tilted his head to the side. "No. Why would we do that?"

She shrugged. "It's the only thing that was odd about the situation. I was bleeding when your blood dripped on me. That blood might have had mine in it too."

He considered her words. And then he considered the implications, if she were correct. "Do you mind if we try an experiment?"

She shook her head, and seeming to know exactly what he was thinking, she pricked her finger and then squeezed two drops of blood out of it, onto the table. She motioned to him, and he moved forward, letting her do the same to him.

They watched the blood until it shimmered and turned to aether.

She peeled it off the table and held it between her thumb and forefinger, like she had before. And then she disappeared.

He blinked, mouth dropping open. "Impossible," he whispered.

"It worked?"

He nodded mutely, head spinning.

He heard her footsteps, and her outline flickered again, near the mirror. "How do I get back?"

"Just...I don't know. Do it. I don't really think about it."

There was a pause, and then finally she shimmered back into existence. Some of the aether filtered down from her hand, powder.

She set the remaining aether down on the table. Together, they stared down at it.

"Burning skies," Vaughn finally said.

This was an incredible discovery. Non-Banebringers, able to use aether? If he had any doubts about going back to the Ichtaca, he didn't now. Yaotel needed to know this. No doubt the researchers would be ecstatic about a new discovery to study.

"Why do you think it works?" Ivana asked suddenly. Her voice was hesitant. As if she was afraid to voice the question.

"I don't know." And he really didn't.

"The way you've talked about it, it sounds almost like it's half-way sentient," she said.

"Sentient is the wrong word. It's more like it's designed to act a certain way given certain situations."

She nodded, as though that made perfect sense. "Then if it's designed to react to Banebringers in some way, perhaps by mixing non-Banebringer blood with Banebringer blood, that subverts the system. Creates a loophole in the law governing it, so to speak."

Interesting theory. "You mean...like tricking it into thinking you're really a Banebringer?"

She shrugged. "Sure. Or maybe not. Just a thought."

He turned to face her. "How did you even consider the idea that it might be because our blood mixed in the first place?"

"It was a variable we hadn't accounted for," she said. "We know I can't use it straight. We know"—she cast him a look—"that I'm not a Banebringer. So there was something else changing the equation. Something..." She trailed off, seeming lost in thought.

He continued to watch her, studying her face. It was then that he *saw* her. Sweetblade the assassin was gone. Ivana the innkeeper was gone. Even the tired face of the woman who had held the babe in that rocking chair was gone. Whatever she had been before this life, it was there, for a moment, in that faraway gaze. He was *right*.

She started, as though suddenly realizing she had drifted off. Her eyes flew to his, and for the first time since he had met her, she flushed. And then the mask went back on again. Her lips pressed together, her eyes focused, and she turned away from him.

He felt like he had just lost something, and he grabbed for it. "Is all of this calculating due to a lifetime's experience creating effective poisons?" he asked, trying to make his tone light.

Her back stiffened, and he wished he hadn't said anything.

But she indulged him. "My father was a tutor for a noble family," she said, her voice emotionless. "I received a quality education." She glanced at the window. The light was fading. "I assume you're leaving as soon as it's dark?"

"That had been my plan."

She nodded. "Good."

"What about you?"

"Assuming our frantic friend from the rubble of my inn follows my directions, Aleena will contact me here. I'll wait to see what news she has."

"And then?"

"I'm going to find my girls."

Chapter Nineteen

Racing Time

Ivana sat with her back against the wall, watching Vaughn while he systematically made a pile of aether chips from his own blood. She understood, now, why he had been so upset earlier, but that didn't mean she appreciated being accosted and accused.

As for now, she was...relieved. She had been afraid that somehow she had become a Banebringer, despite the fact that, as far as they knew, people were never changed at times other than the sky-fire.

And it was also a relief to know she wasn't some sort of freak who could turn invisible for no reason. There was a logical, scientific explanation for what had happened. At least as scientific as things like that came.

"How are you going to deal with that leg?" Vaughn asked, looking up from his task.

"As soon as I can, I'll leave the area and try to find a doctor."

"And what if it becomes a problem before then?"

"A risk I'll have to take."

"Wouldn't it be wiser for you to leave now, instead of waiting for word from your friend?"

"If the only consideration were my own health, then, yes."

He gazed at her. "How very selfish of you," he said, and then looked back down to his pile, adding another sliver of aether.

She gritted her teeth. She didn't have to explain herself to him. The girls were her responsibility, she had taken them under her protection, and it was her fault they were potentially in danger. She refused to leave until she knew what had happened to them. It could be that there was nothing she could do about it at present, but once she knew, she could formulate a plan.

"If you die from an infected wound, you won't be doing your friends much good," Vaughn said.

She knew that. But her best chance at gleaning information was now, not three months from now.

"Look—I'll stick around another day. I can apply more salve for you. That's your best chance."

She felt her stomach tighten. She wanted him *gone.* "No." And she certainly wasn't going to beg him for help.

"If it helps, I'm doing it as much for your workers as you. It's as much my fault they may be in danger as yours, after all."

"Still not necessary."

"Will you threaten to kill me if I stay?"

She rolled her eyes, annoyed that her loss of control around him, yet *again*, had seemed to make him more determined that he was right. "You can do whatever you want," she said. She turned her back on him and lay down on the floor. Even though she had just woken up a few hours ago, she was already exhausted. Apparently the last few days of little sleep and what seemed like endless running had finally caught up with her. "I'm going to rest. If you're gone when I wake...good riddance."

Vaughn watched while she put her back to him, closing him out. He wavered. Another day wouldn't matter to his purposes. If she really didn't care...

The salve would be gone soon, anyway. Then, he would have to either venture out to find more—not a good idea right now—or she would simply have to hope for the best.

He mulled on it more as he worked, and then turned his thoughts to the remarkable discovery they had made that day, which led to considering how the Ichtaca would take the news.

Several hours passed, and he was satisfied with the amount of aether he had managed to stock up. He had just swept all of the scraps into his pouch, when a rapping on the trapdoor startled him. Vaughn froze, listening hard. The sound didn't occur again.

He rose to his feet and retrieved his bow.

"Ivana," he whispered. She didn't respond; presumably deep in sleep.

He crept to the trap door, and then, after a moment of listening again, threw it open, sighting his arrow on the opening immediately.

Nothing happened. However, he did see a tiny bundle tied to the underside of the door. He hesitated, and then removed the package and shut the trap door. For good measure, he sat down on top of it, still a little nervous about whoever had attached the package.

He set aside his bow and turned over the bundle. It was a small leather pouch, cinched at the top with a cord. He glanced toward Ivana, wondering if he should wake her; but he decided to see what it was first. He loosened the cord and turned it over. A necklace fell into his hand—the same one he had observed her wear at the inn—accompanied by a folded piece of paper.

He set aside the necklace and then opened the paper to read it.

Sadly, he couldn't make much of it out. He recognized the language, Xambrian, but it had been a long time since he had studied Xambrian.

He supposed it was time to wake her; she would want to know.

He re-folded the note and put it, along with the necklace, back in the pouch, and went to her sleeping form.

"Ivana," he said again, louder. When she didn't respond, he shook her gently. She still didn't respond, and he drew his hand back, eyes wide. He could feel the heat of her skin through her clothing. He touched her face for confirmation. She was burning with a fever.

He shook her harder. "Ivana!"

She finally stirred and turned over to look up at him, but her eyes weren't focused. "Airell?"

Vaughn sat back on his heels. Airell? As in, Airell, his oldest brother? "No. It's Vaughn. You need to wake up." He held up the pouch. "I think your friend contacted you."

She stared at him for a moment longer, and he wondered if she even understood what he was saying. "Aleena," she whispered. She tried to sit up, but her face contorted, and she fell back and closed her eyes again.

This was not a good sign. He pocketed the pouch and didn't even ask to look at her leg; he simply undid the bandage, and she didn't stir to complain.

The wound itself didn't look any worse—though neither did it look better—but red streaks traveled outward from it that hadn't been there before. A sure sign of infection.

He didn't have any more clean rags, so he was forced to wrap it back up again. "Ivana," he said. "You need to see a doctor. Your leg is infected."

She shook her head faintly.

"Listen to me. This will kill you."

In response, her head lolled back to the side.

"Ivana!" He shook her again, but she was unresponsive.

He cursed and ran a hand through his hair. At this point, he didn't even know if a doctor could help her. It might be too late.

He chewed on his lower lip. She had one chance. He had to take her to a bindblood. But he knew of only one sure place to find bindbloods, and if he took Ivana there...there was no guarantee they'd heal her, and he would be risking his own freedom. But she had saved his life multiple times. He couldn't just leave her here, knowing she would die. It was his fault she was in this mess to begin with.

He would simply have to find her a way out.

It was a task easier said than done. Barden's estate was seventy-five miles from Weylyn City; if it were only himself, and he had a fast and sturdy horse, he could make it in less than three days. But he couldn't carry her seventy-five miles, not and get there in time to help.

So he did something he had never done before. He stole out of the safe house, and then stole two horses, tack and all.

He managed to tie Ivana onto the back of one of the horses by forcing the animal into the house and using the table as leverage for himself. Then, he loaded up the saddlebags with their meager supplies and tied her horse to his. Painfully conscious at how exposed his activities were making them, he then set out for the Ichtaca at the fastest pace he dared.

Vaughn arrived at Barden's estate in the greyish light of pre-dawn on the fifth day. He paused at the top of the hillock that overlooked the estate house to check on Ivana once again. She was unconscious, but alive.

Barely.

She had drifted in and out of consciousness for three days—enough so that he could get her to drink—but hadn't been coherent enough to hold a conversation. The past two days, she hadn't woken at all. He didn't know how much time she had.

He took a deep breath and then let it out slowly. He had made it this far. What would happen next remained to be seen.

If she survived, he was going to be in so much trouble.

He removed their bag from the horse and then untied Ivana. Her unsupported weight slid off the horse and almost hit the ground before he could catch her. He lowered her to the ground and then tied the lead horse to a tree. The horses were tired as well, but he couldn't take the time to care for them right now. He would have someone come out later to retrieve them.

He picked Ivana up in his arms, turned both of them invisible, and staggered out of the woods and down the hill.

He made his way around the wall until he reached a small gate at the back of the estate, hardly noticeable amidst the tangle of ivy that crawled over it. He then worked a single flake of aether out of the pouch at his waist, nearly dropping Ivana in the process, and slid it into a hole on the gate where the lock would normally be.

The gate swung open, and he continued inside. He shoved it shut with his hip and winced at the metallic click it made as it locked behind him. The sentries would know he—or some moonblood, anyway—was here now, but he had unlocked the gate properly, so they had no reason to suspect he was bringing an unauthorized guest.

That was why he was careful to maintain his invisibility as he crossed the yard and entered the groundskeeper's shed. From there, he traveled down a set of stairs and arrived at a heavy metal door. Again, he pushed a sliver of aether into a hole, and there was a click as it unlocked. He opened it...

And was met with half a dozen guards on the other side.

Chapter Twenty

The Ichtaca

Vaughn grimaced and let go of his invisibility. *Great. Just great.*

He recognized all of the men standing at the bottom of the stairway, of course. A couple exchanged looks as he revealed himself, but one pushed his way forward and folded his arms across his large and muscular chest—which he puffed out to an even greater size.

"I hope, for both your sakes, that she's Gifted," he said, nodding toward the burden in Vaughn's arms.

Vaughn rolled his eyes. "Perth," he said by way of greeting. "I think you're hoping the opposite."

Perth flashed him a smile, but it wasn't friendly.

One of the other guards pushed Perth out of the way—Hueil,

one of those who organized guard and sentry duty. They didn't give themselves rank or unit, as if they were some sort of fighting force. They weren't nearly cohesive enough for that.

Hueil didn't smile at him, but neither was his expression unfriendly. "Vaughn," he said with a nod. "Yaotel didn't tell us to expect you." He looked toward Ivana, and his meaning was clear enough. Yaotel didn't warn them Vaughn was bringing someone with him.

"That's because he doesn't know." Vaughn shifted Ivana in his arms. She was heavier than she looked. All that hard-packed muscle, no doubt. "Look. I know I'm in trouble and all that, but can we discuss this later? This woman is in critical condition. I'm hoping Linette or one of the others can help her. It's why I brought her here."

Hueil nodded toward another guard, who turned and took the stairs two by two. When the man had disappeared, Hueil turned back to Vaughn. "Hate to agree with Perth, Vaughn, but I hope she's some Gifted you rescued."

It wouldn't be the first time. Vaughn had brought his share of Banebringers to the Ichtaca over the years. Unfortunately, that wasn't the case this time.

Vaughn crouched down on his knees and settled Ivana on the floor without answering Hueil. Her lack of gifting would be obvious soon enough. He placed a finger to her throat—more to reassure himself, since he had no doubt she was still alive. Her skin was burning so hot he had felt it through her clothing as he had carried her.

Sure enough, her pulse, though weaker than he would have liked, was present.

He had risked a lot by coming here, and not only for himself. Linette might heal her, only to have Yaotel order her executed. If it wasn't too late anyway. Even bindbloods, with their remarkable healing abilities, had their limits.

The ragtag group of guards watched him silently, but no one else moved. They weren't going to let him in without approval. Individualistic they may be, but none of them were lax when it came to the protection of their group from outsiders.

He tapped his foot impatiently, until he heard the sharp rap of footsteps from beyond the guards. "Get out of my way," Linette barked. The guards moved obediently aside, letting her through.

The older woman barely spared a glance for Vaughn. Instead, she knelt immediately by Ivana's side.

Vaughn was surprised to feel his stomach starting to twist in knots as she examined Ivana. Why was he so worried? If she died, she died. He would feel guilty for a while, for bringing her into it, but it wouldn't be the first innocent—if Ivana could be called innocent—to die because of him.

But his internal monologue didn't convince his stomach. "What do you think, Linette?" he asked finally, unable to bear the silence any longer.

Linette shook her head, stray white hairs wafting back and forth with the motion, and Vaughn's stomach dropped. "She's bad off," she said. "Leg's infected pretty bad, and it's obviously spread."

She looked up at Vaughn, and he nodded in confirmation. "She was attacked by a bloodwolf. I did what I could, but..."

Linette stood up. "Move her to the infirmary," she said. "If there's hope for her, we'll need the others."

"Secure room?" Hueil asked.

Linette shook her head and held up the blood-soaked rag that had passed for a bandage over the past day—what remained of his formal tunic.

Perth grinned, while some of the others exchanged glances again.

Vaughn ignored them, taking some measure of relief in the fact that Linette hadn't given up Ivana for lost.

He bent to gather Ivana in his arms again, but Linette stopped him and motioned to two of the other men. "Not you," she said.

"But—"

Linette gave him a hard look, and Ivana was taken from his arms. "Yaotel wants to speak with you, right away." She wrinkled her nose. "Fortunately for all of us, he's about to moderate a meeting, so you might have time to take a bath first." She cast Vaughn one more look before following the men carrying Ivana up the stairs, and it was more sympathetic this time. "I'll send word as soon as we know," she said.

Vaughn went immediately to his rooms to take the aforementioned bath. He didn't mind. He was filthy, and he stank so badly of sweat and sewage he was certain that was how they knew he was coming—assuming no one had noticed the doors opening on their own, of course.

It also gave him time to think. Yaotel could be anywhere from mildly annoyed to furious with him, depending on his mood. Either way, it would likely mean Vaughn would be assigned some unpleasant or tedious task for the next few months, like scrubbing pots or cleaning out the washrooms. Or, if Yaotel were feeling particularly irritable, he might send him on some fool's errand, chasing the most dangerous of what would likely be dead-end leads for the archivists.

When he had cleaned himself up satisfactorily and changed into a fresh set of clothes, he set out toward Yaotel's office.

Huiel soon fell in beside him. "Yaotel's still in the meeting," he said.

"What's this meeting?" Vaughn asked, turning his steps instead toward the meeting chamber.

Huiel took too long to respond.

"Perth is at it again, isn't he?" Vaughn inferred.

Huiel's lips pressed together. "It's not just Perth, Vaughn."

"What do you mean?"

Huiel shrugged. "If you're going there, you'll see."

Vaughn didn't press further. When they reached the meeting chamber, Vaughn and Huiel slipped into the room. It was a medium-sized, circular room, with tables arranged in a half-circle to face the other side. The room itself would hold about half of the Banebringers who lived regularly in the compound. Yaotel usually used it for meetings with researchers or other groups he needed to receive information from or give information to all together. As many as could had tried to cram themselves in, and Vaughn and Huiel had to stuff themselves in the back.

Huiel's words became clear to him almost immediately.

Perth was down front, facing Yaotel. "...much longer can you expect us to sit around on our asses?" he was saying. "For all your and Barton's political wrangling, the Anti-Sedationists are still a minority opinion. Meanwhile, the Conclave grows more powerful." He glanced around the room. "We could *stop* them, Yaotel. You know we could."

There were an awful lot of nods and murmurs of agreement.

Vaughn clenched his fist. Apparently Perth had gained support since had been gone. Perth had been clamoring for Yaotel to start using the Ichtaca for more than research and political maneuvering for as long as Vaughn could remember. Always, Yaotel had resisted, and always before, there had been enough who agreed with him to silence Perth and his comrades.

Vaughn glanced toward Huiel, but the other man's expression was blank.

"All right," Yaotel snapped, holding up one hand. The frustration in his voice didn't bode well for Vaughn's upcoming personal meeting with him. It also didn't bode well for the direction of the Ichtaca. Surely Yaotel wasn't actually considering...?

"I'll make this compromise. While I won't sanction any actions at present, I will allow official combat research and training."

Vaughn blinked. *What? No!* What was Yaotel thinking? This was the first step to fighting, which Yaotel had avoided for as long as Vaughn had been with the Ichtaca. They couldn't engage in fighting. It would be a bloodbath. It would result in too many innocent deaths. It would decimate their numbers, and the resulting monsters that would be spawned would tear apart the land. There was no guarantee they would even win, or what would happen if they did. These were all arguments Yaotel had always seen the reason of, and Vaughn couldn't imagine what had changed his mind.

Perth stepped forward, expression eager. "I'll volunteer to oversee the training," he said.

"No," Yaotel replied, voice hard. "You're too ready to shed blood. I want someone more level-headed in charge." His eyes swept the room again and then landed on Huiel. "Huiel? Would you be willing to step into this role?"

Huiel nodded. "Certainly."

Perth's face turned stormy, but he didn't argue.

Vaughn's head spun. He couldn't believe this. What of Danton? What of the others? Would they say nothing? His eyes searched the room, but Danton's eyes were down on the ground, and the others who had previously supported a less conflict-oriented path were silent.

"I'll trust you to set up arrangements then. Report to me when you think you have a satisfactory plan." Yaotel shook his head irritably. "We're done here."

Vaughn stood riveted in place, anger beginning to simmer in his chest. When everyone else had filtered out, he strode up to Yaotel, who was standing with one hand on the desk, staring into nothing.

"How could you?" Vaughn demanded. "This is a disaster waiting to happen. You're giving Perth fuel. It won't stop here, you know that—"

Yaotel turned hard eyes on Vaughn, arresting his diatribe. "You," he said, "are in no position to make demands. Follow."

Vaughn gritted his teeth and swallowed his rant, though that didn't quench his anger. But he followed Yaotel to his office. He could argue with Yaotel about this later. Surely the man would see reason.

Yaotel sat behind his desk after they entered, elbows on the surface and fingers braced in a triangle. Vaughn closed the door, and Yaotel looked over his fingers at him, face unsmiling. "Sit."

Vaughn did as he asked, resisting the urge to glance at the stuffed head of a bloodwolf nailed to Yaotel's wall. The bloodwolf that had attacked Ivana and him had been the first he had seen in a long time. They typically avoided more populated areas, preferring to prey on the plentiful game to be found farther north, in more heavily forested lands.

"I'm told you brought an unapproved visitor here," Yaotel said, his tone flat.

"I tried to contact you to give you warning," Vaughn said. "But the qixli was giving me problems."

In fact, the qixli had cracked at some point during their many frantic escapes. He didn't tell Yaotel that. They were tricky to make, and he didn't need another black mark against him. Besides, it was theoretically possible that it had simply refused to work for him. The aether was feeling temperamental, or some such.

He almost smiled, remembering the conversation he had had with Ivana about the semi-sentience of aether, but he refrained. He didn't want Yaotel misunderstanding the source of his amusement.

Yaotel sighed and moved his fingers to the sides of his temples. He closed his eyes and rubbed his forehead. "You're such a headache."

"My best quality," Vaughn said.

Yaotel dropped his hands, stood up, and paced to the head of the bloodwolf, passing by three other monster heads in the process. Yaotel liked to collect them, as if in defiance of the gods who had forced their 'gifts' upon them. He looked up at the bloodwolf, hands clasped behind his back, as if trying to determine some mystery hidden there. "You'd better have a damn good reason for bringing her here."

"She was dying. Might be dead already, for all I know. Conventional medical help was impossible, in our situation, and honestly, it might have been too late for that anyway."

Yaotel turned, an eyebrow raised. "And yet she's not Gifted?"

Vaughn swallowed and shook his head. He was going to do everything in his power to keep Ivana's identity a secret. He had a feeling the Ichtaca would be none too happy to find out he had brought an assassin into their midst.

"Then why not let her die? So unlike you. Taking more than a passing interest in a woman."

"It's my fault she was hurt," Vaughn said. "She was helping me escape from a difficult situation, and she saved my own life more times than I want to admit. I couldn't just leave her."

Yaotel was silent.

"What are you going to do with her? Assuming she lives?"

"Does she know you're Gifted?"

He bit his tongue. *Not Gifted. Banebringer.* The Ichtaca had resurrected the old term, refusing to call themselves what everyone else did.

He still thought of himself as a Banebringer. It was what he was, after all. But he never said that out loud.

"Yes."

Yaotel shook his head. "We don't put too much stock in rules here, Vaughn, but there are a very few that are crucial to our survival."

"I realize that."

"If someone were to find out—"

"She's not going to tell anyone about this place."

"So sure? How long have you known her?"

Vaughn coughed. "Erm. Maybe two weeks." If he stretched it a little.

"And you trust her so much, already?"

Trust was a strong word. He shouldn't. He knew that. Yet... "With my life."

Yaotel's eyebrow lifted again, even higher than before, a hint of a smile tugging at the corner of his mouth. "You're sleeping with her, aren't you? Women always make you stupid."

"Only in my dreams."

"Hm." Yaotel's smile faded, and he shook his head. "Well, Vaughn. You're lucky. I'm feeling generous today. If the bind-bloods can save her, I'll let her *stay* alive."

That was a relief.

"But she can't leave here, not yet."

Damn. "Yaotel—"

"I know you say you trust her. But *I* don't know this woman, and I won't endanger everyone here on your word alone."

Vaughn bit his lip. He should have expected this. In fact, deep inside, he had. If Ivana lived, she wasn't going to be happy with him.

Yaotel walked over to the door of his office and opened it. He motioned to Vaughn and stepped out into the hallway. "She tries to leave, she dies. She tries to contact someone on the outside, she dies."

Vaughn followed him down the hall. "You can't keep her prisoner forever."

"No, indeed. Prisoners cost too much. I imagine at some point relatively soon she'll try one of those two options and then I won't have to worry about it."

"And if she doesn't?"

Yaotel shrugged. "She'll have to find some way to offset her cost, and if she's lucky, eventually she'll gain my trust and I'll begrudgingly admit you were right and let her go."

Vaughn ran a hand over his face. "All right," he said. "I don't like it, but I can't say that I blame you."

"You could. But that would be stupid." Yaotel flashed him a smile.

"What about me?"

Yaotel grunted and led him through the door that led to the research wing. They walked a bit in silence, passing windowed rooms where their scientists experimented with blood and aether. Finally, Yaotel stopped and answered his question. "You're a pain in the ass. But I have more immediate concerns right now."

Vaughn blinked. "That's it? No consequence for breaking the rules?"

"Oh, don't worry. I have the perfect consequence for you." He turned and gestured to a single barred window in the wall behind them. "You're going to help me with *her*."

Vaughn glanced through the window, and his mouth fell open. There, curled up in the corner of an empty room, was the crazy Banebringer woman from Ri Talesin's manor.

Chapter Twenty-One

Strange Powers

Vaughn turned to Yaotel, speechless. "How did you...?"

"Know her?"

"We've...met." He restrained a shudder, remembering the powers she had wielded during that encounter.

Yaotel nodded. "Drem told me he thought he recognized you."

"Drem?"

"He was in Ri Talesin's manor in disguise as a guard, trying to find her."

Vaughn blinked. "I see."

"Tell me about your encounter with her," Yaotel said, without explaining further.

Vaughn grimaced. "She exhibited powers unlike any I've

seen or heard of before. Extraordinary strength and endurance. Some sort of...life-sucking or at least face withering power. And...she could, uh...call bugs."

Yaotel had remained impassive throughout his speech, until the last. "Call bugs?"

Vaughn nodded. "It was creepy."

Yaotel rubbed his chin. "Interesting."

Vaughn looked back at the woman, only to find her staring directly back at him.

Burning skies. Creepy is right. "She pulled a saferoom door off its hinges when I met her. I don't think a few bars and a locked door are going to keep her contained."

"This is one of our bloodbane observation rooms," Yaotel said—which meant it was heavily reinforced. "We're also keeping her dosed with a sedative. It seems to be preventing her from displaying too much aggressive behavior." Yaotel moved away from the window and gestured for Vaughn to follow him farther down the hallway.

Vaughn cast a dubious look back, still not convinced about the strength of her prison.

"Now, as fascinating as all of this is, it doesn't even touch on the real issue."

"Which would be?"

"They tried to Sedate her, and it didn't work."

Vaughn stopped, shocked, and turned to face Yaotel. "*What?* How...?"

"How do we know, or how did it not work?"

Vaughn opened his mouth to respond, but Yaotel waved him off. "I'll answer both. We know because Drem was tracking her prior to her capture. We heard some rumors of a Gifted with...*strange powers*...as you put it. She wasn't a menace yet, but was causing quite a panic. Out of season locusts descending on fields. Mice overrunning a granary. Someone tried, foolishly, to put an arrow in her back, and it didn't even faze her. Sources say she just pulled it out, looked at it, and tossed it aside." He stopped in front of another door. "I sent Drem out to try and bring her in. Gifted like her don't do our cause any good."

"And your scientists were fascinated by the prospect of studying an unheard of profile."

He shrugged. "That too. Unfortunately, we weren't the only ones interested. She had at least three Hunters on her back, and one of them got to her before us." He opened the door, and Vaughn went in ahead of him.

They stepped into one of the research rooms. Two of the researchers were huddled over a beaker of steaming aether—the only way they knew to keep it from solidifying, aside from trapping it in an airtight vessel, was to keep it at body temperature or higher. A device Vaughn had never seen before sat on the table next to the flame.

Vaughn recognized both of the researchers, but one in particular drew his attention as the researchers turned. He coughed. Citalli. Great.

Citalli raised an eyebrow at him, and her expression was not friendly.

"Gildas captured her," Vaughn muttered, trying to ignore the look. "That's why she went after him."

"Yes." He waved his hand. "Anyway, they took her in, and we gave up the chase. That was about six weeks ago. Nine days ago,

Drem got wind of another woman with similar abilities. He tracked her down, and sure enough, it was the same woman."

"She escaped?"

"So it would seem."

Impossible. "Perhaps they never Sedated her. Perhaps they were overwhelmed." They knew it happened on occasion, but typically only during the sky-fire, when there was an abundance of new Banebringers.

Yaotel inclined his head. "Like you, we had to assume that somehow they had missed her. Maybe she managed to escape before they brought her to the compound. Maybe there was a slip-up. But just to be sure..."

Yaotel turned to the strange device and put one hand on it. "We've had this for a few months now. Our researchers have been falling all over themselves to see what new discoveries it can help them make, but for our purposes, it proves something crucial." He glanced at one of the researchers. "Saylyn, could you explain to Vaughn what we found?"

The aforementioned researcher, a woman in her fifties, nodded. She moved to the device. "A demonstration is always better." She selected a thin needle from her work table nearby. "May I?"

Citalli, not being called upon specifically, went back to her work, pointedly ignoring them. Or, more likely, Vaughn.

He held out his hand, Saylyn pricked his finger and then squeezed a tiny drop of blood onto a rectangular piece of glass the size of two fingers side-by-side. She set another piece of glass on top of it, causing the blood to spread out, and then slid it underneath a long, vertical tube.

"Take a look," she said. He raised an eyebrow, not sure what it was she wanted him to do, and she tapped the tube. "In here," she said. "Quickly, now, before it changes."

He obediently put one eye to the tube and was surprised that he could see through it. At the bottom, a mass of pale blobs moved lazily around, like the current in a slow-moving river. Amidst the blobs were smaller silvery...creatures.

He called them creatures because while they were still blob-like, it almost looked like they had legs, like a crushed bug. They fought against the current of pale blobs and moved about as though having minds of their own.

"Okay," he said at last. "Why does my blood look so funny?"

"Because you're seeing it at an ultra-magnified level," Saylyn said. "The pale blobs are blood. The silvery blobs are aether."

He looked up from the tube, blinking in astonishment at that revelation. "What?"

She didn't respond to his question. Instead, she motioned for his hand again. He sighed and held it out. He had been pricked and prodded so many times it was a wonder his fingers weren't a permanent mass of scars. She drew another drop of blood, smeared it onto another glass slide, and then dipped a second needle into the steaming aether and flicked a drop of the aether into his blood. She covered the slide once again with a second one and slid it back under the tube.

"Now look," she said. "Quickly, quickly."

He obediently looked again. The drama she had wanted him to see had already started. There were more silvery blobs now, many more, and they had set up a perimeter around the rest of the aether, which were huddled in a mass in the middle. He couldn't tell the difference between the two sides, but the circled aether moved around and around, making the circle tighter, and smaller, until the aether in the middle grew frantic. A few of the blobs struck out at the circle, but they were pushed back. Finally, the two sides became indistinct, and the whole mass of aether writhed, and then fell still.

After a moment, some of the aether started to separate from the circle. And then, incredibly, they began chasing the pale blobs, which had been pushed back from the fight in the middle. A few of the blobs got caught and...eaten? Absorbed? All Vaughn knew was that one moment, they were there, and then they were gone.

The aether continued chasing the pale blobs until they were all gone, and only the silvery squished bugs remained. Some continued to move about, and others maintained the perimeter around the still mass of aether in the middle.

Vaughn looked up. "What in the abyss was that?"

Saylyn looked grim. "Congratulations," she said. "You've just witnessed what happens when one of us is Sedated."

Vaughn backed away from the tube instinctively. "It eats our blood?"

She shook her head. "No. The last was your blood turning into aether from exposure to air. As far as we can tell, it looks like the aether actually consumes the rest of your blood, presumably to survive outside the body?" She shrugged. "That's a guess." She gestured to the slide, and sure enough, where once a smear of red had resided, was now wholly the silver sheen of aether. "The Sedation was the first part that you saw. It seems when we introduce a mix of foreign aether into the blood of Gifted, the foreign aether reacts against the natural aether. When they interact, the foreign aether, for lack of a better term, overpowers the natural aether. It no longer moves. It just sits there, as though shackled."

Vaughn shuddered.

"We've observed this same phenomenon with every single profile of Gifted in the compound, using the same mix of aether that we know the priests use to Sedate." Saylyn waved her hand at the beaker.

That was a relatively new discovery. Three years ago, an ex-priest had joined their ranks and brought with him knowledge of some of the inner workings of the Conclave.

Vaughn eyed the beaker dubiously. He couldn't believe they kept that stuff just sitting around.

She held up a finger, oblivious to Vaughn's increasing agitation at this experiment. "However..." She nodded to Citalli, and she went to a rack of tiny vials of blood. Each couldn't have held more than a spoonful of blood. She removed one, pried loose the stopper, and handed it to Saylyn. Saylyn inserted a needle, gathered a drop of blood, and smeared it onto yet another slide. Then, she added a drop of the Sedation mix. She slid it under the tube and gestured to Vaughn again.

Nothing happened. The foreign aether moved about, ignoring other silvery blobs, which Vaughn assumed were the natural aether—he couldn't tell the difference on sight. And then, after a few minutes, the chase after the red blobs began, on the part of all the aether, until the smear of blood had changed over to silver again. There was no fight. No perimeter. No disturbing imprisoned aether in the center of the sample.

He pushed the instrument away. "Let me guess," he said quietly. "That was blood from the crazy woman."

Saylyn nodded. "It doesn't affect her." She cast a glance at Yaotel. "We thought to check it after we tried to Sedate her ourselves and nothing happened."

Vaughn recoiled. "You what?"

"Yaotel's orders," she said, looking uncomfortable.

Vaughn shook his head. Crazy or not, she was one of them. How could Yaotel have ordered such a thing? It was practically...blasphemous!

Saylyn turned away from them, and Yaotel moved back toward the door. "You can question my methods," he said as Vaughn followed him out. "But we had to know if she had really survived Sedation. Besides. She was out of control."

They walked in silence, back through the research wing, back into the main corridor, while Vaughn tried not to think about what he had just seen. It may have only been a smear of blood, but it had been disturbing to watch.

Yaotel didn't lead him back to his office. Instead, he headed for the library. "Now that you know the background, here's how you're going to help us," he said, pushing the door open to the perpetually dusty-smelling room.

The room was dark, and Yaotel touched the light-plate—a square panel attached to the wall that looked similar to a qixli, but designed for an entirely different purpose. Nothing happened, and Yaotel gave a sign of exasperation. He tried again, and a moment later a pale but pervasive light filled the room.

They walked through the shelves, all the way to the back, where Yaotel stopped in front of another door. He turned to face Vaughn. "There's something about that woman that resists Sedation." His voice grew more urgent. "If we knew what it was, if we could discover..." He shook his head. "Use it, reproduce it." He met Vaughn's eyes. "It could change everything. You understand this? Everything."

It hadn't occurred to him until Yaotel had started speaking, but yes, he understood it. If they could make themselves resistant to Sedation...they wouldn't have to run and hide in fear of the Hunters anymore, and none would dare to kill them, not without completely re-thinking their strategy. The balance of power would shift in their favor.

They could fight.

Was this why Yaotel had agreed to the training? Because he saw a way forward that might make it possible?

Yaotel was watching his face. "I know you disagree with my decision in that meeting," he said. "But if we're going to do this, we're going to do it right. And we're going to do it with every possible advantage." He paused. "Who knows. Maybe we'll discover something that will placate that group a little while longer. Maybe if the priests know they can't Sedate us, they'll work harder to find a diplomatic solution."

Vaughn swallowed, feeling dizzy. This was the worst possible punishment Yaotel could have come up with. He was going to be forced to do research to help the very faction he so diametrically opposed. But he gave a rigid nod. He couldn't argue with the benefit of the potential results of such a discovery, however they were used. And perhaps they *could* be used for a peaceful resolution, if they could be patient enough.

Still. He hadn't yet found the opportunity to tell Yaotel about the discovery he had made with Ivana about her ability to use aether, and he wasn't going to yet. Yaotel would tell the faction that wanted to fight, and they would use it for advancing those purposes. Vaughn would wait to see how this played out.

Yaotel pushed the door open to a much smaller room, even more dusty-smelling than the library, and activated its light-plate as well. The books on the shelves weren't all intact; some were burned, some were old scrolls, some were missing their covers.

Though he had never been in here himself, Vaughn knew what the room was. It was their collection of anything and everything that could have to do with the Banebringers, the heretic gods, how they got to be the way they were...

The Conclave did their best to destroy such texts, when found. The sole task of some of the Ichtaca was to hunt and retrieve them before that happened. They knew so very little, thanks to the Conclave's efforts to wipe out the memory of the heretic gods, and what they did know came from this meager gathering of incomplete knowledge.

Yaotel walked over to a small pile of books that sat on the table in the center of the room. He laid one hand on the topmost book. "Dax brought these back last week. He found them fairly well-preserved in an old shrine in the far north of Fuilyn, almost to the border."

Vaughn didn't need to ask why the Conclave hadn't found them yet. Fuilyn was Setana's northernmost region, mostly mountainous terrain. That far north, on the border with Xambria, the peaks were particularly high—and vicious, so he had been told. No one lived there, and he was, frankly, amazed that

Dax had managed to traverse that land and get out alive.

Then again, he had some vague recollection that Dax was an iceblood.

Yaotel picked up the book and flipped it open, and then held it out for Vaughn to see. "Problem is...no one here can read them."

Vaughn scanned his eyes over the page. "That's not Setanan," he said.

"No kidding. We have *one* woman here who says she's pretty sure it's Xambrian, but she doesn't actually know Xambrian. Just did some business with a trader, back before the Conclave started shutting them out." Yaotel tapped the book. "I read your file; you studied Xambrian."

Vaughn stared at the pages of the book. It was Xambrian. It was most definitely Xambrian. The script was unmistakable. But... "That was years ago, Yaotel. And to say I *know* it is a bit of a stretch." He had a tutor who had taught him what he could, in the space of about six months, before his father had found out and had the tutor executed for heresy.

"Whatever the case, you're the only one here who comes even close to being able to translate it."

Vaughn ran a hand over his face. "Why is this so important now? Is there something that makes you think these are connected to the woman?"

Yaotel slid a folded piece of paper out from between two of the books, unfolded it, and spread it out on the table. "This."

It was a drawing, or perhaps a tracing, of the aether bugs. "Where...?"

"It was painted on the wall of the shrine. There was some

other art too—pictures of the gods, we presume, since they look like other paintings we've found—but this was the most interesting, since we'd never seen anything like it before. Dax copied it the best he could and brought it back. Of course, he didn't know at the time how interesting it really was."

"So you think these books might have something to do with the reason that woman can't be Sedated, because there was a weird painting of aether on the wall where the books were found? That seems a bit of a stretch, Yaotel."

Yaotel shrugged. "Yes. It is. But it's all we have, and if there is *anything* in those books that could give us a hint, we have to find it. Meanwhile, our researchers will be working on the scientific angle."

Vaughn groaned and let his eyes drift over the pile. "This is going to take me forever."

One of Linette's bindbloods slipped into the room, and Vaughn tensed. He whispered to Yaotel, who nodded, and the bindblood left.

He turned to Vaughn. "Well then. You'll have plenty of time to get to know that woman you risked so much to save."

Chapter Twenty-Two

Pretensions

Vaughn didn't even ask if Yaotel was done with him before turning and striding toward the infirmary. The wave of relief that had swept over him on hearing the news that Ivana was alive was more intense than he had expected.

Yaotel caught up with him a short way down the hall. "They've already moved her to a guest room," he said.

Vaughn paused and let Yaotel take the lead. They wound their way back through the common living space, the dining hall, and into the underground portion of the manor that held bedrooms and suites.

Hueil was leaning against the wall opposite a door that Linette was just leaving when they arrived. Linette turned to face them as they approached and held up a hand. "She's sleeping," she said. "And probably will be for another day or so. Let her be for now."

Vaughn halted. "Another day or so?"

Linette cast a glance at Yaotel. "We had to sedate her."

Vaughn stared at her, confused. "Sedate her?"

She smiled shortly. "The old-fashioned kind. Woke up halfway through our work on her and gave us a bit of trouble."

Yaotel growled from behind him and move forward. "What sort of trouble?"

"Nothing to worry about, Yaotel," she said. "Just tried to flee. Tried to grab one of the scalpels and gave us a fright. But between her injured leg and obvious disorientation, we had no trouble containing the situation. No harm done. The poor dear was obviously terrified."

Vaughn had to stop himself from snorting. He would never have applied the moniker "poor dear" or description "terrified" to Ivana.

But Yaotel was giving him a look that made it clear he was the one responsible for her actions. He gestured to Hueil. "Lock the door and keep it under guard. Switch off with Danton if you need to."

Vaughn stepped in front of Hueil, blocking his way. "Look—I don't think that's a good idea. If she wakes up in a strange place and finds the door locked, she's going to assume the worst. I guarantee that's not going to make her...transition here easy."

Vaughn didn't actually know how Ivana would react, but he was sure a simple locked door wouldn't keep her in—and the last complication he needed was her assuming that anyone she met was hostile.

Yaotel glared at him, but relented. "Fine. Keep the door unlocked, but under guard. Let me know as soon as she wakes. If she leaves, follow her. Don't answer any questions. She can go to the common area and the dining hall. If she tries to go anywhere else, stop her."

"And if she refuses to cooperate?" Hueil asked.

Yaotel looked at Vaughn as he responded. "Kill her." And then he turned and walked away.

Linette gave Yaotel's back a disapproving stare, but merely clucked her tongue and left in the opposite direction.

When both were gone, Vaughn turned to Hueil. "All right. I know what Yaotel said, but seriously. If she gives you trouble, send for me before you start using deadly force?"

Hueil chuckled. "No problem. Yaotel's just being his normal grouchy self. I wouldn't worry about it."

Vaughn shook his head. He wasn't so sure, but he wasn't going to argue that point. "All right. See you around."

He headed back to his own bedroom. The exhaustion of the past week was more insistent, now that he knew they were both safe for the time being. And if he had to spend hours on end staring at a language he hadn't studied for more than a decade, he'd need to be rested.

It took Ivana five seconds after she woke to realize she wasn't in her own bed. The mattress was too firm, and the blankets weren't right. She touched her thigh and found her dagger missing, along with its sheath. She sat up, instantly wary, and evaluated her situation.

She was in a small, modest bedroom. It contained the bed she sat in, a bedside table, a chair, and a washbasin and mirror. One door, no windows, and empty of anyone else but her.

Someone had garbed her in an ankle-length nightgown—not hers—and she was clean. The sweat, dried blood, grime, and most notably, stench of the past few days were gone. She sniffed her arm, and a faint citrus scent filled her nostrils.

She pushed back the bedclothes and gathered up the nightgown to examine her thigh. The wound itself was covered by a clean bandage, and after prodding the area experimentally a few times and finding less pain than she would have expected, and after noting the carefully wrapped and secured bandage, she determined that it must have been cared for by an expert.

She slid out of the bed, and her bare feet sank into the thick pile of a rug that covered most of a stone floor.

As she put weight on her right leg, it gave a twinge of protest. However, after a few cautious steps she found she was able to walk—if with a slight limp.

A pile of neatly folded clothes lay on the chair, and she moved to examine them. They also weren't hers. The top garment was an unadorned muslin dress, and underneath was a set of underclothes and a pair of soft leather shoes. She cast another look around the room and then shed the nightgown to change.

The dress was long on her, but otherwise fit tolerably. It wasn't fashionable, but the material was of a high quality.

Someone had kindly left a few necessities at the side of the wash basin—a pitcher of cool water, a chunk of soap, a clean towel, and even a comb. She washed her face and did the best she could to make amends with her tangled hair, and then turned toward the door.

Wherever she was, her best assumption was that Vaughn had brought her here, and it was obvious that she had been taken care of. But that didn't mean she could assume that the environment was friendly toward her. Whoever had seen to her had not thought it necessary that she have her dagger back.

She had her suspicions.

She limped to the door and noted on the wall nearby both a lit lantern on a hook, and a small panel next to it that looked almost like Vaughn's distance-speaking device. She touched it, but nothing happened.

She then tried the handle of the door, half-expecting it to be locked, but it wasn't. Still, she patted her thigh, wishing again she had her blade.

She opened the door.

An unfamiliar man slouched against the wall directly across the hall from her door. He was young, perhaps only eighteen or nineteen, and boyishly handsome. If he was supposed to be guarding her room, he wasn't taking it very seriously. His hands were in his pockets, and he was scuffing one toe against the floor. When she emerged, he appraised her from head to toe, and then he met her gaze and straightened up—but his hand didn't stray toward the short sword at his hip.

She tilted her head and appraised him in the same way he had her. "Dal," she said. "Might I ask where I am?"

The man shifted. "Well, I'm not supposed to answer questions..." He shrugged his shoulders apologetically and then offered a sheepish smile.

She didn't press him. Instead, she looked down one end of the hall and then the other. It stretched in both directions, the occasional door punctuating the wall. "Am I allowed to leave the room?"

"Sure," he said. "Just can't go everywhere." He clapped a hand over his mouth and spoke between two fingers. "That was answering a question, wasn't it?"

The observation drew a smile from her. "I'm sure that one was harmless," she said

He brightened and returned her smile. "I'll tell you if you have to turn around."

"Fair enough." She chose to head left, and he fell in behind her as she walked. So she had a guard, but was free to move about within limits.

The hallway walls were stone, but a thick cream rug stretched wall to wall, and she noted that their way was lit by evenly spaced lanterns. As she walked, she passed a decoration here or there—a painting of some generic nature, a potted plant...

This was no prison, nor a hospital. It looked like the modest surroundings of a minor lord's manor—which was as unlikely as it was curious.

Her guard followed two steps behind, and when she glanced back, his eyes were studying her curiously. "Am I allowed to know your name?" she asked, stopping to face him.

He hesitated, and then shrugged again. "Danton," he said.

"A pleasure to make your acquaintance, Danton. My name is

Ivana, though I suspect you already knew that."

He chuckled, which was affirmation enough, but didn't respond until she started walking again. "Begging your pardon, Da, but...they're saying you and Vaughn are...well, you know. Together." He quickened his pace a bit, to walk by her side instead.

So Vaughn *was* known here. That confirmed her initial conclusion. "Vaughn said that?" She glanced at him.

He shook his head vigorously. "Oh, no. He's quite insistent otherwise."

He had used present tense—meaning, Vaughn hadn't merely brought her here. He was still here, wherever *here* was.

Danton was still talking. "I have no reason to doubt him, especially since everyone knows relationships aren't his thing." He gave her another one of his sheepish grins. "But now that I've seen you, I wouldn't blame him..."

He blushed, as if realizing after the fact what he had said, and looked down at his feet. "And, you know, he brought you here. Can't help the rumors." And then he peeked up and flashed her a smile.

She returned his smile. "I understand," she said. "No harm done. If I were you, I would be more inclined to believe Vaughn's assertion."

His smile widened. "Of course." And then the grin slid off his face as she crossed an intersection of halls and headed toward the door at the end of the one she was walking down.

His shoulders tensed, and he hurried to move in front of her. "Begging your pardon, Da, but you can't go that way." His hand twitched a little closer to his weapon.

"Ah," she said, stopping. "Well, Danton, I know you're not supposed to answer questions, but I might find what I'm looking for sooner if I knew where I was going."

"What are you looking for?"

"Something to eat, of course."

He relaxed visibly, and a full grin broke out on his face. "That I can help with. Follow me."

Ivana followed him for a short ways and then fell in beside him, deciding to hazard a question based on her suspicions of where she might be. "So, what can you do?" she asked at last, careful to scan the walls casually, as if interested in the paintings hanging there rather than her question.

"Pardon, Da?"

"Well, you know. Vaughn can turn invisible and throw water around. What can you do?"

He seemed uncertain, as if not sure if she was supposed to know that information, but unsure what to do since it was clear that she did. "I don't know if..."

She shrugged. "Don't concern yourself, Danton. I don't want to get you into trouble. I was just curious."

Danton stopped, finally, and grinned. "Guess it can't do any harm, seeing as you already know about it." He appeared to tense...and then faded into the wall behind him.

She didn't have to feign surprise or wonder. "You're like Vaughn?" she asked, though there was something different about it. She could see his outline, vaguely, as though his body had made an imprint on the wall.

He returned to his visible self and shook his head. "No. Vaughn's a moonblood. He can actually turn invisible, more or less, depending on the phase of the moon. I'm a lightblood. It's different." He glanced at her, and then, presumably encouraged by what he found on her face, went on. "Look at that painting."

She followed his finger to the painting he pointed at. It was a generic still—a vase of flowers. But as Danton stood pointing, the flowers changed...until the painting appeared to be of a bowl of fruit.

She didn't have to feign interest now. She walked over to the painting and touched the frame, and then traced her finger up toward the fruit. It felt solid enough. If she didn't know any better, she would be positive that it really was a painting of a bowl of fruit.

Yet, a moment later, the painting shimmered, and the vase reappeared.

She turned to look at Danton. "Is this like the hallucinations some of you can cause?"

He grinned and shook his head yet again. "That's a bindblood. They work on someone's mind. I'm not doing anything to *you*, I'm changing what you see."

Ivana paused, staring at the painting. Now *that* could come in handy as well. She wondered if he could change his own appearance. "How?"

Danton scuffed his foot and flushed. "You know...I...I'm not really sure how it works. That's not my specialty."

She changed the subject. "You didn't use any aether to do that," she observed, and when he tilted his head, confusion on his face, she added, "Externally. I've seen Vaughn do it." She held out her hand and rubbed her forefinger and thumb together, as if crushing one of his aether flakes.

"Oh," Danton said. "Yeah. Well...Vaughn is a minority in that regard."

He started walking again, and Ivana kept pace. "Oh?"

"I guess there's some evidence to suggest that when we use aether externally, it creates less of a pull on the other realm. You know, that the monsters come from?"

What she knew of the "other realm," as he put it, was limited to what the Conclave preached against and folk tales. But she nodded immediately, careful not to betray any sign of ignorance.

Thus encouraged, he continued. "So the less we use our gifts, especially by doing it naturally, from burning our own blood, the less we pull monsters through during the sky-fire—in both quantity and strength." He shrugged once more. "At least, that's the theory." He was quiet, but Ivana could tell he wanted to go on, so she remained silent.

"See—Vaughn thinks we've caused enough trouble as it is, just by existing. He says it's our responsibility to be, well, responsible with the gifts. Not cause even more trouble. So he doesn't like to use aether from within."

"And what do you think?" she asked.

He chewed his lip, glanced at her, and then ahead again. "Vaughn rescued me from Hunters. Brought me here. I hate to disagree with him, but..." His voice grew stronger. "Well, no offense meant, Da, but I say until people start caring about what happens to us, why should we care about what happens to them?" His face darkened. "We didn't start this."

Fascinating. "No offense taken," she said, offering a gentle smile.

Still, he seemed relieved when they turned a corner and arrived at a wide archway. He gestured to it, and she looked through. She hadn't been searching for Vaughn, but his presence was immediately noticeable, since he sat at the end of a long table alone, even though the hall was relatively full.

"The dining hall," Danton said, stating the obvious. "Yaotel said you could come here, so I guess that means you can eat too." He tapped his foot a few times. "Here, let me show you."

Vaughn saw Ivana enter the dining hall, as did many others. Glances and whispers followed them as Danton led her through the tables to the serving area, but no one challenged her, which was a relief. There were some here who took it upon themselves to treat all new Banebringer residents with aggressive suspicion. How would they treat a non-Banebringer?

Danton hovered by her side, showing her where to get her food. Vaughn was sure she could have figured it out herself, but she let Danton dote on her, and she rewarded his efforts with the smiles and laughter of her sweet, carefree young woman persona.

Danton walked her over to Vaughn's table. "So, Danton," he said with an easy smile after they had approached. "How many questions did you answer?"

Danton ducked his head and gave his characteristic sheepish grin, but he didn't respond. He merely inclined his head in greeting and bowed low to Ivana before leaving to lean against the archway, keeping an eye on her as he was supposed to.

Vaughn's eyes followed Ivana's movements as she settled nonchalantly down at the table, as if she did this every day.

"Well," he said, after she had set in fully to her meal. "I take it all back. You won't have to lift a blade to find a way out of here. You'll just charm all the guards."

She ignored him, choosing instead to focus on her food.

"You won't find all the guards as friendly—or pliable—as Danton."

She set down her fork and wiped her mouth. "So I *am* a prisoner."

He winced. "'Prisoner' is such a heavy word. It's not like you'll be locked in a dank cell with only water and stale bread to eat."

She returned to her food. "A well-treated prisoner, then."

He couldn't respond to that, since it was true.

He observed her while she ate. She was silent, but it wasn't a cold silence. At least, no colder than normal. "You're not angry with me?" he asked at last. He had fully expected *some* negative reaction to the news that she was trapped here.

"Possibly," she said. "What, precisely, is it that you've done that I should be angry about?"

He gestured widely to the room. "For bringing you here."

"Considering I would likely be dead if you hadn't, I can hardly be angry with you over it."

He studied her, dubious. She seemed sincere enough—or at least, she didn't seem angry—but she was, among other things, a masterful actress. "But—"

"I have already gathered," she said, "that this is a relatively safe place to recuperate and plan my next course of action, so I am content."

He raised an eyebrow. "Really?"

She shrugged. "I'll find a way out, sooner or later, and one way or another." Her eyes traveled around the room, as if at that very moment she was taking stock of her options. They flitted past Danton, and he smiled as he noticed her gaze. She returned the smile and turned back to her food, expression more thoughtful than before.

Danton was totally smitten—and Danton wasn't the most perceptive person in the world. Vaughn frowned as Ivana's words came back to him. *One way or another.* "You hypocrite," he said aloud.

She raised an eyebrow. "Pardon?"

"You'd sleep with Danton in a heartbeat if you thought it'd get you out, wouldn't you?"

She chewed her food deliberately and regarded him silently. He held her gaze, refusing to be cowed.

"If I thought it would work..." She shrugged. "Perhaps."

Vaughn snorted. "At least when I sleep with a woman, they know what to expect. Or not to, in my case."

"Well, then, there's the difference between you and me, Vaughn. I know what I am. And I have never pretended to be a good person."

He wanted to protest. If she wasn't a good person deep down, then why take care of those women and their children? Why take such an interest in the plight of beggars? But he bit it back. Was he really going to argue that point with a hired killer? She was the definition of contradiction.

So he changed the subject. "How's your leg?"

She returned to her food, mopping up sauce with a slice of bread. "Surprisingly whole," she said.

"I saw you limping when you walked."

"I imagine an unfortunate side effect of nearly having my leg bitten in two."

"Does it still hurt?"

"It could be worse."

He frowned. Would it kill her to admit that her leg hurt? He was about to press her, but Danton approached. "Begging your pardon, Da," he said, addressing Ivana, "but if you're almost done, Yaotel wants to see you and Vaughn."

Vaughn grimaced. *Great.* Danton must have alerted him to the fact that Ivana was awake. She had slept through the remainder of the day yesterday, all night, and through lunch today. Yaotel didn't waste time. Though Vaughn was sure his excuse for the meeting was to inform Ivana of the terms of her confinement, in reality, Vaughn knew Yaotel wanted to size her up for himself. See if she seemed like a threat.

And Yaotel was both non-pliable and perceptive. He would see through any attempt on Ivana's part to charm him in a heartbeat, and it wouldn't endear him to her. He wanted to warn her, but there would be no chance, not with Danton there.

He would just have to hope for the best.

Chapter Twenty-Three

Unexpected Foe

Ivana didn't ask who Yaotel was as she, Vaughn, and Danton walked down the hall; she had already guessed he must be the one in charge of...whatever it was that was here to be in charge of. Pieces of what Vaughn had let slip prior to coming here locked into place with everything she had learned since waking, and she had a pretty good idea of what sort of place this was, if not *where*, geographically, she was: a sanctuary for Banebringers.

She didn't know how Banebringers found out about and made their way here, but Vaughn had rescued at least one person, so that was one means. Vaughn had also mentioned research on several occasions. Danton had hinted at it as well. That meant it was more than a safe house; they had an agenda, and apparently, if Danton was to be believed, not all of them agreed.

How they were funded was an unanswered question. The meal she had just eaten hadn't been stingy. A commoner would be lucky to get meat once a week, yet the kitchens here had provided generous servings for, by her rough count, over a hundred people. And while her surroundings weren't extravagant, they were well-maintained.

One disappointment was that, so far, she hadn't seen a single window. Either that was deliberate, or they were underground. The latter would make sense if they were trying to hide their existence, but that was one less mode of escape, when the time should come.

They finally stopped outside a door, and Danton leaned toward Ivana. "Don't worry," he said, "he's not as mean as he appears." He smiled at her and stepped back to wait in the hall, letting Vaughn take the lead.

A gruff voice commanded them entry, and a moment later, she and Vaughn were standing in the office of the reportedly-formidable Yaotel.

He was writing, his head bowed over his desk, and he didn't immediately look up as they entered.

That was, she was positive, purposeful. It gave the impression that he was the one who was going to control this conversation, not any interloper stepping into his space.

Best to be straightforward with this one.

Vaughn folded his arms across his chest. "All right, Yaotel. We're here."

Yaotel ignored him for one more moment, and then set

down his pen and looked up at them.

Ivana blinked.

She recognized him. It was the eunuch from Gan Pywell's harem.

Well. Apparently not.

And as his gaze fell on her, the slight twitch of his eyebrow and surprise on his face told her he recognized her as well.

"You," Yaotel said, rising from his chair immediately. "How did you—where—?" He fell silent, staring at Ivana with furrowed brow, mind obviously working furiously.

And then his face contorted unpleasantly.

Vaughn hadn't known what to expect, but it hadn't been that.

Ivana lifted her chin and met his gaze coolly.

They stood like that for a moment, staring at each other, Yaotel clenching and unclenching his fists in turn, before finally he rubbed his hand over his mouth and sat back down again.

Vaughn had never seen him in such a state. "Uh...do you two know each other?"

Yaotel ignored him. "Well," he said, leaning back in his chair and putting his hands behind his head, the momentary loss of control now surmounted. "Well, well, well. It appears our friend had help."

Vaughn raised an eyebrow and glanced at Ivana. That didn't sound encouraging.

But Ivana remained motionless and impassive.

Yaotel spoke again, addressing Vaughn, but didn't look at

him. "Vaughn, I cannot believe even you would bring an assassin here."

Vaughn choked back a reply. It hadn't been a question, after all, and he wasn't going to confirm anything until Ivana did.

"Hmmm," Yaotel said, eyes flicking toward Vaughn at last, and then back to Ivana. "Well. This changes things." He stood up, rounded his desk, and perched on the edge. Despite his regained calm demeanor, his eyes were hard. "I was going to give you the details of the unfortunate circumstance that you've found yourself in, but perhaps we can come to a better arrangement. Having someone like you around could be useful, if you're willing to play." He raised an eyebrow.

Ivana stirred at last, a frown touching her lips. She met Yaotel's eyes, unflinching. "I accept payment in one way for my services. Coin."

Yaotel returned her frown, and Vaughn jiggled his foot a little. *Come on, Ivana. Don't be so stubborn.* It sounded like Yaotel might be willing to let her go, if she offed a few people for him.

"Besides," Ivana continued, and then paused to sit down in the chair across from Yaotel's desk, uninvited. She mimicked Yaotel's pose from earlier, hands folded behind her head. "I'm taking a break." And then she propped her feet up on Yaotel's desk.

Yaotel gave her a once-over, eyebrow raised. "Have it your way," he said, returning to his chair. "Very well, *Ivana.* You now have the privilege of being the indefinite guest of Gan Barton."

It was Ivana's turn to raise an eyebrow. "Gan Barton? The most outspoken opponent of the Anti-Sedationists?"

"I see you know your politics. I'm sure you also know that

there's nothing more satisfying than hiding from your enemies in plain sight, yes?"

"Barton is a Banebringer?"

Yaotel's mouth turned downward at the use of the term Banebringer, but he shook his head. "No. But a generous sympathizer."

Ivana was still for a moment, and then inclined her head. "I honestly would never have guessed."

"And neither would lesser men—or women. Gan Barton contributes a significant amount toward the expense of running this place—not to mention board in the basement of his rather large manor."

"A mere seventy-five miles from the capital," Ivana murmured. "You have balls."

A wry look passed over Yaotel's face. "I can assure you, they are quite intact."

Vaughn was thoroughly confused by this exchange. They obviously had met, but *how*?

Yaotel picked up his pen and tapped it on the desk. "I am sure you have already guessed the delicate nature of our situation here, and therefore I'm sure you understand why it is we cannot let you go. I have no reason to trust you, and in fact, every reason not to." His eyes narrowed. "Especially knowing that you might sell your services to the highest bidder."

"I would think less of you if you did trust me," She put her feet down and leaned toward the desk. "As long as you understand that I *will* escape, eventually."

"And if you're caught, I'll have you executed," Yaotel said calmly.

"Then I'd best not get caught," Ivana returned, without missing a beat.

"Do I need to keep you locked up? I had intended to give you freedom to go where you please within the common areas of our compound."

"Oh, don't worry. I won't be planning an escape any time soon. Like I said, I'm taking a break. But I'll be sure to let you know when I'm thinking of it. Wouldn't want it to be *too* easy."

Yaotel regarded her silently for a moment, and when he spoke next, his voice bordered on dangerous. "Let us be clear. I don't trust you. I don't like you. If you give me an excuse to get rid of you, I will take it without hesitation. In fact, the only reason I haven't already done so is because Linette would have my head, and I need my bindbloods cooperative." He glanced at Vaughn. "And Vaughn, for whatever misguided reason, seems to trust you."

Ivana said nothing.

Then Yaotel turned to Vaughn. "I want you to know that I hold you directly responsible for anything our uninvited guest does."

Vaughn rolled his eyes. "I figured as much."

"I'd recommend bedding her as soon as possible. That way I can be sure you'll no longer be a potential ally, and you'll be off the hook."

It wasn't the first time someone had repeated back to him the stark reality of his own casual encounters with women, but for some reason, this time, he found himself fighting back the urge to argue. Instead, he shrugged. "Can't say I haven't tried," he said, feigning a nonchalance he didn't feel.

Ivana stood up. "If you two assholes are finished, I have things to do."

"Like stare at the paint on your wall?" Yaotel asked.

"No," Ivana said, giving Yaotel a wicked smile. "Like make other allies." And without even a glance at Vaughn or asking permission from Yaotel, she left the room.

Yaotel didn't stop her. Instead he raised an eyebrow at Vaughn. "I think perhaps you've taken on more than you can handle this time."

To the abyss with him. "She doesn't need a handler," Vaughn said.

And then he left.

Chapter Twenty-Four

Monsters at the Wall

Vaughn spent the next three days pounding his head on the wood of the table in the back room of the library. Sometimes literally.

At first, he assumed he had forgotten more than he had thought. It had been a long time ago, after all, that a childhood tutor had taught him a bit of Xambrian. But after three days, he was beginning to suspect a different cause for his frustration. It simply wasn't possible that he didn't recognize *any* of it. Surely the word for 'god' or some other common word he could remember would have shown up, yet nothing stood out.

After dinner on the third day, he needed a break—and a new tactic. He picked up the book he had been flipping through, tucked it under his arm, and headed toward the research wing.

It was a slim chance, but that woman had started this. Maybe she could help him finish it. Had anyone even tried to *talk* to her?

The researchers eyed him as he strode down the hallway, but no one stopped him. It wasn't as if only certain people were allowed in this area. It was simply that those who didn't need to go here, didn't.

When he reached the room that housed the woman, he stopped and peeked into the window. She was sitting on a cot that someone had kindly provided, head leaned back against the wall, eyes closed. He wondered wryly who had lost the draw to be the one to have to lug a cot in there.

He stopped a middle-aged researcher walking by. "Excuse me," he said, and then searched for a name. He didn't know the researchers well. "Airec, is it?"

The researcher nodded in confirmation.

"Is there a way I can talk to her?" Vaughn pointed at the woman.

Airec looked at him like he was crazy. "She doesn't talk." He started to turn away, as if that resolved the problem.

Vaughn *knew* that wasn't true. "Are you sure?" Vaughn asked. "I mean, has anyone tried?"

Airec hesitated. "I guess when they first brought her here," he said. "But she was more interested in fighting than talking." He frowned. "The only way you could talk to her would be to go in there, and we only do that if it's an absolute necessity."

Vaughn held up his book, letting it fall open to a random page. "See this?"

Airec stared at it. "Uh..."

"Recognize any of it?"

"No."

"Right, well neither do I. I'm about to gouge my own eyes out, and it's possible this woman might be able to help me. I'm getting desperate."

Airec glanced down the hall, as if longing to escape from this, and then sighed. "All right. But I wouldn't go in defenseless. Wait here."

He disappeared into a door across the way, and then came back out with a full syringe a few minutes later.

Vaughn took it delicately. "What's this?" he asked suspiciously.

"A normal sedative, extra strength. If she gets too close, plunge it in anywhere. It won't last long, but it'll put her to sleep almost immediately." He held up a finger as Vaughn tucked the syringe into the inside pocket of his jacket. "Careful. It'd kill you."

He moved over to the window. "I'll stay here and keep watch. Just don't take long. I have things to do."

Vaughn nodded his thanks, took a deep breath, and slipped into the room. He patted the bulge on his jacket to reassure himself.

The woman opened her eyes as he stepped in, and he froze, holding his hands out in what he hoped was a reassuring manner. "I'm not going to hurt you," he said. "Please. I want to talk."

To his relief, she didn't move toward him, but her eyes never left him either.

He held open the book like he had for the researcher. "Do you recognize this?"

She didn't even look at the book. Just stared at him.

All right. He had been reaching. He closed the book and tried again. Maybe she would *tell* him what they wanted to know. "Why can't you be Sedated?"

At the word Sedated, her face changed from impassive to hostile. Vaughn backed toward the door, but it was a good sign. It meant she *did* understand some of what he was saying. "Please stay calm," he said. "I'm like you. I understand."

A hiss left her mouth. "You're nothing like me," she said. Her voice was low and raspy, as if from disuse, which he supposed made sense.

He dared a glance back at the researcher, who was watching through the window. He seemed faintly surprised, but Vaughn doubted he could hear what was being said—only noted that she had moved her lips to speak.

The woman hadn't moved, but she was watching Vaughn with naked enmity.

"I'm not your enemy," he said quietly.

She laughed, and the only word to describe the sound was crazed. Just like her.

"Everyone is my enemy," she whispered. "Everyone." Something akin to despair flashed across her eyes—making her seem, for a moment, almost human. Then it disappeared, and she started rocking back and forth. "Everyone. Everyone. Everyone. Everyone..."

She kept muttering the word, and Vaughn was at a loss. Whatever momentary lucidity she had displayed was gone.

He tried again. "What is your name?"

She stopped muttering and recoiled farther against the wall.

"You'd like to know, wouldn't you?"

He breathed out slowly. She was growing tense, and he had the instinctive feeling that if he didn't wrap this up soon, she was going to attack him.

"All right. Forget the name. Can you tell me what happened to you?"

She hissed again. "You," she said. "You. All of them. All of you! You think you'll stop me." She laughed. "I dare you. I dare you!" And then her posture changed, from merely tense to a wildcat about to spring.

That was it. Vaughn felt for the doorknob, backed through it, and slammed it shut just as she lunged for him.

Airec hurried over to lock it again. Vaughn rested his head against the door, heart pounding. He retrieved the syringe from his jacket with sweaty palms and handed it back to the researcher. He could hear her thrashing about inside the room, and he dared to peek through the window. She was throwing herself against the wall, shrieking.

"I told you it was pointless," Airec said.

"But she talked to me. For a moment, I think she was even coherent."

Airec shook his head. "Did it do any good? No. Not worth the trouble, that's what I say." He shook his head and hurried away.

Vaughn stared numbly through the window and flinched back when the woman picked up the cot and hurled it toward the window at him.

The window was too small for her to squeeze through, thankfully, and he assumed if she could rip apart the walls—designed to withstand some of the worst bloodbane—she would have done so already.

But what about the bugs? Why hadn't she simply called a swarm of wasps, or the like, to torture her captors into letting her go?

He swallowed. Maybe the researcher was right. Maybe they *should* execute her, deal with whatever monster her death generated, and be done with it.

But as he stared at her, he couldn't help but feel sorry for her. Maybe the Conclave's attempts at Sedation had damaged her mind, even if it hadn't suppressed her abilities.

And even though the conversation hadn't exactly been helpful, he was more convinced than ever that they might be able to get something out of her, if they could only figure out how to approach her.

He stared forlornly down at his book. It wasn't like this book was helping.

At that moment, the alarm bells started ringing. He looked toward the woman instinctively, but she was back on the cot, crouched on all fours, eyes half-shut.

Researchers poked their heads out of their doors, some curious, some alarmed. Vaughn started back down the hall; perhaps Ivana had managed to escape after all. He hadn't seen or spoken to her since she had left Yaotel's office; he had no idea what she had been up to.

But when he reached the main hallway, it was clear that something bigger was happening.

"Vaughn!" Someone shouted his name from down the hall, and he spun. It was Hueil.

"Monsters at the wall," Hueil panted when he reached

Vaughn. "Yaotel needs you, now, in the courtyard."

Monsters? *Plural?* Since when did bloodbane outright attack the wall? Sure, they had a stray here or there that had followed a horse or the smell of carrion that some wild dog left nearby, but...

He hurried back to his room to retrieve his bow and arrows.

A quarter of the ragtag assortment of men and women who passed for soldiers had gathered in the courtyard by the time Vaughn arrived. Yaotel was there, barking orders, as well as a few sentries on the walls, shooting into the darkness.

They were no disciplined military unit; Vaughn didn't need orders to know what to do. Yaotel nodded to him once, and he bypassed those standing around their formidable leader, mostly men with close combat weapons of various sorts. He knew from experience that they were the reserve. Banebringers didn't engage bloodbane close if it could be helped; dying attempting to kill one monster only to spawn one that might be worse in its place was no help to anyone.

In a reversal of normal combat, he was the front line—he and anyone who was skilled with a ranged weapon. Unfortunately for them all, it was beyond dark outside the dim ring of light that the courtyard provided. The sky was overcast, and even though the moon was still half full, it was hidden, along with any stars. But the darkness was no enemy to Vaughn; his eyes immediately adjusted, and he could see the bloodbane clearly. There were, indeed, more than one: three, to be exact, all bloodwolves.

And they were hurling themselves against the walls. It was an eerily familiar image, considering the behavior of the crazed woman earlier. The walls held for now, but he could feel them vibrate as the gigantic beasts rammed them in concert. The walls were meant to discourage the roaming monster from getting too close to the manor, as well as to keep curious eyes at bay. But they weren't designed to withstand a concerted attack. The bloodwolves could breach them with enough effort and time, and Vaughn didn't intend to give them that time.

He glanced down the wall. The sentries, naturally, were having trouble hitting the wolves; one managed an arrow into the hindquarter of one wolf, but that only enraged it further. Unless there was another moonblood on duty, he was the only one up here that could see well enough to hit a target. And he was the *only* moonblood among the Ichtaca who could hit a target without fail regardless of the amount of daylight.

He hurried down the wall so that he was standing right over the spot where the wolves were attacking, set an arrow to his bow, and loosed it directly downward.

It pierced the skull of one of the bloodwolves. It yelped, stumbled backwards, and then lay on the ground, twitching.

The other two wolves howled and renewed their attack with vigor. He loosed another arrow, and a second wolf went down.

He reached for a third arrow, and then frowned when he didn't feel the distinctive feathering of the aether-enhanced arrows. He glanced down at his quiver.

Damn. He was out of them. He hadn't even thought to restock when he returned.

He loosed a third, normal arrow, but it was in vain. It

skimmed off the thick hide of the wolf with hardly a scratch.

He turned and shouted to the nearest archer. "I need aether arrows!" The man shook his head and pointed to the ground. The earth was littered with missed arrows; all of them expended on a target the sentries had no hope of hitting in the dark.

There was a crack, and then a hiss of rubble as the wolf made some headway on damaging the wall. He cursed again and ran back down the stair to the courtyard, to be met by another man bearing a quiver of arrows. He traded it for Vaughn's own useless one and ran off.

Vaughn was about to head back up to the wall, when he saw that the wolf had moved to the gate, presumably so it could see where Vaughn went.

They might be vicious, but they weren't exactly intelligent.

It was snapping and snarling at the group standing just inside the bars, where one man was attempting in vain to engage it through the gate with his longsword.

Vaughn set an arrow as he ran, and then stepped right up to the gate and loosed an arrow through the bars directly into the wolf's open mouth.

It fell, and a cheer went up.

Vaughn slung his bow onto his back and turned. Yaotel was already issuing commands. "Get those things in here and burned," he shouted. "And gather up every arrow. Quickly!" The gates were cracked opened and a group scurried through to carry out Yaotel's orders.

While the monsters would have been deadly had they breached the walls, the real danger was an event like this drawing the attention of someone it shouldn't. There weren't supposed to be scores of extra people living here, certainly not taking down monsters with such ease.

There needed to be no evidence that anything unusual had happened in the morning.

Vaughn went out with the group, helping find the arrows that had been lost. He met Yasril, an older moonblood, working with the group. "Nice work," Yasril said as they searched together in the dark.

Vaughn grunted. The bow was as natural to him as using his own arm to reach out and grab something. As the third-born son, he had been destined to take his turn in the United Setanan army as an officer over archers, and his father would have rather gone to the abyss than see his son anything less than the best among the other noble's sons.

Yasril, unfortunately, couldn't hit a ten-foot tree trunk if it were five feet from his face, even though Vaughn had tried to teach him. His arm shook wildly every time he tried to draw the string; even strength training had done no good. Linette said there was something wrong with it, but Yasril wouldn't speak of what that might be.

"That all of them?" The voice of Hueil spoke from behind.

Together, Yasril and Vaughn scanned the area. "Don't see any more," Vaughn said, and Yasril nodded his agreement.

"All right. Head back in. We can do a second sweep in the morning."

They nodded and followed the party back through the gates.

"I wonder what all that was about?" Yasril asked before they parted ways.

Now that he had time to think, Vaughn was asking himself

the same question. Bloodwolves, attacking the manor directly? And three? Unlike normal wolves, bloodwolves didn't hunt in packs; they were isolated and were more likely than not to tear out each other's throats if they ran across each other. And yet here, three had been working together.

It was as strange as the two attacks he and Ivana had survived in the woods.

But, just like the book and the woman, Vaughn had no answers.

Chapter Twenty-Five

Xambrian

Vaughn groaned when he woke and rolled over the next morning to see the book, which he had tossed aside in his room the night before, open and staring him in the face from his bedside table.

He sat up, picked it up, and stared at the meaningless words one more time, as if his lack of knowledge would suddenly disappear. He shook his head. He was going to have to tell Yaotel that he couldn't do it. Whatever language this was, it wasn't Xambrian, regardless of the script. And since he was the only one here who could read the Xambrian script, no one else would be able to tell him what language it *was*.

He set the book back down, got up, and picked up the trousers he hadn't worn or washed since he had arrived here. They stank, and he was going to have to have them burned. But a hard lump in the pocket pressed into his hand when he picked them up, and he fished out a tiny leather pouch. He stared at it. He had completely forgotten about the note to Ivana.

Which had been written in Xambrian.

Ivana was washing her face in the wash basin, not even out of the dressing gown she wore to cover the more comfortable nightclothes she had procured as soon as she figured out who to ask, when there was a knock on the door.

She pulled the gown closer around herself, tied it around her waist, and answered the door. It was Vaughn.

She rolled her eyes, left the door open, and went back to the basin. She had wondered how long it was going to take him to come bother her. She had lain low the past few days, trying to seem inconspicuous and unthreatening.

It was, of course, working. She doubted anyone she had spoken to other than Yaotel would guess what she really was, nor that she had any capability of finding her way out of here without being caught.

Those she interacted with had fallen into three groups. There were those who were obviously suspicious and kept their distance. Then there was the large group of those who were curious, and once they worked up the nerve to talk to her, were easily convinced that she was as innocent as their favorite sister. The third group was the hardest; a handful of the Banebringers had treated her with outright disdain. Based on some of the talk she had overheard, she gathered it was because they thought she was lesser than them; the group was led by a man named Perth.

But it had amused her more than anything else. However much commoners complained about the greed of their rulers, the propensity toward the lust for power and status was common to those born high and low. Most commoners, despite their mostly legitimate gripes, would trade their lives with the same people they spoke out against in a heartbeat, and not for some selfless reason like bettering the lot of their friends, either.

Vaughn was now standing in the doorway, watching her in the mirror as she was watching him. His dark eyes studied her face, and then flicked down to the V of skin from throat to midchest that her dressing gown left bare, causing a spasm of longing to shoot through her.

Annoyed, she dried her face on a towel and turned around. "Did you need something, or did you come to gawk?" she snapped.

He shifted. "How's your leg?"

"Fine," she said, though it still hurt some. She had seen the wound, and while it was much better, it would take time to fully heal.

"Haven't seen much of you. I thought maybe you still needed to rest."

She walked over to the chest of meager possessions she had collected in three days, some legitimately, and some not, and found a comfortable set of clothes.

"You're still limping."

"How observant of you." She had tried not to think about

that. She knew it was possible she would always have a slight limp; she hadn't gone back to the bindbloods to ask. If that was going to be the case, so be it. If not, she'd know soon enough.

He frowned. "Linette says you're lucky they didn't have to amputate it. That's what she first thought when they saw how bad it was." He paused, as if waiting for her to respond, and when she didn't, he went on. "Then she thought you might not be able to walk again without a cane. But apparently the salve I put on it helped to knit the essentials back together well enough, even if it didn't stop the infection."

"Are you trying to get me to express gratitude? Because if so, you have it, such as it is. Is there anything else you needed?"

He shook his head, sighed, and held out the book. "You said your father was a highly educated tutor."

She looked at the proffered book, but didn't take it. "Yes."

"Did he happen to teach you other languages?"

She turned away to lay the clothes out on her bed. "He was more of a science person," she said.

The disappointment in Vaughn's voice was evident. "Oh. I see."

"My skill with languages came from my mother." She turned around to look at him, leaned back against the bed, and folded her arms.

Learn to express yourself well, Ivana, her mother had said once, *"and you'll make something of yourself. Learn to communicate with others in their own tongue, and you'll have their respect as well."*

Ironic that all that knowing those languages had attained for her was the ability to hire herself out to people other than native Setanans, something other Setanan assassins had trouble doing.

Vaughn's eyes lit up. "So you know more than Setanan?"

"Yes."

He held out the book again. "Could you look at this and tell me if you recognize it?"

She hesitated. She wasn't keen on continuing this trajectory with him; he had seen and knew too much of her as it was. But now that her mother's voice was in her head, it was hard to ignore it.

"You can't truly call yourself fluent in another language if you haven't learned about the people who speak it."

Her mother's words would be considered borderline heretical by the Conclave. Pagans spoke other languages, not loyal Setanans. Ivana now supposed that was because the Conclave knew her mother was right, and if there was one thing the Conclave couldn't have, it was people empathizing with those from other lands.

The few foreigners allowed into Setana, mostly for trade, were expected to speak fluent and unaccented Setanan. It was the only way they were allowed to do business here.

She took the book from him and opened it to the first page. The fastest way to get rid of him was to do what he asked. "Xambrian," she said without hesitation. The sharp, square script was unmistakable, all corners and squat little letters as flat and stocky as the strange northerners who spoke it.

To her surprise, Vaughn nodded without questioning her. "That's what I thought, too. Do you speak it?"

"I understand enough to get by."

He gestured to the book. "Try reading it."

She decided to humor him. She glanced down at the page and scanned it. She frowned and flipped to the next page, and then the next.

"I take it back. This isn't Xambrian," she said after about a minute. "It's their script, but not their language."

Vaughn shook his head. "Took me three days to come to that conclusion," he muttered. "I thought I was just stupid."

She raised an eyebrow. "*You* know Xambrian?"

He shrugged and looked away. "Enough to tell that this isn't it."

Curious. "I didn't know language study was on the approved list of courses for noble sons to take."

"It's not."

She raised an eyebrow, and he ran a hand through his hair, looking embarrassed. "When I was fifteen—right after my father, uh, became Ri, my old tutor left our service. My father hired a new one right away. I liked him. He told stories of what seemed to me to be exotic lands and their people—stories that I'm sure were strictly forbidden. But I was interested. So he offered to teach me a little Xambrian, since Xambria was a place he had often visited. It took six months for my father to find out. So ended my language studies."

Ivana set the book down on her bedside table. "What happened to your tutor?"

"He was released from our service." He walked over to the table and tapped one finger on the book. "So it doesn't make any sense to you?"

It was the first time he had tried anything resembling dissimilation with her, and she knew immediately that he was hedging the truth. "Your father had him arrested, didn't he?" Which probably also meant he had been executed. The Conclave took heresy seriously.

Vaughn flipped open the book again and ran a finger over one of the pages. "I think it was the first time I saw my father for what he really was, even if I didn't want to admit it at the time," he said softly, as if to himself. "So it doesn't make any sense to you?" he asked again.

She let the subject drop and instead turned back to the open page. She tried reading it again, but it might as well have been nonsense. "*D'nath qitanah reganthin...*" she read out loud, trying a different tactic. She paused. *That* had been vaguely familiar. She turned the book around so she could see it more clearly and read a few more words, mouthing the sounds as she went. It took a few minutes to work out the sentence, but by the end she was sure, even though it seemed impossible.

"Burning skies," she said softly.

"What?" Vaughn asked, stepping closer to look down at the book, as if to see what she saw. "What is it?"

"It's native Fereharian."

Vaugh stood in silence for a moment. "I thought Fereharian had no written form."

Once again, she was surprised he would know that. "It doesn't. It didn't..." She shook her head, amazed. "But if I'm right..." She picked up the book and sank into the chair nearby, running her finger over the next sentence. "It's not easy to decipher," she said. "I'm fluent in native Fereharian, but I've never seen it in written form." She paused to sound out some more words. "And it's been transliterated into Xambrian, of all scripts, which makes it even more difficult. There are so many Xambrian letters that don't have a one-to-one correlation to Fereharian sounds. Is there a pattern to the way the scribe transliterated it? Was he consistent with his endings?" She stabbed at a word she had just read. "Look, there. I'm fairly certain that's the word for god—*d'nath*—which is a first declension noun, but here it has the feminine ending you would normally expect on a fourth declension noun. Is that a mistake? Was he trying to say goddess and didn't know Fereharian well enough to differentiate? Or is it something else?" She pointed again. "There it is again, with what I think is the right feminine ending..." She trailed off staring at the page, eyes skipping around, mind racing. It was hard to tell. After all, she was only one of a handful of people she knew of who had even thought to categorize Fereharian that way, since it wasn't written.

Vaughn hadn't said a word for the past few minutes, and she realized she had been rambling out loud. She looked up at him. He was staring at her, not as if she were crazy, as she might have thought, but as if he were seeing her in a way he had never seen her before.

That was because he hadn't. She pressed a hand to the page. This was dangerous. It brought back a part of her life she had long buried, long forgotten. A part she would rather leave in the dark.

She shut the book and stood up. She handed it back to him. "There's your answer." She picked up the trousers she had laid on the bed. "Now if you'll excuse me, I'd like to change into something more appropriate."

"Wait," he said, putting a hand on her arm. "You mean to tell me you could actually translate this?"

She shrugged. "Maybe. With enough time and effort." But why would she want to? She glanced at the book. Aside from that accursed awakened part of her that longed to do something that gave her back a little of the life she had left so long ago.

Back when she knew what it was to feel.

Why did some part of her want that again? Feeling brought nothing but pain.

"Help me," he said. "Please. If you refresh my memory of Xambrian, I'm sure I could be of some use. I don't know Fereharian, but maybe I can transliterate for you back into the common script, so it will be easier for you to translate and see patterns."

Yes, that forgotten part of her cried. "Why?"

He let his hand slide from her arm and ran it through his hair instead. "These are fairly recent acquisitions. Yaotel is under the impression they may have some important information in them. I'm the only person here who has any knowledge of Xambrian, and he thought I could translate it. I know now that I can't."

She paused. "What sorts of things?"

Vaughn told her about the crazy woman, about everything Yaotel had said, about the researcher's discoveries, and about what he had seen through the strange device.

"You have a microscope?" she asked when he had finished.

"What?"

"A microscope. The device you mentioned."

"I don't know. I've never seen one before." She had?

"They're a fairly new invention. My father had one he made himself," she said, eyes growing distant again, like they had a few minutes ago. "But we looked at blood once. It didn't look like what you describe. Even without the...aether."

Vaughn shrugged. "I don't know. They say they got it a few months ago and made some enhancements." He tried to bring her back from wherever she had drifted to. "So will you help? If there's anything in those books that might make the connection, we have to find it." He was still doubtful as to whether there was, but the thought of sitting and working through them side-by-side with Ivana made the task more appealing.

Or perhaps it was the thought that if his father knew, he would be horrified. And that filled Vaughn with a sense of satisfaction he rarely felt when thinking of his father.

Ivana was hesitating. He didn't know why. He had seen the spark in her eyes a few minutes ago, when she had started rambling about the language of the book. Had even heard genuine excitement and wonder in her voice. She had closed herself off as soon as she realized what had happened, just like before, back in the safe house, but why wouldn't she want that? Did she *like* being cold and detached about everything?

"It'll be fun," he added, flashing her a hopeful smile.

Her jaw clenched. Finally, she shook her head. "This isn't my problem."

He slumped physically, as if to match the crestfallen feeling inside. But he could hardly force her.

"What gave you the idea that I might know Xambrian in the

first place? Because my father was a tutor?" She raised an eyebrow to emphasize her doubt.

He withdrew the pouch from his pocket, where he had stowed it when he left his room, and handed it to her. "I'm sorry I didn't give this to you earlier, but I forgot until this morning. It...came...while we were in the safe house. When you were delirious."

She uncinched the leather to reveal the pendant and the note inside. She fastened the pendant back around her neck without a word and pressed out the note on her bedside table.

She read silently, and then looked up and stared at the wall. "I've changed my mind," she said softly. "I'll help you."

Relief flooded through him, but also confusion. "What? Why? I mean—"

"It doesn't matter," she said. She glanced at the book as she turned away from him, as if meeting an old friend after some years. An old friend that she had parted with on poor terms. It was the first time he had seen her masks slide so obviously.

He knew better than to press her. "When can we start? Do you need to eat?"

"I need to *dress*," she said.

He grinned, feeling reckless by his success, and let his eyes slide again to the bronzed skin at the point of her dressing gown, only the slightest dip hinting at what might be beneath. "Don't let me stop you."

She frowned at him, and, taking the hint, he turned to the door. "I'll meet you in the dining hall," he said. "And I'll show you where I've been working."

Chapter Twenty-Six

Just Ivana

Ivana frowned at the word in front of her and tried sounding the vowels out a different way in her head, emphasizing different syllables in turn. Finally, she shook her head. She simply didn't recognize the word. "Vaughn," she said.

Vaughn looked up from his place across the table, where he was diligently transliterating Xambrian into the Setanan alphabet.

She spun the sheet of paper around and pointed to the word. "What is that supposed to be?"

He looked at it, flipped back a page in the book, found the word with his finger, and then looked back at the transliteration. "Tlaxchali? Isn't that what I wrote?"

"Let me see it." She slid the book from under his hands and looked at the Xambrian herself. She immediately saw the problem. "You mixed up two letters," she said.

"What? I didn't!"

She pointed out the offending letter. It had two vertical short legs and a long horizontal line joining them across the top, like the profile of a squat table. "See how the ends of the line stick out a tad beyond the legs? You transliterated it as though it were *this* letter." She pointed to another example, which looked almost identical, except that said line didn't stick out. "They're completely different letters."

Vaughn raised an eyebrow, grinning. "Legs?"

She felt herself flush, and she frowned, mostly because he had caught her unguarded. "Don't be an ass. It looks like a table. Would you pay attention?"

He looked back and forth between the letters. "Damn," he said. "You're right. I did mix them up."

"Aren't you using the chart we made?"

He wrinkled his nose, looking sheepish, and shuffled aside a few papers to produce the phonetic chart they had made five days ago, the first task Ivana had insisted on. "I haven't needed it," he said. "I thought I had it down. Why'd they have to make two letters that sound so different look so similar?"

She shook her head. "I don't know." She cast him a dangerous glance, daring him to make fun of her again. "But if you think of it as a *table*, there's an easy way to remember. Table equals the sound *tch*. If it doesn't look like a table, it's *xch*."

"Table equals *tch*, no table equals *xch*," he repeated.

She raised an eyebrow at him.

"What?"

"Say that again."

"Table equals *tch*, no table equals *xch*?"

She burst out laughing. She couldn't help herself. Admittedly, the latter was a difficult sound to make, as it didn't exist in Setanan, but still...

"What's so funny?"

"You sound like a cat about to vomit."

"It's a strange sound!" he protested, his own face reddening now.

She shook her head, still smiling, corrected the word, and moved on.

Truth be told, he had surprised her, and she was rarely surprised by anything. The ease with which he had adjusted to polishing rusty language skills was remarkable, considering the difficulties of the first day. The mix-up was an honest mistake, especially since scribes weren't always careful to distinguish the two letters exactly when writing quickly; just like any language, it didn't usually matter because a person's knowledge of the vocabulary and normal sentence structure was enough to cover ambiguities.

His presence was, to her shock, actually useful. As soon as he felt comfortable with Xambrian again, his transliterations became faster. He had even devised his own system of symbols to mark up his copies, noting where words seemed off, or inconsistent, simply based on spelling.

And there were a lot of mistakes and inconsistencies on the part of whomever had written the book that caused no amount of consternation in the process of translating, but Vaughn's eye for patterns was quickly making the task less tedious.

If she were honest with herself, which she was loathe to be on this point, she found herself enjoying and even looking forward to the time she spent each day working in the library, and not least because Vaughn's constant company wasn't as bad as she had imagined it would be. He had been useful, generally pleasant, and it soon became clear that they shared a common interest.

She felt almost as if she were Ivana again, when she was with him. Just Ivana.

There is no difference. Isn't that what you told him?

It was a dangerous feeling, and she shoved it away, concentrating on her translation.

The smile Ivana had worn a moment ago had punched a hole straight through Vaughn's gut. It was the first time he had seen such a genuine expression from her, let alone heard her laugh like that, and he found himself watching her, hoping to see it again.

But her smile had faded, replaced by the tiny creases in her brow that he now recognized as meaning she was lost in her work.

He took the opportunity of her inattention toward him to study her further.

There was something about this entire process of translating that had relaxed her. The cold mask she usually wore around him had slowly slipped, replaced by one that was, if not completely open, a little less guarded.

His eyes rested on her lips, and the ache started again. Gods, she was exquisite.

"Is there a reason you're not working?" she asked without looking up.

He looked away before she noticed the focus of his eyes. Dare he tell her the truth? "I was thinking about how that's the first time I've seen you really smile," he responded.

The scratching of her pen stopped, and the pen hovered over the paper momentarily before starting again. "Perhaps you should focus on the task at hand," she said.

He ignored her. "Is it really so bad? Letting someone see the real you?" He winced before she could even respond. The last time he had said something like that...

She finally looked up at him. "If you're finished with your work, there are other books to start on."

Her gaze was icy. *Damn.* A step too far.

He went back to his work without a word.

Another two days brought actual results.

"Who is Danathalt?" Ivana asked a short time into the morning session.

"Danathalt? What's the context?"

Ivana scanned over the transliteration Vaughn had provided, and then her translation. "He's a god, I think."

Vaughn frowned, sorting through everything they thought they knew about the heretic gods, and then finally shook his head. "I don't think I've ever heard of that one."

"Don't you know all of them?"

"Not a chance. So far we've found references to over two dozen gods in the pantheon and another half dozen that *might* be gods, but then again, might be some sort of other supernatural creature or being. We don't know all of their names, and not all of them appear to be associated with Banebringers."

She tilted her head, studying him. "How do you know your particular connections to the gods, then?"

"We guess. I'm one of the lucky ones, if you want to count knowing the name of the god who cursed me as lucky. We have an almost complete myth about Thaxchatichan, the goddess of the moon."

She had stopped writing and looked cautiously intrigued. "What's the story?"

Vaughn wrinkled his nose. "Uh, I don't know, something about how she murdered her brother's wife, and, outraged, her brother chopped off her head and threw it into the sky, where it became the moon."

Ivana raised an eyebrow. "How pleasant."

"You have no idea." The stories they had about the heretic gods were grisly. They were always fighting amongst themselves, starting wars, murdering each other, using each other's blood and body parts in gruesome ceremonies...it was no wonder the Conclave's pantheon was so readily accepted. They were much tamer.

Except when it came to their apparent unanimous hatred of Banebringers, that is.

"How does she create her Banebringers? Wouldn't she be dead?"

"Can't believe everything you hear," Vaughn said, smiling.

"And yet there may be truth to some of it."

He raised an eyebrow. "I wouldn't have taken you as religious."

She snorted. "Only if 'religious' means knowing that whatever gods there are, I'll be living in the darkest corner of their version of damnation."

The matter-of-fact statement jarred him. He didn't think much about life after this one. As a Banebringer, he was automatically barred from whatever happy place existed for pious servants of the Conclave's gods, so what did it matter? The Ichtaca always joked about how they were all destined for the abyss. But she was serious.

He shifted, unsure of how to respond. "So what does the book say about this...Danathalt?" he asked, changing the subject.

"Not sure yet," she said. "The content has finally changed. I think we're about to get a myth, instead of religious drivel. I'll tell you when I have more." She went back to her translating.

In the seven days they had been working, she had translated about half of the first book. They hadn't discovered anything profoundly new; the first part had been old hymns, some of which they had copies of in other sources. Then there were the elaborate descriptions of religious rituals, complete with the exact measure of every grain of barley—and drop of blood from what animal—to bring to sacrifices and feasts. Some of the precise vocabulary had tripped even Ivana up, who seemed to have a good handle on Xambrian and was fluent in Fereharian.

But myths were interesting. You had to read them through the lens of realizing that they were mostly ridiculous, of course, but Ivana was right: it was there that the secrets of Banebringers and their connection to the gods that they so desperately wanted to re-discover were buried.

Facts as simple as a name and domain could open up possibilities. They were always exploring new ways to use their powers, of course, but occasionally a myth would reveal an area to explore they hadn't even thought of. That was how they had come to invent the qixli—when they had finally linked Taniqotalin, god of the sunrise and sunset, of all things, to the Banebringers they had been calling lightbloods, for their ability to produce light at any given moment.

But they had a myth about Taniqotalin doing precisely the same thing, in an effort to win a contest with his arch-nemesis, Tiuhtanah, the goddess of warriors. But he hadn't done it to blind her, but to somehow use the light to call ahead to his own minions who were waiting in ambush for Tiuhtanah—against the rules of the contest, of course, but they were gods. Who cared about rules?

The discovery of this myth had sent a flurry of activity through the Ichtaca who had been assigned to research, and after extensive testing and months of failed experiments, they discovered that lightblood aether could also be used to communicate over long distances. Lightbloods themselves could do the same thing by burning their own blood, but only with other lightbloods, so that had limited usefulness for Banebringers as a whole.

"You sure you've never heard of Danathalt?" Ivana said after a while.

"Positive. Why?"

"If I understand all of this correctly, he's the god of the abyss. That seems pretty important."

Vaughn frowned. "God of the abyss? What's the myth?"

"He raised an army comprised of inhabitants of the abyss to march on heaven to overthrow..." She paused, mouthing sounds wordlessly for a moment. "Zilo...ziloxch...."

"Ziloxchanachi? He's the head god, in most myths." He grinned at her. "And we call him Zily for short. His name's a bitch to pronounce."

She blinked at him, as if unsure whether he was jesting or not. "Well, apparently they had a severe falling out," she said. "Do you have Banebringers who are connected to him?"

Vaughn shook his head. "Not that we know of. You'd think he'd show up more, being the head god and all, but he doesn't do an awful lot. Mostly sits around and watches the other gods kill each other. Doesn't seem to approve, but he doesn't stop it either."

"Maybe that's Danathalt's grievance."

"Maybe. It doesn't say?"

"Not that I've found yet."

"Huh." Vaughn shrugged. "Well, I don't know if that gets us too far. I don't know of any Banebringers who can summon armies of the dead."

"Not just the dead. Also monsters and other nasty creatures."

He raised an eyebrow. "Other nasty creatures?"

"Yes. You know. Insects. Spiders. Snakes. Rats." She grimaced. "Everyone knows those come from the abyss."

Vaughn blinked. "Wait." He stood up, rounded the table, and leaned over to see her translation. "Insects and rats? It says that?" He didn't wait for an answer. He read her translation himself, out loud.

"*And so Danathalt summoned to himself the inhabitants of the abyss*

Discontent souls by hundreds, seeking revenge

Horrors by thousands, seeking blood

Every creepy crawly creature by tens of thousands—"

He broke off, dubious. "Surely it does *not* say 'creepy crawly creature'! Are you actually trying to translate this?"

She held her hands out to the side. "Perhaps you would prefer, 'Creatures that crawl on their bellies, and with multitude of legs, every creature detestable in the eyes of mortals.' But that's awfully long-winded, don't you think? Creepy crawly is much more concise and conveys the meaning just as well."

He stared down at her. This was the second time she had revealed a whimsical side, so incongruous with everything else he knew about her. He couldn't help it: he laughed. "Well, one thing's for sure, they'll never be seeking you out as a liturgical poet."

She actually smiled again, that genuine smile he had seen a few days ago, and her eyes shone with amusement. "No, I don't imagine they will."

He grinned at her in response, and for a moment, he was certain he saw it. There wasn't a hint of Sweetblade, or Ivana the charmer, or anything else. It was just her. Ivana.

She was beautiful, and the urge to reach out and touch her lips, to feel the curve of her smile against his fingers—aw, damn, why lie to himself? against his own mouth—was so strong that he knew she could see it. He didn't care; she already knew he wanted her, but for another instant, something else flickered across her own eyes. Longing, almost thirst.

She broke the moment first, which was just as well. She probably would have stabbed him if he had kissed her.

"Is there any significance to this?" she asked, looking back down at the paper. "You seemed like you had a thought."

He retreated to his side of the table and leaned over the Xambrian-Fereharian hybrid, staring at the words, which were mostly nonsense to him.

"I don't know. Just that woman. The one we're keeping prisoner. She could summon...creepy crawlies." He flashed a smile at her, hoping to regain the comradery of earlier.

She didn't return it. "Perhaps this Danathalt is her patron."

"Perhaps. But that doesn't explain why she can't be Sedated, which is really our concern." He tapped the table a few times with his pen. "Maybe it's time to have another chat with her."

Chapter Twenty-Seven

Danathalt

Vaughn stood confined again with the crazy woman. He patted his side pocket, reassuring himself that the syringe was there. Another researcher stood at the window, fidgeting.

As before, she didn't move toward him. She merely watched him. But this time, the enmity was already in her eyes.

This may not have been a good idea. He decided to be direct. "Do you know who Danathalt is?"

If the Ichtaca hadn't known, he wasn't sure how the woman would have found out, but he wanted to see her reaction.

It was worth the risk. Her eyes widened in a human-like expression of surprise, and for an instant...hope?

And then it was gone. She sneered at him. "You think you're

clever. Naming me."

Vaughn blinked. "Naming...you?"

She laughed, high and shrill. Wild.

A prickle ran across the back of his neck. Naming her. Naming *her*. He looked at her hard, watching her eyes. They were hard, colder than he had ever seen even Ivana's. As he stared, a knowing, spine-chilling smile spread over her lips.

He took a step back toward the door. "Danathalt?" he whispered, horrified.

She laughed again. And kept laughing.

He fled the room before she could even prepare to lunge at him. As he shut and locked the door, she howled.

The researcher—he couldn't remember her name—was staring at him oddly. "What's wrong?" she asked. "You're pale."

"I need Yaotel. Now."

Yaotel stood across from Vaughn where he had found him in the hallway, arms folded and eyebrow raised. "Possessed," he stated flatly. "You think she's possessed. By a god."

"I don't know what exactly it is," Vaughn said. "But I'm telling you, it isn't natural. Somehow, he's there. Or *someone* other than her is there. Controlling her."

Yaotel glanced down the hallway. A triad of people were headed their way, talking animatedly and laughing. He took Vaughn's elbow and steered him into a nearby empty room. "Vaughn, you need to cut this out."

Vaughn's mouth dropped open. "You don't believe me."

"I believe there's something strange about that woman. But

being controlled directly by a god? And one we've never heard of? That's, frankly, crazy."

"I *told* you, I just found a myth about him in one of those books you wanted me to translate."

"Yes, I've been meaning to talk to you about that. The archivist told me your *friend* has been joining you back there."

Vaughn ran a hand through his hair. He had wondered when Yaotel would hear about that. "You told me she had to find a way to contribute, didn't you?"

Yaotel's lips pressed together. "Allowing her access to our most sensitive documents wasn't exactly what I had in mind."

If Yaotel was irritated, then so was Vaughn. What did he have against Ivana, anyway? So she was an assassin. Was that a reason to dislike her so much? "What, now that you've found them, you plan on keeping all the information to yourself? How is that better than the Conclave?"

A muscle jumped in Yaotel's cheek, and Vaughn knew he had taken it a step too far.

"Look," he said, before Yaotel could speak. "You want them translated, she's going to have to do it. It's some weird hybrid language, and I simply don't have the knowledge."

Yaotel's jaw twitched a few more times, but finally he jerked his head, which Vaughn took as reluctant acquiescence.

Vaughn steered the conversation back to the original subject. "All I know is what I told you. Danathalt is the god of the abyss. The myth indicates he can summon creatures of the abyss—which seems to include—" He broke off, choking back a laugh as he realized he had almost said "creepy crawlies." "Insects and vermin," he revised.

"I'll give you that perhaps this Danathalt is her patron, since we've never seen a profile like hers before," Yaotel said. "But possessed?"

"I don't know," Vaughn said. "I just know that she was talking like...like it wasn't actually her. And I keep getting this feeling like the real person is in there somewhere, desperate to be let out."

Yaotel grunted. "We already know she's nuts. Maybe she thinks she *is* Danathalt."

Vaughn had to admit that was a distinct possibility.

Yaotel rolled his eyes. "But I'll try talking to her myself—only because I can't ignore it. But if you want my opinion, I think spending so much time in that back room is causing you to have an over-active imagination. We've never heard of such a thing before—"

"And that's stopped us from learning new things?"

"—and more importantly, I'd rather not waste time entertaining the implications of such a thing if it all comes to naught."

Vaughn was silent. He was trying not to think about that himself. If this Danathalt could somehow control his Banebringer...why couldn't any god?

It wasn't a pleasant thought, certainly not one that Yaotel would want rumors spread about before they knew more.

"Just keep working," Yaotel said. "Right now, I'm more concerned with the Sedation angle, and this doesn't get me any closer to that."

"Unless possession by a god keeps you from being Sedated," Vaughn muttered.

Yaotel threw him a sharp look and headed back toward the research wing.

Vaughn sighed and leaned against the wall. Maybe he *was* crazy. Maybe *she* was crazier than he'd originally thought. Maybe he needed some fresh air.

Alarm bells started to ring, and he pushed himself away from the wall, startled. *Again?*

"What's with the bells?" Ivana asked, without looking up, once Vaughn had slipped back into the room.

"It means there's a threat to the compound," Vaughn said. It had been worse, this time. This time, it had been a pair of bloodhawks, who could simply fly over the walls. Fortunately, he had already re-filled his quiver with aether arrows, and while Linette and her team would be busy tending to a slew of nasty gashes for the next few hours, no one had been killed or mortally wounded. "The first time, we were attacked by three bloodwolves. This time, it was two bloodhawks."

"And this happens often?" Ivana asked.

"No. I...honestly don't know what's going on." He hesitated. It seemed coincidental that both times they had been attacked had been shortly after he had talked to the crazy woman. But was it worth mentioning?

Ivana looked up. "Spit it out."

He was apparently quite transparent. He slid into the chair across from her. "Danathalt could summon bloodbane, right?"

"I assume that's what it means by *horrors*," Ivana said. "And it's pretty well-accepted that bloodbane come from the abyss."

She raised an eyebrow at him, as if to obtain his confirmation.

He shrugged. "We haven't found anything to contradict the idea."

"So?"

"So…I wonder if the crazy woman has something to do with it. Bloodwolves are solitary, and yet they attacked in a group. Bloodhawks typically don't prey on people. A menace to livestock, but…" He rubbed his chin. "And I've *never* heard either of those monsters attacking a walled estate."

"Other monsters do?"

"Well, no, not typically for no reason. But the more overtly vicious ones might follow someone and cause trouble if they get angry enough."

"Like our friend from the city."

He shuddered, remembering that behemoth. He didn't want to think about what would happen if one of *those* showed up. It would smash their puny walls with one swing of its fist. "Yeah."

"So you think she might be summoning them."

"It's a guess."

"Why?"

That was the problem. "I don't know. To try to escape? Because I annoyed her?"

Ivana was silent for a moment, studying him. "A reasonable hypothesis, given the evidence," she said at last. "Though if she's trying to escape, she'll need more than a few monsters, it sounds like."

Vaughn shook his head. "I don't know," he said for what felt like the hundredth time that day.

"Was she the one sending monsters after us?"

Vaughn blinked. "What?"

"If your hypothesis is correct, and she's summoning monsters...could she have been sending them? It sounds like it's pretty unusual for the bloodwolf and bloodhawk that attacked us to have acted as they did as well."

He had pondered that before, but he hadn't seen that connection. "That hadn't occurred to me. But why would she do that? I was no threat to her after I was gone."

A wry smile touched the corner of Ivana's mouth. "Because you annoyed her?"

He snorted. "Always a possibility." He craned his head to look over at what she was translating. "Anything new?"

"Right now, I seem to have run across a list of epic battles between gods and their outcomes."

He wrinkled his nose. "Great." He stood up. "Well...if you don't mind, I'm exhausted. You don't have to continue without me."

She shrugged and shifted a piece of paper. "It's fine."

She said nothing else and didn't look at him again as he slipped back out of the room, wanting nothing more than to fall into bed and sleep for twelve hours straight.

When Ivana was sure Vaughn had left, she slid the note from Aleena out of her pocket and spread it out flat on the table, reading over it again.

They used Xambrian as their "code" because so few people knew it. And in the unlikely scenario that someone, first, got ahold of a message, and second, knew Xambrian well enough to decipher the contents, it probably wouldn't be someone who was going to run to the Conclave or city guard. Admitting one knew how to translate profane languages, regardless of the content of said message, was a good way to get oneself thrown into prison—or hung.

Still, that didn't mean Aleena had spelled everything out in her note. There was no reason to take chances.

Met K. Ivana assumed that meant the man she had run into, since his name was Kayden. That simple phrase meant a lot. First, it meant Aleena hadn't been captured with the rest of the girls. That didn't surprise Ivana. She had trained her well.

Second, it meant that Kayden had managed to follow her instructions and meet with Aleena. That *did* surprise her. She had expected the man to flee. That would have been the sensible course of action.

All accounted for, but not with me. No one had been killed, but they weren't with Aleena. That, too, hadn't surprised Ivana, since she knew from Tenoch that there had been no bodies, but that they had been captured. Still, it was a relief to have the information confirmed by a second source.

Don't worry about me. Got a job in a workhouse. Will look out for others until you return. In other words, she had managed to get into the workhouses under honest cover, in order to find out what had happened to the girls. This had been the chief source of relief from Aleena's note. Ivana had trained her to take over the inn if something happened to her, but with the inn and girls gone, she hadn't been sure what Aleena would do.

When Ivana had left, she had been wondering if she could trust Aleena at all.

She was gratified that she had taken it upon herself to continue working as Ivana's eyes and ears, doing exactly what Ivana would have done had she been there. In fact, she seemed to expect Ivana to return and take over. Ivana, of course, planned to do just that, as soon as she had fully recovered and formulated a plan. Of course, that was difficult when she was being held prisoner and not allowed to contact anyone on the outside.

K still around. Noble, but clever. Got me better position. So the man had been a noble—and had, incredibly, used his influence to get Aleena in deeper. Ivana assumed he had been serious about doing whatever it took to find Caira. The final part, however, had been the most shocking.

Assembly has them with the exceptional. Don't know why yet. Ivana read it for the hundredth time, trying to figure out if it could mean anything other than what it seemed to. But *assembly* was the word they used exclusively for the Conclave, partially because it was the closest translation into Xambrian of the word, and partially to keep the unlikely person who could read it from automatically knowing what they were talking about.

Tenoch had hinted that though the girls had been taken to the workhouses, they hadn't kept them there. It wasn't unusual for unwanted people to "disappear" from the workhouses. Not too many. Maybe one every six months, or so. No one other than Ivana's "type" knew or cared, of course. Why should the average person care if a beggar they didn't know existed in the first place didn't last long in the workhouses? They were a rough place.

But to this day, Ivana had never been able to discover where it was those people went. If Aleena's message was correct...

They had taken them to wherever the Conclave kept Sedated Banebringers.

Banebringers had to be Sedated, not executed, due to the practical problem of the monsters their deaths would summon. That left the problem of what to do with the hundreds—thousands, now—of Banebringers who were little more than vegetables. For the safety of everyone, or so the Conclave assured the populace at large, they were kept in an asylum somewhere. They were fed and cared for, but locked up for good. Eventually nature would take its course, since Banebringers weren't immortal, and the Conclave's cloistering away of the Sedated also ensured that no rogue bloodbane could escape when one of their charges expired.

Aleena had managed to infiltrate their ranks at least to the point that she knew where the girls were. It baffled her. Why would the Conclave need non-Banebringer nobodies in the same place they kept Sedated Banebringers? What were they doing in that fabled asylum?

One thing was certain: if there were answers to her questions, she was being held captive in the second best place to find them.

Chapter Twenty-Eight

Fire and Ichor

The next two weeks were relatively uneventful. No more attacks. No more discoveries. They had finished translating the first book and had almost finished the second. So far, nothing seemed to link the books to the pictures Dax had found on the wall.

On the fifteenth day, after lunch, Vaughn met Yaotel coming from the research wing. He gestured to Vaughn when he saw him, and Vaughn stopped.

"Just talked with the woman," Yaotel said.

About time. "And?"

"She stared at the wall," Yaotel said flatly.

Vaughn gritted his teeth. No way. He *knew* he had seen a spark of intelligence in her eyes. She might be crazy, but she wasn't *that* kind of crazy. She was baiting him.

Yaotel must have seen the expression on his face, because he shook his head. "Look, I don't doubt your story about what she said to you. The researchers confirmed that they saw her talking. But I'm of a mind to think she's just lost it."

"Maybe."

"Just keep at those books," Yaotel said. "There *must* be something there."

Vaughn stared after him. He was beginning to think Yaotel was a little over-obsessed with the books. They hadn't found anything substantial yet, and Vaughn was starting to doubt they would. He understood that Yaotel wanted to know why the woman couldn't be Sedated, but...

He turned toward the research wing to peek through the window at the woman.

As soon as he had a view, she looked directly at him and gave him a wicked smile.

Alarms started ringing.

"Bloodhawks again!" Yasril shouted, pointing into the distance

A chorus of cursing rose from those below, and Vaughn looked in the direction Yasril indicated. Sure enough, three bloodhawks were headed their way, flying close together.

He sighted the closest and then let his bow drop. They were moving strangely. Then his eyes widened. They were *carrying* something!

Yasril had seen it as well. He shouted a warning to the guards waiting in the courtyard below, and then scurried down off the wall.

Vaughn wasted no time in loosing an arrow, and then another. Two bloodhawks went down, one after the other, but the third hurtled over the wall with the arrow of another sentry in its wing. It crashed to the courtyard behind the wall and let go of its burden: bloodcrabs, one held in each claw.

As with all the names they had given bloodbane that looked anything like normal animals, "crab" was a generous term. They were so-named because their bodies were flat, circular shells, they had six or eight legs sprouting from underneath, and they tended to live near water.

But as always, that was where the resemblance stopped. It was as though someone had taken the idea of a crab and inserted it into their worst nightmare. As if a crab the size of a small bear wasn't bad enough, their legs, instead of ending in pincers, ended in sharp, needlelike protrusions that could rip a man to shreds simply by walking over him. If you got close enough to one—which wasn't a good idea—you could see its mouth, hanging open under the shell like a gaping cavern.

And as with all bloodbane, they were strong.

Vaughn had once seen one of these things pluck a fisherman from its boat with its front two legs, and then drag him screaming down into the water.

His body had never come back up—only a spreading stain of blood.

And now they were inside the wall, thanks to that bloodhawk.

He finished the bloodhawk before its fury at the injury could do any damage and turned to the bloodcrabs.

Men backed away from the monsters, and only the stupidity of the crabs kept any of them from becoming the first victim. There were only two bloodcrabs, and two dozen men—the crabs scuttled in one direction, halted, and then in another, confused by all the potential targets.

Unfortunately, all the confusion was also making it difficult for Vaughn to get a straight line of sight. The shells on those things were hard as steel, and even his aether arrows would have a hard time piercing them if he didn't place it just right. He had learned that the mouth was the best bet, but that required the crab to rear.

Which would require it to be attacking.

He was momentarily distracted by the sound of scrabbling against the wall outside. He looked down and was horrified to see the four crabs that had been dropped by the now-dead bloodhawks trying to wedge their needle-like legs into cracks in the wall to climb it—and they were making slow progress.

Great. Just great.

Yaotel's voice rose above the din. "No!" A few men were trying to seek shelter back in the manor, and one of the crabs had followed.

They would be slaughtered if they became cornered in the groundsman's shed.

Vaughn loosed an arrow, and it stuck in the crab's shell for a moment and then fell to the ground. It didn't hurt it, but it did distract the crab momentarily, and then men scattered out into the courtyard.

Vaughn stared down at the scene in frustration, feeling helpless. Their lack of coordination as a fighting team was never more obvious than it was now. They weren't even trying to work together. If a few men could corner one, run out, and then let the others attack from behind...

He hated to admit it, but this was a point in Perth's favor. If they trained their abilities for combat, they would likely know better how to use them together—and how to *work* together.

But who could have imagined they would have to fight against a concerted attack of monsters?

Another arrow flew through the air, and it promptly skewered the leg on one of the crabs.

He turned to see Tharqan a few meters away down the wall. "Nice one," Vaughn shouted.

Next to him, Tharqan was their best archer, but he wasn't a moonblood. Tharqan gave him a quick nod and turned back to the skirmish, looking for another opening.

"Would being closer help?" a voice said in his ear.

He turned, startled, and then Danton appeared next to him.

"If I can get an arrow buried hard into its mouth, it's dead," Vaughn said.

Danton gestured to him and Vaughn followed. As the two slipped down the wall, a fireblood named Thrax decided to let loose a little magic.

He stood with legs spread and hand held out, and fire leapt from one of the torches on the wall and wrapped itself around one of the bloodcrabs.

Others backed away from the heat and squinted against the sudden flare of light as he held the maelstrom tight.

The crab shrieked, an inhuman sound that he had never heard a real crab make, and Thrax shouted with glee. "Roast crab, anyone?"

Vaughn had never seen a Banebringer use their magic in such a way. Apparently Thrax was one of those who was training with Hueil and Perth.

Vaughn could see Yaotel grimacing, glancing out at the wall, as if expecting a stranger to be peeking over to watch the show. But what could he say? It was either that, or they die.

Vaughn turned invisible just as Thrax let go. The crab's shell was black, smoking, and one of its legs had disintegrated, so it stood lopsided on the ground. Still, it struggled to rise.

The other crab turned from pursuing a man who had blockaded himself in the guardroom, trying to stab its legs through the wooden door, and Vaughn could have sworn its eyes flickered with rage.

It charged Thrax.

"Now's our chance!" Danton shouted. He sprinted behind the crab and then became a blur of color against a horrifying background: the crab reared, and Thrax turned only just then to see what was happening.

Vaughn darted the other way, lifting his bow as he ran.

And then, Thrax disappeared. Or, rather, he faded, and in his place was a yapping dog.

The crab dropped back to the ground, startled.

It didn't last long. It reared again, looking down at the dog, but it was too late. Vaughn was already in place. As close as he was, the arrow drove right through the mouth and into the soft flesh under the shell. Perfect shot.

The crab convulsed in the air and then dropped. The dog ran away, and a moment later turned back into Thrax.

Danton saluted Vaughn from across the crab and took off in the other direction.

One convulsing, dying crab, and one blackened husk, smoking in the night air.

Vaughn barely had a moment to feel satisfied, because a scream tore his attention back to the wall, where the first of the four crabs from the outside were making their appearance.

Damn.

Thrax pulled out a jet of fire again, and the first crab tumbled from the wall and landed on its back. Vaughn put an arrow in its underside, just to be sure. The second crab had started scrabbling down the stairs, its needle-legs a nightmarish clicking against the hard stone, and the third went the other direction, directly toward Tharqan.

Vaughn shouted a warning, and Tharqan took off down the wall toward the other stairs, the crab close behind.

The fourth crab went up in another flare, but the second had made its way to the bottom and surprised three men who had been taking shelter against the wall.

Before Vaughn could do anything, it had stabbed one of them through the stomach.

"No!" Vaughn shouted, and that mobilized everyone else. They massed on the crab, hacking at its shell with aether-enhanced axes and swords. Vaughn turned invisible again, darted in, and dragged the man back. A trail of blood was left in his wake.

Damn. Damn. Damn.

"I need a healer!" he screamed.

They were already there. A bindblood took the man from

Vaughn as he reappeared, and he felt rather than saw the flurry of activity around him as they raced to stabilize him before they had yet another bloodbane to deal with—and who knew what kind. It could be anything from a harmless bloodsprite to the behemoth that had attacked them in the city.

He couldn't even see the second crab, surrounded as it was. He turned his attention down the wall, where Tharqan had finally made it down the stairs and was fleeing back toward them, the crab's needle-legs clicking close behind.

Vaughn ran straight toward them, lifting his bow. The crab was faster. It reared. Vaughn shot the arrow.

Tharqan bolted past him, the arrow embedded itself into the crab's mouth, and before Vaughn could slow his momentum to dart out of the way, the damn thing had fallen right on top of him.

The smell of ichor permeated his hair and his clothes, and he almost vomited when he felt it dripping into the corner of his mouth.

He managed to avoid getting stabbed by the thrashing of the crab's legs, and then the crab lay still. He pushed it off himself, disgusted.

"Vaughn!" Danton was running his way, and Vaughn waved him off as he staggered to his feet. "I'm fine," he said.

Danton stopped. "Good. That's the last one. No casualties."

Vaughn glanced toward where the healers had been. They were gone. "What about...?"

"Bad off, but they think he'll live."

Vaughn closed his eyes and sank to the ground as the energy of the past few minutes seeped out. He opened his eyes and

stared dully at the cracked remains of the second crab. Someone had obviously thought to get out a hammer.

"You all right?" Danton asked.

"I need a bath."

"It was her," Vaughn said grimly, standing in Yaotel's office after he had wiped off the worst of the crud from the crab. "I'm
certain of it. Every single time I've been down there, it's been
followed by an attack. And they keep getting worse."

Yaotel was obviously agitated. "Then stop going down there!"
He threw his hands in the air and placed them against the wall.
"You think she's summoning them?"

"If Danathalt is her patron? Likely."

Yaotel cursed. "I can't let her go. I can't kill her." He cursed
again. "Barton is supposed to have guests arriving tomorrow.
How in the abyss am I going to clean up the mess out there?"
He whirled on Vaughn, glaring at him. "And for what? We've
learned *nothing*." He ran a hand across his balding head. "I've
given Perth and crew permission to hone their gifts for combat,
but if I don't come up with a way to stall them, I'm going to
have a fight on my hands—right here in the compound."

Vaughn regarded him, a little stunned. He had never seen
Yaotel get so worked up before. So *that* was why Yaotel was so
agitated about finding an answer in those books. He did still
want to prevent war between Banebringers and the rest of the
world; he had simply cracked under the pressure that Perth and
the others were putting him under, felt he had to compromise.
Now, he was feeling the press of time.

Vaughn's irritation at him lessened a bit. In fact, he felt sorry for the man.

"Why couldn't her patron have been damned Zily? Then all she'd do is sit around on her ass." Yaotel cursed one last time. "You stink. Go take a bath."

Vaughn slid out of his office. *Gladly*.

Chapter Twenty-Nine

Etiology

"You didn't show yesterday," Ivana said without looking up as he entered the back room.

"Sorry," he said. "Another attack the night before last. I was beat."

She shrugged. "I'm not sure that I need the transliterations anymore, anyway. I think I've got a handle on translating directly from the Xambrian."

"Was that a subtle hint that you prefer to work alone?"

"Nothing subtle about it," she said.

Vaughn sat down in the chair across from her and studied her for a minute. "Why are you doing this?"

Silence.

"It has something to do with that note from your friend,

doesn't it?"

Of course, she didn't answer.

Vaughn wasn't stupid enough to think she was doing this out of the kindness of her heart. She had an ulterior motive, he just wasn't sure what it was yet. He considered sneaking into her room and trying to find the note. Between her lessons and their work, his Xambrian was passable again.

But that was foolish. If the note was that important, she probably kept it on her. And there was only one way to solve *that* problem.

That particular fantasy of his didn't seem likely to happen, however.

"What are you grinning about?"

"Huh?" *Oops.*

Her eyes were dark with disapproval, almost as if she knew where his thoughts had gone.

"My older brother and I—the second oldest—used to write notes in codes," he said, turning the subject away from one that would likely arouse her ire. And back to secret notes.

She rolled her eyes and continued working.

Maybe he could annoy it out of her. "It drove my younger brother crazy, because he never could figure the code out." He smiled at the memory of lazy summer afternoons, too young to have real responsibilities, but old enough to know when to flee the estate after their schooling was done for the day, lest their mother engage them in some tedious task.

And then he halted, his chest tightening momentarily, and he pushed it away. "Our oldest brother always thought we were foolish. Especially after he came of age. Airell was always like that. Thought he was better than the rest of us."

There was a snap, and Ivana cursed. Vaughn glanced over; she had broken the tip off her pen. "How in the abyss did you do that?"

She glared at him, as though it were his fault, tossed the pen aside, and snatched up Vaughn's, which lay unused in front of him. That was a bit of an over-reaction when she was usually so cool.

And then he remembered. Airell. She had said that name once, hadn't she? When she was delusional. Obviously thought Vaughn was him.

Coincidence?

"Did you know Airell?"

Tenseness rippled through her body. "Pardon?"

"Airell," he repeated. "My oldest brother."

"How in the abyss should I know one of your brothers?"

He shrugged. "You mentioned the name when you were delirious. Back at the safe house. You seemed to think I might be him, for a moment."

"As you say, I was delirious." Her voice was cool, edging on cold. "What was the attack this time?"

The shift in subject was abrupt, for her. He sensed it would be dangerous to press her, so he let it drop. For now. But his curiosity had been aroused. She was an expert at hiding her emotions; for his question to provoke a reaction so powerful a reaction? There had to be a connection. But what was it? And was it also connected to her hatred for his father?

What had his family done to her?

"Three bloodhawks and six bloodcrabs. We almost lost

someone this time. Not good."

"And if you lose someone..."

"Yeah."

"Any way of knowing what kind of bloodbane will be summoned?"

He shook his head. "As far as we can tell, there's no link between type of bloodbane and type of Banebringer. There *might* be a correlation between how much a Banebringer uses their powers and the strength of the monster, but we don't exactly go around killing each other to find out."

"Makes sense," Ivana said.

"Not killing each other? Obviously."

She rolled her eyes. "The possible correlation between Banebringer powers and the bloodbane that get summoned. If it's true that when you use your abilities it creates a greater draw on the spiritual realm at the sky-fire, it makes sense that stronger monsters would be attracted when the veil tears when one of you dies."

"Well, I guess that's—" He halted. "Where did you hear that?"

"What?"

"The thing about...using our abilities drawing more monsters."

"Danton."

He tapped his finger on the table several times. "I see you weren't kidding when you said you were going to find other allies."

"Of course I wasn't kidding. But I learned that the first time I talked to him."

He shook his head. "That kid is completely infatuated with

you. If you're going to use someone, can you please leave him out of it?"

She didn't respond to that. "He said you were the one who brought him here."

"Yes. Rescued him on the way to wherever it is they take Banebringers for Sedation."

She turned back to her work. "Seems like with the ability to make oneself blend in with one's surrounding, he could have escaped easily enough on his own."

"The kid was fifteen, barely even knew what he could do yet. Besides, blending in doesn't do much good if you're trapped in a steel cage." He knew that all too well. He craned his neck to look at the book in front of her. "Found anything else interesting?"

"Actually..." She picked up the original, flipped back a few pages, studied them for a moment, and then looked back at her translation. She frowned.

Vaughn sat up straighter. This sounded promising. "Ivana?"

She stared at the page hard again and then turned it around so Vaughn could see it. "What does this mean to you?"

He read silently. The passage described a battle—apparently the epic battles between gods that Ivana had been translating, and this one was between Danathalt and Ziloxchanachi. And it seemed that many of the other gods had taken sides, for there were several named on both sides, some that he recognized, and some that he didn't.

Vaughn became lost in the story for a moment—even the endless list of warriors that the head god had summoned to his side in heaven, since he had never heard of the creatures before. He had to assume they were some sort of heavenly beings, or perhaps "good" monsters, since they were enumerated, rather than named.

In the end, Ziloxchanachi and company won, casting Danathalt back into the abyss with his armies with a proclamation:

And Ziloxchanachi was so angered at the rebellion that he swore on his own name that no longer would the father of gods engage in the petty schemes of his sons and daughters. "Your blood and the blood of your subjects be on your hands!" And then he cursed them, saying, "As you have schemed against each other, so you will be bound. God to god, in blood and strife."

The story ended there. "Interesting to have more information on Danathalt, but does this have something to do with Sedation or our friend in the basement?"

Ivana tapped her finger on the translation. "You told me that Ziloxchanachi sat around and did nothing."

"Well...that's what we knew about him up until now. But perhaps that's not precisely true?" He raised an eyebrow. "Still not seeing the connection."

She picked up the page and read from it aloud. "No longer would the father of gods engage in the petty schemes of his sons and daughters. *No longer.* That seems to suggest that he had been involved before then, at least enough to now swear he wouldn't be."

Vaughn stared at her, brow furrowed. He didn't want to admit again that he wasn't seeing it, lest she think him dense. So he sat in silence, furiously thinking. To give credence to the idea that he was making progress in his thoughts, he got up to go look at the translation again, for himself, leaning over Ivana's shoulder.

And then it dawned on him. "This is old," he said.

"*Yes*," she said. "Well, sort of." She stood up and started pacing. "While the myths don't always agree in details, this is likely an etiological story explaining why it is that the most important god apparently did nothing. It's meant to take place *before* the other myths." She waved her hand, as if to stave off an objection. "Whether it was penned before the other myths is irrelevant."

She was clearly excited. Ivana. Excited. Her cheeks had taken on a slight flush, and her eyes sparkled. Even a long length of hair had fallen out of place, tickling the side of her throat, which only served to enhance the image of the slightly eccentric professor. He couldn't help but smile.

She stopped pacing abruptly. "Why are you smiling?"

"You're doubly appealing when you use the word 'etiological,'" he said, before he could stop himself.

Predictably, her eyes flashed.

"What?" he asked, holding his hands out to the side in defense. "Is a man not allowed to appreciate the fine intellect of a woman?"

She snorted. "I wasn't aware you knew how to appreciate anything in a woman other than a fine body."

He met her eyes. "You're not just any woman, though, are you?" Had he really said that? Did he actually *believe* that?

And then, he wasn't certain he was still breathing. The surroundings faded, and for a moment that seemed to paradoxically stretch out forever and yet be over before it started...he wanted to take her in his arms, breathe her, kiss her, know her.

Something flickered in her eyes. "Stop," she said. Her voice was tight.

The moment passed, and he turned away, disconcerted. "Stop what?"

"How many women have you told that to? You're not going to seduce me with smooth talk."

He wanted to protest. He hadn't ever told a woman that before, in fact. But she wouldn't believe him. Why should she? He didn't blame her, and he wasn't sure he wanted her to believe him. He wasn't sure if he wanted what he obviously wanted.

The path those thoughts led down were uncomfortable, so he retreated to a safer place. He stepped closer to her. "Does that suggest that there might be some other way to seduce you?"

She didn't move back, and for a heartbeat, he thought she might be receptive. But then she spoke, softly. "Perhaps you should know that there are only two reasons I will sleep with a man," she said. "First, if I want to use him."

He grinned. "That sounds exciting."

Her eyes turned to flint. "Second, and more likely, if I intend on killing him."

He swallowed. A subtle reminder of whom exactly he was dealing with. It had been easy to forget. But he didn't want to remember. His fear of her had eroded, and he had no intention of allowing her to put the layers back.

"I see," he said solemnly. "You like women."

She arched one eyebrow. "I shouldn't have to explain this to you," she said. "My job is dangerous and my identity everything. I can't afford to engage in anything that might erode my reason."

"Ah. How sad."

"No sadder than your sleeping with so *many* women in order to keep your heart intact." She gave him a shrewd look and turned away.

It was his turn to blink. "That's ridiculous."

She ignored his assertion. "Logical deduction."

Ridiculous, he asserted to himself again. He slept with so many women because he didn't want commitment. He didn't *need* commitment. Because he couldn't get drunk, damn it all, and what else was there? "You have no idea what you're talking about. And how did this get turned around on me?"

She smirked. "You bandied words with a woman of fine intellect."

This subject had thoroughly run its course, in his estimation. "So the story is old, or meant to be taken as old. But how does this help with what Yaotel wants?"

She eyed him, still smirking, and then looked back down at the papers on the table. "I'm not positive that it does, but..." She hesitated. "I don't suppose there's any way you could get me into the research wing to take a look at some blood and run a few experiments?"

"Probably. Yaotel won't be happy when he finds out, but..." He shrugged. He really didn't care.

Chapter Thirty

Aether

Ivana followed Vaughn down the halls, down a set of stairs, until they reached a long hallway punctuated by doors and windows facing out. It wasn't as comfortably decorated as the rest of the manor, but it wasn't stark either. Merely more practical, the walls dressed in beige and brown, and a tighter knit, less-plush carpet beneath their feet.

Vaughn led her into a room two-thirds of the way down the hallway. One long table encompassed the perimeter of the room, with cabinets and racks and vials and—yes—the microscope, much more elaborate than the simple one her father had built. He would have fainted in ecstasy at the sight of such resources.

There was one other person inside, who turned as they entered and then paused, eyes darting back and forth between Vaughn and Ivana a few times before finally resting on Vaughn with a distinct look of distaste.

Great.

"Is she allowed to be down here?" the woman asked.

Vaughn didn't even look at her. "Nice to see you too, Citalli. Ivana needs to verify some of our recent experiments with the..." He coughed and gestured to a microscope sitting on a side table. "New device. For our research for Yaotel."

The woman hesitated, and then shrugged. "Very well." She walked to the other side of the room and busied herself at the table against that wall, but Ivana could see her casting sidelong glances their way every so often.

Vaughn gestured to the room. "Well. Do whatever it is you need to do."

She walked over to the microscope and ran her hand down one side. The body was metal, rather than wood, like her father's had been.

It was still beautiful. "Show me what you saw before."

Vaughn nodded. "Look at your own blood first."

Ivana glanced toward the researcher, but she didn't seem intent on providing any aid, so Ivana opened the cabinet above the microscope. Sure enough, the cabinet held a long row of glass slides. She selected several, along with a blade. The razor was encompassed in a long tube until the end, where it came to a slanted point. She used it to prick her own finger and smeared a drop of blood on the slide. She put it under the microscope and looked through the lens.

She couldn't help but gasp. "Burning skies," she muttered. "I can't believe how magnified this is...how?"

"Um...lightblood aether. Or so they tell me."

Of course. The magical properties of that particular type of aether must cause the light to be refracted at a higher rate, thus resulting in a greater degree of magnification. Fascinating. She shook her head and went back to the task at hand, studying her blood. She set the slide aside. "Your blood."

He wiped off the edge of the razor and pricked himself, and then copied what she did. "Quickly," he said. "If you want to see it."

She observed what he had told her. Tiny, almost bug-like blobs, scurrying around the blobs that she had seen in her own blood. As she watched, they started to consume the blood itself, until they were finished, and slowed, and then froze altogether. The sample took on a shiny, silvery quality, though she could still see the frozen aether-bugs. She pulled back and looked at the slide. Sure enough, it had turned to aether.

She set it aside. "All right. Now I need to see what happens when the Sedation formula is mixed in."

Vaughn looked at the researcher. "We need a sample of the Sedation formula."

The researcher ignored him.

"Citalli," Vaughn said, more loudly. "I'm talking to you."

The researcher—Citalli—cast him an irritated look, but moved to a beaker over a flame. The aether within was liquid. She carefully drew a small amount into a syringe and then handed it to Vaughn, who handed it to Ivana. Vaughn gave her another sample of his blood without being asked, and she squeezed a drop of the formula into it, and then quickly slid it under the microscope.

It was just as he had said. The foreign aether bugs, distinguishable because they were part of the silvery substance slowly swirling through the blood, cornered and surrounded the native aether bugs until they froze, with the exception of tiny tremors. Thus done, they proceeded to eat the rest of the blood, until the entire substance had turned to aether.

"Huh." She picked up the syringe. "So this is a mix of many different types of Banebringer blood?"

"That's what our ex-priest said," Vaughn replied. He eyed the syringe nervously, and she rolled her eyes and set it down.

"Relax. Why do they use so many types?"

"No idea," Vaughn said. "You'd have to ask him."

"Because it works," Citalli said from behind, engaging for the first time. Ivana turned to look at her.

She shrugged. "Perrit doesn't know why it works, and he said the priests don't know why either. But using only one or two types doesn't appear to work, whereas using as many as possible does."

"Presumably they harvest the blood for the formula from the Banebringers they have in their asylum?"

Vaughn shuddered, as though he had never thought of that.

"Presumably." Citalli gave Ivana a look of distaste and turned away.

"Who is your patron?" she asked Citalli.

"We don't know," she said. "But I'm a charmblood."

Vaughn smirked, and Ivana could tell he was refraining from making some remark about that. Clearly, there was some history between those two.

"Good enough," Ivana said. "Can I have a sample of your blood?"

She frowned, but did as she was asked, smearing a sample onto a new slide Ivana laid out for her. She then snapped her fingers at Vaughn. "Your blood. On the slide. Quickly."

Vaughn obeyed, and Ivana looked at the sample under the microscope.

As she had predicted, nothing happened. The aether—she couldn't tell them apart—ate the blood jointly, and then froze. Vaughn stole a look when she was done. "Where is this going?" he asked, clearly unimpressed.

"Do you have someone with Xichtantal as their patron here?" Ivana asked, ignoring his question. It was a guess, and based on the myth Vaughn had described to her and later, her own research into it, she was fairly certain it was a correct one.

Vaughn raised his eyebrow. "A sunblood? Yes. Several."

"Do we have samples of their aether? Pure, not mixed with anything else?"

Again, they both looked at Citalli. She sighed and gave up her show of indifference. She opened a cabinet nearby. Inside was a long row of vials set into racks. Tiny labels were underneath, and she ran her finger along them until she found the one she was looking for. She pulled it out and held it up to the light, shaking it slightly.

"Ah," she said, shaking her head. "Cork was compromised. I'll have to heat it before you can use it. Sorry."

"Heat it?" Ivana said to Vaughn while Citalli did just that.

"It solidifies under two circumstances," Citalli said, either because she thought Ivana was talking to her, or because she thought Vaughn wouldn't know the answer and was finally deciding to be proactively helpful. "First, when it's exposed to air. Second, when it cools. Possibly a combination of the two, but we know that if we heat it—or even if it's really hot outside—it will liquefy again, momentarily, until it cools back down. We also know that if we contain the liquid aether in a fairly airtight container, it will stay liquid for longer, depending on *how* air-tight, regardless of how cool it is."

"Fascinating," Ivana muttered.

"It's liquefying," Citalli said, shaking the vial over a flame. "It doesn't take much. Whatever you need it for, now is the time."

"Your blood again," Ivana said.

Vaughn obediently squeezed out another drop of blood onto a slide, and Citalli provided a needle to dip into the vial. A small drop stuck to the end, and Ivana tapped it into the blood sample, and then quickly put it back under the microscope.

She breathed out slowly. Burning skies, she was right. She was *right*.

The aether was acting the same way as the formula, even though it only contained one type of aether.

"You sure this is *only* sunblood aether?" Ivana asked.

"Positive. Why?"

"Take a look. Quickly."

Citalli cast her a curious glance and then looked through the microscope. She took one long look, blinked, and then stared at Ivana. "That's impossible. It's not the formula. It's—"

"—her rival," Vaughn cut in, after taking his own look. "Burning skies."

"*Whose* rival?" Citalli asked. "What are you talking about?"

"My patron, Thaxchatichan. Xichtantal is her rival, the brother that cut off her head." He put one hand to his face and ran it over the entirety of it several times. "Damn."

He saw it. It took him a little longer, but he finally saw it. Ivana nodded at him in acknowledgement.

Citalli was already preparing another slide, needing to see for herself. She pulled another vial out of the cabinet, mixed a drop of aether from each vial together, and put the sample under the microscope. "Impossible," she muttered again.

She started working with a flurry, pulling the entire rack of vials out of the cabinet and combining different aethers. Ivana moved aside to let her do whatever she needed to. As far as Ivana was concerned, she had substantial evidence that she was right.

"Iceblood and fireblood," Citalli muttered. "Of course. I understand now." She mixed another set of aethers together and then frowned. "I would think..." She shook her head. "Doesn't happen with lightblood and darkblood."

"Doesn't necessarily follow that because they're opposites, they'll be rivals," Ivana put in.

"True," Citalli said, sounding excited now, and apparently finally unconcerned that Ivana was the one giving suggestions. "What would be the opposite of a beastblood, after all?"

"Beastblood?" Ivana was trying to figure out what that particular gift would mean.

"It's how we make the weapons that kill bloodbane," Vaughn said. "Their aether somehow repels them, so we seal it in weapons, making them more effective."

"Do you know the patron?"

"Um, Tiuhtanah, I think."

"Is that the one who had a contest with the lightblood god?"

"Taniqotalin? Yes." Vaughn slapped his forehead and turned to Citalli. "Try lightblood aether to combat beastblood."

She looked at him askance, but did as Vaughn asked.

"That's why your arrows work so well?" Ivana asked, returning to his earlier comment while Citalli worked.

"Yes."

"I knew you couldn't be that good."

Vaughn chuckled. "Thanks. Appreciate your confidence."

"Do you have to be a Banebringer to use the weapons?"

"Yes," he said. "You have to activate it, just like with any aether." He didn't mention the possibility that they could mix a non-Banebringer's blood with a beastblood's and create weapons that person could use, so Ivana didn't either.

To the abyss with the Conclave. This group of Banebringers had discovered a way they could arm non-Banebringers against bloodbane, but because the priests were so blind with hatred toward Banebringers, they'd never be able to reap the benefits.

Ivana shook her head. Stubborn fools.

"It works," Citalli announced. "Lightblood versus beastblood." She didn't appear to be talking to them directly, as she went right back to work.

Ivana glanced at Vaughn, wondering if he had yet followed this theory to its end. He looked...*disappointed* wasn't the right word...*frustrated*, perhaps. So she guessed he had.

"We've never seen a profile for Ziloxchanachi," he said quietly, confirming her guess. "That's why she couldn't be Sedated. Zily is Danathalt's rival. We'd need aether from one of his Gifted to Sedate her."

Gifted? He hadn't used that term with her before, though he had mentioned they used to be called that once. She had heard others there using it, however. "Just because you've never seen one, doesn't mean one doesn't exist."

Vaughn shrugged. "Doesn't matter. We don't need information on how to Sedate a Gifted with Danathalt as the patron. We needed a way to replicate whatever kept her from being Sedated." He stared at the formula, looking morose. "We can't replicate not having a rival."

"*Can't* is a strong word," Ivana said. "You have more information now than you did before about how Sedation works. That's got to count for something."

"Something," Citalli put in, still working. "But whether it will be useful..."

"Granted," Ivana said. Not all discoveries led to what one was hoping for—or even anything helpful.

The door swung open behind them, and heavy footsteps stopped. "What's going on in here?"

Aw, damn. Vaughn glanced at the doorway, where Yaotel stood, arms folded across his chest, staring at Ivana. Which researcher had tattled? Anyone walking by could have seen them working through the windows in the wall.

He had brought Perrit, the ex-priest, with him, however, which suggested that Yaotel had guessed they were here because they had made a discovery and thought an ex-Conclave's perspective might be useful.

Vaughn moved between Ivana and Yaotel. "We made some headway with the translation," Vaughn said, "and Ivana wanted to test a theory."

Yaotel snorted. "What, she's a scientist now too?"

Ivana's face was ice. "Yes, in fact," she said, matching Yaotel's withering look with one of her own.

"Is there anything you're *not* good at?"

"Art," Ivana retorted. "And music."

Yaotel ignored her and went back to speaking about her in the third person. "She's not allowed down here. Damn it, Vaughn, you know better."

Vaughn frowned. What was he, a child? "You told me this was important. I did what was necessary."

A muscle jumped in Yaotel's cheek. What was his problem, lately? Ivana had done nothing but help since she had arrived; granted, she would probably run given the opportunity, but Yaotel could give her a little regard at least.

"What have you learned?"

Vaughn looked at Ivana. She was the one who had figured it out. Who had thought to test it. And she understood it better than he did.

But she nodded to Citalli, giving the ground up. "Show him."

Citalli moved Yaotel through all of the same steps Ivana had gone through, ending with the dramatic example of a single Banebringer's aether taking on another's.

When finished, Yaotel looked less perturbed, but he had a frown on his face.

Ivana took back up the narrative. "In short, our theory is that Sedation works by pitting the aether of two rival gods against each other. The reason your prisoner can't be Sedated is because the formula the Conclave uses is missing the aether of her patron's rival, Ziloxchanachi."

"Ziloxchanachi doesn't have Gifted that we know of," Yaotel said.

"Hence the reason the Conclave doesn't have any aether to Sedate her with."

Yaotel frowned and turned to Perrit. "Does the Conclave know this?"

"No," Perrit said. "They only know that the formula works." He glanced at the microscope. "And they don't have any microscopes nearly this powerful, so I don't know if they could figure it out scientifically even if they wanted to. It'd have to be extreme trial and error, and since they don't know nearly as much as we do about the heretic gods, I don't know where they'd get the idea to even try experimenting."

"Why bother, when what they're doing works," Yaotel muttered. He gestured toward Vaughn. "Why did the sunblood aether win over the moonblood aether, though? Seems like if it's as simple as rivalry, it'd be a fight, and whoever wins, wins. But that's obviously not the case, since Sedation works every single time."

Ivana gave him a look of grudging respect. "A good question," she said. "Perhaps if pure aether invades blood that hasn't been consumed yet, the aether wins against half-blood, half-aether, every time." She looked at Citalli. "Have you noticed this at all?"

Citalli rubbed her chin. "Well, the sunblood aether we took from the vial did win against Vaughn's fresh sample, but when I started mixing only all-aether samples, the winner was unpredictable. Sometimes it was one, sometimes it was the other. But we'll have to get more fresh samples to be sure."

"Great," Yaotel said. "So the only way to combat Sedation—half of the time—would be to turn all of our living blood into aether while still inside our bodies." He didn't sound serious, just grumpy.

"I'm pretty sure that would kill you," Citalli put in. "Since the only way we know to turn blood into aether is to expose it to air.

Yaotel rolled his eyes back. "Yes, thank you, Citalli." He sighed. "Keep working on it," he told her. "Get the whole team on it, pool your thoughts on the matter. You never know."

Then he turned to Vaughn. "So. Looks like our books were likely a dead end."

Vaughn shrugged helplessly. He felt let down. It was a tremendous discovery, but it didn't *help* them. "It's looking that way, for now."

Yaotel closed his eyes. "Not what I wanted to hear. But it was always a stretch." He opened his eyes. "Perrit," he said. "Get the slaying team together. I'm done with that woman."

Perrit inclined his head and left.

Vaughn blinked. "You're going to kill her?"

"You're the one who told me you thought talking to her was only making her mad, making her summon bloodbane."

"But she's the only Gifted we know of who has Danathalt as her patron!" Citalli put in, looking appalled. "We've barely studied—"

"Have the researchers collect as many samples as they dare," Yaotel said. "But she's too dangerous to keep around."

Vaughn could only stare at him, his gut feeling like a hole had been punched through it. "You're going to kill her," he repeated.

"Was I unclear the first time?"

"Since when do—"

"I didn't ask for an argument."

They didn't *kill* Banebringers. They rescued them. What was Yaotel thinking? Surely there was a better way. "You're no better than them," he said through clenched teeth.

Yaotel turned his focus fully on Vaughn. "Pardon?"

"You don't like her powers, so you're going to have her killed."

"I do what's best for the people here, and this is what's best."

"And what if what's best is starting a war with the Conclave?" Vaughn shot back. Yaotel had always been neutral in that fight. Always.

The room went silent. Yaotel met Vaughn's eyes. He didn't answer. And that was when Vaughn *knew*. He had finally given in, given up on a less drastic and more peaceful solution. His last lead had been a dead end.

"Do you know how many people would die?" Vaughn said softly.

"People who hate us."

"Leaving aside that Banebringers would die as well—they hate us because they're ignorant," Vaughn said. "And can you blame them, with the destruction we've caused?"

Yaotel's face twisted. "Not our fault, not our problem."

"The Conclave is the enemy," Vaughn insisted. "They hold the power, the knowledge—"

"The *enemy*," Yaotel interrupted, eyes blazing, "is anyone who would see us wiped out of existence, merely for being alive." He jabbed a finger at Vaughn. "Your family betrayed you," he said to Vaughn. "But at least your town didn't try to lynch them. Being *noble* has its benefits. Never forget that." And with that, he turned on his heel and walked out.

Even Citalli was pretending she hadn't heard anything. Vaughn was seething. As if he hadn't seen the mobs. As if he hadn't been the victim of one before. As if his own father hadn't burned down towns as punishment for sheltering him, even unknowingly. Yes, they all suffered because of the existence of Banebringers. All of them. And he didn't care what Yaotel said: the Conclave and their dogs were the reason.

And with the excuse of research gone, Yaotel's ire would soon turn back to Ivana, who had remained quiet throughout the exchange. Frankly, Vaughn was sick of it.

They left the research room together and walked in silence down the hall.

"I'm sorry," Ivana offered at last.

"For what?"

"That we didn't come up with something that would help."

Vaughn grunted. "There are more books. Yaotel might have given up, but I haven't."

"I don't think Yaotel is going to let me continue working with you."

Vaughn stopped to face Ivana. "Yes. That's another matter. Why does he seem to hate you so much? How do you know each other?" He might as well ask, since she had brought it up.

Ivana looked down the hall, both ways, but it was empty.

"I'm not certain," she said quietly. "But it's possible I inadvertently killed someone who mattered to him."

Vaughn raised an eyebrow. "Inadvertently?" Was there anything inadvertent about being hired to kill someone?

"Collateral damage. It happens."

Ah. *That* kind of inadvertent. They started walking again. "When did you meet him?"

"On a job about six months ago. I had disguised myself as part of Gan Pywell's harem, and your leader was also apparently in disguise, though I don't know why, as the eunuch in charge of us."

Understanding flooded him. Yaotel had been trying to rescue his sister, who had been essentially enslaved into Gan Pywell's service after Yaotel had changed into a Banebringer, years ago. Vaughn knew that the rescue attempt had gone poorly, and that Yaotel had been particularly gruff and withdrawn for a while after he had come back. "Gods, Ivana. I'm pretty sure that must have been his sister."

"Well. That would explain it."

"That would *explain* it? That's all you have to say?"

She stopped again and turned to face him. Her face was hard. "You seem to forget who you're dealing with. You trust me and you shouldn't. When it comes to it, I will do what is necessary to protect myself and my own interests, and nothing more. It's what I am, and it's who I am. Don't forget that."

She seemed to think that was final, as she turned and left him then. But he set his jaw. He refused to believe it. He had seen someone else inside her, someone who was different, someone he was convinced she had deliberately buried. He just wished he knew how to draw that person out, once and for all.

Chapter Thirty-One

Memories in Blood

Ivana had just bathed and was getting ready for bed, when a knock on her door interrupted her preparations. She tugged her robe tighter around herself and answered the door. Vaughn stood there, clutching a small satchel in one hand. His eyes darted down the hall and back, and he shifted from one foot to the other. "Can I come in?"

Ivana hesitated, but shrugged and let him in. By the time she had closed the door and turned around, he had dragged the one chair in the room to the other side of the bedside table, so that there was a chair on one side and the bed as a seat on the other.

He sat in the chair and started removing items from the satchel.

The first item that came out was a knife—sharp, but not designed to be a weapon—the kind one might use to pare fruit. That was followed by a second, similar knife. Then a teacup saucer, a needle, and last, a coin purse.

Ivana drifted closer, standing at the side of the table looking down at the assortment of items as Vaughn stashed the satchel under his chair.

"What *are* you doing?" she asked.

He placed one knife closer to the bed, and one in front of himself. He sat for a moment, staring at the table, and then said softly. "Helping you get out of here."

Ivana froze. "What?"

He looked up at her. "I haven't told anyone about our discovery. That a non-Banebringer could use aether."

"Why in the abyss not?"

His jaw twitched. "Because Yaotel is an ass, and I was being petty. But I'm glad I didn't. Because now, we know something they don't know, and it might help you." He gestured to the bed. "Have a seat. This could take a while."

She understood now what he was going to propose. They were going to make her own stash of aether to use—specifically the kind she could use to turn invisible. Useful when trying to escape, certainly, but...

She wasn't ready to escape yet. How could she explain that to him, without giving away the content of the note from Aleena?

She perched on the edge of the bed and stalled. "You used the term Gifted earlier."

"Yes. It's what the Ichtaca call themselves."

Well. That explained the dirty looks when she used the term Banebringer around here.

"But you don't?"

He shrugged, but said nothing else.

"You know," she said, as if she had just thought of it. "Just because I can turn invisible doesn't mean I'll be able to escape right away."

"No," Vaughn said. "But if the opportunity presents itself, I want you to have every available advantage."

"Why are you helping me?"

He paused. "Because Yaotel is an ass, and I'm being petty."

She raised an eyebrow, and he sighed and ran a hand across his face. "Because now that I know why Yaotel hates you, I'm convinced that he's never going to let you go. You'll rot here until he decides he's done with you, and then come up with an excuse to be rid of you. He's not a cruel man, but he carries grudges."

She shook her head. That only half answered her question. Why would he want to risk Yaotel's trust in him to help *her*?

"You realize that I would betray the Ichtaca if it became expedient for me to do so?"

He glanced at her, but said nothing.

"All right," she said, shrugging. "I won't turn down free help. What's the best way to go about this?"

He pushed the knife closer to her with one finger. "Same way I make my own aether, except once you have a few drops, try to squeeze them onto the saucer. We'll mix it, wait for it to turn to aether, and then peel it off." He held up the purse. "You can keep it in here. Ready?"

Ivana picked up the knife and skimmed one thumb along the blade. It was sharp enough to make a tiny slice in her finger even as careful as she had been, merely a paper cut. Plenty sharp enough for the task.

"I would recommend your forearm," Vaughn said. "Shallow cuts." He demonstrated. "You keep pricking your fingers, they'll quickly become sore."

Ivana followed suit. She was unprepared for the rush of emotions and memories that followed as the knife bit into her arm.

Sitting in the closet that passed for her room, alone but for a razor and her own skin. Her own blood had been the first she had let, long before her mentor had set her to taking out easy targets. Burying the pain and guilt in physical punishment. It had helped somehow, before she had found more permanent ways to deal with it.

At least, what she thought had been permanent.

It had been years since those marks had faded into paper thin scars, barely visible unless you were looking for them. He had seen them once. He didn't know what they were.

"Ivana?"

She looked up. Vaughn was watching her, his own blood already glistening red on the plate. "We have to be quick."

She took a deep breath and scraped a few drops of blood off with her fingernail, and then onto the plate. Vaughn immediately mixed the blood with the needle. Then, they waited.

He looked at the cut she had made. "I'm sorry," he said. "I guess I figured since you're so...ah...handy with a knife already, it wouldn't be that big of a deal for you to draw your own blood."

"It's fine," she said, unsettled that he had noticed her own discomfort. She deflected. "That researcher didn't seem to like you much."

Vaughn grimaced. "Citalli? Uh, yeah."

"What'd you do to her?"

"Well, I think she was hoping for a little more than I gave her."

Ivana snorted. "What, all the women around here don't already know what to expect?"

"She's the only woman from here that I've slept with."

"I find *that* hard to believe."

"I try to avoid women that I have to see again on a regular basis," Vaughn said.

"Well. That makes sense," she said dryly. "What happened with her, then?"

"It was when I first came here. She was angry at Perth for some reason—they were together at the time—and was trying to get back at him. She told me they were no longer together and just wanted some temporary comfort." He shrugged. "I didn't question it, and I'm certain the fact that she's a charmblood didn't hurt her skills of persuasion. Unfortunately, she was hoping for a little more than one night and was furious when I refused. As a consequence, she holds a grudge against me, and Perth hates me."

Ivana shook her head. "For once, Vaughn, I can sympathize with you. Women who are so petty deserve what they get."

He smiled and pulled a sliver of bindblood aether out of the pouch at his side. He crushed it and rubbed it into the first cuts he had made, and then offered it to her. "Keeps it from scarring," he said. "Shallow cuts like these will be gone in the morning, without a trace. Learned that somewhere along the way."

She accepted his administration of the aether. "You do this all the time?"

He shrugged, watching while the latest mixture of blood started to shimmer, and then fade to silver. He pried it off the plate with his knife and set it aside, and then made another cut. "You get used to it."

"But not everyone does it."

He was silent for a moment. "Not everyone cares that using our gifts could end up causing even more harm."

"Yet you care enough to do this to yourself? Even without hard evidence?"

"Like I said. You get used to it." He shifted and then gave a weak chuckle. "Honestly, it's not so bad. There's something almost..." He shook his head and fell silent.

"Comforting about the pain?" she asked, before she could help herself. It was too raw, too close. *Damn it, get control, Ivana.*

He didn't look up. "Thanks. As if I wasn't already enough of an aberration."

She looked at his forearms. She had never noticed them before, but they had a myriad of paper thin scars, fading into non-existence, from long ago, before he had discovered he could put bindblood aether on the cuts, no doubt. So much like her own. "It wasn't meant to be a slight," she said quietly.

He looked up at her, studying her face.

She didn't know what led her to do it. Maybe it was the feeling that mixing her blood with someone else's was somehow intimate. Maybe it was the weeks, even months of time with him, flirting with the dangerous notion that someone might begin to *know* her...flirting with the dangerous notion that there was someone else to know.

Maybe it was simply seeing her own weakness displayed so openly on someone else.

She put down her knife, loosened her robe, and slid the right side off her shoulder, baring her entire arm to him.

He looked at the generous amount of skin that her nightshift displayed first, of course, but then at her arm. He stared at the scars. They were hard to see, but he would know what he was looking for, since he had seen them before.

"At least you have an excuse," she said.

"I don't understand," he said, not taking his eyes off the scars.

She slipped the robe back over her shoulder. "Don't you?"

He met her eyes.

Her chest felt tight. She felt exposed. She didn't know why she was doing this to herself. She nodded toward the most recent cut on his arm, where he had failed to siphon the blood off. "Your blood is turning."

He cursed and looked away to peel the aether off his arm. He tucked it into his own pouch, hanging at his side, and didn't look at Ivana again.

Maybe she had made a mistake. Maybe he had no idea what she was talking about.

They continued in silence for a while, until he suddenly broke it. "None of those are fresh," he said.

"No. They're not." She had traded drawing her own blood for drawing the blood of others. The former hadn't erased the pain, it had just allowed her to control it. The latter, on the other hand, had desensitized her to pain, until she no longer felt it.

At least...until recently.

She could see his mind turning it over. Trying to puzzle her out. Drawing conclusions. She could tell he wanted to speak, but he wasn't sure what to say.

"How did you know my brother?"

She made one cut a little too deep and sucked air through her teeth with a hiss. She quickly put her arm over the saucer, not wanting to waste the especially heavy trickle of blood that ensued.

That had not been what she had expected.

"I believe we've already been over this," she said. She was *not* discussing this with him. She didn't care how vulnerable she was feeling right now. She was simply *not* going to tell him.

"I'm not trying to be nosy. Really. I'll admit he was an arrogant ass, but this is still my brother we're talking about. What did he do to you?"

She slapped the knife down on the table. "Destroyed my life," she said through clenched teeth. "That's all you need to know."

He raised an eyebrow. "That's rather dramatic."

Something inside her snapped. "Do you know that at the university, my father was thought to be one of the most promising young scholars there? He could have stayed. He could have become a teacher of more than snotty-nosed noble brats. But as prestigious as that would have been, young scholars barely make enough to provide for themselves, let alone a family. He met my mother. So he took a job as a tutor. It paid better. We were comfortable enough. He should have stayed at the university. He would have lived longer."

"My brother killed your father?"

"No, your *father* killed my father, because your brother was a self-absorbed ass who couldn't take responsibility for his own actions, and your father was an arrogant, cold man who probably cared more for the mice in his stables than some commoner." What was she doing? She hadn't spoken of this to anyone. Ever. She spoke, and she didn't believe the words coming out of her own mouth. She wanted to be angry. She wanted to hate him. She wanted to believe it was his fault.

She only hated herself, as she always had, and that made her angrier than anything else could have.

Vaughn didn't say anything. He just watched her, knife held limp in his hand.

"Your *brother* took advantage of a girl who didn't know any better, who was naïve enough to believe the honeyed words of a handsome noble when he spoke of love, when all he really wanted was a free whore."

She had said the words so many times, but to her girls. About their situations. That the men were as much to blame, probably more, than they were. In every case, it was true. Every case, except hers. Because she couldn't bring herself to believe her own advice.

The dam had been compromised. It had been leaking for months. Now, it broke, and the pain welled up like the blood from her broken skin.

She knew the truth. It was her fault, her fault her father was dead, her fault they hadn't had the resources after her father's death to care for her sick mother, her fault her sister was the gods knew where in slavery.

Her fault she had run. Her fault. She should have known better. She *had* known better.

She had known Airell was trouble, but she had been so desperate to prove herself, so desperate to be thought of as a woman, that she had pretended she hadn't known. Even when she pressed him on when they could be together, she knew it was a lie when he had always said, *soon, love, soon.* But by that time, she was so ashamed of herself, ashamed for falling prey to him, ashamed of, at times, *liking* it, she couldn't bring herself to admit it.

Until it was too late. Until she had happily announced she thought she was pregnant, sure that would bind him to her.

Stupid, stupid girl.

She had never seen him again.

"He got you with child, didn't he?" Vaughn asked.

She gritted her teeth. She had already said too much.

"I've seen the stretch marks, Ivana. I can add."

Shut up. Shut up!

She only knew one way to get him to shut up.

"When my father demanded compensation for my virginity and an allowance for the child, Gildas told him he should have thought of the consequences when he didn't keep his whoring daughter under control. My father challenged him to a duel." Foolish man. Swordplay had never been his strong suit, but he had been blinded by love. Love that Ivana had so desperately sought, when it had been there all along. "Your father ran him through with a sword about five seconds into the fight.

"Without my father's income, we couldn't afford to live. The pitiless noble he worked for let us stay on his estate just long enough that, after my mother fell sick and died, he felt the need to try and recoup his losses by selling me and my sister into slavery. When they came for me, I ran. My sister wasn't so lucky."

Ivana could hear her own heart thudding in her chest, anger, shame, frustration warring. She wanted to strangle Vaughn for making her feel this way. She wanted to hate him for being a specter of her past come to haunt her these past months, and she most certainly wanted to despise him for pushing her to open herself up to him in a way she never had to anyone else.

"What happened to the child?" Vaughn asked.

"Premature birth. Died a few hours later." After all of that. She hadn't expected to care. She had. Could still remember holding the tiny, silent body, too numb even to cry. She had cried later, when her had mother died. When she was alone, and scared, and helpless in the months and years that had followed. And then one day, she had found the tears were simply no longer necessary. One day, she had stood over a corpse and found herself as dead inside as the body at her feet.

The room was silent. She couldn't look at Vaughn. Why, oh why, had she chosen to speak at all? Because they shared scars?

Vaughn scooped up the pile of aether they had made into the coin purse. "I would recommend keeping it on you. I don't know if they're searching your room."

She was suddenly immensely, deeply grateful to him that he didn't try to pursue the subject. She took the purse and put it under her pillow, but not before removing a sliver and tucking it between her breasts. She had nothing to attach the purse to at present, but it couldn't hurt to be prepared. She walked to the wall and put her hand on it. She didn't know if it faced outward, but it felt like the place where a window would have been had it been above ground.

There was a rustle from behind her, and then he joined her at the wall. In his hand was a larger knife. Long, slender. For cutting vegetables. He handed it to her, hilt first.

"Not your dagger," he said. "But should you need something. Don't let them catch you with it."

She took the knife, held the blade up to the light, and turned it. It was functional, if not elegant. She'd have to figure out a way to carry it discretely without impaling herself, though. She didn't have a sheath. Maybe she could "borrow" a few scraps of leather from somewhere and make one for herself.

Vaughn was still talking. "Yaotel would be highly displeased, to put it mildly, if he finds out I helped you." He hesitated. "I realize that I didn't put you under a condition of silence when I offered you the help. And I realize that should it become useful to you to tell someone, you probably would..." He didn't say, *betray me*, but that's what he meant. "But..." He shrugged. "There it is."

She set the knife down on the table. So he did understand her, knew what he was risking, and yet he helped her anyway.

She didn't understand *him*.

He ran a hand over his face, made to speak, stopped, and then finally spoke. "I know what it is to be used," he said quietly. "I went to my fiancée for help, after I had been changed. She made it clear that the only reason she had been with me was for the wealth and power my family would offer." He paused. "I had thought she loved me. I had thought I loved *her*." He hesitated. "I know it's not the same thing, but..." He trailed off, fiddling with the cuff of his sleeve.

No, it wasn't. "I miss the moon," she said.

"Not the sun?"

"It's been a long time since sunlight held any warmth for me." Darkness, on the other hand, had become her friend, her companion. It was peaceful, even in chaos.

"I know a way up onto the roof. There's a guard, but I can get past one guard easily enough." He paused. "Want to risk it?"

She stared at the wall, and longing filled her. "Absolutely."

Chapter Thirty-Two

Science and Moonlight

It had been a while since Vaughn had been up here, but it had always been his favorite haunt, especially on nights he couldn't sleep. It wasn't much: a tiny balcony cut outside a window from an empty room on the topmost floor of the manor. It was mostly hidden from prying eyes by the slope of the roof, yet allowed an unhindered view, for himself, of the moon and the forest beyond the walls.

The guard was at the stairway to the upper floors. Banebringers weren't supposed to leave the underground compound that served as their home by any other way than the secret entrance in the shed; it wouldn't do to invite the curiosity of strangers should a Banebringer wanderer stumble across a guest or servant of Gan Barton.

Invisibility was useful. The guard at the door was always bored, and tonight he was dozing against the wall, meaning Vaughn didn't even have to create a distraction to open the door and slip by, which is exactly what he and Ivana had done, using his invisibility.

Ivana stood away from him, hugging her arms around her chest and staring up at the moon. She was still wearing her robe over her nightshift—had stopped only to don a soft pair of shoes—and the night air was cool.

But it was peaceful. The change in her countenance was visible. Her face smoothed, the hard lines at her eyes and mouth all but disappearing. She didn't smile, but neither did she look as tense as she had earlier.

It had never occurred to him that someone might deliberately do what he did for a reason other than creating aether. But now that it had, he understood it. There were days when he almost looked forward to replenishing his stash. He had always thought he was crazy.

Then again, perhaps comparing himself to a killer wasn't the best sign that he was sane.

He breathed deeply and closed his eyes. He was never sure if the moonlight and night air relaxed him because he had some tenuous connection to an ancient moon goddess, or if it was only a personality quirk that made him prefer moonbeams to sunlight.

He was still trying to digest what she had told him about his father and brother. It wasn't that it was hard to believe—it wasn't. As Vaughn had learned since his exile, his father cared about the family's—or perhaps only his own—reputation more than anything else. He wouldn't have cowed to a common man claiming that his eldest son had sired a bastard on his daughter. Offering compensation and support would have been admitting guilt, and Vaughn had known even as a child that his father never did that.

As for the casual manner in which he dispatched Ivana's father...

A good judge of a man's character was how he treated his servants. While his father hadn't been overly cruel—beating them because he was angry about an unrelated matter, for instance—neither did he hold them in any regard. Ivana was right. They, and any commoner, might as well have been mice in the barn—or more likely, the cats that caught the mice. They served a purpose, but beyond that, their existence was inconsequential to him.

His brother?

Airell had been arrogant, selfish, and their father's prized son in every way. Vaughn had never been close to him, and the constant comparisons between the eldest and the younger three by their father had done nothing to encourage brotherly affection on their part, and everything to encourage a sense of entitlement and conceit on Airell's. It was because of Airell's known taste for women—and a lot of them—that his father had thrown Vaughn's former fiancée at Vaughn, hoping to cure what he had worried was a flaw in his masculinity.

Ivana's story, at least as it concerned his own family, was not only plausible, but entirely likely, on all points. That he had heard nothing about specifics to tie her story to events he knew was not noteworthy; his brother's escapades were so accepted that at thirteen or fourteen, the age Vaughn must have been at the time, it would have been only another rumor among many, quickly dealt with and swept under the rug.

That Ivana had been a victim, however...

His gaze drifted to her, and he wondered. Wondered what had happened from there, after she had run. How she had ended up as an assassin, of all things. Whatever she might say, whoever she might be right now, it was clear to him that the person she once was, was not, in fact, dead. And he had an incredible urge to try and resurrect that person.

The person who loved language and science and moonlight.

She turned her head to glance at him, and he looked away. Not only because she never liked it when she found him staring at her, but also because the feelings stirring inside him were uncomfortable. Unwelcome. Downright frightening.

He wasn't supposed to *feel* anything, other than pure, unadulterated lust. It was why he never slept with a woman more than once.

So much for that. That he hadn't slept with her didn't seem to matter in this case. Perhaps that was the most frightening part.

"So not only have you given me advantages, you've now given me an escape route," Ivana said softly, studying him.

Vaughn looked over the edge of the stone half-wall that surrounded the balcony. They were at least fifty feet up. "I don't know if scaling the manor wall from here would be particularly wise," he said.

Her eyes roved back and forth over the wall as if she were gauging the difficulty of the climb. "I've climbed worse," she said. "But you're right. And a sudden distraction could be disastrous."

"Trying to keep yourself invisible would certainly qualify as a distraction," he reminded her. "It takes time to master before it becomes second-nature."

She paused, digesting that. "Any tips?"

"Control," he said. "Learning how much you need to burn to accomplish your goal and controlling your use of it accordingly. It's the single most important aspect and hardest to master. But the last thing you want is to run out of aether in the middle of an escape attempt."

She turned to look back out beyond the manor. "Could we be seen up here?"

He pointed to a spot on the wall. "There's only one point where a sentry's regular route would allow him or her to see into this particular spot, and they're looking outside the walls for threats, not within." As he spoke, a sentry strolled into just that spot. As expected, the sentry didn't so much as glance in their direction. What possible reason could he have, after all, for watching the manor itself? When the sentry had left their line of sight again, Vaughn continued. "Unless, of course, something draws their attention."

"Like an escape attempt, perhaps?"

"Indeed."

"Still," Ivana said, stepping back. "Perhaps it would be better to go in rather than risk it. If I were seen up here..."

Vaughn didn't want to go in. He had never seen her so relaxed, and, for that matter, it had been a while since he had felt so relaxed himself. So instead, he stepped close behind her.

"There are other ways to ensure we can't be seen, if you're concerned." He placed one hand lightly on her waist and burned aether to make them both invisible.

She stilled at his touch, and the tangible sign of her recognition of his proximity, whatever she thought of it, was enough to send a thrill through him.

Ah... She smelled faintly of lavender, courtesy of the soap she had used while bathing, no doubt, and he had to stop himself from leaning in to take a deeper breath. He didn't *think* she would appreciate it. At least, she wouldn't admit it if she did.

She didn't draw back, however, and after a moment, she relaxed again.

Perhaps it was the fact that she didn't move away from him that encouraged him to say what he said next. "I'm not my brother," he said softly.

She shifted.

He persisted. "Any woman who sleeps with me knows exactly what she is and isn't getting from me. I would certainly never tell a woman I intend to bed that I love her."

She snorted. "No. Just that her scars, about which you know nothing, are like rivers of liquid pearl."

He blinked, momentarily confused. And then remembered. *Ah. Right.* He had bedded one of her women, hadn't he? "Is that why you dislike me? Because I slept with one of your ladies? Or is it because I look like my brother?"

"Ohtli is a grown woman," she said, ignoring the latter comment. "If she wants to make stupid decisions, that's her right. Might not leave her long in my employment, but I can't pretend she couldn't have said no."

Was it a compliment that she didn't think he was a rapist?

"But perhaps if you understood a little bit more about her," Ivana went on, "about how her desperation to see herself as more than the slime on the bottom of your boot has led her to seek the approval of men, any man, who would say something vaguely complimentary to her, you would have thought twice about it."

He refused to feel guilty. As Ivana noted, her "girl" was a grown woman, and she could have said no. "How can I know more about a woman if I only intend to have a casual encounter?"

"How, indeed," she said dryly.

"Look—when you sleep with a woman long enough, she starts getting *ideas*," Vaughn retorted. "My life is not one I can invite a woman into. How could I provide for a wife and an inevitable family? What I do is for their protection."

"You know what's crazy?" Ivana responded. "I think you actually believe you're being chivalrous."

"It isn't about chivalry," he said.

She shifted again, tossing her head, and despite their argument, the wave of lavender that washed over him was intoxicating. "You're right. It's about protecting yourself."

So he wasn't allowed to try and understand her, but she was allowed to analyze *him*? That hardly seemed fair. "That's ridiculous. Women are like liquor to me. And that's all there is to it."

He realized in hindsight that what he had said was far more revealing than he had intended it to be.

She turned enough to look up at him, a wry look on her face. "That much is obvious."

He let out a long breath. He had intended to draw *her* out, and instead she had turned it around on him again. This conversation was long overdue for a subject change. "I'm sorry for what my father and brother did to you and your family. It wasn't right."

She looked at him askance, as if knowing exactly what he was doing, and then turned back. "My own choices are what did this to me and what brought me to where I am and who I am. You don't have to apologize for anyone."

He dared to ask. "Why, then, have you chosen this life? Do you enjoy killing?"

"I feel nothing about it one way or the other."

Burning skies, how did one get to that point? "Then surely you didn't *choose* anything. Whatever the circumstances were, I can't imagine—"

"There is always a choice," Ivana said, her voice hard.

"But that doesn't make it *who* you are!"

"My actions are what define who I am, and nothing else."

"So be someone different."

There was a long silence before she spoke, more softly. "There comes a point when redemption is simply no longer possible, Vaughn."

A sudden gust of wind blew, and it was cold. Ivana shivered, and Vaughn drew her closer against himself reflexively. There was no point in arguing with her further. "We can go in," he said.

She didn't pull away. Instead, she turned again and tilted her head back to look up at him. "Perhaps that would be best," she said. Her voice sounded odd, tight. It thrummed with tension left unexplained.

He looked down into her eyes, and his entire body went taut as he felt the warmth of her own body beating into his own, felt the curve of her waist against his hand. Burning skies, he had never wanted a woman so badly.

He let his hand slide up her waist, to her ribs.

She closed her eyes and let out a long breath, and when she opened them again, her eyes were burning. And that was when he was finally sure. She didn't mind his touch. She welcomed it. She was *enjoying* it, and had been all along.

It was all the encouragement he needed. He leaned over and pressed his lips to hers.

Chapter Thirty-Three

Unmasked

She ought to have killed him. She ought to have knifed him. At the least, she ought to have punched him.

But Ivana didn't do any of those things. Instead, she found herself tilting her head back farther, turning toward him more fully, leaning into his kiss. The tension that had been thrumming through her body since the moment he had stepped close to her demanded nothing less than full acquiescence.

Then, when he pulled back far enough to look at her, as if to gauge her reaction, she had a moment for her brain to kick in.

She stepped away before he could kiss her again, her mind and body both feeling like a raging, flooded river about to crest over its banks. This was not good. She had to escape, before she made a stupid decision.

She had no excuse that wouldn't sound like an excuse, so she merely said, "This was a bad idea, for many reasons. Good night." And she turned, walked to the window, pulled it up, and climbed back through it, the way they had come. She had the sliver of aether with her; she hoped it worked.

"Ivana," he said from behind her.

She ignored him, and again when he called a second time. If he called a third, she didn't hear him. She was already on her way back down the servant's stairs, safely, she hoped, invisible.

Vaughn stared through the open window, one hand caught in his hair.

He let go of his hair and slid the hand down to rub his face instead.

She had kissed him back. She *had* kissed him back. He could still taste her lips, gods, as soft as he had ever imagined, her warmth leaning against him. And his heart was beating wildly at the surety that she wanted him, as well.

Then why had she fled?

A bad idea, she had called it. She wasn't just referring to the risk of being caught. *I'd recommend bedding her as soon as possible. That way I can be sure you'll no longer be a potential ally,* Yaotel had said. Was that it? Did she think he would bed her, and then no longer help her?

Wouldn't he? Yaotel's words had stung, but they were true. Had been true.

But...what if, just this once, what if, only with her, he allowed himself to enjoy something more? What if...

It *was* a bad idea. He was already too emotionally invested in her. But *Temoth*, her lips...

He wanted her so bad, it hurt. Would she take him, if he could convince her? Could she even be convinced?

He glanced again at the window, wavering, his body urging him one way, and his mind warning him another.

As usually happened, his body won.

Ivana heard her name being softly called outside her door as she lay on her bed, staring up at the ceiling, cursing herself for losing control, a failing she had an awful lot around Vaughn. She closed her eyes. *Go away.*

He was persistent. "I know you're in there. Don't make me wake everyone."

She gritted her teeth, went to the door, and opened it a crack. "Go away," she hissed. She tried to close the door, but he stuck his foot in it.

"Just hear me out. Please."

Don't let him in, foolish girl. Don't do it.

She wasn't afraid of him. She was afraid of herself.

"Ivana? I'm begging you."

She let him in.

He closed the door and turned to face her. She hadn't bothered to extinguish her lamp yet, and she could see his pupils, dark and large in the dim light, but he didn't approach her.

She hugged her arms to her chest. "What do you want?"

"I'm sorry," he said, spreading his hands. "I shouldn't have kissed you without asking."

"You're forgiven. Now leave."

He stepped closer. "Ivana...can we be honest with each other?"

Her throat tightened. "Absolutely not."

"I want you. More than I've ever wanted a woman before in my life."

She snorted, trying to force herself into apathy, even though his words made the throbbing worse. "That's only because you can't have me."

"Most likely." He took another step toward her. She took a step back, and he stopped. "But unless I am mistaken...you want me too."

She swallowed. She wanted to deny it. Should have denied it and insisted that he leave again. But it was true.

Somehow, he had cracked her walls and squirmed his way through them. He knew more about her than even Aleena, the only other living person who might have a claim to understanding her—and that only because she was exceptionally perceptive, not because Ivana had opened herself to her.

But Vaughn, he had given her a taste of what it might be like to be just Ivana again. She hated him for it, she feared it, yet longed to give in to it...

He must have taken her silence for acquiescence, because he dared to take another step toward her. There wasn't anywhere else for her to go, except to back into the wall behind her, so she didn't move. He took another step, bringing him close enough to touch, and then into her personal space, close enough to lean forward and kiss again. Her heart started pounding.

"Deny it," he said, reaching out with his hand and laying the back of his palm against her cheek, let it slide down, and then turned it in time to let his fingers brush over her lips. "Deny it, and I'll leave. I swear."

It was so unfair. Her lips burned at his touch, and she knew that *he* knew exactly what he was doing to her. He was far too experienced not to. He was playing with her, making it harder for her to speak words she didn't mean.

Just say it. Make him leave and be done with it.

"We don't always get what we want in life," she whispered instead.

Despite his earlier apology, he leaned forward again and brushed her lips with his own. He could sense he was winning, damn him.

"But when what we want is so easily in our grasp..." he murmured back against her lips, and then kissed her again, softly. "Why not take it?"

"Because I need allies, not trysts," Ivana choked out. He didn't move, but let her words tickle his lips. She didn't move either, though she knew it belied her statement.

He pulled back again, far enough to look at her eyes. Something warred in his eyes, and a moment later, she knew what. "It doesn't have to be like that," he said.

Her breath caught in her throat. Those words were too familiar. "Your pardon?"

He touched her face again, this time moving his hand to push her hair back, and then cradle the back of her head. "It could be different, this once. For me. For us."

"Just a little longer, love, and you'll see. We can be together."

She laughed, and it came out sounding more nervous than

she had wanted. "You just finished enumerating all the reasons you never sleep with a woman more than once, and now you're telling me you've changed your mind?"

His eyes flashed eagerly. "But that's just it. You and I...we're different. I *know* you won't ever expect or want anything more from me." He hesitated, and then placed one hand on her waist again. "When we finally go our separate ways, or when we get tired of each other—whichever comes first—we can mutually part and it won't matter. No broken hearts. No unfulfilled expectations." He let his hand drift up again. "We're the perfect lovers, Ivana, for as long as we have each other."

But it was different. It was different, wasn't it? He wasn't promising her forever, and she didn't want forever. She just wanted to be *known*...

His hand reached her side and hovered there. Almost tentative—a question.

The warmth that had been pulsing through her body grew more insistent, drowning out the voice of warning in her head.

It took sheer force of will to stop herself from turning reflexively toward his touch.

Ivana ran her tongue along her lips, and he watched her, hunger in his eyes. And then he looked back up at her, met her own eyes. "When is the last time you did this for yourself?" he whispered.

That broke her. She closed her eyes and sank against him. "I hate you," she said, and then opened her eyes and looked back up at him.

He smiled and touched her face with his free hand. "That's what I'm counting on." And then he kissed her again.

Vaughn had broken Sweetblade, the hardened assassin, and his head was still spinning from the achievement. She melted into him, casting off any lingering pretense of resistance, parting her lips to allow his tongue to sweep into her mouth.

This was quite possibly the worst decision he had made in his entire life.

He was going to get what he wanted, and the cost was going to be enormous.

But he couldn't stop himself. Against all odds, he had convinced her, and now she was offering herself to him. He couldn't change his mind now. Right?

No. No way he could change his mind now. His mind was fogging, and any semblance of rational thought was already fleeing.

He untied her robe and pushed it off her shoulders. Though he half-expected her to shrink back, changing her mind as their dalliance grew more heated, she didn't. She merely exhaled as his hands explored her body with one less layer of fabric between them and her flesh.

She tugged his shirt off and ran her hands across his chest.

No. She was serious.

He kissed her again. Her obvious pleasure intoxicated him further, in a way a woman's pleasure never had.

He was losing himself in her, to her, and he felt like he needed a reminder of the terms of their engagement. He slid up, pressing himself close against her, sighing at the warmth of her body against his, and he kissed his way around to her ear.

"You don't have to worry," he whispered. "I never tell a woman I intend to bed that I love her."

He might as well have punched her. Ivana shoved him back and slithered away from him. "Get out," she hissed.

He stumbled back, blinking, obviously stunned. "What?"

"Get. Out."

"Don't worry, I never tell a woman I intend to bed that I love her..."

"I love you. Just a little longer, and we can be together."

He was so different from his brother, that he was in reality just like him. She didn't even know if that made sense logically, but it was what she felt.

He still didn't move. His eyes flicked across her, and he licked his lips. "I don't understand."

She bent down and picked up his shirt, and then hurled it at him and went to the door. "I don't know how to make myself more clear."

He caught the shirt, but his face was pained as he adjusted himself. "Ivana...please..."

"You have a hand, and I'm sure you know how to use it." She threw open the door and pointed to the hallway. "Get out of my room and stay out."

He stared at her, mouth open. "Do you *want* me to tell you I love you?"

She didn't have the energy for an explanation. She didn't even know if she had one. All she knew was that this had been a terrible idea, and its fulfillment would come at too high an emotional cost. She couldn't afford such a cost, not now, not ever.

She couldn't be that person again.

"No. I want you to leave."

He slowly pulled the shirt back on, seeming to finally believe her. He started to speak as he went out the door, but then shook his head, and left.

She closed the door behind him and then leaned against it, eyes closed. She had *let* him seduce her. She had allowed him to make her vulnerable, and in that state she had dared to reach for the unattainable—and yet what she feared more than anything: to stand unmasked, and perhaps in that terrifying state, find a way to be whole again.

But she would never find either in his—or any man's—arms.

She slid down the door and put her head against her knees. She may have hated him, but even more, she hated herself.

He didn't understand. He couldn't understand. She had let this go on for too long, had *let* him get to her because he was right: the old Ivana was still buried inside her, deep down, and she wanted out.

Well, she wasn't going to let that happen. She wouldn't allow herself to be vulnerable again. She would rescue her girls, and then that person would die, once and for all.

Chapter Thirty-Four

Servants of Danathalt

Vaughn had no idea what had just happened. It was obviously the comment about never telling a woman he intended to bed that he loved her, but that made no *sense*. Why in the abyss would that matter? It was intended to reassure her—and himself—not upset her.

Damn woman. Damn women! Damn all of them. He pounded his fist into the wall once, and then strode down the hall toward his own rooms, fully intending on taking Ivana's biting advice.

He was stopped a few steps from his door. "Vaughn? Vaughn!"

He turned. "What?" he snapped.

A young researcher he had seen around, but didn't know

well, halted, seeming taken aback by his tone. "Uh, thought I'd find you in your room, not wandering the halls." He paused. "What are you—?"

"Never mind," Vaughn growled, mood darkening every moment he was being kept from relieving his aching loins.

"We need you down in research," the researcher said.

Xavin. That was his name. "What in the abyss could you possibly need me for in research at this time of night?"

"That woman is acting crazy."

"Great. And the grass is green."

"She's asking for you."

What in the— Vaughn gritted his teeth. "Can't this wait?"

"She's being quite...insistent."

Superb. Just superb. Vaughn put one hand against the wall and leaned forward, taking several deep breaths, and then pushed himself back. "Fine."

By crazy, they meant she was throwing things around her cell again, including herself. And howling. And screaming vulgarities at the top of her lungs. He could hear her all the way down the hall.

The moment she laid eyes on Vaughn, she stopped, and smiled sweetly. "Ah," she said. "I knew that would eventually work. People will do almost anything to make someone stop acting insane."

Vaughn fingered the syringe he held behind his back. "I'm in no mood for your games," he said. "What do you want?"

"They're going to try and kill me," she stated calmly, as if she had been commenting on the amount of wildflowers that had grown in the upper field that year.

Vaughn started and glanced toward Xavin and now Saylyn, who were watching from the now-broken window. Xavin and Saylyn exchanged glances and then shrugged. *Didn't hear it from us*, the gesture said.

"You want me to sympathize?"

"No. I want to tell you that they won't succeed. They can't hold me back. And even if I die, another will rise in my place."

Vaughn shivered. Was this a promise from a crazy woman, or a threat from Danathalt? "Look, woman. If you don't have anything useful to say, I have other things I could be doing—"

"Do you know why I called you here?"

"I have no idea," Vaughn said. He was about ready to plunge that syringe into her neck, immediate threat or not.

"Because I like you." She smiled again, and it was half-coy and half-grotesque. "I just wanted you to know that. It's nothing personal, you understand, not between Thaxchatichan and I. And for what it's worth, I hope you survive."

"Great," Vaughn said. "Got it." He turned and left the room, handed the syringe back to Xavin, and started to head back down the hall. *Damned crazy woman. Crazy just like the rest of them, just a different kind of crazy.* Waste of—

The alarms started ringing.

Within minutes, there were people rushing down the halls, shouting, strapping on weapons—pulling on pants as they ran. It was the middle of the night, after all.

Vaughn stopped in his room for his bow and quiver and followed the increasing stream to the hidden entrance. It didn't take long for him to hear the rumor that this attack would be much worse than the others—combined.

It also didn't take long for him to realize why.

The moment he stepped outside, he could hear them. The scrabbling of needle-legs. The howling. The screeching. The growling.

It sounded like every damn bloodbane she had summoned thus far had made an appearance, and possibly more.

He sprinted for the wall, took the stairs two-by-two, laying an arrow to his string as he ran.

Tharqan was already on the wall, an arrow held loosely to his bowstring, but he hadn't drawn it. He was staring.

Vaughn joined him—and stopped breathing.

Bloodcrabs scuttling back and forth. Bloodwolves pacing. Bloodhawks circling the forest. New monsters as well. He saw at least one bloodgiant—a distant and thankfully smaller relative of the behemoth that had attacked them in the city, but still plenty dangerous. They liked to stalk travelers in the Dusty Hills, throwing boulders down on their heads in narrow passes—and then feasting on their flesh.

Bloodspiders with their poisoned fangs. The spiders themselves were *only* the size of dinner plates, but one bite from those fangs would leave a grown man convulsing and dead within an hour if he didn't receive the antidote. They didn't even congregate in this part of the continent, preferring to inhabit the humid forests to the east, dropping on unwary passers-by.

Bloodbats, normal-sized, but a spelunker's nightmare. They didn't let go once attached.

Even bloodrats. Individually, they were merely a nuisance, but in number they were deadly to anything—or anyone—they swarmed.

Creatures they had no name for—unlike any he had ever seen before—all of them terrifying.

And they weren't attacking yet. They were *congregating*: pacing, chittering, growling and snapping when they saw people on the walls, but staying put.

It was like a scene from a nightmare. It *was* a nightmare.

He lifted his bow and sighted the nearest bloodwolf, but hesitated. Tharqan looked at him. "I haven't attacked yet," he said. "I'm afraid doing so will break whatever it is that's holding them back."

Vaughn didn't know what they were waiting for—but whenever they decided to attack...

Tharqan was right. Not worth risking it. He lowered his bow and glanced back at the manor house. Lights glowed in a few of the windows; either the bloodbane had been noticed, or someone had alerted the staff.

Then he flicked his eyes down to the courtyard, to discern how organized they were this time. The training had apparently been beneficial; it looked like they were in units.

Good. Maybe that meant they had a strategy.

He turned back to the horrors outside the wall. Other archers had joined them on the wall and were spreading out, but all held, following Tharqan and Vaughn's lead.

It was only after they were in position that a tall figure

strode to the front of the pack of monsters. At first glance, he looked human, with human clothing and long, black hair tied back. But he then turned his face toward those watching on the wall.

This was no human—at least, no living human. His skin had the pallor of a corpse, and his eyes were the white, pupil-less orbs of all bloodbane.

He looked directly at Vaughn and smiled.

The monsters stilled, waiting.

Vaughn's heart started beating faster. He didn't know what this creature was, but it seemed to have control of the others, and that couldn't be good.

"Servants of Ziloxchanachi!" the corpse-thing cried, lifting its arms in the air. Its voice was melodic, strangely soothing, and carried easily. "Your declaration of hostility has not gone unnoticed. Consider this a warning."

What the—? It talked? *Since when did bloodbane* talk?

The corpse left its arms up, and an expectant hush fell over all those gathered there. And then it dropped them.

Vaughn's first arrow was flying through the air before the corpse's hands had returned to its sides. Time slowed, and it seemed like Vaughn could watch the progress of its flight. The corpse cocked its head, also watching the arrow. The moment before it would have pierced it in the heart—assuming it had one—a bloodhawk swooped down in front of it, taking the arrow through the wing instead.

The corpse smiled, shook its head, and disappeared into the advancing throng.

Vaughn cursed. Waste of a good arrow.

Time returned to normal, and the abyss broke loose.

At first, Vaughn thought they might barely have the upper hand. The archers collectively knocked three bloodhawks out of the air almost immediately, along with their charges—bloodcrabs carried again in each claw. The first coalition of bloodbane sent to take down the wall, led by the bloodgiant, faltered at another hail of arrows.

But it didn't take long to realize that while they had the initial edge, they were far outnumbered. And unlike their previous encounters with the monsters, they were learning.

Bloodhawks started dodging, wheeling and turning in the air, swooping at the archers themselves, causing them to reel back or even flee from the wall. One went down—the bindbloods were tending to him already.

Only Vaughn and Tharqan had a hope of hitting the bloodhawks with their new maneuvers, and Tharqan had the disadvantage of not being a moonblood—for the enhanced sight as well as the ability to confuse the creatures by turning invisible.

Vaughn had the disadvantage of not being able to be everywhere at once.

And he couldn't stop the spiders. Dozens came, climbing over the dead bodies of the bloodwolves and bloodgiant who had tried to ram it down by brute force, up the walls.

Archers backed away as the creatures came, which allowed the remaining bloodhawks free reign to fly right over their heads and drop their packages inside the walls.

Shouts rang out from the courtyard below, but Vaughn didn't have time to look. A half-dozen spiders had just crested the wall, ten feet from where he stood. They took a few seconds to congregate, and then they headed right for him.

He backed away, shooting arrows as quickly as he could, but they were too fast. He cringed back right before they reached him, expecting the bites of dozens of fangs—

Fire exploded in front of him, licking at his face, causing him to stumble back in shock, almost off the edge of the wall. Thrax gripped his arm, pulling him upright.

The spiders had collectively burned to a crisp.

"You singed my eyebrows!" Vaughn accused Thrax.

Thrax barked a laugh, slapped him on the back, and then jogged back down the wall, looking for more creatures to set on fire.

Vaughn's attention was drawn by another group headed toward the wall. A second bloodgiant, and a half-dozen bloodwolves. This time, the bloodgiant was carrying a huge wooden shield, blocking Vaughn from finding a good shot.

The aether arrows might excel at cutting through monster hide, but they could be stopped by a thick piece of wood as much as any arrow.

So he started on the wolves.

The wall vibrated as the bloodgiant rammed into it. It wouldn't take much to breach, and, desperate, Vaughn took down two of the bloodwolves closest to him, and then shot at the bloodgiant's exposed leg.

The giant howled, but shook the pain off like it had been stung by a bee, and if anything, renewed its attack with more vigor.

Another vibration.

"They're going to break through!" he warned anyone who could hear him below, though they had their own troubles, by the looks of it.

A glance told him that spiders were spreading out over the courtyard, bloodhawks were diving at prey, and bloodcrabs were chasing down men and women in pairs, separating them from their comrades.

Thud.

He shot the last bloodwolf that was with the giant, but the giant was still going strong. If there were more bloodwolves—and Vaughn had a suspicion there were—they were hiding in the forest now.

Smart. Waiting until the giant broke through. How and when had they grown so intelligent?

Tharqan had tried to get him from the other side, but a swarm of bloodbats dove at him. He flailed with his arms, almost losing his bow, trying to keep them back by causing turbulence in the air where they flew. Vaughn watched helplessly. He couldn't shoot an arrow into that; even if he could hit the bats, he would chance hitting Tharqan.

A flare went up from the courtyard, another fireblood attempting to burn the spiders off a man who had just gone down under a dozen of them, screaming.

The spiders went up in flames, but so did the man.

Yasril ran to the man's aid, directing a stream of water from the well to douse him. It worked, but the man lay convulsing, bleeding from a dozen wounds. Bindbloods raced in to drag him out of the fray, back into the shed, which had, at present, escaped the monsters attention.

Thud.

The bloodhawks were leaving him alone now, and all the other creatures were waiting, out of sight. He couldn't shoot at bloodcrabs from up here, and there were too many spiders to waste arrows on, especially if the firebloods had them under control.

So he waited, arrow nocked. The moment that wall was down, he knew more bloodbane would come streaming out of the woods.

With a crack, the stone finally split, and after another smash from the giant, the wall caved in.

The giant roared and charged.

The forest exploded with monsters.

When the alarm bells rang this time, Ivana groaned and pulled her pillow over her head. Was she ever going to get sleep?

They kept ringing. She heard shouting. She lifted her head, listening. More shouting than ever before. She got up and went to the door, opening it far enough to stick her head out. People were rushing past her, paying her no mind.

It almost seemed the entire compound was being emptied.

This couldn't be good. She shut the door, turned around, and put her back to it. Or was it?

She threw on her clothes and snatched up the knife Vaughn had given her, along with the pouch of aether. She plucked a piece out, burned the aether, and slipped out her door.

She knew it wasn't perfect. It was only the third time she had tried using it, after all. But either it was good enough, or people were too busy heading toward the exit to pay any attention. So she headed the opposite way, toward the stairway Vaughn had shown her. The guard was gone, and she made it to the balcony without issue. From there, she could see the entire fight.

Hundreds of bloodbane were engaged in a concerted attack on the manor. The first attempt at breaching the wall failed, but winged monsters flew right over to deposit their deadly burdens, and the spiders climbed unhindered.

She considered her options. Now would be the perfect time to escape. No one would even notice in the chaos. But she hadn't obtained the information she needed yet, and if the Ichtaca fell like this, she would never gain that information. Now would also be a perfect time to prove herself, gain some trust. If indeed Yaotel would ever trust her. But what could she do?

Vaughn was in the midst of the chaos, standing on the wall. He almost got swarmed by spiders, but a fireblood caused the whole pack to go up in flames before they could reach him.

In fact, Banebringers were now using their abilities with abandon. Ice, fire, water, flashes of light, tiny windstorms...and those were only the most obvious uses. Whatever training they had done had clearly helped.

An idea formed in her head. She looked down at the pouch in her hand. She knew exactly where she could obtain more than moonblood aether. And if she had a full range of aether at her disposal, mixed with her own blood... Had they even considered the many ways their own abilities could be used? From what

Vaughn had said, Yaotel had just recently started allowing them to think about it.

Ideas pumping through her brain, she headed back down to the compound and toward the research wing.

To Vaughn's horror, not a handful, but dozens of bloodwolves streamed from the woods, accompanied by more crabs and more grotesque creatures he had no name for, all heading for the breach.

Arrows flew from his bow and the others', but it was a paltry amount compared to the number of bloodbane coming, and Vaughn was running out of arrows.

He saw a flash in the woods, and for a moment, the corpse-thing reappeared, looking grimly satisfied, and then disappeared back into the woods.

That thing. It was what was controlling the horde of bloodbane. It was one thing to summon a few bloodwolves and bloodhawks and have them carry a few bloodcrabs. It was another to get the monsters to work together, to have strategy and thought.

If he took that thing down...

He scanned the woods frantically, but even his eyesight couldn't pierce the dense foliage.

The sky suddenly brightened, and Vaughn glanced down.

Danton had summoned light. A lot of it.

The monsters recoiled momentarily, giving a large group of men a chance to attack en masse. Shells shattered. Spiders burned. Bloodwolves yelped. A group of bloodbats began swirling around in a small tornado.

An iceblood paved the ground in front of three charging bloodwolves with ice, and they slipped and slid, giving half a dozen others the chance to skewer them on pikes.

Yaotel had even entered the fray. As a beastblood, it was difficult for him to use his magic up close to monsters without chancing being killed, but with the monsters distracted, Yaotel jumped on the back of a bloodcrab, pushed his hands onto the shell, and roared.

The crab almost threw him off, but a moment later...

The shell *exploded*, leaving a very gory but satisfied Yaotel in the middle of the mess.

Vaughn blinked, duly impressed.

The maneuver hadn't been without cost, however.

The beasts quickly regained their composure, and now a dozen Banebringers found themselves in the middle of a very dangerous situation.

Vaughn felt in his quiver. Three aether-arrows. Damn.

He scanned the chaos, trying to be rational, trying to look over the many people in immediate danger and decide, in the long-term, what would be best to spend his arrows on.

The blood giant was brushing off attacks—and people—like gnats. It had finally noticed that they were dragging injured Banebringers into the shed, turned, and headed directly toward it.

Vaughn drew his bow, sighting the giant's head. He loosed the arrow.

The giant turned at the last moment, distracted by Perth, who had stepped in to engage the bloodgiant up close, and

Vaughn's arrow went wild.

Vaughn cursed.

As much as Vaughn hated the man, he had to admit he had balls.

Still, Vaughn was tempted to put an arrow through him for causing him to waste an arrow as well as miss a perfect shot.

The bloodgiant *laughed* at Perth, who was hurling icicles at its legs. A deep, resonating laugh that vibrated the clothes on Vaughn's back.

He raised a hand to smash at Perth, and Perth darted out of the way, narrowly missing being obliterated.

Vaughn raised his bow again, but the giant kept moving, in unexpected ways, trying to follow Perth.

He was so focused on the battle in front of him, he failed to see the bloodhawk diving at him from behind.

The bow flew from his hands as the beast barreled into his back, and Vaughn toppled off the wall.

He braced himself for collision with hard stone, but landed on something remarkably soft instead: a bloodwolf that had happened to be running by. The wolf snarled, flailing to get out from under the sudden weight that had crushed it, and Vaughn rolled to the ground.

Of course, now he had a bloodwolf breathing on his face.

He turned invisible and rolled.

The wolf howled and turned in circles, sniffing, and Vaughn dove after his bow.

He had almost reached it when a nameless creature with two heads, six hooves, and lots and lots of teeth stomped on it.

A crack sounded, and when the creature moved on, not seeing Vaughn, Vaughn crawled over to his bow. It had been shattered in three places. Useless.

He clenched the broken pieces of the bow, infuriated. That bow had been with him since before he had fled home. It had been a gift from Teryn.

He spun around, reaching for the nearest source of water, intending to drown the fanged horse-thing by shoving the water down its double-throats. He didn't even know if it would work. He had never tried it before. He'd probably kill himself.

But he didn't get the chance to try. Someone stumbled into him, not aware he was even there, and he lost his concentration, as well as a line of sight on the horse-thing.

Being invisible had its advantages, but not in the middle of a crowded battle. He reappeared, startling the man who had walked into him, and went in search of another bow.

A shout went up from the direction of Perth and the bloodgiant, and he spun to look.

Perth was down, bleeding from one side of his head, arm hanging crookedly at his side.

The bloodgiant advanced on him, bloodlust on its warped face. It ripped a piece of wood off the roof of the shed and raised it, obviously intending to skewer Perth on its jagged edge.

Suddenly, it went rigid, and blood started to spurt from its throat. It roared, smashed into the side of the stable, caving in the wall, and then fell with a thud, narrowly missing crushing Perth, who lay barely conscious on the ground.

Everyone, including the monsters, stopped fighting to turn and see what had happened.

Ivana appeared on the bloodbane's back, holding a kitchen cleaver dripping with blood.

Everyone else shook off their surprise and went back to the battle. Not Vaughn. He stared at her, shocked to see her there, shocked at what she had done. How had she managed to slice through that giant's neck, when her dagger hadn't worked on the behemoth? Sure, the giant was smaller, but it usually took aether-enhanced weapons to get through bloodbane hide that easily.

He shook himself, realizing that standing stupidly in the middle of the battle wasn't a good idea, and when he looked back, she was gone.

Also, he was still weaponless. He turned invisible again, darting for the nearest open space from which he could take stock.

The shed had been crushed, sadly. Fortunately, no one had been inside. The bindbloods had been dragging the injured back into the manor itself.

Unfortunately, the hidden entrance had now been exposed. Another nameless creature, this time a horse-sized lump with about a dozen arms started prying at the door.

He started. They could *not* get inside the manor!

Anyone nearby realized it as well.

But they were losing Banebringers fast. Dozens had already been removed for injuries, or had fatigued beyond immediate recovery from over-use of aether, leaving behind a smaller and smaller fighting force, forcing those who would normally not fight to join the fray.

Xavin, the researcher, swung a hammer at the lump's back at

the same time a fireblood wrapped it in flames.

The wooden shed went up, but so did the lump.

Moonbloods worked to douse the shed. Incredibly, when the fire was out, the lump was still standing and still prying at the door, despite a giant *dent* in its back from the hammer. The metal door had a dozen divots in it, and Vaughn could see it bowing at the sides.

Maybe now was a good time to try the water trick. The well was nearby.

He slunk as close to the lump as he dared, and then—

Huh. He didn't see a mouth. Did it have a mouth? Did it have lungs? Did it even *breathe*? This was a problem.

Xavin tried again with the hammer, and the creature turned, quicker than seemed possible, wrapped him in its dozen arms, and squeezed.

They watched, horrified.

Xavin simply...popped.

A spray of bloody mist and gore filled the air, followed by an almost elegant shimmer, as the same spray turned to aether mid-flight.

The air nearby split. *No, no, no!*

Vaughn held his breath. He had never prayed before, unless he counted ritual visits to the shrines before he had changed, which he didn't. He prayed now.

Thaxchatichan, if you give a damn about any of us...

It was short, but Vaughn hoped a god would get the point.

A bloodrat scurried out of the tear. Followed by two dozen more bloodrats. And then the rip disappeared.

Vaughn sank back in relief.

Sure, bloodrats could be annoying, and if you let a dozen of them cover you, their especially sharp teeth could bring a man down, but considering all the alternatives...

The swarm went up in flames almost instantly, and the fighting resumed.

The lump...smiled...licked a few patches of skin off itself, and turned back to the door.

So it did have a mouth!

Vaughn crept even closer, trying to see it. It was nothing more than a slit in the lump's hide, and it was *vertical*. No wonder Vaughn hadn't seen it. He had been looking for a mouth under the thing's eyes.

He summoned the water, heart pounding. He hoped he didn't kill himself with the effort of using his powers in a new and unpracticed way.

He should have practiced more. He should have joined the training; what could it have hurt to hone his skills a little?

The water reached him, and he shoved.

At first, it merely splashed onto the lump, since its mouth was closed. But the lump turned, surprised, and its mouth opened.

Vaughn pushed even harder, willing the water down, down, down...

The lump lurched backward, many arms flailing in the air. It fell onto the ground, gurgling, retching, and still Vaughn kept at it.

Finally, the lump fell still, and a cheer went up among those around him.

Vaughn let go, and the excess water ran out of its slit-mouth onto the ground

He swayed, feeling dizzy. Too much, too intense, not enough control.

Inspired, Banebringers who worked with elements started afresh all over the courtyard. He saw a monster explode in flames from the inside-out. Another froze—literally—and then shattered when someone else hit it with a sledge hammer.

Vaughn used his solidified aether to turn invisible again—so he could find a good spot to rest until his blood regenerated. At present, he was only a liability.

Unfortunately, despite the work of those left, they were losing. As much as the death of the lump inspired them, the first Banebringer death seemed to inspire the bloodbane.

They had been lucky up until now. Three more Banebringers died when a handful of bloodcrabs initiated a coordinated attack on them. A half-dozen harmless bloodsprites flitted out of the first hole, but the second two holes spit out a bloodwolf each. The bloodwolves overwhelmed those standing closest to the tears, causing even more deaths.

Before long, the ground was covered in a fine silvery powder, aether crushed by the trampling of many feet.

He scanned the area, looking for Danton. He found the youth fighting another grotesque creature. It had a body like a worm, except it was covered in carapace like a beetle, and had the many legs of a millipede. Vaughn shuddered. Bug-haters' nightmare.

Danton was holding his own, however. The creature was as dumb as a worm, and though it sported the razor-sharp teeth of many bloodbane, it was confused by Danton's illusions, constantly slithering toward and snapping at the wrong thing.

Finally, someone came to help, and while the beast was chasing a butterfly, of all things, another Banebringer clove the stupid creature in half with an axe.

Ivana appeared a few more times. She was using his aether extensively, disappearing and reappearing at convenient points in the battle, somehow using whatever weapons happened to be dropped. Most of the time, she cut and chopped her way through monsters as though she were using the aether-enhanced weapons herself, which continued to confuse him. It shouldn't work, unless she had managed to make a beastblood aether mix with her own blood and apply it to the weapons.

Suddenly, when Banebringer deaths were summoning bloodbane as fast as they could take them down, the tide changed.

Vaughn stood, confused. There were no fliers left and now more Banebringers than monsters left alive. He saw another bow on the ground and picked it up—but it was over. And they had...won?

The remaining monsters left in the courtyard retreated, as if called back by a singular mind.

Vaughn's stomach dropped out of him, certain that the corpse-thing had signaled the retreat, and that they were in store for some new horror.

But then the corpse-thing itself made an appearance, stepping regally through the breach in the wall as if it had been created for its use.

It went up in flames. Vaughn felt a wash of relief.

Well. That settles that.

Except...the flames grew, brighter, larger, until a whirlwind of fire and ash forced everyone nearby back, and then it disappeared as suddenly as it had started.

Out of the smoke and silence a melodic laugh sounded. The corpse-thing—he *really* needed a better name for it—stepped forward, and its white-orbed eyes were now wreathed in flame. It held out its hand, and a tiny flame floated above it. It turned its hand experimentally, as if curious about the flame, and then hurled it at the nearest man.

This time, the man went up in flames.

A moonblood quenched him, pulling him back as he screamed.

The courtyard stood in shocked silence.

Magic. The bloodbane had just used magic. Impossible. They were tough, but not magical.

The corpse chortled with glee.

A moonblood shot a jet of water toward it, and an iceblood refined the water into a dagger of ice right before it struck the corpse's stomach. It impaled it, and it looked curiously down at the ice sticking through it, touching it.

When it looked back up, its eyes had taken on a shimmery cast. It grinned, and a moment later, was hurling tiny icicles through the air toward anyone and everyone, until the giant icicle was gone.

"Anyone else want to try?" it asked, stepping forward again.

This was no ordinary bloodbane.

Vaughn turned invisible, stepped closer to the corpse-thing, and held an arrow loosely to the string of his new bow. His last one. Would it even matter if he shot it through the heart?

To his surprise, the creature looked right at him. Not through him. At him. It could see him.

"Go on then, *moonblood*." The word sounded almost like an insult. A mockery.

Vaughn dropped his invisibility, since it didn't matter anyway, drew and loosed the arrow. It was a perfect shot. The corpse threw up a wall of ice at the last moment, stopping the arrow in flight. It hung in the middle of the wall while everyone stared.

My gods.

"I trust you've taken my warning?" it said. No one replied. No one dared.

And then Ivana appeared directly in front of it. She held out her hand, and it went rigid, eyes wide in shock.

She twisted her hand, face contorted in concentration, and it started to bend backward.

It screamed.

She kept her hand up, kept walking toward it, and it kept bending, bending, bending...

"You've allied with them?" it screeched, sounding indignant.

A sudden crack. It dropped to the ground, limp, and Ivana dropped her hand. She walked over to it and nudged it with her foot. It didn't move.

Then Yaotel made a gesture with his hand, and Perth, Hueil, and two other men Vaughn didn't know well surrounded Ivana. She held up her hands. She was currently weaponless.

"Seize her," Yaotel said.

Chapter Thirty-Five

Implications

Vaughn followed as Perth and Hueil dragged Ivana through the smoking ruins of the shed and back into the manor. He tried to keep Ivana in his sights. She was walking calmly, head held high, and not struggling at all against her captors. But when she glanced back, just once, her eyes were ice.

Many of the uninjured—or at least not seriously injured—Banebringers stayed behind. The walls had been breached, and they knew a handful of bloodbane were still roaming in the woods.

Besides that, there was a gigantic mess to clean up, as quickly as possible.

But the procession through the manor's halls was nevertheless long. It was led by Yaotel, and Danton had come along, as well as the other two men who had originally seized Ivana. Perth and Hueil, of course, held Ivana's arms firmly, and Perrit the ex-priest trailed behind—as well as a few stragglers: Bane-bringers who had been healed satisfactorily by the bindbloods emerging from the infirmary, a few who had ignored Yaotel's order to start cleaning up and followed anyway...

All in all, at least a dozen people entered the meeting chamber. No one sat. Those who weren't actively involved in guarding Ivana were standing around nervously, wondering what this portended. Or curiously. Or eagerly.

As for Vaughn...

He thought he was going to throw up. He didn't know if it was the residual effect of the battle, or the fatigue and terror and horrific sights were finally catching up to him, or over-use of his aether, or if he were worried for Ivana. Or all of them. He had no idea what Yaotel intended by this.

"Search her," Yaotel said.

Perth eagerly obeyed and performed a search for weapons that ended up being more like a systematic groping. Vaughn gritted his teeth, feeling the sudden urge to slug the man. But Ivana leveled a cool stare at Perth that made him instinctively quail, though he tried to cover it up by coughing and picking at the blood that had dried on the side of his face.

Maybe *she* would slug him. That would be almost as satisfying.

"Easy, Perth," Hueil said, frowning at Perth.

Vaughn knew he had always liked Huiel.

Perth pulled out a slender package that was tucked into the

back of Ivana's trousers, looking triumphant. He let the make-shift wrappings fall off, revealing a kitchen knife.

Vaughn winced. The knife he had given her. Not weaponless, then.

Perth slid it across the table that was at the front of the room to Yaotel. Yaotel glanced at it, frowned, and shook his head.

"She tried to escape," Perth said before Yaotel could speak. "You ought to have her executed."

That was it. Vaughn was going to punch him. Or maybe strangle him. Yes, that was more fitting. He felt himself inching forward, fist curling into a ball.

Danton spoke up, timidly. "I don't know if coming out to help defend the manor counts as an escape attempt, Yaotel."

"She's clearly dangerous," Perth spat back.

Vaughn lunged at him. "She saved your worthless life!" Vaughn shouted, shoving the man back against the wall.

"Enough!" Yaotel said. "Perth, shut your hole. Vaughn, control yourself, or I'll have you thrown out."

Vaughn stepped back, matching Perth's glare.

Perth rubbed his head. Vaughn had almost forgotten the man had suffered a pretty hard blow to the head. Probably had a massive headache. Maybe dizzy. Being shoved against a wall wouldn't have helped.

Vaughn grinned savagely. Good.

Yaotel massaged his temple. "Now. Perth, your concern is noted, but I agree with Danton. She made it outside the manor. If she wanted to escape, she could have easily slipped away without endangering herself." He looked at Ivana. "Which brings me to the point. When did you become Gifted?"

"I'm not...Gifted," she said, her voice even.

Yaotel frowned. "Lying about this isn't going to help you."

Ivana lifted the hem of her shirt, revealing a bloody gash across her waist. It had stopped bleeding, but it hadn't turned to aether. "Does that look like aether to you?"

Yaotel's frown deepened. "Then how," he said, "did you do what you did out there?"

There wasn't even a moment of hesitation before she responded. "Ask Vaughn."

He grimaced. *Yeah. All right, then.* She *had* warned him, after all.

The room fell silent, all eyes on him. Even Ivana was looking at him, but her eyes were unreadable. He shifted uncomfortably. The last words they had exchanged hadn't exactly been friendly.

"You had better explain yourself," Yaotel said. "Now."

There had been an unmistakable flash of hurt in Vaughn's eyes when she had given him up. *Good.* He had become far too comfortable with her. He needed a hard lesson.

Vaughn didn't attempt to dissimilate. "We discovered that when you combine the blood of a Gifted with the blood of a non-Gifted, it creates an aether that the non-Gifted can use."

Yaotel blinked, several times. The silence of the room took on a stunned feel.

Vaughn kept talking. "We created a stockpile of this aether for her use, at my suggestion. Obviously, she used it tonight."

"When did you discover this?"

"Shortly before we arrived, by accident."

"And you've said nothing about it before now?"

Vaughn remained silent.

"And you specifically set out to create this...mixed aether to help her escape."

"I gave her options, should she grow desperate. I should point out, she chose to use those options instead to help defend all of you." He cast his eyes around the room, meeting the gaze of each person in turn.

And still he defended her? Burning skies, this man was unbelievable. What did she need to do, take off a few of his fingers?

Yaotel held up his hand. "All right. We'll deal with that later. Let's go back to the aether. You're telling me a non-Gifted could use aether if they were to mix their own blood with that of a Gifted."

Vaughn hesitated. "Well. I only know about our tests with my own blood. But I assume so, given the abilities she used during the battle."

"Test it. Now. I want confirmation." He gestured to Hueil. "Hueil."

Huiel pricked himself with a knife and then held the knife out to Ivana. She almost snorted. Had he really just done that?

No matter. She accepted the knife calmly, pricked her own finger, and put her hand out. Huiel smeared his finger onto hers. She set the knife down silently, right next to her hand, while everyone else was staring at her finger.

It turned to aether a minute later.

"What does it do?" she asked Huiel.

"I'm a windblood," Huiel said.

Wind. All right then. She imagined turning the aether into a tiny whirlwind.

A sudden breeze wafted across the room. Papers skittered across the table at the front, and Ivana's hair rose and sank. The aether on her finger had turned to powder.

Yaotel let out a long breath. "This is..." He shook his head, apparently at a loss for words.

A shaky voice spoke up. "Could I...say something?" Perrit. The ex-priest.

Yaotel waved his hand.

Perrit looked troubled. No, beyond troubled. He looked shaken. "Do you realize the implications of this?"

"I'm sure there are many," Yaotel said. "What are you referring to?"

"The priests," Perrit said. "I never rose high enough in the ranks to learn how they did their magic. Since I was rejected, I've often thought it ironic how so much of what they did mimicked Banebringer powers, to a lesser degree, and how the sacred texts never mention magic as a gift from Yathyn." He hesitated, glancing around at the faces watching him, and then down at his feet. "Perhaps irony isn't the right word."

"What are you saying, Perrit?"

"We know the priests keep Sedated Banebringers somewhere, presumably to care for them in a humane manner and to keep the rest of us safe from them when they die. What if...what if they're doing more than just caring for them? What if they're—" He broke off, seemingly unable to continue.

My gods. "Harvesting their blood for their own use," Vaughn finished softly for him.

The silence turned to whispers as everyone repeated what they had heard to each other, making sure they had heard correctly, making sure they weren't crazy.

Vaughn's head was spinning. An idea was forming, the barest outline of an idea, but... "This could be it," he said, and then repeated it, louder. "This could be it."

The whispers dropped off.

"Don't you see?" he said to everyone in the room. "If this is true, then it means that the priests are living a lie. At the same time they damn us, they themselves use the very magic they've condemned. And call it a gift from Yathyn, when in reality it's a gift from the heretic gods."

Saylyn, ever the researcher, broke in. "But how could they use aether from Sedated Gifted? Wouldn't the aether be useless once they've rendered it neutral with the Sedation formula?"

Vaughn blinked. He hadn't thought about that. "Unless they aren't actually Sedating everyone," he said. "Or there's another factor we're unaware of at work. Have we ever experimented with aether directly from a Sedated Gifted?" He glanced around, half-expecting Yaotel to stop him, but even he was listening. "Maybe they're all hypocrites. Maybe Yathyn doesn't care. Maybe Yathyn doesn't even exist. I don't know, but whatever is going on—"

A sob broke the air, and Perrit swayed back and forth, and then fled the room.

They all allowed a moment of silent pity for the priest. Most of them treated the Conclave's damnation as a joke. No one believed it. Or at least, no one knew what to believe.

But Perrit...Perrit had always kept his faith in Yathyn, choosing instead to believe that the god had rejected him—that he had some offense or sin in his life that had damned him. To have that belief questioned...

Poor man.

But Vaughn was growing too excited to linger over it for long. "Yaotel," he said. "This could be our salvation. If the general populace knew about this—"

"It wouldn't make a difference," Yaotel said roughly. "No one is going to miraculously accept us back into society because the Conclave is proven corrupt. Most people believe that anyway, to some degree."

"No." Vaughn shook his head. "No. You're right, of course. The prejudices run too deep for that. But it's a seed of doubt. There are already those who support us—Gan Barton isn't the only one. And there are those who doubt, but are too afraid of being branded heretics themselves to speak up. The Conclave's fall would strengthen those people, giving them a voice. Yaotel, this could swing the political tides in our favor. Even the king might be convinced, given enough time and effort." Without war. Without massive bloodshed. Without Setana being ripped apart in a bloodbane's claws. "The power of the Conclave has only grown strong in the past century. It doesn't run so deep into Setanan heritage that it will be impossible to uproot."

Yaotel shook his head, slowly. He still wasn't convinced. What would it take? "What would you have us do? March into the Conclave and declare their corruption, without any evidence? You think they would take kindly to that?"

"No, of course not. We'd need a plan, a way to get them to reveal it themselves..."

"Except that this is all still theory. We don't know for sure the priests are harvesting aether from Gifted for their own purposes. It could be coincidence. It could be ignorance. The only way to know for sure would be to know where the Sedated are kept so we can find the evidence. And we don't know."

Vaughn deflated. Yaotel was right. There was no point in even brainstorming plans until they knew for sure Perrit was right. As quickly as hope had flared, it died.

"I do," Ivana's voice said.

"What?" Yaotel said.

"I know where they're kept." She paused. "Or, at least I know someone who could tell us."

Yaotel stared at Ivana, incredulity on his face. And then: "Out," he said. "Everyone but Vaughn and the woman, leave now."

The others left reluctantly, wanting to hear the rest of this, but Yaotel's voice had the ring of authority that compelled obedience.

When the door had slammed shut behind the last person, Yaotel pinned Ivana with an impressively intimidating stare. "Explain."

Not that she was actually intimidated. She shrugged. "I told you. I know someone who knows where Sedated Banebringers are kept. She's on the inside, in fact." She used the term "Bane-bringer" deliberately, trying to irritate him.

"And you've waited all this time to tell me this? You didn't think that might be useful information to us?"

"Contempt and disdain are hardly the tools with which to win someone's trust," Ivana said, matching his gaze without flinching.

Yaotel shifted and looked away. "You're telling me now. Why?"

"Because I have something to gain now," Ivana said.

"Your freedom?"

"My freedom has never been in question. I'm here because I've chosen to stay here."

Yaotel's face darkened at that, which was precisely Ivana's intent. She was in control. She was the one manipulating his moods, not the other way around.

"What I stand to gain is your help," she continued, as if nothing had happened.

"Our help," Yaotel said, disbelief in his voice.

"A trade," Ivana said. "Mutually beneficial. I can see, despite your endeavors at making it seem otherwise, that you're intrigued by Vaughn's proposal."

Yaotel was silent. He rubbed his hand over his face, and then spoke as if the words were being dragged out of him. "What do you want from me?"

"Simple. I want in."

"Why in the abyss would you *want* to be part of a plot to infiltrate and expose the Conclave? What possible advantage could that have for you? Unless you have a death wish, that is."

Finally time to play the card she had been holding close, for the right moment. "The Conclave has imprisoned some people who are important to me. I can't imagine their intentions are benevolent. I want to find them and rescue them. I can't do it alone."

Yaotel sighed and sat down for the first time. "I can't let you go. I don't trust you."

She rolled her eyes. If she wanted to leave, she could. But she would continue playing, for now. She needed his help. "If you won't let me go myself, then I need someone to go in my stead to deliver a message and obtain the information we need from my contact."

"I'll go," Vaughn volunteered. He had remained silent the entire time and didn't look at Ivana now. "It's my idea. I'll take the risk."

Yaotel looked dubious. "You think you can handle it?"

The door flew open. "Yaotel! There's a problem—the woman—she's, she's dead!" Airec stood in the doorway, panting.

Yaotel looked up sharply. "What do you mean, dead? She was alive when the attack started. Who killed her?"

"No one, Dal. She's just...dead. Collapsed on the ground of her cell. No pulse."

"And the bloodbane?"

"As far as we can tell, no bloodbane was summoned. We've already tested her blood, and it doesn't turn to aether. She's no longer Gifted!"

Ivana raised an eyebrow. How was that even possible?

Yaotel stood up. He addressed Vaughn and Ivana. "Work out the details. Let me know when we have more information."

Yaotel strode out of the room with Airec, leaving Vaughn and Ivana alone together for the first time since...had it really only been hours before?

She went over to the table and started rummaging around in drawers until she found a clean piece of paper and a pen and ink. She sat down at the table, dipped the pen in the ink, and started writing.

Vaughn shifted from one foot to the other, uncomfortable in the sudden silence, and wishing she would say something.

Finally, he broke the silence. "How did you do that?"

She didn't look up. "Do what?"

"Whatever you did to that...corpse-thing? It was like you were controlling his body."

She paused in her writing and then looked up at him, eyebrow raised. "With your aether?"

"*My* aether?"

"Don't you realize how much water the body contains? In your blood, your bladder, your bones, your organs..." She raised a second eyebrow. "Have you people never dissected anyone?"

He certainly hadn't. He didn't know about the researchers.

"Of course, I couldn't be sure if that thing's biological makeup was the same as ours—so I didn't even bother to try and be more precise. I just grabbed whatever I could and tried to break it."

Vaughn's mouth dropped open. "Burning skies," he whispered. The possibilities swirled in his brain. Could he make someone's bladder explode? Someone's heart? Drain all the blood to one side of their body? Break bones? The power...

He was going to be sick.

"Granted, it wasn't easy," Ivana said, going back to writing as if she hadn't just imploded Vaughn's brain. "Didn't know if it would work, especially with my inexperience. But I'm certain that with practice, you could do some pretty precise manipulation of the body." She tucked a strand of hair behind her ear. "My contact is, of course, Aleena. I'm including anything pertinent in this message, which you will give to her."

He had liked Aleena. And she had *almost* helped him. This couldn't be so bad.

Ivana dipped her pen again and let it hang above the inkwell. "Don't underestimate her." She put the pen back to the paper. "She'll be naturally and rightfully distrustful of you, given that I disappeared in your company. She's better at reading people and seeing through facades than even I am. This note, even in my hand, and even in Xambrian, won't be enough to convince her that you're my agent, not my captor."

On the other hand...

"She'll likely ask you some questions to try and feel you out. Your best chance is to be perfectly honest."

"That I can do," he said, relieved. Deception wasn't his best attribute.

"If she asks you to tell her something only I and someone I trusted would know, how I gained the inn would be a promising topic."

He snorted. "Let me guess," he said.

Ivana ignored his comment. "I was plucked from the workhouses by an older gentleman whose wife and children had died in a fire decades earlier. He had no other family and wanted someone to leave his inn to."

Vaughn's mind was spinning, trying to piece together her story. Ran away from slavers, ended up on the streets and in a workhouse? But...wait...when had her training as an assassin come in? She had mentioned that like it had come directly after her flight.

"He also wanted...companionship."

Vaughn didn't ask. He didn't need to, because he could guess—trading her body for food, shelter, and a possible future? He studied her, wondering. He had asked her, that night, when the last time she had slept with someone for herself had been, because he had an inkling that it had been awhile—and thought that might break down that last barrier. And it had worked—at least temporarily.

But had she *ever* done so, since his brother—if even that counted? Her body had been a tool, her entire life, a means to an end, and nothing more.

And for the first time in *his* entire life, he felt a pang of guilt. What had he been asking for? To give herself to a man in a way she hadn't done since she was fifteen years old?

This business of knowing a woman before sleeping with her was a pain in the ass—and conscience.

"I tired of that. When he became severely ill some time later, I helped hasten the inevitable. Aleena knows this story. No one else does. It will probably convince her that I sent you."

"Probably?"

She shrugged. "There are other ways to get information out of someone than my telling them freely. She may question you further, she may not. It depends on how she feels about you. She's perceptive; I'm hoping she'll sense that you're genuine."

Vaughn was feeling a little uneasy about taking this on. This wasn't in his skillset. "What about that pendant? The one you gave to that man, presumably to convince Aleena you had sent him?"

Ivana's hand went to her collarbone, touching an invisible chain. "I had no time for anything else. It was a gamble. But I'm sending you to collect information, sensitive information that she will be wary of giving out let alone admitting she has—not least because it will put her own life at risk. I sent the man solely to give information. Different situation. The pendant wouldn't be enough. It could easily be taken off my dead body."

What must this woman's mind be like, always thinking about such things?

"All right," Vaughn said, though he still felt unsure.

Ivana signed the note with a flourish and put the pen down. She folded the note in quarters, stood up, and brought it to Vaughn. "Are you sure you can do this?"

Not really. "Yes."

"It's possible you may have to do more than just talk to Aleena to get the information your leader needs."

"I know."

"Don't screw it up."

"You're not the only one with stakes in this," Vaughn said. "I won't."

Ivana looked dubious, but she handed him the note anyway.

He tucked it into his pocket. "Um, how will I find her?"

"The standing plan is that if there is ever a situation where I appear to have been compromised, she is to visit a particular location, if at all possible, once a week, for exactly one half an hour, to see if I send any message. Unless she's been compromised herself, I have no doubt she'll be there at the planned time and place."

"Which would be?"

She cast him an irritated look. "I'm getting there. Down at the docks, at an inn and bar called *The Quay*. She'll be sitting at a table in the corner, having a drink. Thursday night at ten."

Three nights hence. *Damn.* "That doesn't give me much time."

"Then you'd best hurry."

He had been hoping for a good night's rest. He would have to settle for a few hours. "I suppose now you're going to tell me not to be conspicuous?"

"Dress like a commoner and go about what you're there to do, and you'll be fine. You look intimidating enough not to attract attention from those looking to rough up someone weaker than themselves, and meetings in dark corners of inns are pretty commonplace. You won't be bothered unless you invite trouble. You want to work in that questionable part of town, you learn to turn a blind eye to anything but your own business, so don't invite trouble."

Great. Just great. That didn't make him feel at *all* better.

She started toward the door.

"Wait—Ivana," he said.

She stopped and turned, one eyebrow raised. Her expression was still unreadable. Impassive.

Emotionless.

He didn't know what he intended to say. He was sorry? She had been acting as though nothing had happened. Perhaps a bit more cool than she had been of late, but she exhibited none of her fury of a few hours ago, nor any embarrassment. As if it was what it was, and now it was done.

Was that all it would ever be? Was there *nothing* to say?

If so, he didn't know what or how to say it. He didn't even know if he *wanted* to say it. So instead, a single word dropped from his lips. "Why?"

"Why what?"

"Why..." He struggled and felt like a coward for what he said next. "Why didn't you escape when you had the chance?"

She studied him, and then answered calmly. "Because I knew enlisting the aid of your people was my best hope for rescuing my girls."

"Ah."

She moved toward the door, as if to leave, but then stopped as she passed by him. "Oh, and in regards to your original question—"

"I didn't ask another question," he cut in, feeling panic rise in him. Maybe he *didn't* want to talk. Best to let it go. No need to belabor the point.

"In regards to your original question," she repeated. "Do you know what they call a woman who agrees to be a bottomless bottle of liquor for man?"

He swallowed. "I—"

"A free whore."

"Ivana, that's not—" He stopped when he felt the flat of the knife she had retrieved against the side of his neck.

She bent her head in close to him, almost as if she were going to kiss him. But instead she leaned around to put her lips next to his ear. "I made that mistake once," she said softly. "And I don't intend on making it again." She turned the blade and let it drop so that the sharp edge skimmed across his skin as it fell.

He winced at the sting of the cut and stepped away from her.

She met his eyes, and they were hard. "Report to me as soon as you return."

Then she left—the impact of her words leaving Vaughn feeling like someone had socked him in the stomach. She had it wrong. He hadn't been trying to use her, not like his brother.

He touched his neck, wet his fingers with the blood there, and then held up his hand to watch it turn to aether. Or had he?

Chapter Thirty-Six

New Allies

The streets near *The Quay* were surprisingly busy this late at night. Revelers just getting started, traders of wares best left for darkness, whores...

The last he eyed with interest. It had been far too long, and being around Ivana all the time was starting to make him hurt. He didn't typically hire women to meet his baser needs—usually didn't need to—but he was feeling desperate of late.

But not now, as he was in a bit of a time crunch, and not here. If he were going to hire a prostitute, he would seek out nicer neighborhoods. Pricier, but their handlers were more concerned about controlling disease and keeping their establishments worthy of the upper-class men who would seek entertainment there.

He shoved aside such thoughts. He needed the brain in his skull for this job.

He pushed open the door to *The Quay*. It was clean, dimly lit, and loud. It smelled of fermenting ale and faintly of fish. He wasn't sure those two smells went together, but no one else seemed to mind.

Aleena, he reminded himself. He looked around and finally spotted a lone figure at a corner table in the back. He approached cautiously, trying not to look like he was headed there until he was sure it was her.

He cast a glance that way—

She looked over at him.

He had once observed that Aleena didn't seem the type to be involved in this business. The look she gave him made him reconsider that observation. It wasn't malicious or even hard, like Ivana's tended to be. Just...chillingly penetrating.

He slipped into the empty chair across from her and gave her an easy smile. "Well, fancy meeting you here."

She didn't return the smile. Instead, she pinned him with that same, penetrating gaze. Without looking away, she gestured to a passing waiter. "An ale for my friend," she said. "Cider for me, if you please."

The waiter nodded, and they sat in silence until he brought two foaming mugs and plunked them down in front of them without a word. Aleena slid a setan across the table, far more than needed to pay for two drinks. The waiter pocketed the coin and left without another glance at them.

She leaned forward. "It has been months since I have had news of my mistress, and the last I heard, you were in her company. No amount of charm is going to gain my trust. Where is she?"

The smile slid off his face. Perhaps this wouldn't be so easy after all. He fumbled in his jacket pocket, pulled out the folded bit of paper and handed it to her. He had tried to read it—couldn't help himself—but his Xambrian simply wasn't good enough without a lexicon to make out much more than some basics.

She took the paper and unfolded it, eyes remaining on him until she had smoothed it flat on the table, and then she finally looked down at the note.

Vaughn waited. He tried not to look around or jiggle his leg or chew on his lip, and he didn't know if he was succeeding.

"Interesting," Aleena said. She touched the corner of the paper to the candle on their table and then tossed it in the middle to wait while it turned to ash.

She took a sip of her cider. "A secret society of Banebringers, hm?"

Vaughn swallowed and couldn't help but glance around them. But the tables around them were conspicuously empty, and it was far too loud to be overheard by those beyond. Not being able to read the note, he didn't know exactly what Ivana had told Aleena. He had hoped that perhaps it wouldn't be necessary to reveal that information, but he supposed that was naïve. If she was going to help, she'd have to know what was going on.

"And are you one of her captors?"

"She's not—well—" He pressed his lips together. *Honesty, Vaughn.* "No. I brought her there to save her life, not to have her imprisoned. Unfortunately, she hasn't been allowed to leave yet. But she's been treated well, I promise. She's not locked up and fed only bread and water. Just restricted."

"Ivana doesn't deal well with restriction. Why didn't she come herself?"

Aleena didn't even seem to think it was in question that Ivana could have escaped such circumstances to come herself if she wanted to. "I—I think she feels that cooperating with them—us—is her best bet for rescuing the girls. But I don't know all her logic. She didn't explain herself fully to me."

Aleena regarded him silently, eyes studying every minutia of his face, as though it revealed his thoughts.

Who knows. Maybe it did.

"And why should I trust you?"

"I—the note is written in her hand," he started weakly.

"A forgery," she said. "Easily done, by someone skilled enough."

He blinked. She sounded so certain. Had he lost already? "No! It's not. I mean—" He took a deep breath. She had already read that he was nervous and not particularly keen on this whole endeavor, and she knew someone like him would easily panic and give something away. She was trying to unsettle him.

"Tell me something that you could only know if you had gained her trust enough to become her agent."

Gained her trust? Is that what had happened? He doubted she would ever admit it, if so. And yet, she had accepted his aid. Shared a private part of her past with him so that he could do this.

He opened his mouth to repeat Ivana's instructions, but

nothing came out. All Vaughn could see was Ivana, brow furrowed as she poured over an obscure text in a forbidden language, Ivana, tugging down her robe to show him the scars on her arms, Ivana, head tilted back, eyes closed, as she let down her defenses to allow herself the pleasure of his touch.

"It's a mask," he whispered.

"Your pardon?"

He raised his eyes to meet Aleena's. "It's a mask," he repeated. "She's hard and cold. Yet—though she would never admit this—something inside of her wishes she weren't what she is, but she feels powerless to do anything about it." *Past the point of redemption.* Maybe she had admitted it. To him.

And then he had ruined everything.

Aleena sat back in her chair, a look of surprise on her face for the first time. "My," she said, and Vaughn struggled to regain his sense of composure.

"While my instincts tell me you're sincere, I feel compelled by due diligence to base my trust on more than instinct." She tilted her head to the side again. "What was the name of Ivana's former master—the man who taught her everything she knows?"

Vaughn's head snapped up and despair filled him. "I have no idea," he said.

To his surprise, Aleena nodded. "Good, because neither do I. If you had gained that information, it would have to have been through torture or means other than her own lips." She drained the rest of her cider and stood up. "I'm satisfied, but I can't give you the information you want tonight. It's too sensitive for this place."

Vaughn stared blankly up at her, not sure what she wanted.

"There's a retaining wall for an orchard within the city, but just outside the northern gates of the palace. The king allows commoners to come and pick a limited number of apples at this time of year, leading up to the harvest festival. Meet me there tomorrow at two in the afternoon."

She didn't bother to wait for his confirmation. Instead, she stood up, nodded to the waiter who had brought them their drinks, and left.

Vaughn was left staring into his untouched ale. Why bother?

He drained it anyway, as if to justify to himself that he had no other recourse than what he did next to drown his sorrows.

He looked too scruffy for this place, but coin talked when clothes didn't. Still, they made him bathe, took his clothes to wash while he would be occupied, and provided him a plain but clean robe to don in the meanwhile.

He had specified no preference in the type of woman—at this point, he didn't care—but he started when a bronze-skinned, obviously native Fereharian entered the room.

She was achingly beautiful and dressed to accentuate it, and his body responded almost immediately.

Good. I need this. I deserve this. Damn woman, playing with my mind, playing with my emotions. Well, she wouldn't keep playing with his body, not tonight.

The companion—that was what they called whores in places this upscale—smiled at him and seated herself on the divan. She patted the seat next to her. "Dal," she said. "I am at your disposal. What is your pleasure tonight?"

He went to her, reveling in the closeness of such near-naked perfection as he sat down where she indicated. Unexpectedly, a thought encroached on his mind—a stray wondering at what had brought her to this place, literally and figuratively.

Her face was so friendly, so open, it was hard to believe she didn't want to be here. Surely she enjoyed it as well. Especially in such a place as this—they wouldn't think well on their prostitutes being mistreated, not here. She was lucky; not all establishments were so kind. She was taken care of.

But not, perhaps by those who should be taking care of her. Would any woman really chose this, every night a different man, never knowing what sort of man, called upon to be and act and do exactly what she was told, and have to pretend it was her pleasure to do so?

Perhaps some would. He didn't know.

But what about her? Not likely.

He felt his desire waning, and irritation grew in its place. This was *not* what was supposed to happen.

"Dal?"

He swallowed and swept his eyes over her, pushing away such inconvenient thoughts, trying to stir himself back to where he had been a moment ago.

This was all her fault! All her moralizing and high and mighty thoughts, coming from an assassin of all people—

The woman seemed to sense his hesitation. Of course she did. She was good at this. She put her hand to his robe and fingered it. "If I may presume?"

He nodded numbly, barely noticing as she slid the robe off

his shoulders, leaning in close as she did so. Her body, lightly clothed as it was, brushed his chest, and fire swept through him. Until she kissed his neck, and he breathed in sharply.

Though her skin might have been the same approximate color, and her hair as silky and dark, she smelled nothing like Ivana.

And she looked nothing like Ivana. Her skin was too perfect, too smooth, too youthful—aside from a large, dark freckle on the side of her neck, which someone had attempted to cover up with makeup.

Ivana hadn't worn makeup since they had been with the Ichtaca, and he didn't think she suffered for it. Perhaps her complexion wasn't perfect, and, away from her inn, she had worn her hair pulled back, giving her a more severe look.

Until she had loosened it, and it had spilled around her shoulders. Until he had seen the lines around her hard eyes fade as she had melted against him. Until he had run his fingers along those scars, evidence of imperfection, evidence of a pain he didn't even begin to understand, hadn't tried hard enough to.

This woman was imperfect as well. He knew it as surely as he could see it, once he looked hard enough—all covered discreetly, of course. A freckle here. A dimple in the wrong place there.

A mask.

His manhood failed him, then. She *was* beautiful, but he didn't want this woman. If he tried hard enough to think about nothing else, he could probably perform, but that would take too much energy, and he was tired.

She pulled back from him, sensing that whatever it was she had been doing wasn't working. And she finally gave up, tilting her head. "I wonder," she said quietly, "if you really want to be here."

He stood up and pulled the robe back over himself, turning away from her. Never in his entire life had he failed to perform for a woman. Not once. Not one, single, damned time.

Ivana had ruined him, completely.

"Who is she?" the nameless beauty asked from behind him, still seated.

Perceptive. He could almost hear Ivana whispering next to him. *And has anyone ever noticed that about her?*

"A pain in the ass," he said. *Or balls.*

He thought she stifled a laugh in response, but he wasn't sure. Perhaps she had merely sneezed. "A long talk with the woman in question might be better than other means of relieving your frustration," she said.

Ha. He didn't think Ivana would respond well to that. He shook his head. "It's complicated," he said.

"It usually is."

He turned then, one eyebrow raised. "Are all companions versed in counseling as well?"

She smiled. "You would be surprised."

He sighed. "I'm sorry," he said, though that was an odd thing to say to someone whom he had hired to please *him*. "I...it isn't you."

"I know," she said. "I don't suppose you would admit that to my handler?" Though she was smiling, her face was strained.

Punishment if there were complaints? If a man had been

unable to achieve arousal to his satisfaction, for whatever reason, it was unlikely that he would admit his failure, thus making her bear the fault, however unjustified, if he chose to mete out his frustration rather than hide it.

"I won't blame you," he promised.

She nodded, relief evident on her face.

He knocked at the side door, into the dressing area, and an attendant opened it. The man, a eunuch, raised his eyebrow. "Finished already, Dal?" He cast a look into the room, frowning at the woman.

"Sometimes a man just needs a quick fix, you know?"

The eunuch stared at him, and given the high timbre of his voice, perhaps he didn't know.

"Uh...yeah. Are my clothes ready?"

The man bowed. "Washed, but still drying over the hearth."

"Don't care." He wanted out of here. Now. He didn't look back at the woman as the attendant closed the door behind him.

On his way out, he was sure to praise her exceptional beauty and skill and gave her a ridiculously generous personal tip.

It felt like a hollow gesture.

The next day, Vaughn found Aleena basking in the sun near the entrance of the orchard. He brushed himself off, trying not to look offended at the rough search he had had to endure to get in the orchard. A commoner wouldn't be offended. A commoner would be grateful for the tithe of free apples.

"Tell me," Aleena said when he reached her. "Do you think

the standing ordinance that commoners can pick the apples from this orchard before the harvest festival is generosity on the part of the king, or a way of obtaining free labor?"

Vaughn grunted. "You sound like Ivana."

Aleena smiled. "She's an exceptional woman." She stood. "Walk with me, Vaughn."

He had never told her his real name, so the note must have told her. He kept pace with her as she walked, and they wound their way through the trees, avoiding the poor already up on ladders, eagerly plucking apples from the trees under the watchful eye of the orchard's caretakers. They would receive a tenth of any apples they picked, for free.

Or, rather, in exchange for picking the king's apples for him.

Aleena led him to the far side of the orchard, where few had wandered yet. The orchard was enormous.

She plucked a ladder from an untouched pile and hoisted it against the tree without any struggle.

Strong, Vaughn noted. Not someone to underestimate, despite her plain appearance. She climbed the ladder, and together they worked, she plucking them, and then handing them down to Vaughn, who held up the increasingly heavy basket. When they had a full basket, she finally descended the ladder.

She went over to the caretaker, gave him the basket, and the caretaker selected a portion of the apples and let her wrap them in a large cloth. She slid one arm through the loop she had made at the top and gestured to Vaughn to follow.

He glanced back at the tree and then around the orchard. What in the abyss did any of this have to do with the information she had for him? They had been here for over two hours, and still she gave no hint that she had any intention of doing anything other than picking apples.

They left via a different gate and spent another fifteen minutes walking around the palace wall, toward a poorer part of the city—surprisingly close to the palace, but at its backside and well-hidden from view by trees, where no one important would ever see it. Finally, Aleena stopped and sat down next to the wall in the shade of a tree. She tossed an apple Vaughn's way and then selected one for herself before tying the bundle back up.

"Um," Vaughn said as they sat. "Do I dare ask why we just spent two hours picking apples?"

Aleena nodded beyond the trees. "Not a half mile from here is a workhouse. Ivana delivers her portion of the apples to them every year. I didn't want her work to go undone because she's currently indisposed."

Vaughn shook his head, no longer surprised by such revelations about the assassin. "And you had to bring me along?"

She turned to him and gave him a wide smile. "Made it go faster, didn't it?"

He stared at her, incredulous.

"However..." Aleena took a bite of her apple with a loud crunch and then continued to speak around the fruit in her mouth. "You might also be interested to know that *that* is the workhouse the girls were taken to."

"So they're there?"

"Not anymore," Aleena said, and then looked up. "Ah. There we go."

A man was headed their way. He had the pale skin of someone from Fuilyn. And the clear blue eyes and blond-white hair of a Fuilynian of pure noble blood. Fuilynians always seemed washed out to Vaughn, like someone had dunked them in a tub of bleach.

The man stopped when he saw Vaughn, and then glanced at Aleena.

"It's all right, Kayden," Aleena said. "He's a friend."

The man—Kayden—joined them, and Aleena tossed him an apple. He held it, obviously perplexed, and then sat on the other side of Aleena. "What's this about?"

Vaughn was glad he wasn't the only one who was confused by this encounter.

"Kayden, meet Vaughn. Vaughn, meet Kayden."

Kayden nodded curtly to Vaughn, and he realized with a start that this was the man Ivana had sent to talk to Aleena, back when they had fled the smoldering ruins of her inn. He had only seen him in the dark, and all but the darkest skin tones looked similar with his night vision.

Vaughn nodded back.

"Vaughn comes with some welcome news from Ivana. We are, apparently, to receive some help from a rather unusual source in freeing the girls."

Hope flared in the man's eyes, and he leaned forward eagerly. "It's been months, and with all my resources, I haven't figured out a way to get her out. What can this man do?"

"This man, and his friends." Aleena held up a hand. "But first, let's get Vaughn caught up. I took a job at the workhouse where I knew the girls had been taken, hoping to find and retrieve them easily. But by the time I started work, they had been moved." She glanced at Kayden. "I had unexpected help. Kayden used his influence to help me obtain a better position, one that allowed me information about where they had gone." She smiled wanly. "Lots of coin, noble blood, and a pretty face will do a lot that even I can't do."

Vaughn studied her. She didn't think she had a pretty face? She wasn't the exotic beauty of the prostitute the night before, but she wasn't homely by any means.

"The Conclave has them," Vaughn said, filling in the blanks from what Ivana had already told them.

Aleena nodded. "Part of my job is managing the rooms of the topmost priests' personal stash of whores."

Vaughn winced. Conclave priests were supposed to be celibate. That some paid little heed to their vows was no revelation—Perrit had told them that much, though he personally, the poor, pious man, had never indulged in such wickedness.

"The position is, of course, a significant step up from managing the washwomen in the workhouse, and one instilled with a certain amount of trust, since I see a lot I'm not supposed to."

At this, Kayden's chest rose, and he stared off into the distance, looking troubled. For a noble to have used his name to guarantee a person for a position of confidence, knowing that the person was exactly the opposite...

If he were discovered misusing his power, his family would not fare well. What had motivated him to do such a thing?

But Vaughn brought his focus back to what she had said. "They've been made whores for the Conclave?"

She shook her head. "No, I don't think so. At least, not yet. I'm also in charge of bringing them food and emptying chamber pots. I don't know what the Conclave is doing with them otherwise, but they appear to be unharmed, physically, anyway. I can't converse with them without raising suspicion. But if they were whores they would be with the other whores, not locked up with their children." She waved her hand.

"But the whores they've collected are housed near the same place where they house the Sedated Banebringers." She raised an eyebrow at Vaughn. "And that, I think, is where your interest in this lies."

Kayden started and turned to Vaughn with wide eyes.

Vaughn gave him a helpless smile. "Sorry," he said. "I'm afraid your help is coming in the form of demonspawn."

The man closed his eyes and muttered under his breath. A prayer, perhaps? But he said nothing else.

"So you *do* know where they keep them," Vaughn said softly.

"Yes. There's a compound far, *far*, beneath the palace, underground. It connects to the temple. It's quite extensive. I've never been to that side, so I don't know what they do with them there, but I've heard the talk. I don't think it's just keeping them comfortable until they die."

At the same time that Vaughn felt hope, he felt disappointment. He had been hoping Aleena would know more of what was happening. But this alone was more than they had known for years.

And even this little bit was incredible. *This* was how the Conclave kept the populace safe from bloodbane spawned at a Banebringer's death? By putting the lot of them beneath a *capi-*

tal city? What if by some catastrophe, all of the Banebringers perished at once? Could they actually contain the army of bloodbane that would be spawned?

So much for the altruistic excuse for Sedation.

"It's your turn, Vaughn," Aleena said. "Ivana didn't explain everything to me in her note. What do your people want in return for helping us rescue the girls? To rescue the Sedated? Forgive me, but that seems unwise."

Vaughn tried to gauge Kayden's trustworthiness, but it hardly mattered. Aleena apparently trusted him, and he needed her help. "No," he said. "We want to bring down the Conclave."

Chapter Thirty-Seven

The Intruder

Aleena's eyes glinted. "Yes," she hissed.

Vaughn paused and raised an eyebrow.

"You think you're the only type of person the Conclave has labeled demonspawn?"

Vaughn hadn't the faintest idea what she was talking about, but he wasn't going to question it. If she *wanted* to help, all the better.

"Regardless," he said, "we need evidence. We have reason to believe that the priests are involved in some activities that would severely undermine the credibility of everything they teach about Banebringers." He wasn't going to explain further until he knew for sure. No reason to start rumors too early.

"And I suppose you want me to get this proof for you,"

Aleena said.

He took a deep breath. Since Aleena didn't have the information he needed, he knew what he would have to do next. "No. I only need you to get me in and out without being detected. I'll take care of the rest." Even as he said it, he could feel his heart start to pound faster. Sure, he could waltz around invisible, but that didn't mean he was an expert at sneaking. And if he were caught...

He didn't want to think about the ramifications, and not only for him.

"Only?" Aleena asked. "Forgive me, but you don't seem the type to make such a task an *only*."

"Except for this." He promptly turned himself invisible and then back again.

"Ah," Aleena said, eyes appreciative. "I forgot about that."

Kayden, on the other hand, was staring at him like he'd grown a second head.

"Indeed. You don't need to do anything more than leave a door open, so to speak, long enough for me to slip inside, point me in the right general direction, and then leave a way for me to get out."

"If, truly, no one can see you? Should be easy enough on my part," she said. "I typically work the night shift, starting at around eleven. I enter through the western gate of the palace complex. Be at that gate at quarter till eleven and follow me. I'll give you till one to be back at the same door we'll enter through, when I'll make an excuse to leave." She tapped her apple core on her knee. "I'm not going to do anything to confirm you're around. If you're not there at either time, you're on your own, or you'll have to wait until tomorrow."

Vaughn swallowed and nodded. "Fair. I'll be there."

And he was. This was one appointment he had to keep.

At first, he was afraid he'd missed her. He had arrived at precisely quarter till. But after about five minutes, he saw her walking toward the gate.

True to her word, she didn't look around, didn't look at all like she was doing anything other than headed to work. He slipped in behind her as she passed by him, trying to match his pace exactly to hers, so the guards at the gate didn't hear two pairs of footsteps on the gravel.

She nodded to the guards, who obviously recognized her, and they opened the smaller door in the large gate, which was closed for the night.

It was interesting that they accepted her identity so easily. Vaughn tucked that information away for future reference.

Aleena couldn't do anything to keep that door open longer, since the guards were in control of it. He nearly ran into her trying to slip through right behind, as they didn't open it very wide or leave it open for long.

The scuffle he made on the gravel as he did so didn't seem to attract any attention, thankfully.

She didn't even flinch. She kept walking, entering the palace complex through a servant's door. She shoved it open far enough that he could slip right through after her, but didn't catch it on her way in.

Thankfully, the hallways inside were quiet at this time of

night. He followed her, without meeting anyone else, down a long corridor, passing kitchens, washrooms, servants' quarters...until she turned and descended a long, dimly lit stairway. It turned several times, switching back and forth, until it finally opened up into a guard room. Four guards lounged there, rolling dice and looking bored.

One of the guards looked up. "Looking forward to the harvest festival?" he asked, rising.

"Nah," Aleena said. "I hate apples."

The guard searched her for weapons and then unlocked and opened the door for her.

Vaughn blinked. He *knew* that wasn't true. She had just been eating—

Oh. It was a code phrase.

Again, he slipped through right on her heels. The heavy metal door shut behind her with a clank, and his stomach lurched. What had he gotten himself into?

The door opened up into a large room. More people scurried about here, with only brief stops for conversation here or there.

No one greeted Aleena. She crossed the room and turned down another corridor, which soon turned from stone to wood-paneled, even underground, which seemed an extravagant expense.

It was then that she pulled out her own ring of keys, stopped, and unlocked a door. Again he followed her, but it was only a storage room. She pulled a pile of sheets into her arms, and Vaughn frowned. Was he going to follow her around while she worked all night?

But no sooner had he thought it, than she kicked the door

closed behind her. She looked around. He hesitated and then reappeared.

She nodded. "The area you're looking for is farther down the hall, through another door, and to your right. Keep going. You'll find it."

"What if there are more locked doors and guards?" he asked.

She raised an eyebrow. "I do believe you said, 'Get me in and out, and I'll take care of the rest.'"

He had said that, hadn't he?

"Don't forget. Two hours." She pulled open the door, wormed through with her pile of linens, and left the room. He slid through as the door closed and stood in the hall, looking both ways, feeling bewildered.

All right, he thought. *I'll just wing it.*

He headed in the direction she had indicated.

Vaughn met no resistance as he traveled down the halls. He passed a few doors, but none were locked, and no one was around to see them open of their own accord. Until he reached the end. There, once again, was another heavy metal door, and more guards.

Damn. Okay, think, Vaughn.

A distraction? "Help!" he yelled.

All but one of the guards came running, and he slipped past them in the opposite direction. The final guard was attentive, watching the corridor they disappeared down, but still on guard. Vaughn sidled up to him as close as he dared. He had a ring with a few keys at his waist, and Vaughn wished Ivana were the one doing this. She could no doubt pick the lock with the guard standing there, none the wiser.

He spied a pitcher on the table, and when the guard wasn't looking, he knocked it over. The guard started, surprised, and while he was distracted, trying to clean the mess up, Vaughn plucked the key ring from his belt, praying he wouldn't notice.

He had keys. Now what? The guard would surely notice the door opening.

He tried to think. Water. Water, in the body. How could he use that knowledge to get rid of the guard without hurting him?

Tentatively, he reached out toward the guard, concentrating on his bladder. It was harder than he thought. He couldn't see the bladder, didn't know how much water was there. He pulled a little on the water he sensed there.

The guard stood up abruptly.

Vaughn tugged on it again.

The guard put his hand on his crotch and crossed his legs. "Burning skies," he muttered. "What did I drink?"

Vaughn tugged again, a little harder. He could feel the aether burning in his blood, more than he normally burned at once.

"Oof," the guard said, and fled down the hallway, leaving Vaughn alone in the guardroom with the keys. He shrugged, unlocked the door, and entered the hall beyond without resistance. He kept the keys. Never knew when they might come in handy. Maybe the guard would think he'd lost them in the privy.

Vaughn passed a few priests in the halls, but they were wide enough that he could easily evade them. The floors had rugs, so he didn't have to worry about footsteps being heard.

The compound was a maze, so he decided to follow one of the priests and hope he was going somewhere interesting.

It turned out to be a good plan. He didn't have to wait long.

The priest led him to a large room, and when Vaughn slipped in after him, his breath caught in his throat.

The room was long, and the walls were lined with beds, most of which were occupied by sleeping people. Subjects?

A second priest was already in the room, moving from bed to bed, checking each patient, making notes, and Vaughn stood to the side, watching. He just needed some sign that their hypothesis was true.

The priest he had followed moved over to the priest in the room, who was younger, and looked over his shoulder at his notes.

"Heard they're choosing a Fereharian this year for Harvest Hunter," the older priest said to the other.

Vaughn felt his jaw lock. Harvest Hunter. Sounded so benign, like someone out to hunt deer for the table.

But the harvest festival was more than a celebratory conclusion to the year's harvests. It was also a religious feast, honoring the Conclave's gods as well as beseeching them to protect the people from further infringements by the heretic gods.

Vaughn returned to listening to their conversation.

"...two dozen Banebringers this year, alone."

The other priest whistled. "I guess he deserves the honor then."

They must still be talking about the Harvest Hunter. The

Hunter who was honored for being the most dedicated Hunter that year. Usually someone was chosen because of their record—how many Banebringers they had brought in, but politics definitely played a part in the "honor."

He grew irritated as they continued discussing the merits of the Hunter in question. This was all very fascinating, but it didn't help his mission, and time didn't stop for small talk among priests.

"They say he lost two sons to a bloodbane, years back, and that's why he's so dedicated now."

"I'm sure currying favor with the Conclave has nothing to do with it," the other priest said.

They laughed.

Vaughn's ears pricked up. Lost two sons to a bloodbane? And from Ferehar?

He felt sick.

"Well, what's the status?" the younger priest said. They both turned to look at the bed nearest to them, and Vaughn looked as well. A young man lay there, asleep or unconscious.

The older priest shook his head. He gestured to a table nearby, which held some tubes of blood. They also had a...what was it Ivana had called it? A microscope. The man drew a bit of the blood out of the vial and smeared it on a slide, and then gestured for the younger priest to take a look.

"No change."

The two priests huddled over the blood sample, and Vaughn moved closer, trying to figure out what they were studying.

The older priest picked up a two-sided glass slide—it looked a little like a miniature version of a qixli—and slid it into an empty slot on the microscope. "Even with more magnification."

Vaughn frowned, even though he felt satisfied. If they were using aether to make more powerful microscopes like the Ichtaca, then that meant one of two things: they had a Banebringer who was working with them, or they were using the formula he and Ivana had discovered by mixing their own blood with the aether of a lightblood they kept un-Sedated but imprisoned—or Sedated, if that worked. Either way, it was exactly the sort of activity they were hoping to prove.

The priests murmured over several vials of blood and samples, shaking their heads, obviously frustrated by whatever experiments they were running...

Vaughn did a double-take. Blood? Blood in vials? Blood on the slide—yes, still blood. They had set aside the old one, and it showed no signs of turning to aether.

He looked back at the man on the bed, and then the realization hit him. These weren't Banebringers. He had assumed these were some of the Sedated Banebringers, kept in this lab for experiments or harvesting. But if this blood had come from that man...

He moved over to the bed and peered down at the man again. What were they doing with non-Banebringers?

He glanced around the lab, looking for some obvious explanation. The priests had started arguing, in even lower voices.

"...*know* it's possible."

"...not without..."

Vaughn couldn't get any closer without chancing bumping into one of them, so he used their moment of inattention to move down to the other end of the lab, where a door was partially opened. With one last nervous glance at the preoccupied priests, he pushed the door open a crack so he could slip through. It creaked, and he cringed and looked back.

They hadn't noticed, and he let out a breath. He slipped into the room.

He froze, and panic swelled in his chest. The overwhelming urge to flee swept over him, but he caught it before he could do anything rash.

The creature in front of him wasn't moving. Its eyes weren't open. It didn't even look...fully formed.

It was the corpse-thing he had encountered at the attack on the Ichtaca. Or, at least, it was one of the same class of blood-bane.

Though the thing obviously wasn't alive, his heart beat faster as he moved closer to inspect it. It was hung on the wall by a hook stuck into its back, like someone's discarded jacket.

Voices came closer, and he glanced around, looking for a place to duck out of the way. He scurried into a corner as the two priests entered the room and appraised the creature hanging on the wall.

"I disagree," the older priest was saying. "We lost control of the last one after she escaped."

Vaughn blinked. *She?* Surely they weren't talking about...

The younger priest grunted. "We have to keep trying; eventually we'll figure it out, even without her."

The other priest shook his head. "We've got a hundred vials of blood from mortal and monster alike that say differently. Until he sends us another tool, we're wasting our time."

Vaughn blinked. *Monster?*

The younger priest glanced back through the now fully-open door, as though expecting someone out there to be listening. "Good riddance, I say. If we can work without Danathalt, all the better. I don't trust him."

Vaughn felt like he had been struck. Danathalt? *Danathalt?*

"Hush," the older priest said. "Don't speak his true name, even here. Our purposes align; that's all that matters."

The younger priest rolled his eyes, but inclined his head, their argument apparently finished.

Vaughn took a step backward, head spinning with the deluge of information. They knew about Danathalt? They had been *working* with Danathalt? What did that mean? The crazy woman? Burning skies, had he been right? Had she actually been possessed by the god himself?

What was the Conclave *doing*?

The priests had left the room, and the older one—the same he had initially followed—was headed toward the main door.

Vaughn jogged back through the lab, wanting to slip through on his heels. He barely made it, catching the door on his hip on his way out. The priest looked back quizzically, and Vaughn cringed. The door shut with a click, and the priest shrugged and kept walking.

Vaughn hesitated. He probably had an hour left. He should go. He still had to figure out how to get out of here. But a simple mission to obtain evidence that the priests were using aether contrary to their own holy laws had turned into something more, and he had to use the opportunity to find out all he could. He hurried after the disappearing figure of the priest.

The priest popped his head into another room where the

door had been propped open. "Everything going okay, Sanlin?" He must have received an affirmative, because he kept walking.

Vaughn paused to look in himself. There—there was what he was expecting to see. A few beds, a priest drawing his own blood, and a tray of aether flakes in front of him, a label on the front.

He wanted to see what it said, but he also wanted to continue following the priest. He chose to keep following. The priest stopped to speak in a few more rooms, which held more of the same. Different types of Banebringers, perhaps? Different labs to create different aether? But if they were drawing blood from these Banebringers to use in experiments, that meant they couldn't actually be Sedated, could it? Wouldn't their blood be useless, otherwise?

Or was there something they were missing?

The Ichtacan researchers needed to get on this.

Finally, the priest entered another door at the end of the corridor, and, distracted by the latest room they passed, Vaughn didn't make it behind him. He was left alone in the corridor. A corridor connecting rooms full of vegetable people and priests harvesting their blood.

He shivered. He was running out of time. But he stopped to investigate the last interesting room, first. It looked like a storage room. A deep cabinet with hundreds of square drawers took up both walls. Each drawer was labeled with a name.

He pulled one open. It held aether—hundreds and hundreds of slivers of aether. Each was in a little compartment of its own, meticulously labeled with words like *fire* and *wind*.

The personal stashes of aether for the priests who used

them, to replenish their stock, he guessed.

Vaughn retraced his steps. There was no doubt, now that the priests were blatantly flaunting their own rules. But what else were they doing? Something with creating monsters, something with normal people, something with *Danathalt*? Unfortunately, he didn't have time to investigate further.

The door he had come through had only been locked on one side. He pushed it open, and in a moment of brilliancy, he burned some aether he had from a lightblood and disguised himself as a priest. It wouldn't last long—he had no practice with using aether that way—and it might be imperfect, given the it wasn't aether of his own profile.

But it worked long enough for the guards to glance up, dismiss him, and go back to their games. After all, why would an intruder be...extruding?

He arrived at the final door just as Aleena did. She pushed the door open and held it there for a moment, smiling at the guards. "All right," she said as he edged by her. "I've managed to get away." She let the door slam shut.

The guards whooped and patted one of their number on the back, who sheepishly got up. Without another glance, Aleena joined him and the two scampered down the hall together.

In a few minutes, Vaughn was back outside, hurrying away from the complex. He would have to meet back up with Aleena later to give her his report, but he wouldn't feel safe until he was on his way back to the Ichtaca.

Chapter Thirty-Eight

Harvest Ball

Ivana was with Vaughn in Yaotel's office, waiting while the man digested what Vaughn had just told him.

She had already heard it, of course. Vaughn had come to her first, as she had asked.

Yaotel was sitting still in his chair, fingers pressed to his temples, eyes closed. She would have thought he was praying, but she doubted he prayed.

Vaughn had forgone a chair and was leaning back against the wall, arms crossed, while Ivana took up her place in the chair, feet propped up on Yaotel's desk.

"Do you realize," Yaotel said at last, opening his eyes, "how incredibly risky this would be?"

"Riskier than declaring war on the world?" Vaughn asked.

He pushed himself away from the wall. "It just makes sense, Yaotel. This is a way of pushing our cause, exposing the Conclave, with no, or at least limited, bloodshed."

"But if we fail—"

"I'll admit, failure is a problem."

"—instead of helping our cause, we may well be hurting it."

"We're not helping anything by sitting here doing nothing."

Still, Yaotel hesitated. Ivana could understand why. He was no doubt weighing the risks and benefits of various courses of action. It was a calculation she was used to herself.

Vaughn moved forward and put his hands on Yaotel's desk. "Yaotel, we have never had an advantage like this. We have information, and they don't know we have it. We can use that against them." He pushed himself back, meeting Yaotel's eyes. "Or would you rather *Perth* use the information against them in his own way? You can't keep this secret forever."

A wise move, on Vaughn's part. As she understood it, after years of existing in secret, Yaotel's little clan of Banebringers was growing restless. He was caught between a faction pushing for blood, and a smaller faction urging him to continue the long game of politics. He had to do something. Now *something* was staring him in the face. How could he refuse?

Again, Yaotel was silent for a moment. "Are you sure we can trust this woman—Aleena?"

Vaughn looked at Ivana.

"Yes," she said. She knew that now, without a doubt.

Yaotel snorted. "I don't even know if I trust *you*, and you're asking me to take *your* word that we can trust someone else I've never met?"

"She helped me, didn't she?" Vaughn put in.

"For what reason, though?"

"Does it matter?" Ivana said. "All that matters is that she's eager to help. Her motivations are her own." Ivana, of course, knew why Aleena had so readily agreed to helping Vaughn obtain his evidence, but that wasn't hers to share.

"As long as she doesn't get in the way."

"She won't."

Yaotel looked resigned. "I suppose I'll have to let you go."

"If you want me to coordinate any plan with her? Obviously."

His jaw twitched. "All right," he said at last. "Make your preparations, and let me know what you need from me."

Three weeks later, Ivana was staring at herself in a mirror, feeling ridiculous. Her hair swept up on top of her head in a pillar, with gels and clips to hold it in place. An evening gown to rival the wealthiest lady's. Jewelry. Makeup.

She had never tried to impersonate a person of real privilege. Her appearance—skin color, hair, features—marked her too easily as a native Fereharian, and no pure-blooded Fereharian was also of noble blood.

Vaughn's family had a mixed heritage, and so he wasn't as obviously Fereharian as she was. His skin wasn't as dark, his hair too light of a brown to not have some Weylyn or Arlanan blood mixed in.

That was why she wasn't going to play the part of a noble. No one would accept that. Instead, she was the daughter of a prosperous merchant from Ferehar. More believable—anyone could become wealthy through trade.

Still, without Vaughn vouching for her, even that was a stretch from the backwater region of Ferehar.

She turned away from the mirror, eyes sweeping her room once more for threats, out of instinct more than anything else.

Their party had spent the previous night at an inn in the wealthiest part of Weylyn City, awaiting the eve of the Harvest Ball—which happened at the culmination of the week-long harvest festival activities.

A knock sounded at her door.

And the evening was about to begin.

Ivana opened the door to Vaughn. His eyes swept over her unashamedly, and he took her hand and planted a smooth kiss on the back of it. "My dear, you look stunning," he said, and stepped into her room.

She rolled her eyes and jerked her hand away to close the door behind him. "We're not there yet."

Not only the daughter of a wealthy merchant. A daughter who was now engaged to a prominent noble who was about to reappear after nine years of absence—and who was presumed dead.

"Just practicing," he said, giving her his best charming smile. Indeed, unlike her, he seemed at home in the expensive dress clothes he had donned. He radiated charm and sophistication without even trying, and he reminded her far too much of his brother in that moment.

She narrowed her eyes at him. "Before we go forward with this evening, perhaps I should make myself clear, once again. I am playing a part. I am not your fiancée. I am not your partner.

I am not even your friend."

The smile slipped off his lips. "Still? Does everything we've gone through mean nothing to you?"

"Certainly," she said. "It means I've taken a barely tolerable thorn in my side and turned it into a somewhat useful tool."

He wasn't deterred. "Is that Ivana speaking, or Sweetblade?"

She gritted her teeth, but before she could speak—or perhaps injure him—a knock sounded, and then a voice outside the door. "Da? Dal? Are you ready?"

They were all already playing their parts, as they had been since they had left the Ichtaca. The inn was in an uproar, trying to make way for all of their "servants" and meet the needs of their important guests. Ivana knew all too well what the poor proprietor and his staff must be going through.

Vaughn offered Ivana his elbow, and she rested her hand on his forearm, mentally switching to the role she had to play for the next few hours. Their carriage was waiting.

The ride to the palace was tense. Vaughn and Ivana didn't speak, not even to make small talk. They both knew what was coming, and there was nothing left to say.

Besides, if Vaughn spoke anymore, he was sure he would vomit.

He focused on the woman sitting across from him, pushing aside thoughts of what was to come. She *was* stunning. The current fashion for the wealthy was teasingly modest—as though a woman was trying to see how much she could get away with without being scandalous. As a result, the dress that had been modified for Ivana for such an occasion as the Harvest Ball was in keeping with that style. The back of the dress was full and ended in a high collar on her neck—a departure from off-the-shoulder and even open-back styles of the trend before this one. But that was the back. The collar, while high on the back of her neck, was open at the throat in a sweeping V right to where her cleavage started. The floor-length dress hugged her, covering most of her skin yet emphasizing her curves. At her waist, the seamstress had cut tiny slits, allowing the barest hint of flesh to flash through when she moved.

Thinking about Ivana wasn't helping either. Her words to him had bothered him more than he wanted to admit.

He slid a finger inside his belt, feeling the underside, reassuring himself once again that the aether he needed was tucked securely in a tiny pocket there. He couldn't bring a pouch of aether into the ball—it would be found, and that would ruin everything. So he had to hide it where he could. No one was going to strip him, after all.

Ivana's was in her hair. A convenient place for storing just about everything—including a tiny penknife—though he didn't doubt she had also strapped a dagger to the inside of her thigh, safely hidden under the skirt of her dress.

Vaughn had no weapons. There was simply no way to smuggle them in without relying on an already over-burdened Danton. Vaughn was depending on others to get his bow to him when the time came.

The carriage stopped, and the door opened. "Dal Teyrnon. Da Serina."

Ivana had to use a different name, since her identity had

been compromised. Of course, someone might recognize her from Ri Talesin's dinner, but dressed fully to a part so different from the one she had played before, it was unlikely.

Aside from the one person whom they *wanted* to recognize her, of course, and they had no doubt he would.

Their "footman" was Danton, standing by to see that every one of their men and women made it where they were supposed to be without question.

The whole plan depended on this first stage. Everything had to go perfectly if they were to get into the ball. If they didn't get in—or if they were discovered—it all fell to pieces.

Ivana let herself be helped down from the carriage by Danton. To his credit, Danton didn't ogle her, playing the part of the serious footman perfectly. Vaughn climbed down himself and took Ivana's arm again.

The driver—one of theirs, of course—moved the carriage away so the next one in line could let out its passengers, and Vaughn and Ivana headed straight for the pillars that flanked the entrance of the palace ballroom, accompanied by their footman, Ivana's maid, several guards, and a few nameless servants who would go to the servants' area to await any orders their masters might have. A total of a dozen people, including Ivana and himself, would be slipping into the ball—all Banebringers. All illegal. All risking their lives for this. All depending on him.

Not to mention the other half dozen who were staying with the carriage—the driver, more guards, the stable hand—for the other part of their mission.

It was an impressive entourage, and it drew stares.

Good. That was as they had hoped. They were met at the door by the herald, a priest, and another servant, dressed in the palace livery. The ballroom beyond was already full of light, conversation, dancing, food, and most importantly, lots and lots of people.

The herald bowed. "Good evening, Dal, Da." He looked at Ivana, and Vaughn tensed, hoping it was merely the curious glance of someone noting her Fereharian heritage.

"Your cards?"

Danton produced their cards, which announced their identities both for the purposes of alerting everyone there who had arrived, and to prove they belonged there.

Gan Barton had been instrumental in some of the behind-the-scenes preparation for this ruse.

"Da Serina of Ferehar," the herald announced, reading the lady's card first, as was proper. The lack of a family name, only a region, made it clear she wasn't noble. He handed the card to the servant waiting nearby. "And Dal Teyrnon of House—" He broke off, staring at the name.

Vaughn could feel his hands sweating. Burning skies, this was insane. This was crazy. This was never going to work.

The herald cleared his throat, looked at Vaughn, and then back down at the card. "Dal Teyrnon of House Ferehar."

That was it. It was out in the open now, for better or worse. Nine years of being a fugitive, nine years of hiding...it was all over. All for this chance to change all of their lots forever.

The herald bowed low to Vaughn, but his hands twisted together. The name of the House *was* a region, which could only mean Vaughn was of the Ri's family. The herald was no doubt versed in every noble and their families—a good memory was important for the job—and Vaughn wondered if he was unnerved because he didn't realize there was an additional member of the Ri's family, or if he had heard of Vaughn's name and knew he was supposed to be dead. Either way, it would soon mean an investigation on the part of someone.

Sure enough. The herald, a picture of duty, handed the cards to the priest, and then turned to the servant and whispered in his ear. The servant nodded and scampered off. The herald turned to the next set of guests, while the priest took his turn. "My apologies," he said, "but we must perform the tests."

Vaughn sincerely hoped that his face wasn't as flushed as it felt. "Of course." He held out his hand and waited for the prick. The priest scraped the blood off Vaughn's finger onto the back of his white card, and then moved on to Ivana, and then to each servant in their entourage as they filtered through the line.

Vaughn tried hard not to look at Danton. Ivana had warned him to never look at anyone doing covert work, but also not to look like he was trying not to look.

It was difficult. Was he doing his job? Was it working? Maintaining an illusion on twelve—eleven, not Ivana's—different cards all at the same time? Vaughn couldn't handle the suspense.

It could all end, right here, before it even started.

The priest was obviously satisfied by what he saw on the cards. He set them aside, nodded toward Vaughn and Ivana to indicate they could enter the room, and ushered their servants down a back hallway to join others. Vaughn was proud of himself. He didn't even look to see if Ivana had successfully swiped the cards off the table where the priest had placed them with the rest, hundreds of tiny cards, all in neat piles...

"Relax," Ivana whispered in his ear. "I have them."

Could she feel him trembling?

He turned to look at her, and she smiled, charming, beautiful, a hint adoring, and his stomach flipped. For a moment he thought the smile was for him. Then he remembered she was supposed to be his fiancée.

Then they were there. Standing in the midst of the Harvest Ball. It was extravagant. Every noble family that could be there, would be, along with their servants and guards.

Including his own family.

It had been years since he had attended one of these, and he suddenly felt very old. The last time he had stood in this room, he had had a real fiancée on his arm. He had been walking on clouds, avoiding his oldest brother but wondering what mischief he and his next oldest brother could still get into at their age, while Teryn tagged along.

Pouring lupque into the punch would have been frowned upon at age eighteen, and being engaged and in love, he could no longer have flirted openly with other women. He had thought himself a man.

He had been a boy.

The pang of loss he felt in that moment was real. Not for the crystal chandeliers, not for the gold embroidered tapestries, not for the marble floors, not for the sides of beef and fruit and cheese and wine spread out on long tables throughout the room.

But for the family he had once had. No, that wasn't right. For the *illusion* of family that he had once had. Ignorance was sometimes the easiest way to live, and the loss of that ignorance was the hardest part of his exile.

He felt pressure on his hand from Ivana's. "I wouldn't mind a bite to eat," she said. "I'm famished."

The hint was clear. They had a few hours to waste before the meat of their plan went into motion. He couldn't just stand around. He had to look like he was enjoying himself.

"Of course," he said, rousing himself into motion. But no sooner had they started heading toward the nearest food table, than he saw none other than his father heading their way.

He had been counting on his father's terror of someone finding out that his son was not only alive but a Banebringer to keep him quiet. There was a reason he had been presumed dead, when his father knew full well that Vaughn was alive.

They had also been counting on the fact that he would recognize Ivana. He would immediately assume Vaughn was here to attempt to have him killed again, which would distract him from their real purpose.

He was about to find out if his assumptions had been true. Of anyone in this room, his father had the power to expose either of them.

"Teyrnon?" his father said. "My gods, Teyrnon. Teyrnon!"

His father wrapped him in a tight embrace, and tears shone in his eyes when he pulled back. "We thought you were dead, bless Yathyn, we thought you were dead! How...?"

He was an amazing actor. So amazing that for a moment, Vaughn almost believed his father was happy to see him again. But his grip was a bit too tight, and he was too congenial. His father had *never* been so glad to see him.

Presumed dead was the key. For this ruse, they had needed to verify what exactly had happened to the Ri of Ferehar's sons in the official record. They had only recovered one body—Vaughn's younger brother—but Vaughn's had never been recovered. His father had reported him presumed dead, dragged off by the monster for later consumption—as evidenced by the trail of blood and gore leading into the woods.

Though he had seen and even spoken to his father numerous times over the years, it was the first time since he had fled home that they had stood as equals. With the father who had not only betrayed him, but had actively sought to wipe out this blemish on their family name. He hadn't known how he would feel.

Now he did. He felt nothing, unless emptiness was a feeling. This man was a stranger to him. He had no father.

So it was relatively easy for him to smile and clasp his father's shoulders. "Father," he said. "I'm so sorry I didn't announce my coming. I wanted it to be a surprise."

They were attracting a crowd. "But how?" Gildas asked again.

Vaughn grew solemn, repeating the story as he had practiced over and over to Ivana, until he sounded nothing but perfectly sincere. "The monster that..." He swallowed. *That* grief was real. "That took Teryn. It dragged me into the woods, but I was alive, father. It left me for a time for a later meal, I suppose, not realizing I was in a condition to escape. But I woke, and I did escape, barely. I could hear its roar of anger as I fled."

"And you didn't come home?" Gildas asked, feigning confusion.

Vaughn shook his head. "My memory. Something happened. I had no idea who I was, where I was...

"I was found and taken in by a generous merchant family of, at the time, modest means. They cared for me and my wounds and I worked with them for a long time after. Just a month ago, an accident left me wounded, but I found my memory completely restored. Of course, I immediately tried to find my family." He ducked his head. "I...confess. I thought it would be great fun to simply show up at the Harvest Ball. What a way to return to society, yes?"

Gildas clasped his shoulder again. "A way to give your old man a heart attack!" He didn't question Vaughn's story. It wouldn't stand detailed scrutiny, but it was believable enough for their purposes.

Gildas turned to Ivana, and Vaughn held his breath.

The glimmer of recognition was definitely there. But he kept up the charade, as Vaughn had hoped he would. "And who is this lovely woman with you?"

Vaughn turned to Ivana and smiled. She was smiling shyly back at him, just the right mixture of nerves and adoration. Vaughn marveled at her ability to take on roles, even when she was standing in the presence of the man who had killed her father and destroyed her life. "Meet Serina, a daughter of the merchant family. We fell in love and were engaged before my memory returned." He rubbed at his chin, feigning concern. "I hope...I hope that won't be an issue, father. They aren't noble, but their family has grown in wealth over the years and is of no small means now."

"I am merely happy to have you back. I will dote on any daughter-in-law you choose." Gildas took Ivana's hand and kissed the back of it. "Cheris is here somewhere," he said to Vaughn, though his eyes were still on Ivana.

Why had he brought Cheris up? She knew he was a Bane-bringer; was that supposed to be some sort of warning?

"I hope she won't be too put out. She's still unmarried."

What? Really? Why had she not moved on? "Ah—" Vaughn said. "I'm afraid that was simply far too long ago..." And he had no desire to see her again.

"No, no," Gildas interrupted. "No hard feelings, I assure you."

"What about Airell?" Vaughn pointedly avoided looking at Ivana. He fervently hoped they would not run across him. Ivana had said she could handle it if he were there, but Vaughn had his doubts. He had experienced firsthand just a smidgen of the pent-up rage she still harbored toward Airell. Would she really be able to hold it together long enough not to put her penknife through his eye, and thus ruin the entire plan?

Gildas was one thing. Oh, Vaughn was certain, presented with the right opportunity, she would take it—but she had already spent her wrath on him once.

Airell?

He had a feeling, as far as she was concerned, there was no pit of the abyss deep enough for him.

"He's not here yet, that I know of." Gildas smiled. "I'm to be honored tonight, as you will see, so I came up early, while he took care of wrapping up business at home. He shouldn't be far behind."

On the contrary, Vaughn hoped he *was* far behind. "Mother? Glyn?" He had to admit he had been cautiously excited about seeing Glyn after all these years. He had missed his second oldest brother sorely, and as far as he knew, Glyn had no idea he was alive, let alone a Banebringer.

Gildas shook his head. "Glyn is off in Cadmyr with the United Setanan. He's an officer now, you know." Of course. The second-son, skilled at the sword. "Your mother, sadly, had to stay home this year. Took a cold, recently, and felt it would be best not to be out and about. But as soon as the ball is over...please, come home with us. You and your fiancée. We will be delighted to receive you."

Vaughn was sure he would. "Of course, father," he said, bowing. They both knew that would never happen.

He touched Ivana's elbow, meaning to guide her away, but Gildas stopped him by putting his own hand on her arm. "Before you go off to enjoy the ball, may I have a dance with your fiancée?"

Vaughn glanced at Ivana out of the corner of his eye. "I don't think—"

Ivana bowed, smiled at Gildas and offered her hand. "Don't be silly, dearest. I couldn't turn down a dance with my future father-in-law."

"A woman of sense," Gildas said. He inclined his head to Vaughn, who seemed distressed at this turn of events.

His concern was misplaced.

Ivana hated Vaughn's father. He was a calloused, arrogant

noble, the man who had killed her own father, and in so doing, destroyed her life.

But he was not Airell.

Airell was the reason her entire life had gone so terribly wrong in the first place. Had taken her innocence and left her to deal with the consequences alone. Her own foolish fault, to be sure, but that had only made it harder to bear.

The pain he had wrought in her had been the reason she had sought refuge in in the idea of Sweetblade to begin with.

At the mere mention of his name—at the present possibility that he might show up at the ball at any moment...

Perhaps it was a good thing, after all, that he wasn't here yet.

Gildas led her out into the midst of the floor and pulled her smoothly into the proper hold, but his grip was unnecessarily tight.

Fear, anger, or something else?

"So. Serina," he said. He looked down at her, and though a smile was on his face, his eyes were hard.

"Dal," she said, favoring him with a sweet smile in return.

His eyes flicked around them once, and then looked back at her. "I don't know what you and the demonspawn have planned, but it isn't going to work."

She tilted her head and fluttered her eyelashes in an obviously exaggerated manner. "My only plans are to marry and bed him as soon as possible."

He looked as though he had bitten into raw starleaf.

"I'm so sorry. Did I scandalize you?"

He snorted. "We are surrounded by dozens of guards and priests, and may I remind you that I am no stranger to a fight myself."

She let her smile grow just a bit more sinister. "I'm aware. And I can assure you, I won't make the same mistakes next time."

"You obviously didn't take my message to heart."

"Have you ever been bitten by a bloodbat, Dal?"

Confusion flickered across his eyes. "Ah...no?"

"Like most common bloodbane, what they want most is to get away, but if you get *in* their way, they bite and don't let go until one of you is dead." She leaned a little closer. "Your fatal error will be that you think *you're* the bloodbat."

At that, he finally looked just a little rattled, but he just frowned, trying to shrug it off for her benefit. "I hope you do bed him," he muttered. "He always was a bit of a prude."

Prude? *Prude?* The thought of Vaughn as a prude was so hilarious that she lost control and laughed—sort of. It came out as a choked sound as she tried to hold it back.

She pulled away from him, fanning her face. "Oh," she said. "I—" She coughed again, this time in earnest, having sucked some saliva down her throat upon inhaling. "I'm so sorry. A fit has come upon me. Pardon me. I could use something to drink."

She moved away from him, and he trailed behind. She poured herself a drink, and then gave him a saccharine smile. "May I get you something as well, my lord?"

His jaw twitched, and he stalked away.

Vaughn found Ivana standing alone near the drink table. He

hadn't intended on having to leave her alone with one of the men who had ruined her life, but she didn't seem any worse for it. In fact, she seemed uncharacteristically amused.

Ivana drew close to him, and he instinctively put his arm around her waist, holding her near as he bent down so she could put her lips to his ear. "He's terrified," she whispered. "And he's convinced we're here to kill him."

"Good," Vaughn said.

He led her out onto the dance floor himself, tired of talking to people. Next, it would be a cousin, or some other person to congratulate him on his return from the dead, posturing to see if striking up an old acquaintance would help or hurt them politically. Had he actually enjoyed this, once?

"What mischief have you gotten into?" he asked her. Ironically, he felt as though she were the only genuine person in this room.

She raised an eyebrow at him.

"You didn't poison his drink, did you?"

A wistful look passed over her face. "A splendid idea, but he wouldn't take one from me for some reason."

"Sometimes," he said, "you frighten me."

"Only sometimes? Clearly you need an object lesson," she said, now cheerful.

Well, cheerful wasn't the right word, but compared to her normal moods...

He felt himself warming at her pleasure. At her proximity.

"All right," he said, feeling emboldened by her disposition. "I confess. Sometimes when you ought to frighten me, you simply...intoxicate me."

"There's something wrong with you," she said.

"Probably," he admitted. "But you can't deny that you look rather ravishing."

She snorted.

"I mean it," he said. "You do know you're beautiful, don't you?"

She looked out across the dance floor, silent for a while. When she spoke, her voice was cool. "I obviously pass muster for enough men that I'm able to use them." She looked back to meet his eyes, all joviality gone.

Was that supposed to be a reference to her earlier remark? That, apparently, all he had been was a tool?

The words of the companion floated back to him. *Perhaps a talk would be better than other ways of dealing with your frustration.*

Impossible. He couldn't talk to her. She had made it clear that she wanted nothing to do with him. And frankly, did he even want to talk to her? What did it matter?

Yet, he simply could not let go of the brief period when he had seen her, known her, and then he had ruined it, and Sweetblade had returned from her respite. Could he somehow bring Ivana back?

His heart started pounding. This was the perfect opportunity. He could try talking to her now. She was trapped. She couldn't run away, it would be too obvious. They were stuck here until the plan was ready to be set into motion.

"Ivana," he began.

"Don't."

She knew. She *knew*. "But you don't even—"

"I've said all I want to say on the matter."

He forced the words out. "But I haven't."

Her jaw twitched, but she didn't say anything else, so he pressed on. "Look. Let's not play games. You know I want you. I can't deny that." His eyes traveled down her throat, to her chest, and beyond. A familiar ache began in his groin.

Focus, Vaughn. He looked back up at her face. "But that gives me no right to...what I mean to say is..." He took a deep breath. "I'm sorry."

She lifted her eyes to his, and they were dark and unreadable.

"What I did was...you're right. I sensed that you were vulnerable, and I used that to manipulate you, acting solely in my interest rather than your own." His throat was dry, and he swallowed a few times. "I want you to know, whatever you may think of me, I respect you too much for that. I shouldn't have acted that way and I...I'm sorry."

He had no idea how she would take it. He hoped that a genuine apology would be received well, at least.

Her face was blank, and she made no reply.

"I visited a prostitute while I was in the city to meet Aleena," Vaughn said. The words slipped out in desperation.

She raised an eyebrow, looking faintly amused. "What, do you want a reward? I don't think they hand those out for being a man."

"That's unfair," Vaughn said, feeling the need to defend his gender. "Not all men are—" He stopped short. *Are what? Like me?*

"No. I suppose you're right. I have met a few decent men in my life, my own father being one of them." They reached the side of the ballroom, and he stepped to the side, bringing her around in a smooth twirl. "What's your point?"

His pounding heart beat even louder, until he was sure she would hear it. He hadn't intended on bringing this up, but it was too late to take the words back now.

"I didn't get far. I'm embarrassed to admit that I had trouble...ah...performing."

"I'm still waiting for the point."

"Do you know why?"

"No. And neither do I care."

"Because all I could think about was you."

She wasn't looking at him. She was looking beyond him, at the ballroom. Probably attentive to what they were supposed to be doing here, unlike him.

She didn't say anything for a long while, leaving him alone with his pounding heart and squirming stomach, wondering if, in an attempt to prove his sincerity, he had alienated her further.

She finally met his eyes again. "Here's the problem, Vaughn. Every woman deserves your respect, not only one that you happen to be infatuated with at present.

"In fact, perhaps you should consider the possibility that *you* deserve to respect *yourself* more than that."

He stared at her, not knowing what to say.

She didn't look away, holding his eyes in a vice.

Who was this woman who had reached into his soul and bared it so completely?

The room hushed, and they both turned toward the front, where a priest was holding up his hands for attention.

Vaughn's heart started pounding again, for a different reason. This was it.

Chapter Thirty-Nine

The False Prophet

"Blessed guests!" the priest said, smiling. He gestured to the king, who was reclining on the dais behind the priest. "On behalf of the crown and the Conclave, I welcome you to the annual Harvest Ball!"

The guests, well-relaxed by good food and wine by this point in the evening, cheered and clapped without reserve.

"Let us begin with a prayer for endurance."

Vaughn scanned the room with half-lidded eyes while the priest began his chant, taking note of the doors, looking for his people. Of course, they weren't all visible, but by now, they should have all carried out their various tasks. If any had failed or had been compromised, this was going to go sour, fast.

Between common knowledge, non-so-common knowledge

from Gan Barton's spies, and the information Aleena had provided, they were able to piece together a map that went all the way down to the door to the Conclave's underground facility. There were, of course, more entrances than the one Aleena had entered through, but they were all guarded. They couldn't have any old person wandering in.

He saw Danton standing near one of the doors leading to the kitchen. Not as Danton, of course, but as a pre-agreed upon illusionary disguise so that no one would recognize him as someone who had come with Vaughn. A full body appearance change was difficult to pull off, but Danton had always been exceptionally skilled at using his powers—and unashamed in doing so—and could do it for a limited amount of time.

He met Vaughn's eyes and nodded.

Vaughn licked his lips and bowed his head with the others. Everything was in place, then. This was going too smoothly. Something was going to go wrong.

It was like Ivana had prepped him. *Never count on Plan A working out to your expectations. There are always unexpected events getting in the way, no matter how hard you try to control them. Always have a Plan B, and a Plan C if you can manage it. But in the end, be ready to improvise.*

When the prayer was finished, the priest called on the king.

The king was largely a figurehead at these balls. It was a religious event, in theory, so he merely presided. But it was with the king's approval that they chose the Harvest Hunter.

The king smiled broadly as he announced, as Vaughn had expected, his father as the Harvest Hunter. There were cheers of anticipation as Vaughn's father mounted the dais. It was customary for the Harvest Hunter to give out additional boons.

The ceremony surrounding the naming of the Harvest Hunter was irrelevant to Vaughn. Vaughn's father said some prayers, received a gift, announced some boons. He didn't mention his resurrected son; he probably didn't want to draw attention to him.

Then came the most important part of the ceremony. Together, about a dozen priests joined hands and made a circle on the dais. They chanted while another priest made ablations at an altar of incense. With a snap of his fingers, the offering went up in fire, causing the predictable murmur of appreciation to run through the room.

The smoke turned to a face before their eyes—the face of Yathyn, the head of their pantheon. At least, so they said. Vaughn had no doubt, now, that it was done with lightblood aether. An illusion. It was a symbol that their offering had been accepted and their prayers for safety in the coming year had been heard.

They made a few more demonstrations of magic. They healed a few minor ailments of guests who volunteered and re-froze the ice sculpture that was melting on the main food table. Now that Vaughn was looking at it through different eyes, he saw clearly that everything they did had a counterpart Banebringer ability. They didn't do anything a Banebringer with the right profile couldn't do. The chanting, the incense? Unnecessary, designed to draw attention away from the similarities between what they did and what the Banebringers could do.

Then, the room quieted as two guards—their own men, of course—entered, holding a limp figure between them. The woman they held there was alive, but her posture was one of hopelessness.

It was Citalli, no doubt exuding her charmblood aura to the maximum. Vaughn tensed as the priest glanced toward the woman, waiting for him to notice the switch, but he didn't. That part was going smoothly, at least.

Vaughn clenched his fists. Their annual demonstration of their power over the heretical gods: Sedation. No magic to it, Vaughn knew. It was science. And they didn't know it wouldn't work on this woman. At least...he sincerely hoped the syringe had also been switched as it was supposed to have been, or they were dooming one of their own to a terrible fate. He looked for Yasril, but of course Vaughn couldn't see him. He would be invisible.

"Ri Gildas, would you do the honors?" one of the priests said, producing and handing the syringe to Vaughn's father.

"Gladly," Gildas said.

He felt Ivana press his arm. This was him. It was all him.

Damn, damn, damn. His entire body was thrumming with the frantic beating of his heart. He pushed his way through the crowd until he reached the front.

"Stop!" he cried, voice seeming to come from someone else.

He was going to die. He was so going to die.

The interruption was enough to cause the ceremony to halt, as every face turned toward him.

His father, for his part, was frozen. Vaughn could see the fear on his face, could almost hear his thoughts. What was his demonspawn son about to do? His father had no idea how he had made it past the priest administering the tests—likely assumed, as they wanted, that this was part of some elaborate plan to finally assassinate him—

He had no idea at all.

Vaughn forced himself up the dais.

"What is the meaning of this?" the priest demanded at last, finally realizing someone had dared to interrupt a sacred ceremony.

"Blasphemers!" Vaughn shouted. "Hypocrites!"

The priest stared at him, obviously nervous. They weren't expecting this, which was, of course, the point.

Vaughn's father just looked confused.

"Guards," the priest said in a raised voice. "Take this man away. He's obviously had too much to drink."

No one came to his rescue. Vaughn smiled grimly. That was because all of their guards had been replaced with his own people or otherwise dealt with.

"Guards?" the priest asked again, to the two holding Citalli, as Vaughn came closer.

They didn't move.

"Liars!" Vaughn continued to shout. "They have allied themselves with the very powers they preach against!"

A hundred murmurs swept the room. Curiosity. Surprise. Wonder at what Vaughn was talking about.

"But Danathalt has betrayed you," he proclaimed, raising one arm slowly to point at Citalli.

Now the faces of the priest, and some of his comrades, paled visibly, while the crowd became more confused by the moment. He could hear the whispers. "Danathalt? Who is Danathalt?" "What does he mean?"

The head priest looked around wildly, then at the throne. *Where are the king's guards?* his eyes seemed to ask. *In fact...where is the king?*

Called away, of course, on important business, Vaughn answered smugly in his head. They hadn't wanted to chance the king being caught up in this.

"Who are you?" the head priest demanded. "What blasphemies are you speaking?"

"So hear now the judgment of Yathyn: your power over this woman is void." He looked meaningfully at his father, the Hunter, who held the syringe, unmoving, obviously still trying to work out how this was going to get him assassinated.

And no one else moved to apprehend Vaughn—not even one of the other priests. They weren't battle-priests, though a few slipped toward the doors behind the dais, either to make a hasty exit, or to rouse more help. They weren't stupid. They knew by the lack of guards that Vaughn had more going on here.

The rest of the room was riveted. Prophecy was mentioned in the holy texts, but no one had ever heard one. They might think him crazy, but they were too curious to do anything but listen.

Vaughn met the head priest's eyes, issuing a challenge.

The priest made a sound of disgust. "Give me that," he said to Vaughn's father. With a flourish, he injected the Sedation formula into Citalli's arm. Citalli cried out from the pain of the needle, which was no small size.

The guards held her firmly, and everyone waited.

Nothing happened, other than that Citalli raised her head and gave the priest a crooked grin.

The priest stepped back and looked down at the empty syringe in his hand.

Another murmur went through the room. Did this man really have the power to do this? Vaughn imagined them saying. And why was Yathyn so upset that he would even save a Banebringer?

Of course, no one but Vaughn and his party knew that the syringe had been replaced with aether that would be harmless to Citalli, a charmblood. It had been part of what they had been doing behind the scenes, while Vaughn danced himself into place. The crowd would think Yathyn was angry at the priests, and the priests would think—soon, anyway, if they didn't already—that this was Danathalt's new 'tool.'

"I warned you," Vaughn said.

It was Citalli's cue to start laughing maniacally.

She appeared to throw off the guards with ease, and then lifted her hands in the air. There was a whisper of wind, and a far off hum, and then a hundred winged insects burst into the room and started swirling around Citalli's head. She kept laughing, holding her hands in the air. "You thought I needed you?" she shrieked, eyes flashing wildly.

Her performance, mimicking the crazy woman, was magnificent, and Vaughn found himself admiring her once again.

When she leapt toward one of the priests, attempting to get her hands on one, they scattered. Citalli just stood and laughed, as if she found the whole scene terribly funny.

The head priest whirled, panic on his face. "Stop them! Stop them!"

Anyone left who might have been able to comply seemed

confused by who the priest was referring to, and so no one moved to do anything.

The head priest turned on Vaughn's father, rage on his face. "You! *Your* son!"

Vaughn's father, who had already been backing down the dais, fled.

Well, that was easy. Vaughn had anticipated that they would have to incapacitate his father.

"The doors are locked, Holiness," one of the other priests called.

"All of them," called another, from the other side of the room.

Now a wave of terror swept the ballroom. A raving prophet was one thing, and a maniacal woman with a swarm of insects had already infected the room with fear, but no one liked being told they were locked in. Vaughn sensed the panic growing, and he saw Ivana slipping unnoticed toward the side of the room.

"Your reign of deceit is over!" Vaughn declared, while Citalli continued to laugh and make insects fly all over the room.

"I gave you a gift," Citalli screamed. "My very own Banebringer, for your use! Yet you lost her!" She raised her hand slowly and pointed at the two priests Vaughn had overheard talking. "And you blaspheme my name, the name of Danathalt, your god!"

With no guards left to order around, the priests finally did what Vaughn had hoped they would. Panicked, and with no other recourse, they had to stop Vaughn and Citalli themselves.

They had no time for chanting or incense. Citalli was already spouting off too much knowledge.

At the raised hand of one of the priests, fire leapt from the candles in one of the chandeliers and toward Vaughn, while another two priests hurled the ice sculpture toward Citalli, fashioning it into ice needles as it flew.

Fortunately, they were prepared. The lance of fire dissolved into a wash of sparks as a gust of wind hit it, and the ice needles hit a wall of ice before reaching Citalli and shattered.

Still, Vaughn's heart skittered at the near miss. Trusting others to shield him, impromptu, from whatever the priests might throw out was terrifying. But he went on with the plan.

"Hypocrites! Liars!" he shouted again. "You," he said, pointing into the crowd. "You! Search them. Find evidence of their betrayal!"

Out of the crowd, the familiar faces he had pointed to approached the dais. The priests huddled together, obviously frightened as a half dozen of Vaughn's men and women forced them into a circle, searched them, and started divesting them of the bags of aether Vaughn knew they had to have hidden on them. One of them tossed a bag to Vaughn. He hurled the bag into the room, and the profane substance scattered across the marble floor. "Aether!" he proclaimed to the crowd, which had compressed back against the walls of the room, as far from the dais as possible, and then turned to the priests. "I defy you to try your magic now!"

None of the priests tried. One spat. "We don't need tests of faith to prove—"

"Silence!" Vaughn roared. With a raise of his hand, the priest suddenly stopped speaking. The crowd also fell quiet, though whether that was due to Vaughn's command or because he knew he had started glowing, he didn't know. But the priest's eyes bulged, and he clawed at his throat. "I ask you," Vaughn said, pitching his voice loudly. "Who are the true demonspawn? Those who have no choice, or those who profane everything they preach to gain power through the blood of their enemies?" He gestured with his free hand to the aether on the floor. Those nearest to where it had fallen had backed away, eyeing it with fear, as though the aether itself would spawn monsters.

The priest's face was turning blue, and another priest who was nearby was frantically pressing on his throat, trying to figure out what the problem was. Vaughn finally let go, and the man fell to the ground, gasping.

A handy trick. A terrifying trick. Vaughn still couldn't believe he had been able to do this all along. The body is mostly water, indeed. Leave it to Ivana to come to a conclusion that should have been so obvious to them.

It was a simple plan. All they needed was a public space to accuse the priests, accompanied by evidence the priests themselves supplied. Not everyone would believe, but everyone would talk, and the priests couldn't control hundreds of people. They would have a terrible time handling this scandal. There would be questions, and an investigation—not least because the Anti-Sedationists would, of course, demand it. All without bloodshed.

Now, Vaughn and his people just needed to slip out, disappear, lay low for a while and wait for politics to take its course, with help from Gan Barton and others—

Someone in the crowd shrieked, and Vaughn whirled.

Just in time to see Citalli collapse onto the floor, a knife in her back. The blood puddling on the floor started shimmering and turned to aether.

Vaughn cursed. *That* wasn't supposed to happen!

The priest who had stabbed her backed away. He obviously hadn't thought through the consequences of his actions, and his mouth worked silently as the inevitable tear started in the air above their heads.

No! No, no, no!

Perth, who stared at his fallen lover with horror, echoed Vaughn's thoughts out loud.

Now the room did panic. The guests stampeded to the doors, though they had just been told they were locked, and those closest started banging on them, demanding to be let out.

Chaos ensued, and in the midst of it, a snarling bloodwolf leapt through the tear, laying into a guest before anyone could even do anything.

And Vaughn had no weapons. Not yet. He spun to the circle of Banebringers. Some of them were supposed to have weapons. One of them—

Someone tossed Vaughn his bow, already strung, and a quiver, and he sprang into action.

There weren't supposed to be any deaths. No one was supposed to get hurt.

He fastened his quiver to his belt, drew his bow—

And incredibly, one of the other priests jumped on his back, causing the arrow to go wild.

Vaughn rolled to the ground with the priest, and came up fuming. "You idiot!" he shouted.

"You're no prophet, demonspawn!" the priest yelled, a wild

fervor in his eyes. His declaration spurred the other priests to action.

Vaughn's eyes widened as—in the midst of a bloodbane attack—several of the priests took advantage of the fact that he was distracted going after the monster to attack *him* instead.

Vaughn hadn't counted on the fact that the priests could have religious fervor. He had simply thought them all corrupt frauds.

But they believed—at least some of them, despite their hypocrisy—that the Banebringers were really the enemy. He loosed an arrow at one priest who had hurled himself in his direction, and hit him in the knee, while Thrax struggled with another, trying to fend him off Vaughn without hurting him. Their orders still stood. They couldn't kill people, and they weren't supposed to use their magic. The only Banebringer in that room any onlooker should have known about was Citalli— who was now dead.

But Perth and the group he led started shouting from a corner of the room. The bloodwolf had finished the grisly task of tearing apart a few more people, and Perth and a handful of other guests had been backed into a corner by the bloodwolf. Perth's eyes blazed, and he started hurling ice daggers at the monster. A fireblood with him followed suit, and soon, the ballroom was on fire, smoke gathering near the ceiling.

Damn.

The bloodwolf was dead, but the guests around them frothed with fear, and in their panic, attacked Perth and anyone else using magic. Another Banebringer fell, and another bloodbane was summoned—this time, one of the hideous creatures they had no name for.

The Banebringers on the outside had finally unlocked the doors—no one was going to keep people in here with that horror stalking around—but there were hundreds of people trying to squirm through the doors, trampling, falling—

This was turning into a disaster.

The real guards had finally made it back into the room.

Vaughn gestured to his group of Banebringers, and they split. Thrax threw a few fireballs at a window low to the ballroom floor, creating a gaping hole in the bricks, and Perth's group fled, guards on their heels. Vaughn sincerely hoped none of them were caught. Except maybe Perth.

Another group pushed through the panicked people still left at the main doors, helped along by the guards swinging weapons in their wake.

That left Vaughn, Danton, and Tharqan. They stood, Danton glowing, Tharqan holding a spinning whirlwind of debris above his hand.

The remaining guards noticed them. Time for Plan B.

They fled into the bowels of the palace.

Chapter Forty

Rescue

"I still can't get over the fact that we're invisible," Aleena whispered to Ivana as they crept along the empty halls. "Do you know how often this would have come in handy?"

"Don't get used to it," Ivana said. She was glad to be reunited with Aleena, but she was also reminded of how much the woman liked to talk. "We're not likely to keep a moonblood around for our aether-harvesting pleasure."

Aleena cast her a sly glance. "You sure?"

"Positive."

"I didn't think he was that bad."

Burning skies. What had Vaughn *said* to Aleena?

"We could lock him up." She grinned. "I bet he wouldn't

mind."

Ivana had interrogated Vaughn on his meetings with Aleena, and while he had hedged regarding the initial meeting, she had let it go. He had convinced her, somehow, and she knew it wasn't by seducing her, so that was good enough for Ivana. Now she wished she would have pressed.

Aleena had obviously taken even more of a liking to Vaughn in the process.

"Do you talk, as a matter of course, while sneaking?" Ivana asked Aleena.

"No, but usually I'm alone. This is a rare occurrence."

Ivana heaved a heavy sigh. "Hush," she said. "I hear something ahead."

Aleena fell silent, attentive.

It was shouting. Ivana pressed back against the wall, and Aleena did the same. She hoped fervently that the aether didn't choose that moment to be finicky.

A moment later, a few guards ran around the corner, passed by them in a gust of wind, and then disappeared.

Nice of those above to draw so many of the guards away. They had passed more than one guard post left unattended. That was part of the point, of course, as far as their aid to Ivana went, but they were doing an exceptional job of it.

"Nice dress, by the way," Aleena whispered when the guards were gone.

Ivana shot her a withering look. Aleena was supposed to have more practical clothes for her, but as of yet, they hadn't found time to stop and change.

So she was slinking about the hallways with hair as high as a tower in a hip-hugging dress.

"Wish I looked so good," Aleena continued, ignoring Ivana's look.

"It's exploitation and exemplary of everything that's wrong with our society," Ivana snapped. "And women fall into the trap as much as the men who encourage it."

"You should have been a priest," Aleena said.

Ivana snorted, and Aleena smiled. They both understood the irony of that statement.

"It's just here," Aleena said at last, turning a corner that ended in a door. "Is your friend here?"

"No idea," Ivana said. "I wouldn't be able to see him, would I?"

An older man materialized out of thin air. Yasril, another moonblood. He was going to keep the girls invisible while they escaped. "I'm here," he said. "Are we ready?"

Ivana let go of her own aether. "One hopes."

Yasril smiled. He was a genuinely nice person, one you couldn't help but like. Had a bit of a tremor in one arm—no doubt from some injury long ago—but was fairly adept at sneaking around, all the same. He had made it down here without detection, anyway, though she supposed being invisible helped...

Aleena pulled a key out of her pocket and unlocked the door. They slipped through, passed the whores' rooms, and reached a secondary door. That led through a darker corridor, closer to the priests' area of the complex, and where they kept Ivana's girls as well as, Aleena said, other non-Banebringers.

Aleena hadn't known what they had done with them before

Vaughn's expedition, but they all knew now that there was some sort of experimenting going on.

Ivana hoped they had at least left the children alone.

Aleena unlocked another door, and they slipped through.

Ivana drew up short. The children were there, but no women. She turned to her second. "Aleena?"

"You sure you know where you're going?" Tharqan said to Vaughn as they darted down the halls, guards hot on their heels.

"Pretty sure," Vaughn said. In fact, he recognized the area now. There was the last guard door—

The door was unguarded, but locked. Tharqan blew it to bits—literally—with a forceful gust of wind.

They continued down the halls, which weren't empty. The noise of the door being destroyed had drawn some attention, and a few priests poked their heads out of rooms. They wore confusion on their faces, no doubt wondering why three men dressed for a party were running pell-mell down the halls. Apparently word of the tumult above hadn't reached these depths yet.

But when the guards appeared behind them, their faces changed to shock, and then fear. Vaughn led their small group into the first room he had entered. The beds, as before, were mostly full with unconscious victims. Vaughn kept running, all the way to the back, despite the shouts of the priests, and the guards skidded to a stop behind them.

They looked around, astonished, their quarry forgotten at

the sight in front of them.

"What in the abyss...?" one of them muttered.

"Kill them!" a priest shouted from behind. The guards whirled, expecting it to be a command to take out Vaughn and his friends. Instead, they found themselves under attack from panicked priests.

Exactly as Plan B was supposed to go.

Except Vaughn couldn't let those guards die; they were now a critical part of the rumor mill that needed to be turning furiously by the day's end.

He shot an arrow through the heart of one of the priests, while Tharqan took out another. The remaining priests fled.

Vaughn looked down at the dead priest, bile rising in his throat. The second man he had ever killed.

He swallowed and looked up at the guards, who were still stunned by the change of events.

"Not what you expected?" Vaughn said.

"Don't talk, demonspawn," one of them snarled, but the others didn't look so sure.

"We should go," one whispered, tugging at his shirt.

"He's right," another said. "I don't want to be caught down here, accused of killing priests. Let's leave the demonspawn to them."

They fled, though one glanced back at the horror hanging on the wall behind them, and took in the beds again as they left.

He couldn't guarantee the guards would talk—they might be too frightened. But with the rest of the city talking, they might step forward if it became convenient. Say, if a certain political party paid them.

Danton and Tharqan were staring at the corpse-thing. "That thing is creepy," Danton said, shivering.

"Tell me about it," Vaughn said. His pocket started glowing.

He looked out into the main room again. No one was in sight. He shoved the door partially closed and pulled the qixli out, activating it. "What?" They couldn't stay here long; they had to leave before reinforcements showed up—more guards or worse, battle priests.

It was Ivana. Yaotel had let her make her own qixli for this occasion. It was the only way she could get one to work. "The girls aren't here, Vaughn."

He focused on the molded face pressed into the silvery substance. "What? Isn't Aleena with you?"

"Yes," the tinny voice said. "I'm in the right place. The children are here. But no girls." Vaughn opened the door to the room and peered back out, looking at some of the beds. They were mostly women, and he recognized one of them.

"Damn," he said.

"What?"

"I think they're here. I recognize, uh, you know, that one, that I, uh..." He didn't even remember her name. He really was *that* bad, wasn't he?

"Ohtli?"

"That's it."

"Where is here?"

"In the labs—I don't know what they call them. But they're unconscious."

Ivana cursed several times and then held an indecipherable conversation with someone else on her end.

"I'll be there in a few minutes," Ivana said. "Can you stay put?"

He glanced at Danton and Tharqan, who were nervously peering out the main door to the lab. "I shouldn't," he said. "But I will."

"All right. Try to see if you can wake them, meanwhile."

The face disappeared.

Vaughn left the room with the creepy corpse-thing, shutting the door firmly behind him. "Here's the deal," he said, and explained what was going on.

Tharqan fidgeted. "Vaughn, if we don't leave now..."

"I can't leave her girls here. She helped us because of this."

"I'll stay," Danton said quietly.

Tharqan rolled his eyes. "Fine."

"Help me figure out if there's a way to wake these women up. They'll be hard to get out of here otherwise."

Danton kept watch at the door while Tharqan and Vaughn moved about the room, examining the women lying on the beds. He didn't know what was causing their unconsciousness, but they all had needles stuck in their arms connected to bags of fluid, so he pulled the needles out, hoping it would help.

Nothing happened right away, but after a few minutes, one of them began to stir. Of course, it was Ohtli.

She blinked, looking up at Vaughn groggily.

"Come on," he said. "You have to get up. Shake it off."

She didn't move, and Vaughn tried to pull her up. She found the strength to pull away. "You're with them?" she asked, shrinking back.

"With who?"

Her head was obviously clearing. "Them. The priests. They're trying to turn us into Banebringers, or something like that."

Vaughn gaped at her. *That's* what they were doing? Was the corpse-thing some sort of gross failure? His stomach turned as he thought about the possibility that it had once been a human being.

No time for theorizing right now. "I'm with Ivana," he said. "And some friends. We're going to get you out of here."

That woke her up. She sat up and swung her legs over the side of the bed. She stumbled as she tried to stand, and Vaughn helped her. "Where? Where is she? We knew she'd come..."

Other women were waking up now. One was already sitting up.

"Guards!" Danton shouted.

"Look, try to get the rest of the women together. We're in a bit of a pinch here."

Danton backed away from the door, and a moment later, the entire room turned into...

A jungle?

The women were animals. Vaughn turned around. He had a tail.

The grim-faced guards who entered the room halted, confused. "What in the abyss?" one muttered. Where Tharqan had been a moment before, now stood a lion, and it roared at them. The guards backed away. "This is crazy," one of the guards said. "Damn priests and their experiments. They can't pay me enough to deal with this."

Apparently, the others agreed, because the guards left, and Danton dropped the illusion. He stumbled back, gasping.

Vaughn rushed forward. "Take it easy," he said. "Sit."

"That...took a lot out of me," Danton said.

"Yeah, you turned an entire room into a jungle."

"Was it pretty impressive, at least?"

"You couldn't see it?"

"I think I sort of blacked out for a moment. It was weird."

Loss of blood. "Just rest. No more illusions for a few minutes, until you feel better."

Danton nodded, but Vaughn was concerned. They had all used a lot of magic that night, and while their blood would regenerate nearly as quickly as they had used the magic, they could overdo it.

The women were fully awake now, some of them scared witless by seeing all of their friends turned into jungle animals. They huddled together in a group, looking at Vaughn, Danton and Tharqan with wide eyes.

Tharqan took up the post at the door. "I hear something," he said.

Vaughn looked at Danton. His eyes were closed, and his face pale. He couldn't help this time. Vaughn readied his bow, arrow held loosely on the string...

"It's us," a voice said, and then Ivana and Aleena appeared.

Vaughn let out a breath, relieved, and put the arrow back in his quiver.

"Where's Yasril?" Danton asked.

"He went ahead and took the children out," Ivana said. "They'll meet us later."

Then there was no more time for talk. The women surrounded Ivana, effusive in their adoration of their rescuer. They hugged and clung to her, some of them crying.

She looked a little overwhelmed and patted one of them on the back. "There, there," she said. "We're getting you out. Don't worry."

"We knew you'd come," another woman said. "We knew it."

"Are you all right?" she asked. Vaughn had never seen her look so uncomfortable, even in her dress from earlier. She had changed, at some point, and was wearing black trousers and a coarse shirt with a pair of boots.

"We're fine," the woman said. "A little groggy right now, but nothing they've done so far has caused permanent damage." She paused, worry creasing her brow. "The children are out?"

"They will be," Ivana said. "They're in good hands."

"I hate to break up this reunion," Tharqan said, still looking out the door, "but we need to go."

Ivana looked at Vaughn. "Buy me another minute," she said. Her girls were still overwhelmed by the thought of rescue, and most a little dizzy-looking. She wanted to be sure that when they left, they wouldn't leave any collapsed on the ground behind them.

Vaughn nodded and gestured to Tharqan and Danton. They held a hushed conference, and Tharqan and Danton slipped out of the room, no doubt to guard more distant points, while Vaughn kept watch over the door.

Caira was outright sobbing. "Deteen," she said. "My baby."

"Don't worry," Ivana assured her. "I promise, they'll be fine." The older children would see that the youngest weren't left behind, and she had full confidence in Yasril's abilities to get them out—high praise for someone she had so recently met. The children had taken to him immediately; he struck the figure of a kindly grandfather, and they trusted him.

Ohtli had pulled back and was regarding her solemnly. "You came for us," she said quietly.

Ivana waved her hand in the air, dismissing them. "Of course I did, foolish girls. I didn't pluck you out of misery to leave you in worse."

The girls had quieted and were all looking at her—even Aleena.

Aleena stepped forward. "I think what she means to say, Ivana, is thank you."

Ivana shifted. "Are you feeling up to getting out of here yet? We don't have a lot of—"

"No," Zyanya said, cutting her off. "We've had a lot of time to talk, and we all agreed, when you came—"

Caira took up her speech, though through her tears. "You have to know. We know you're not one for a lot of affection, but what you've done for us—"

"You've given us hope," Ohtli said, still quiet.

"Made us believe in ourselves again—"

"Given us back our dignity."

Ivana looked around the sea of faces turned toward her. To her horror, she felt her throat tighten, for the first time in a decade. "Foolish girls," she said again, trying to push it away. "Trust me when I say I'm no one you should honor or emulate."

But they wouldn't let her continue. "We don't know exactly what happened to you, before you met all of us," Ohtli said, "but we know it wasn't anything less than what we've been through."

"You've said it to us a thousand times, in a thousand ways," Zyanya said, "and not always in words. It's time you heard it for yourself, because we all agree that you don't believe it for yourself."

"It wasn't your fault," Caira said, tears still shining in her eyes.

"You deserve better than self-loathing," Zyanya said.

"Whatever happened, you didn't deserve it," Ohtli finished.

Ivana choked. Tears rushed to her eyes, before she could stop them. She was afraid to speak. She didn't deserve this sort of outpouring. They had no idea what she was, who she was, how utterly she had ruined her family by her choices. It was different, so different...

"They're right," Aleena said, standing a little back from the group. "It's time you started believing your own advice."

Ivana closed her eyes, and the tears spilled over. A sob escaped her lips. She couldn't help it.

She had heard it said that tears could be cleansing. She always thought it was a ridiculous sentiment, but she felt it now, as tears rolled down her cheeks, and her shoulders shook silently. The girls surrounded her and collectively held her.

Years of despair and self-hatred and regret washed out in those tears, brought to light by a group of foolish girls who had no idea what they were saying. And yet were only repeating back to her the words she had told them, time and time again.

She had never felt such love. Love.

She didn't deserve such love. Damn them all...

"Our actions may define us," a voice said in her ear. "But they don't determine our destiny." She turned to see Aleena standing there, eyes wet with tears herself.

Ivana took one long, shuddering breath, embarrassed, uncomfortable, speechless.

Ohtli pushed everyone back. "Pull it together girls," she said. "It's time to let Ivana do what she does best."

They all nodded sagely.

Kill people?

"Rescue people."

Chapter Forty-One

The Assassin and the Ri

"Let's get out of here," Ivana said, joining Vaughn at the door at last.

He had tried hard to ignore the conversation ensuing behind him, feeling like an intruder on a private moment, but it was impossible.

Ivana's eyes were red, and he looked away from her, uncomfortable, and nodded. Aleena joined them.

"How is your aether?" he asked them.

"Running low," Aleena said, and Ivana nodded.

"All right. Use it for yourselves, then. I'll take care of the women. Danton and Tharqan have their own."

Ivana turned to give the group of women instructions, and they listened attentively, no arguments. Complete trust.

Aleena led the way, followed by Tharqan. Vaughn and the women linked hands, with Vaughn in the middle, and Danton and Ivana brought up the rear.

The entire group slinked down the hall in an awkward chain. If they ran into anyone, it was going to be a challenge getting past them while keeping them all invisible, but they had to press forward.

The halls were strangely quiet, and it unnerved Vaughn. Even with the fight above drawing the guards away, this was too easy. Aleena led them down different corridors than the ones they had entered through and headed for a different exit.

They had just crossed a large chamber, and the women were starting up the stairway, when Vaughn heard a familiar voice from behind the group.

"You didn't really think I would let you leave, did you?"

Vaughn froze. Aleena looked back down the stairs, while Ivana turned toward the source of the sound.

How had Gildas seen them?

Then he realized he could *see* Ivana and Aleena looking toward the sound. Their aether was failing—either because it had chosen this moment to be finicky about who was using it, or because they were running out. Either way, Ivana's figure was solid again, while Aleena's was flickering in and out.

Gildas was headed for Ivana.

He glanced back up the stairway, where the entire group of women had also halted, waiting for Vaughn. "Don't stop," he hissed. "Go!"

Danton and Tharqan re-appeared. They moved among the women, linked hands when them, and then the entire group disappeared. Vaughn let go of his own invisibility, hoping that Danton and Tharqan had enough to keep them hidden for a little longer.

Aleena pushed her way back. "Deal with it," she said. "I'll make sure they get out."

Vaughn reached for his bow, heart hammering. Could he kill his father? It would be so easy, right now. Gildas wasn't even trying to move out of the way, just sauntering toward Ivana, and now himself.

"Go," he said to Ivana, coming to stand next to her.

She didn't budge. "My best chance for the girls to get out is to make sure they're not followed," she said. Her eyes were trained on his father almost eagerly.

Of course. What she said was true, but this was his father they were talking about. The man who had killed her own father, and in so doing ruined the lives of her entire family. She wasn't going to pass up a second chance to kill him.

"You can't do it, can you?" Gildas asked, smirking at Vaughn's bow. His arrow was still held loosely to the string. He hadn't even tried to draw.

Stupid. He could have killed him five minutes ago. He remained silent, ashamed. Yet was it ironic to be ashamed that he couldn't work up the nerve to kill his father? Shouldn't that be admirable?

What a life he led.

Gildas' eyes flicked to Ivana, who had slid her dagger out of its sheath. "Ah, the assassin. I wondered if this all had something to do with those women we took from your inn. But how did you convince my worthless son to help you? A trade, perhaps? His services for yours?" He unsheathed his sword, not a dueling sword, nor ceremonial, like all weapons were supposed to be in the ballroom. "No matter. Will you dance with me again, girl?"

Ivana didn't move.

"Where is your syringe?" Vaughn asked, trying to take the attention off Ivana. Perhaps he could distract Gildas and she could slide that blade in. There were two of them, and only one of him. "Why don't you just inject me and get it over with?"

"Oh, no," Gildas said. "I'm tired of Hunting you, boy. I want you gone, for good."

Vaughn blinked. "But—"

Gildas' expression changed from relaxed to fierce. "Summon a whole swarm of them, for all I care." He tilted his head to the side. "I wouldn't, if I were you."

Vaughn raised an eyebrow, confused, but then he realized Gildas was talking to Ivana, who had slid around to the side, trying to get into a better position. She paused in her movements.

"But I feel as though we've been playing this game for so long I ought to give you a fair chance. A duel?"

"You know I've no skill with a sword. That's hardly fair," Vaughn said.

"Very well. You choose your weapon then."

He licked his lips. It didn't matter what weapon they chose. He had no skill with melee combat—at least, not enough to win against Gildas.

Vaughn flicked his eyes to Ivana's. She was looking back. They had both had the same thought, and a small smile played on her lips. But could she take him? He raised an eyebrow, and she nodded, ever so slightly.

"Daggers. I assume you have one on you? And Sweetblade will stand for me."

His father frowned. "That's—"

"A tradition with plenty of precedent. You're the one who wanted one last game. You'll change the rules now?"

Gildas shrugged. "Very well. But if I win, she dies, and so do you."

Vaughn jerked his head in acquiescence and stepped aside for Ivana to take his place.

Vaughn's father rolled up one trouser and extracted a dagger sheathed there. "Let's dance, girl."

Gildas was arrogant, but Ivana could tell he wasn't certain of the outcome of this fight. Ivana wasn't either—she avoided direct confrontations unless necessary, and the last fight she had had with Gildas hadn't ended so well.

Once one of them made the first move, it would be over quickly. Fights like this were close and brutal. Whoever got the blade in the right place first would win. He was stronger and larger than her, so she would need to depend on speed and skill to get in the right spot before he could pin her.

"So," Gildas said, circling her. "Teyrnon must be paying you very well, as I see you didn't take my hint, Sweetblade." His mouth curled up in a smile, as if enjoying the deliciousness of facing the woman he had exacted his punishment on.

"I don't need payment to kill you," Ivana said. It came out

fiercer than she intended.

Gildas raised an eyebrow. "Ah. I see. What offense did I cause you, then? Did I throw your family out of my estate for some indiscretion? Beat your father?" He smiled wickedly. "Sleep with your mother, perhaps? I always did enjoy a good romp with a pretty serving girl."

Hypocrite. Damned hypocrite. "No," she said. "I'm a 'whore' your favored son sired a bastard on. But I doubt you remember."

She honestly *didn't* expect him to remember. He had probably dealt with so many commoners in like fashion that she could have been a bug he accidentally stepped on.

But to her surprise, he tilted his head thoughtfully. "*That* girl? I remember. Airell had a beating that smarted for a week after that. Had to learn the rules of playing that game; bastards aren't good for the family. Cause political trouble if you don't deal with them early on. One or two slip through every once in a while, of course, but..." He narrowed his eyes. "So. I killed your father. Stupid man threw himself at me. I suppose now you have a bastard child to insist I pay for? Did you not learn your lesson the first time?"

Ivana didn't respond to that. "Gildas, if you die at my blade, you can die in the knowledge that it's what came of your lesson. Congratulations for creating your own murderer."

And she lunged.

The scene in front of Vaughn changed as Ivana lunged at Gildas. He tensed. The two mingled in a tangle of arms and blades flashing. Blood stained the ground, but he didn't know whose.

A moment later, Gildas groaned and stumbled back, doubled over. At first, Vaughn thought she had stabbed him in the stomach, but then he realized she had just kicked him in the groin. Not an allowed maneuver in a duel, but he doubted Ivana cared.

She also didn't care about giving her opponent time to recover. She pressed the advantage and was on him before he could even stand.

It looked as though she would win, but then—

Gildas simply...struck her. His blow hit so hard that she flew through the air for a couple feet before hitting the ground. Her hand smacked against the hard stone, and her dagger flew out of her hand, skittering across the floor out of her reach.

It was just like it had been back in Ri Talesin's manor; he had wondered it then and wondered it again now. How did he have such strength?

"Filthy whore," Gildas said, straightening. He advanced on Ivana, brandishing his dagger and ready to end the duel. Vaughn had no doubt she would be dead in seconds if he didn't act.

Anger lanced through him. He was exhausted. He might very well kill himself. But he burned blood and reached for the water in his father's body. He stiffened and slowed.

Vaughn fought to remain in control of the feat. He wasn't skilled at this. His vision blurred, but it wasn't enough to prevent him from pulling his bow out and loosing an arrow into his father's back.

His father's mouth formed a surprised 'o,' but Vaughn saw no more, because a wave of weakness pushed him to his knees.

The room swam in front of him, and he felt strangely cold. Too much. It had been too much, but he wasn't dead, so he would live—assuming his father didn't.

He felt a rush of wind, and then a shout.

He tried to look, but felt only cold stone against his cheek.

Chapter Forty-Two

Death

Ivana struggled to push herself up before Gildas reached her.

It turned out she didn't have to. He became rigid, and Ivana saw Vaughn reach for his bow out of the corner of her eye.

Gildas blinked and turned to face his son, who had fallen to his hands and knees. Blood blossomed from the arrow in Gildas' back, and yet he still managed to change direction and lurch instead toward Vaughn.

He started to lift his dagger, and she propelled herself onto his back and slit his throat.

Gildas staggered. The dagger fell from his hand; he fell to his knees, and then finally collapsed onto the ground.

Ivana retrieved her dagger and moved cautiously toward Gildas. She nudged him with her foot to turn him onto his back. He didn't appear to be breathing, but it couldn't hurt to be sure this time.

Dead already or not, she felt grim satisfaction at plunging her dagger into the heart of the man who had killed her father.

Only when the blood pulsing from his body had slowed to a trickle did she turn back toward Vaughn. He was laying facedown, cheek pressed to the stone floor.

"Vaughn," Ivana said, shaking him. "Vaughn."

He groaned. "I'm alive."

"Then we need to get out of here."

"A minute," he said. "Just a minute."

Ivana tapped her fingers impatiently against her thigh, and then shook him again. "Vaughn!"

Vaughn stirred, and then pushed himself up. He looked first around the room.

Gildas lay face-up, a broken arrow protruding from underneath him, in a pool of his own blood.

His mouth worked, and then he looked at Ivana. "Is he dead?"

"Yes," Ivana said. Amazingly enough. The man had the strongest constitution she had ever seen. "And I made sure he stayed dead this time."

He glanced at Gildas again and then turned away.

"What happened?"

"He didn't take kindly to your putting a hole in his back, so he tried to kill you before he died. I stopped him."

"So you saved my life."

"Or I prevented a bloodbane from coming through." She stood up. "Let's go. I don't know if they have guards standing by."

Almost as if in response, the sound of jangling armor and footsteps sounded distantly down one of the adjoining halls, and both of them rose to their feet and started for the stairs.

Toward freedom? Toward safety? Toward...what, exactly, for her? Was mere survival enough?

She hesitated.

"What are you doing?" Vaughn hissed as he placed one foot on the bottom stair.

"Staying behind."

"Why in the abyss would you do that?"

"To slow the guards down." She would kill as many of them as she could, of course, but even she had her limits, especially when already exhausted.

The guards were getting closer. "So, what, you're going to stay and sacrifice yourself?"

She was silent. It was a fitting end. A just end. And why not? It would take so much energy to repair what Vaughn had broken. She didn't know if she had it in her. Not after today, not after the outpouring of her girls and her own tears.

"I can't let you do this."

Damn it, why wouldn't he just *leave*? "Don't be ridiculous."

"I'll stay," he said. "You go with your girls. It's where you belong."

She didn't belong anywhere. Kayden had offered to take the girls to his family estate, far to the northeast in Fuilyn, and from there they would find new places for them. But her? There was no place for her. Only more of the empty darkness that had consumed her life since she had started down this path.

A new voice spoke from behind them. "Both of you are idiots. Go and make sure the others get on their way safely."

Ivana started. *Danton?*

"I'll take care of it," Danton said, more insistently, and then placed one hand on each of their chests and pushed them back into the stairway.

The guards burst into the room.

Vaughn touched Ivana's arm and wrapped her in invisibility. Despite Danton's orders, they both stood there, watching the scene unfold.

Except Danton was no longer Danton. He was Vaughn's father, in every perfect detail. And the corpse on the ground?

Vaughn stared. He caught even Ivana staring. It was her own.

The guards—a good half dozen of them—skidded as one to a jumbled halt. "Ri Gildas?" one of them asked as he extracted himself from the group. "We heard there was a problem..."

"Taken care of," Danton as Vaughn's father said. He gestured to the corpse.

"Good, good," the spokesman said, nodding. He was obviously relieved not to have to deal with it himself.

But they hesitated when they saw what Danton did next. He removed one of the lanterns from the wall, broke it, and spilled the oil over the corpse. He then promptly lit it on fire.

"Ri Gildas?" another guard asked. "What...?"

Danton spat on the corpse. "The assassin my demonspawn son worked with." He nudged the corpse with his foot, encouraging the flames. "She doesn't deserve anything better than this."

He looked up. "Go on. Tell your superiors that the ringleader was the assassin Sweetblade, and she is now dead. Tell them also that I'm starting in immediate pursuit of the Banebringer Teyrnon and his associates." He turned around, facing Vaughn and Ivana, though he surely couldn't see them.

The guards nodded and filtered back out of the room.

As soon as they were gone, Danton collapsed against the doorway, his illusion disappearing. "I know you're still there," he said.

Vaughn let go of his invisibility. "Danton?"

He closed his eyes. "I'll be okay. I'll be right behind. Don't worry. Go. Just go, please." He glanced back. The corpse had almost been consumed beyond recognition, which was, of course, the point.

"Don't you understand?" he said, but he looked at Ivana. "You're dead. Do you want to be found alive again?"

Ivana stared back at Danton. "You just—" she started. Risked everything for a woman he barely knew. The illusion might not have worked. He could have been killed or captured himself.

He smiled, almost wistfully. "I know. Now would you get out of here?"

Ivana turned and started up the stairs, though her compliance was involuntary. Her conscious self was too much in shock to argue.

Vaughn followed her in silence while they slipped out of the door and past guards in the invisibility Vaughn provided, on the way to the rendezvous point with the women, their children, Yasril, and Tharqan.

Ivana breathed a sigh of relief as they left the palace compound. They had all made it this far, and with what Danton had done, they would have no problem making it much, much farther before someone realized that Ri Gildas wasn't coming back.

And as for her...

She was dead.

No. Sweetblade was dead.

Was she angry? In one foolhardy move Danton had ensured that she—Ivana—would have to start over. Rebuild a reputation under a name other than Sweetblade.

Or...not?

She didn't have to. She could truly start over. Anywhere, as anyone. She had the resources to do whatever and go wherever she wanted. Did she want to continue on the path she had chosen so long ago?

If the past months had taught her anything, it was that she wouldn't be able to just leave that life and move on. The ghosts of her past would haunt her, and she would have new burdens to add to those that she had run from in the first place. She would have to find a way to deal with them. A different way. A potentially more painful way.

She couldn't do it before. What made her think she would be able to now?

Her head was still reeling with the possibilities by the time they arrived at the rendezvous point. Her girls immediately swarmed her, and she had to push aside her own problems for later contemplation.

Eventually, the girls drifted away, crying or laughing and hugging each other and their children for the hundredth time.

She gestured to Aleena, who hung back. "Is everything ready?"

Aleena nodded. "They've just been waiting for you."

What? Not "we?" "They?"

Aleena hesitated.

"You're not coming," Ivana stated.

"No. I...I think it's time I made my own way, Da."

The two women looked at each other. Aleena was tense, as if expecting Ivana to demand that she stay.

Or as if expecting a threat.

Ivana closed her eyes. Whatever she did going forward, there were people who would pay to know that the person behind the assassin known as Sweetblade was alive. Which meant she had to trust anyone who knew her real identity to continue to keep it a secret.

Her real identity? Was that what Sweetblade was? And yet Sweetblade was dead, and so likewise was that identity. How did she function now? Who was she without Sweetblade?

Did she trust Vaughn? This whole affair had begun because she had needed to get rid of Vaughn, who knew her identity. Some impish god was cackling at the delicious irony that now, in the end, she would choose to trust him with that very thing.

But what of Danton, whom she hardly knew? Yaotel, who

hated her for good reason?

If she could trust all of them, certainly she could trust Aleena.

She could take this step, at least. If she thought of it as an experiment, the idea of such final trust wasn't so terrifying.

She opened her eyes. "Good luck...my friend," she said quietly. "If you ever need anything..."

Aleena visibly relaxed, and then she smiled. "The same to you, Ivana."

With that, she turned and walked away—and Ivana couldn't help but feel that by letting her go, she had given up a part of herself. Now she had to figure out what would take its place.

Vaughn hung back as Ivana's girls gathered around her. Yasril and Tharqan were taking seriously their role of guarding the entrance to the old, closed off sewer exit from the city. They were on the east side; there wasn't a lot of traffic here, so it was their best bet for making an undetected exit.

"You ready?" Tharqan asked him.

"Ready?"

"To get out of here."

He glanced back at Ivana.

"The smart one, Aleena—she's already got it all figured out," Tharqan said.

"We donated some blood while we were waiting, so they have some resources," Yasril added.

Ivana was having a side conversation with Aleena. "All right," he said. "Just...give me a minute, okay?"

Tharqan and Yasril exchanged glances and then shrugged. "Guess we should wait for Danton," Tharqan said. Then he hesitated. "He is coming?"

"Hopefully," Vaughn said.

He stepped aside and caught Ivana's eye as Aleena left her. She pulled apart from the group, farther back into the tunnel.

She immediately handed him the qixli, a poignant symbol of the inevitable.

"Thanks," he said, wanting to say more, not knowing what to say or how to say it. "What will you do?"

"My primary concern is getting my girls to safety. The life I provided for them is no longer viable, but I need to at least make sure they get safely to Fuilyn with Kayden and Caira."

They both turned to look at the aforementioned couple. Caira was in the process of handing Kayden her son. She was crying.

He shook his head. That was obviously another story.

"You?"

He turned back to Ivana. "Disappear," he said, and then flashed a smile. "Literally and figuratively." He hesitated. The inevitable was upon him. "So. I suppose this is where we part ways."

"Indeed."

He met her eyes, and his stomach twisted. "It's been..." He began, but he didn't know how to continue. Instead, he reached out a hand to touch her face.

She closed her eyes, briefly.

It was enough. He turned both of them invisible as he pulled her into his arms and pressed his lips to hers once more.

She accepted the kiss, but didn't return it. He pulled back, looking into her eyes. "Disappear with me, Ivana," he said.

She started to shake her head.

"After you've secured the future of your girls, of course."

"Vaughn..."

"Just a...companion for a lonely road."

She gazed back at him. "Vaughn, I have the opportunity to start over. I don't know exactly what that means for me yet, but whatever I decide to do, I'm not going to begin this path the same way I began the other."

"I'm not my brother," he said softly.

"No. Though I hate to admit it, you are a better man." She paused. "But you're close enough where it counts."

He sucked in air through his teeth, trying to ignore how that smarted.

Pity touched her eyes. "You'll get over it. I have full confidence in that." She let go and stepped away from him.

He would. But he knew she would be in his dreams for a long time to come.

She touched his cheek briefly. "Take care of yourself, Vaughn."

And then she walked away.

He watched her until she disappeared into the distance with her women and Kayden, without a glance back.

Not even a single glance back, damn it.

Danton and Tharqan appeared a moment later. "Ready?" Tharqan asked a second time.

Vaughn tore his eyes away from the place where she had been lost to his sight. "You made it back," he said to Danton, relieved.

"I told you not to worry," Danton said, his boyish grin back in place.

Vaughn looked back at the city. Smoke curled up from the palace district. "I have a feeling we're going to want to be far away from here when the Conclave dogs come hunting."

"Besides," Tharqan said, coming up beside him and slapping him on the back. "We've got a lot to do yet. You know. A government to overthrow. Gods to discredit." He grinned, and Vaughn smiled back.

For the first time in nine years, Vaughn felt hope. Not only for himself, but for all of his kind. That things could turn around.

Whatever the priests were up to, it would all be exposed soon.

But Tharqan was right. They still had a long road ahead of them.

"All right. I'm ready."

ABOUT THE AUTHOR

Carol lives in the Lancaster, PA area with her husband and two energetic boys. She loves reading (duh), writing (double-duh), music, movies, and other perfectly normal things like parsing Hebrew verbs and teaching herself new dead languages. She has two master's degrees in the areas of ancient near eastern studies and languages.

For more information on upcoming books, visit
www.carolapark.com

Made in the USA
Middletown, DE
23 May 2021